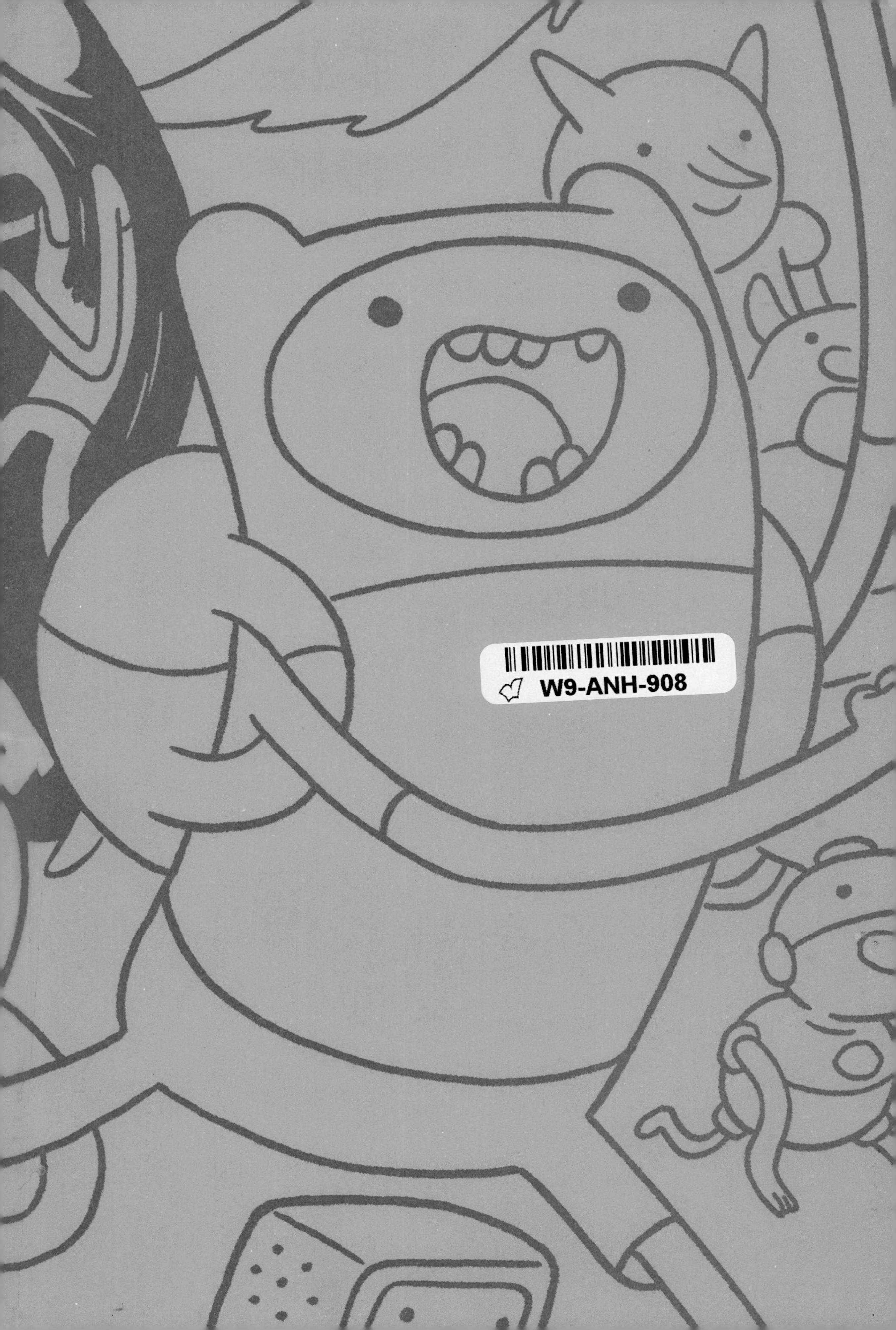

PUBLISHED BY KaBOOM!

ROSS RICHIE ~ CEO & Founder

MATT GAGNON ~ Editor-in-Chief

FILIP SABLIK ~ VP-Publishing & Marketing

LANCE KREITER ~ VP-Licensing & Merchandising

MATT NISSENBAUM ~ Senior Director of Sales & Marketing

PHIL BARBARO ~ Director of Finance

BRYCE CARLSON ~ Managing Editor

DAFNA PLEBAN ~ Editor

SHANNON WATTERS ~ Editor

ERIC HARBURN ~ Editor

CHRIS ROSA ~ Assistant Editor

ALEX GALER ~ Assistant Editor

WHITNEY LEOPARD ~ Assistant Editor

JASMINE AMIRI ~ Assistant Editor

STEPHANIE GONZAGA ~ Graphic Designer

KASSANDRA HELLER ~ Production Designer

MIKE LOPEZ ~ Production Designer

DEVIN FUNCHES ~ E-Commerce & Inventory Coordinator

VINCE FREDERICK ~ Event Coordinator

BRIANNA HART ~ Executive Assistant

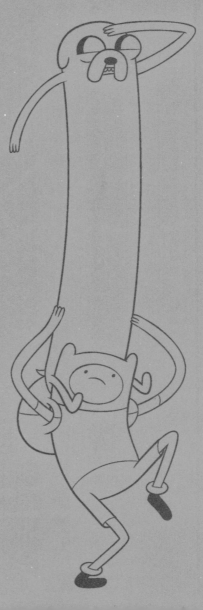

ADVENTURE TIME™

MATHEMATICAL EDITION
Volume Two

kaboom!™
CN CARTOON NETWORK.
FREDERATOR

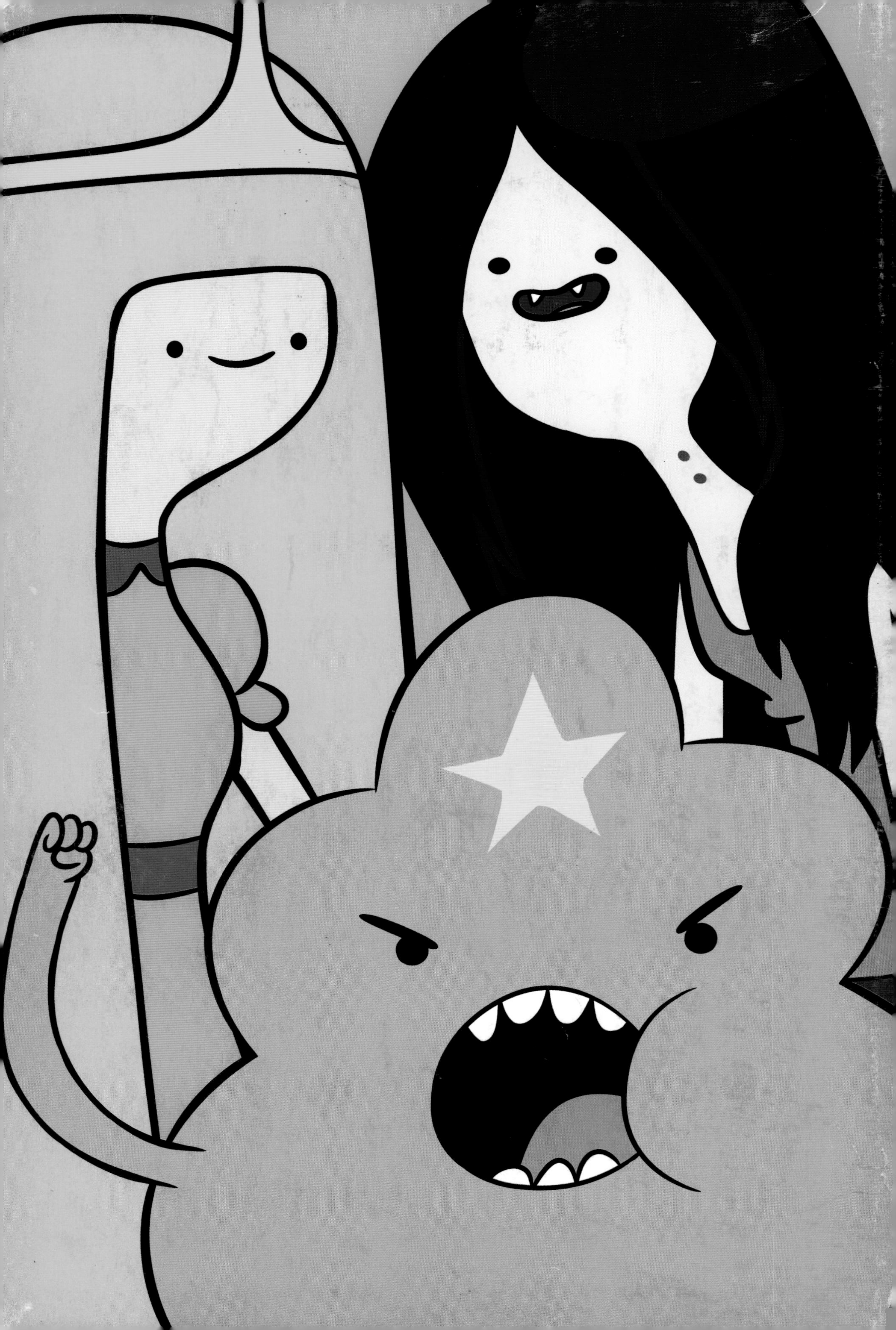

CREATED BY
Pendleton Ward

WRITTEN BY
Ryan North

ILLUSTRATED BY
Shelli Paroline and Braden Lamb

ADDITIONAL COLORS BY
Lisa Moore

LETTERS BY
Steve Wands

"ADVENTURE TIM"

ILLUSTRATED BY
Mike Holmes
COLORS BY STUDIO PARLAPÁ

EDITED BY
Shannon Watters

TRADE AND COVER DESIGN BY
Stephanie Gonzaga

SAN DIEGO COMIC-CON EXCLUSIVE COVER BY
Aaron Renier

With special thanks to
Marisa Marionakis, Rick Blanco, Curtis Lelash, Laurie Halal-Ono, Keith Mack, Kelly Crews
and the wonderful folks at Cartoon Network.

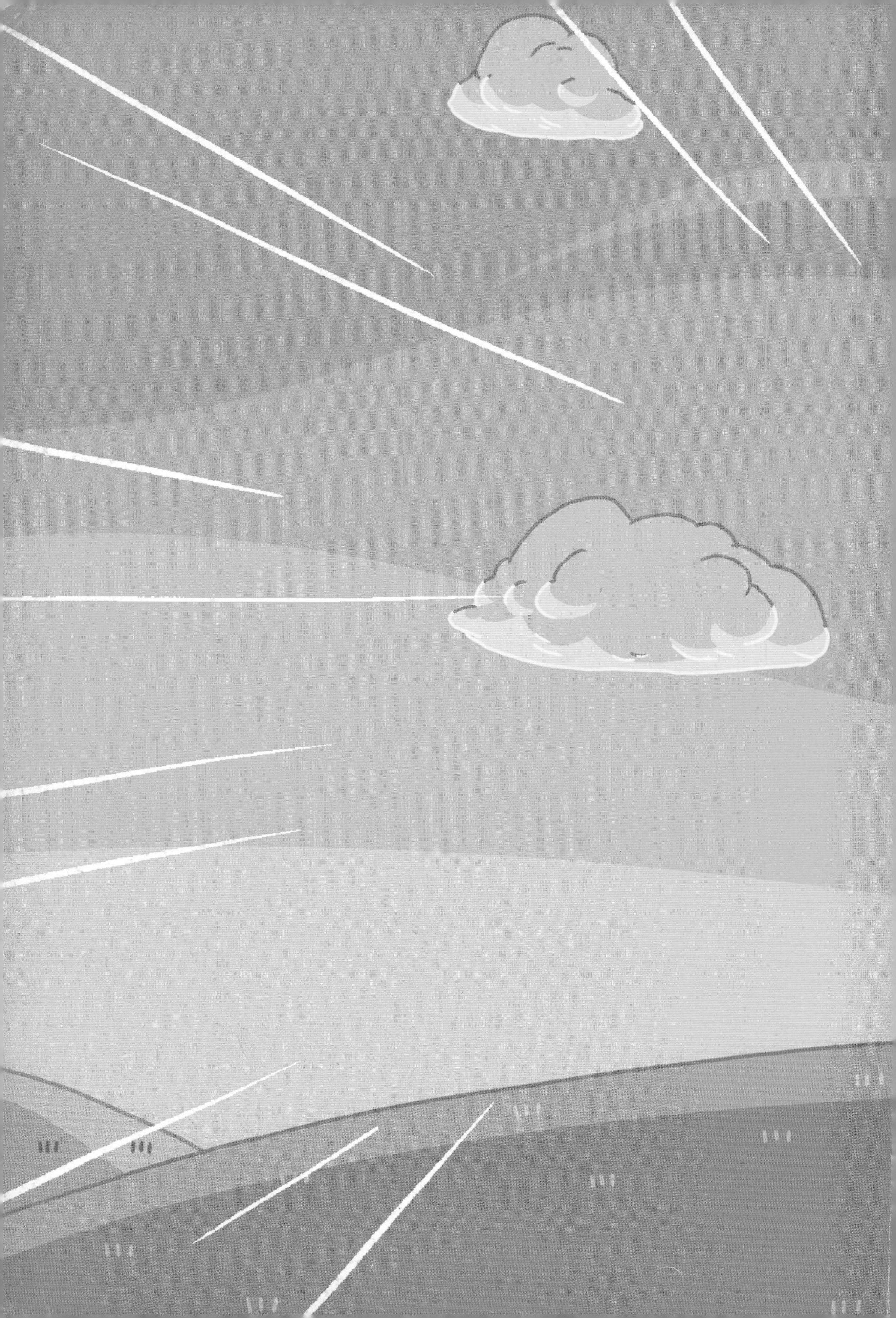

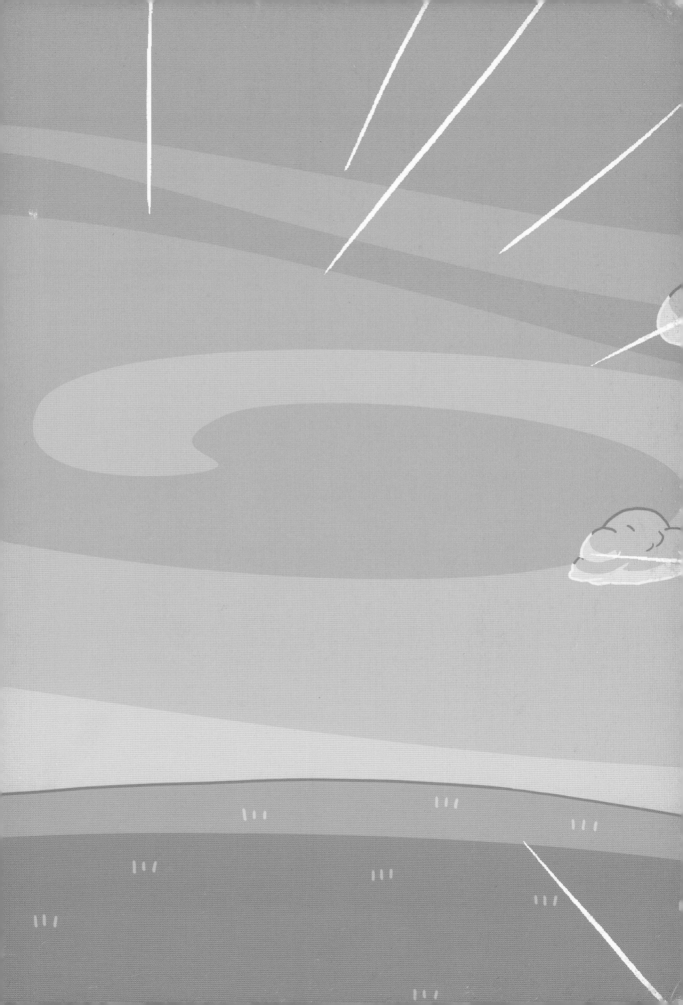

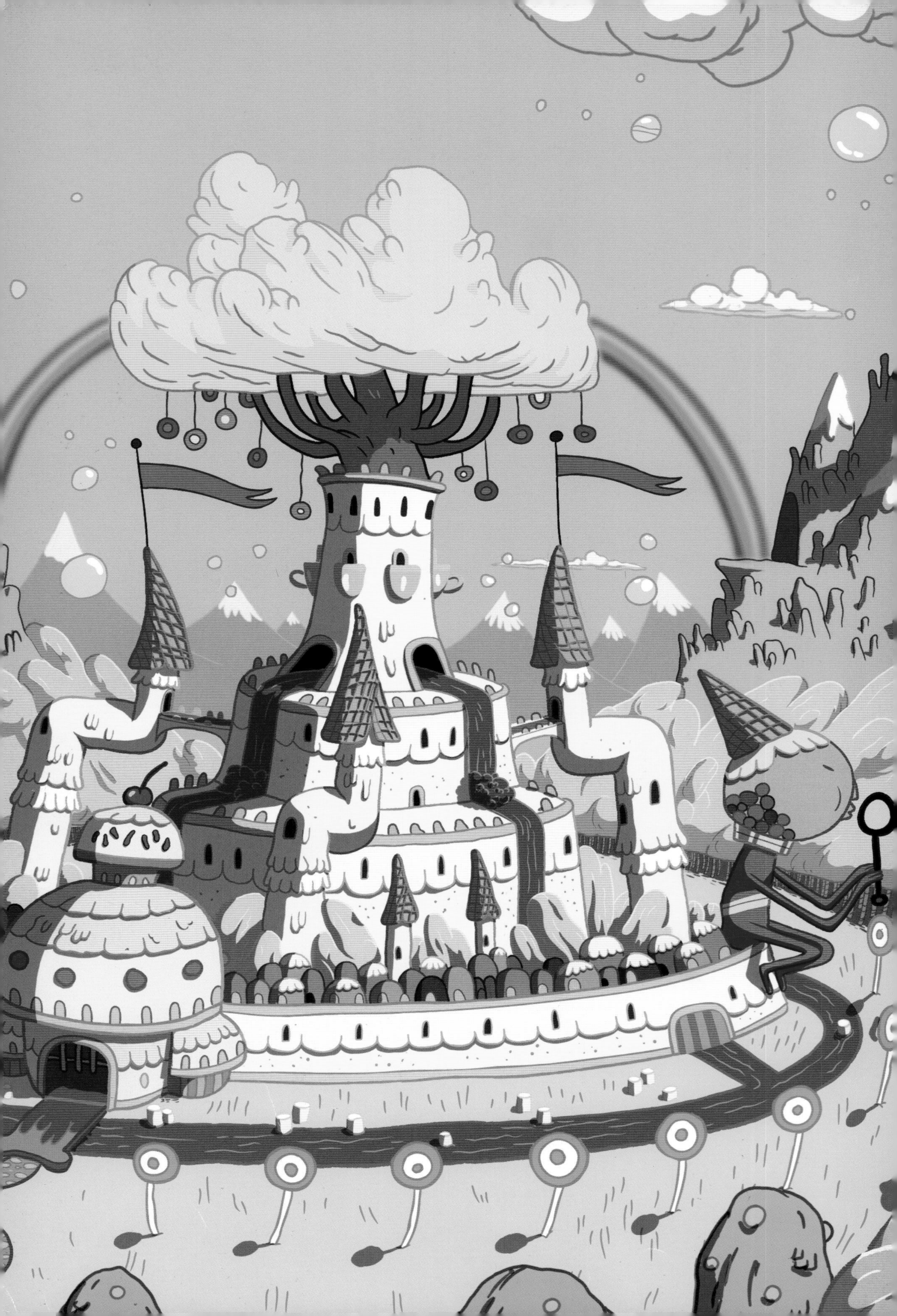

CHAPTER ONE

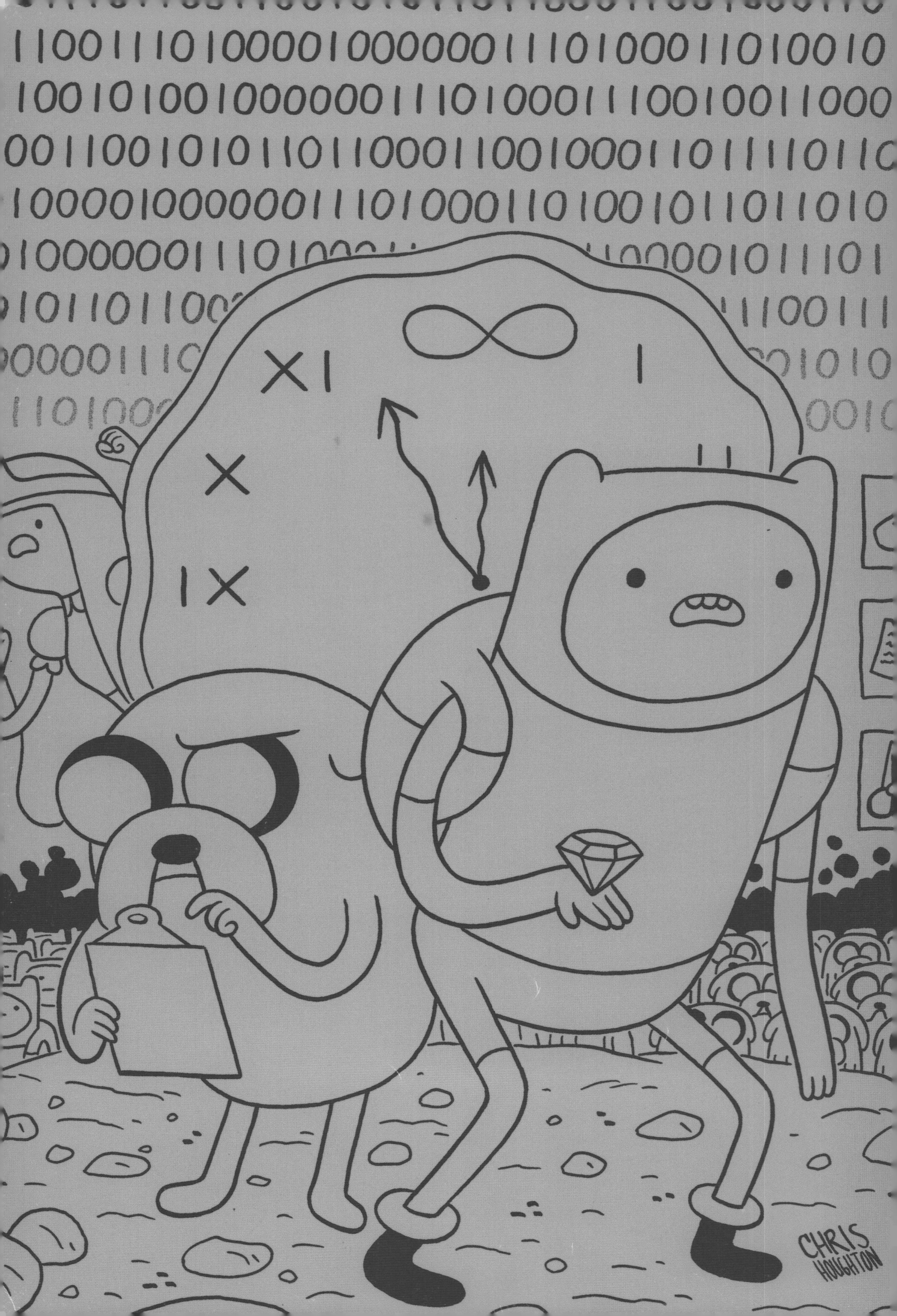

XI
I
X
IX
CHRIS HOUGHTON

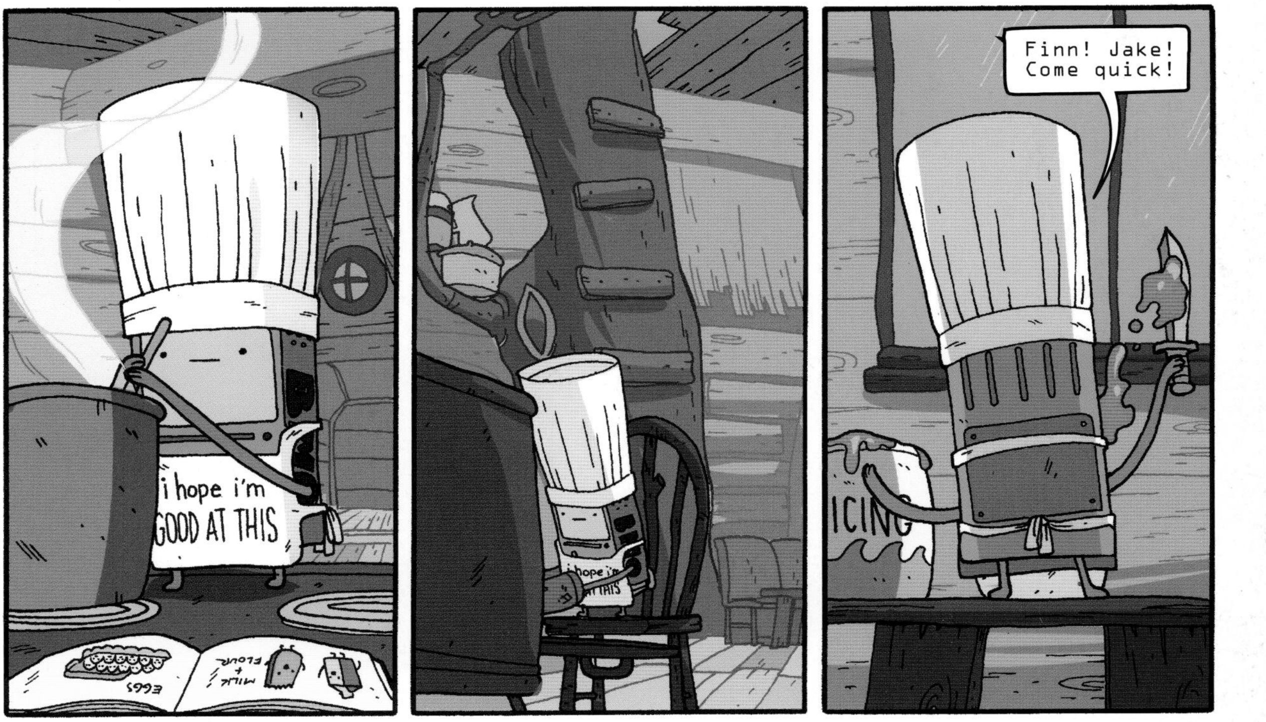
i hope i'm GOOD AT THIS
i hope i'm GOOD AT THIS
Finn! Jake! Come quick!
ICING

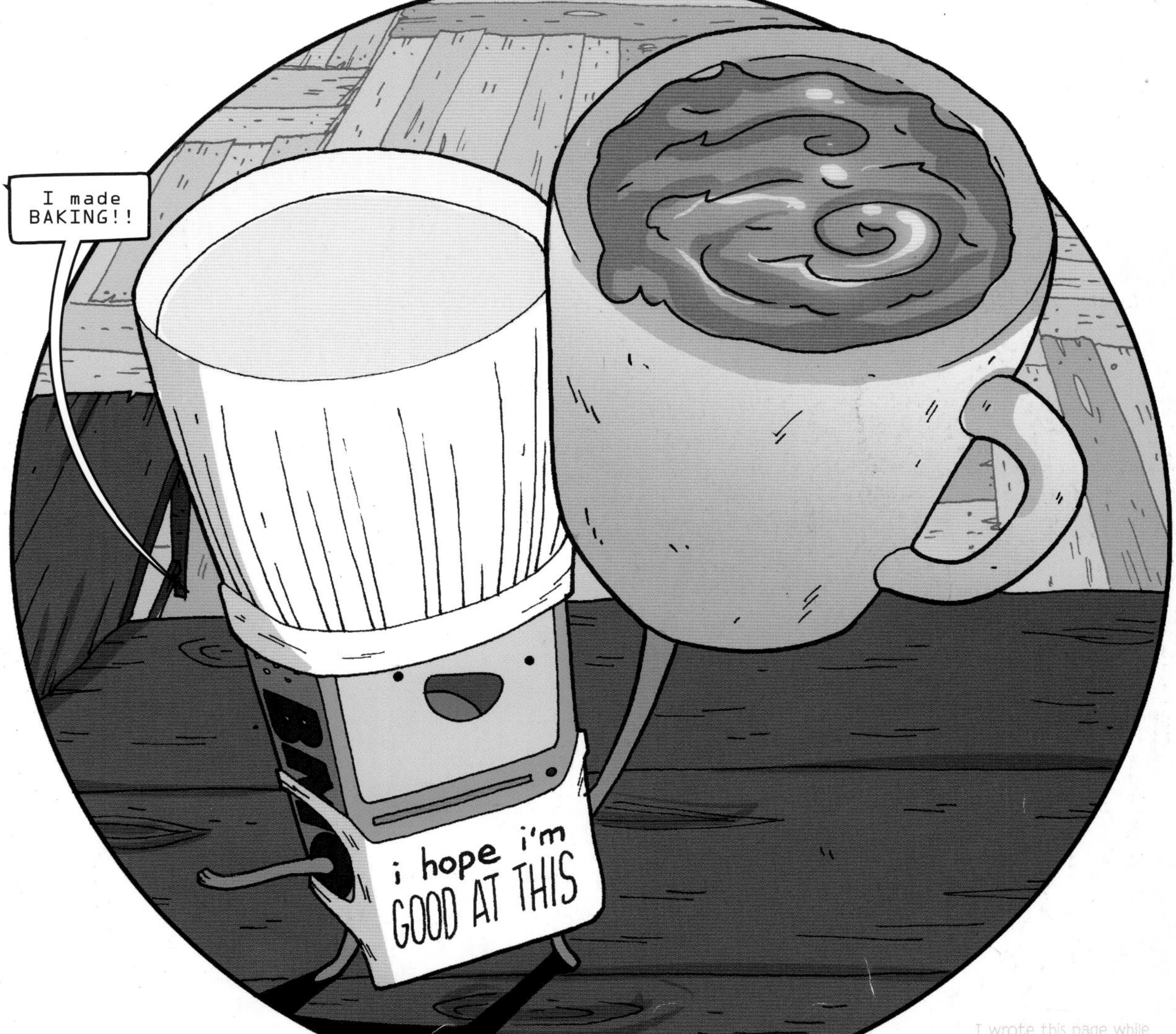
I made BAKING!!
i hope i'm GOOD AT THIS

I wrote this page while eating baking. It was a singular moment of perfection.

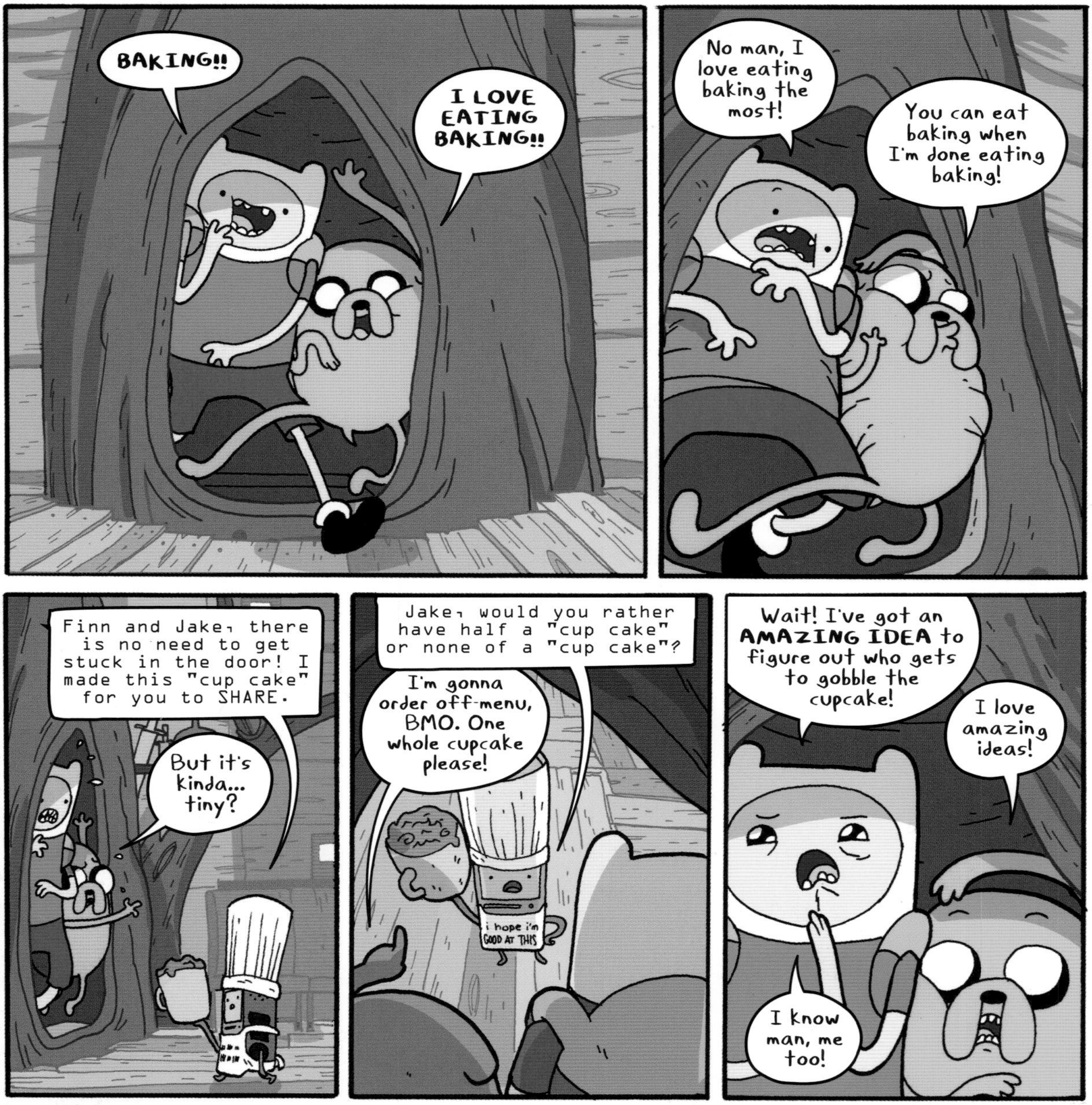
BAKING!!
I LOVE EATING BAKING!!
No man, I love eating baking the most!
You can eat baking when I'm done eating baking!
Finn and Jake, there is no need to get stuck in the door! I made this "cup cake" for you to SHARE.
But it's kinda... tiny?
Jake, would you rather have half a "cup cake" or none of a "cup cake"?
I'm gonna order off-menu, BMO. One whole cupcake please!
i hope i'm GOOD AT THIS
Wait! I've got an **AMAZING IDEA** to figure out who gets to gobble the cupcake!
I love amazing ideas!
I know man, me too!
BMO, give us a challenge!! Then whoever completes the challenge best gets to eat the whole cupcake!
TOTAL MATH. But BMO, make the challenge "who can be the most Jake-like", okay?
I'm super terrific at that.

My editor insisted that the next scene be cut, so you'll just have to IMAGINE sixteen pages of Finn and Jake, still stuck in the doorway, talking about their feelings.

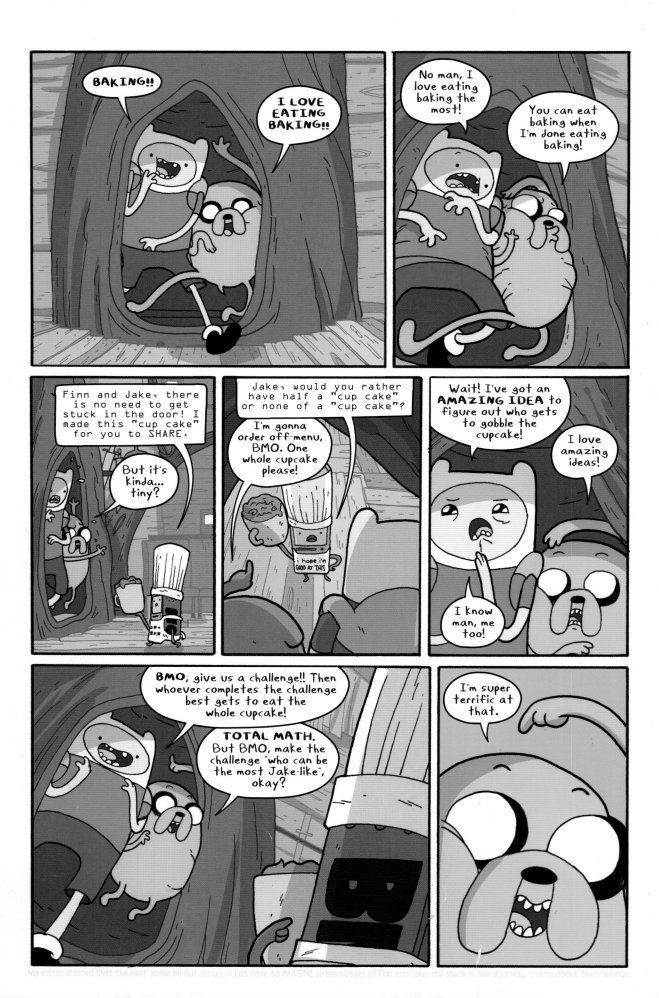

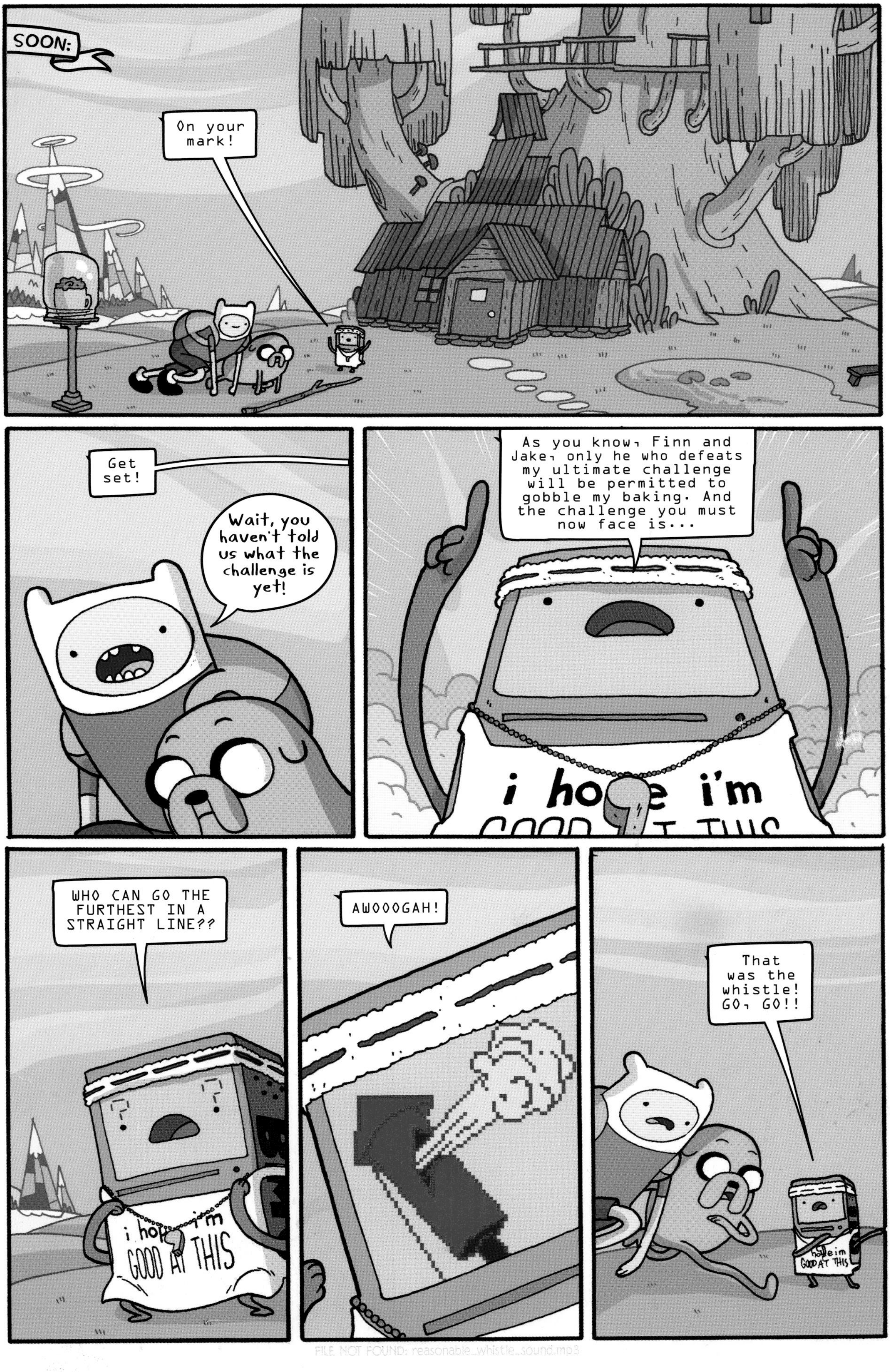
SOON:
On your mark!
Get set!
Wait, you haven't told us what the challenge is yet!
As you know, Finn and Jake, only he who defeats my ultimate challenge will be permitted to gobble my baking. And the challenge you must now face is...
WHO CAN GO THE FURTHEST IN A STRAIGHT LINE??
i hope i'm GOOD AT THIS
AWOOOGAH!
That was the whistle! GO, GO!!

FILE NOT FOUND: reasonable_whistle_sound.mp3

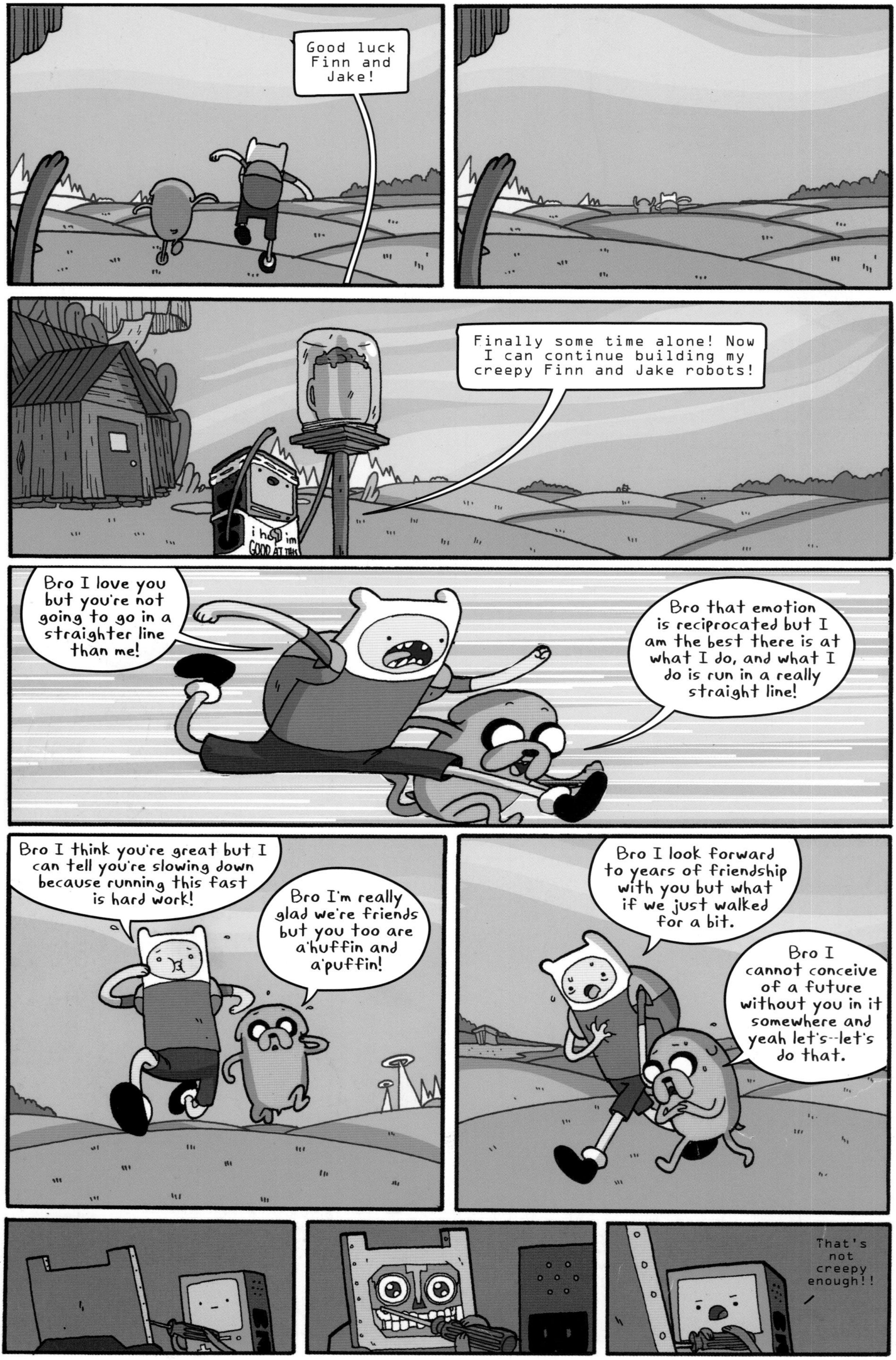

Good luck Finn and Jake!
Finally some time alone! Now I can continue building my creepy Finn and Jake robots!
Bro I love you but you're not going to go in a straighter line than me!
Bro that emotion is reciprocated but I am the best there is at what I do, and what I do is run in a really straight line!
Bro I think you're great but I can tell you're slowing down because running this fast is hard work!
Bro I'm really glad we're friends but you too are a'huffin and a'puffin!
Bro I look forward to years of friendship with you but what if we just walked for a bit.
Bro I cannot conceive of a future without you in it somewhere and yeah let's--let's do that.
That's not creepy enough!!

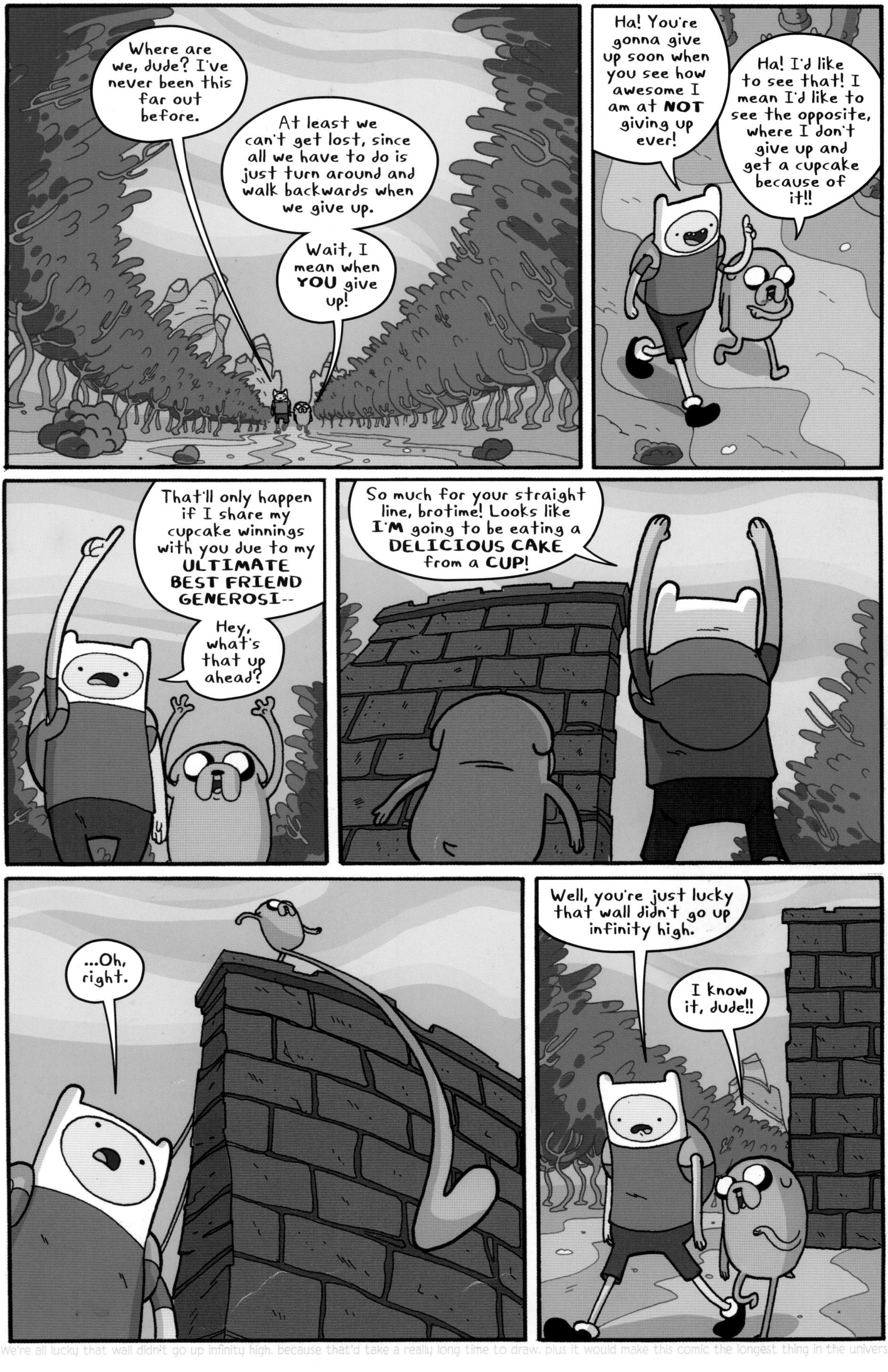
Where are we, dude? I've never been this far out before.
At least we can't get lost, since all we have to do is just turn around and walk backwards when we give up.
Wait, I mean when YOU give up!
Ha! You're gonna give up soon when you see how awesome I am at NOT giving up ever!
Ha! I'd like to see that! I mean I'd like to see the opposite, where I don't give up and get a cupcake because of it!!
That'll only happen if I share my cupcake winnings with you due to my ULTIMATE BEST FRIEND GENEROSI--
Hey, what's that up ahead?
So much for your straight line, brotime! Looks like I'M going to be eating a DELICIOUS CAKE from a CUP!
...Oh, right.
Well, you're just lucky that wall didn't go up infinity high.
I know it, dude!!

We're all lucky that wall didn't go up infinity high, because that'd take a really long time to draw, plus it would make this comic the longest thing in the universe!

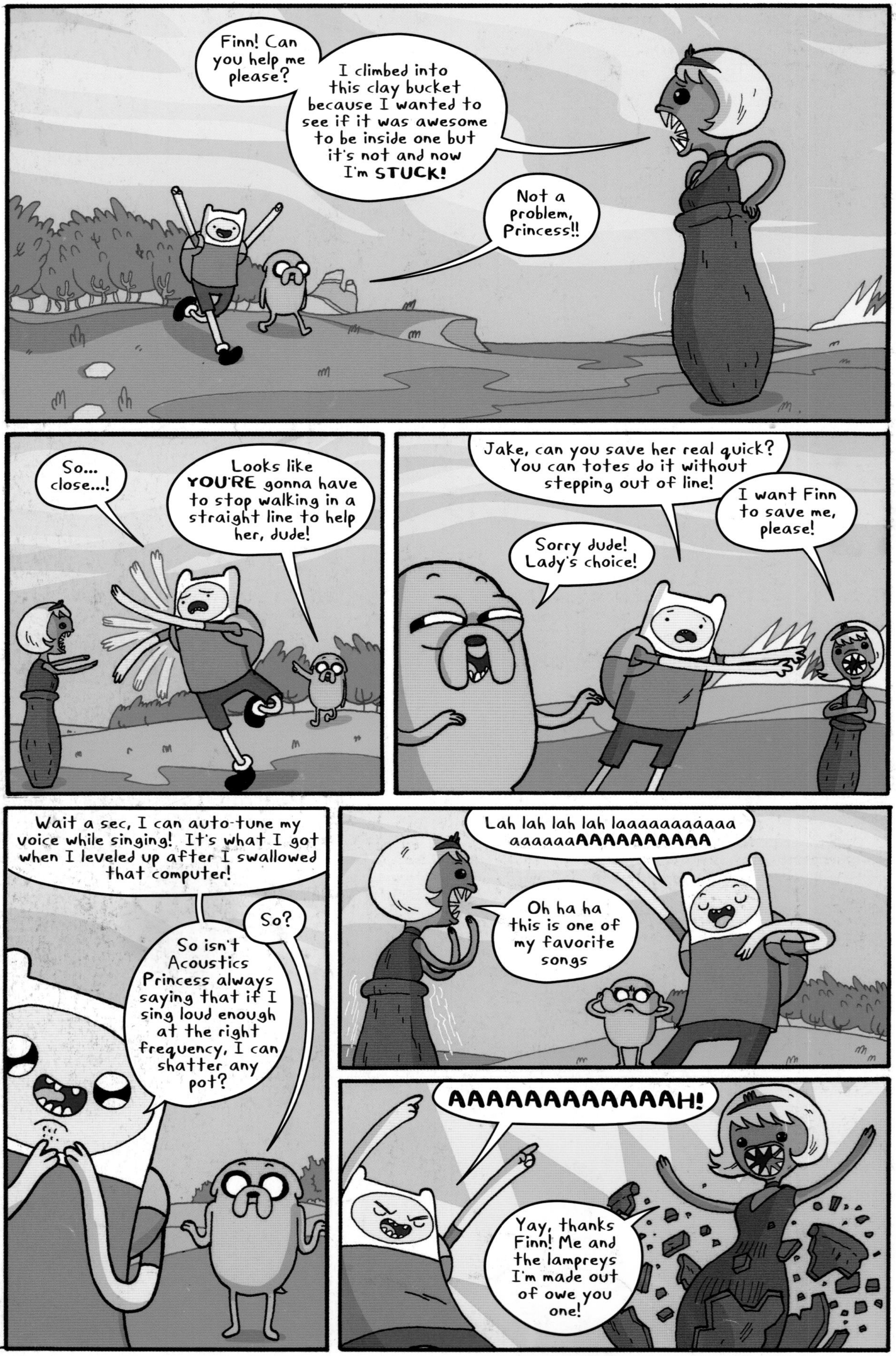

Finn! Can you help me please?
I climbed into this clay bucket because I wanted to see if it was awesome to be inside one but it's not and now I'm **STUCK!**
Not a problem, Princess!!
So... close...!
Looks like **YOU'RE** gonna have to stop walking in a straight line to help her, dude!
Jake, can you save her real quick? You can totes do it without stepping out of line!
I want Finn to save me, please!
Sorry dude! Lady's choice!
Wait a sec, I can auto-tune my voice while singing! It's what I got when I leveled up after I swallowed that computer!
So isn't Acoustics Princess always saying that if I sing loud enough at the right frequency, I can shatter any pot?
So?
Lah lah lah lah laaaaaaaaaaa aaaaaa**AAAAAAAAAA**
Oh ha ha this is one of my favorite songs
AAAAAAAAAAAAH!
Yay, thanks Finn! Me and the lampreys I'm made out of owe you one!

Yes, Acoustics Princess! You mean you haven't...*HEARD* of her?

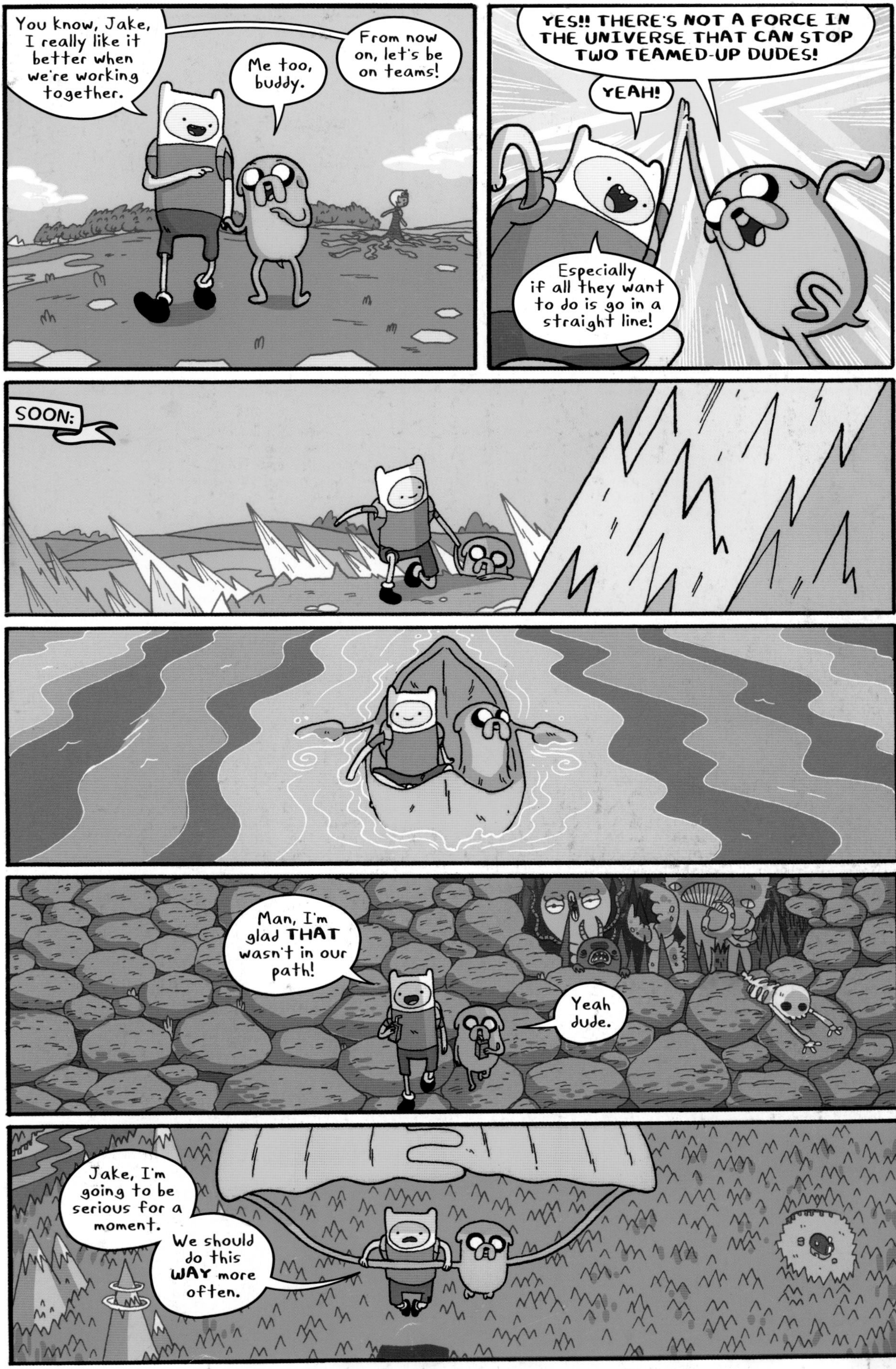
You know, Jake, I really like it better when we're working together.
Me too, buddy.
From now on, let's be on teams!
YES!! THERE'S NOT A FORCE IN THE UNIVERSE THAT CAN STOP TWO TEAMED-UP DUDES!
YEAH!
Especially if all they want to do is go in a straight line!
SOON:
Man, I'm glad THAT wasn't in our path!
Yeah dude.
Jake, I'm going to be serious for a moment.
We should do this WAY more often.

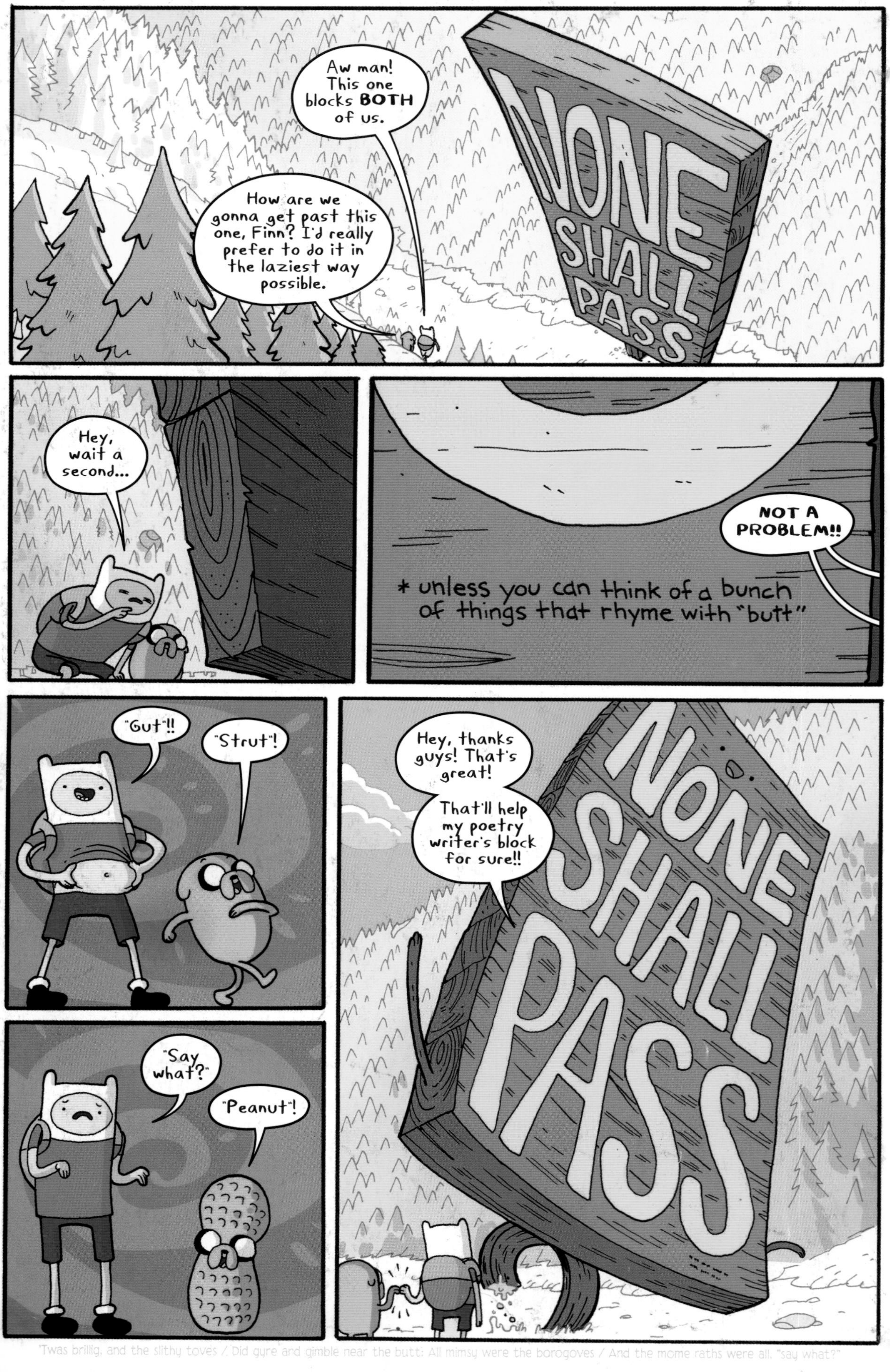
Aw man! This one blocks **BOTH** of us.
NONE SHALL PASS
How are we gonna get past this one, Finn? I'd really prefer to do it in the laziest way possible.
Hey, wait a second...
NOT A PROBLEM!!
* unless you can think of a bunch of things that rhyme with "butt"
"Gut"!!
"Strut"!
"Say what?"
"Peanut"!
Hey, thanks guys! That's great!
That'll help my poetry writer's block for sure!!
NONE SHALL PASS

'Twas brillig, and the slithy toves / Did gyre and gimble near the butt: All mimsy were the borogoves / And the mome raths were all, "say what?"

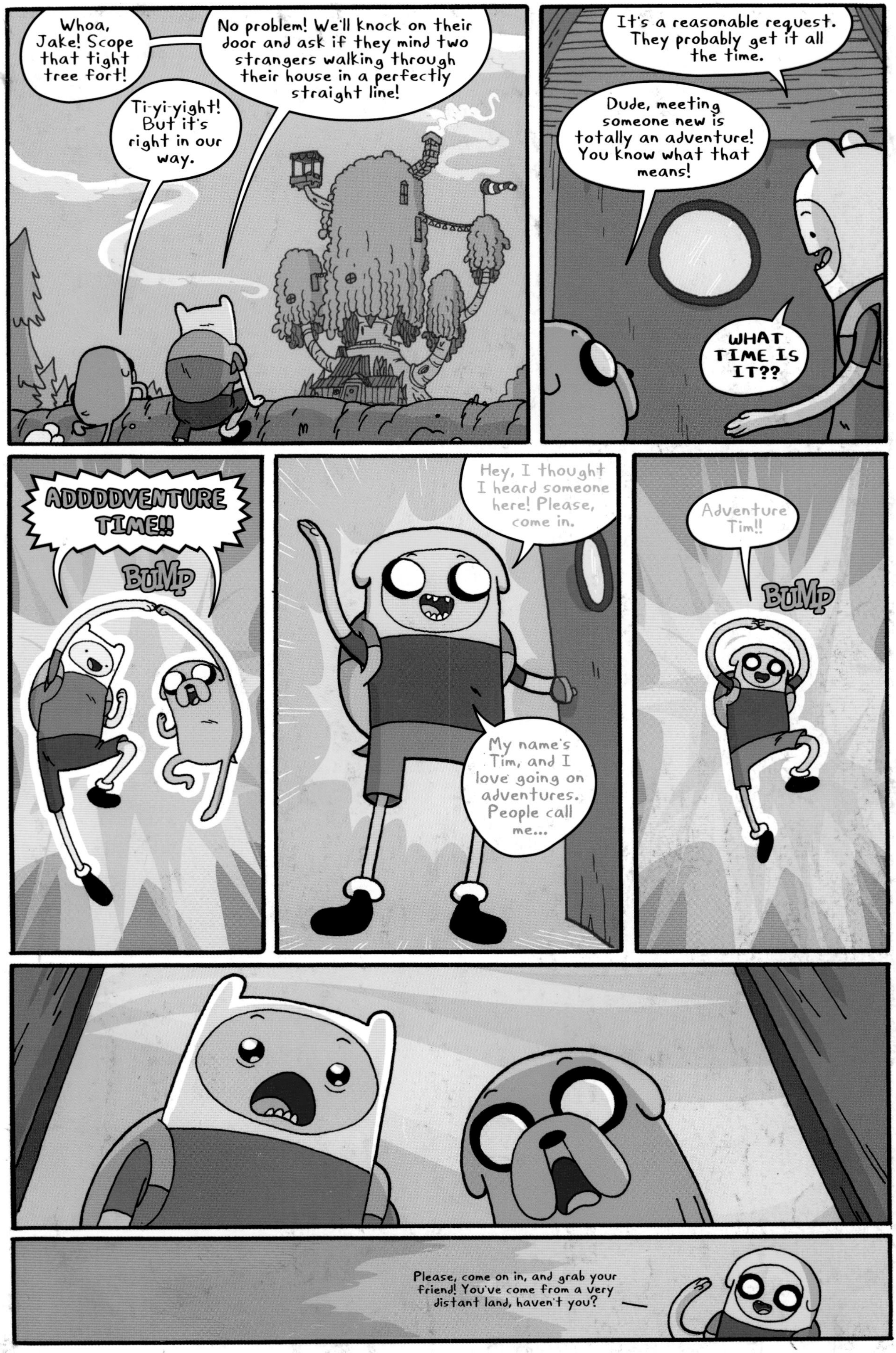

Whoa, Jake! Scope that tight tree fort!
Ti-yi-yight! But it's right in our way.
No problem! We'll knock on their door and ask if they mind two strangers walking through their house in a perfectly straight line!
It's a reasonable request. They probably get it all the time.
Dude, meeting someone new is totally an adventure! You know what that means!
WHAT TIME IS IT??
ADDDDVENTURE TIME!!
BUMP
Hey, I thought I heard someone here! Please, come in.
My name's Tim, and I love going on adventures. People call me...
Adventure Tim!!
BUMP
Please, come on in, and grab your friend! You've come from a very distant land, haven't you?

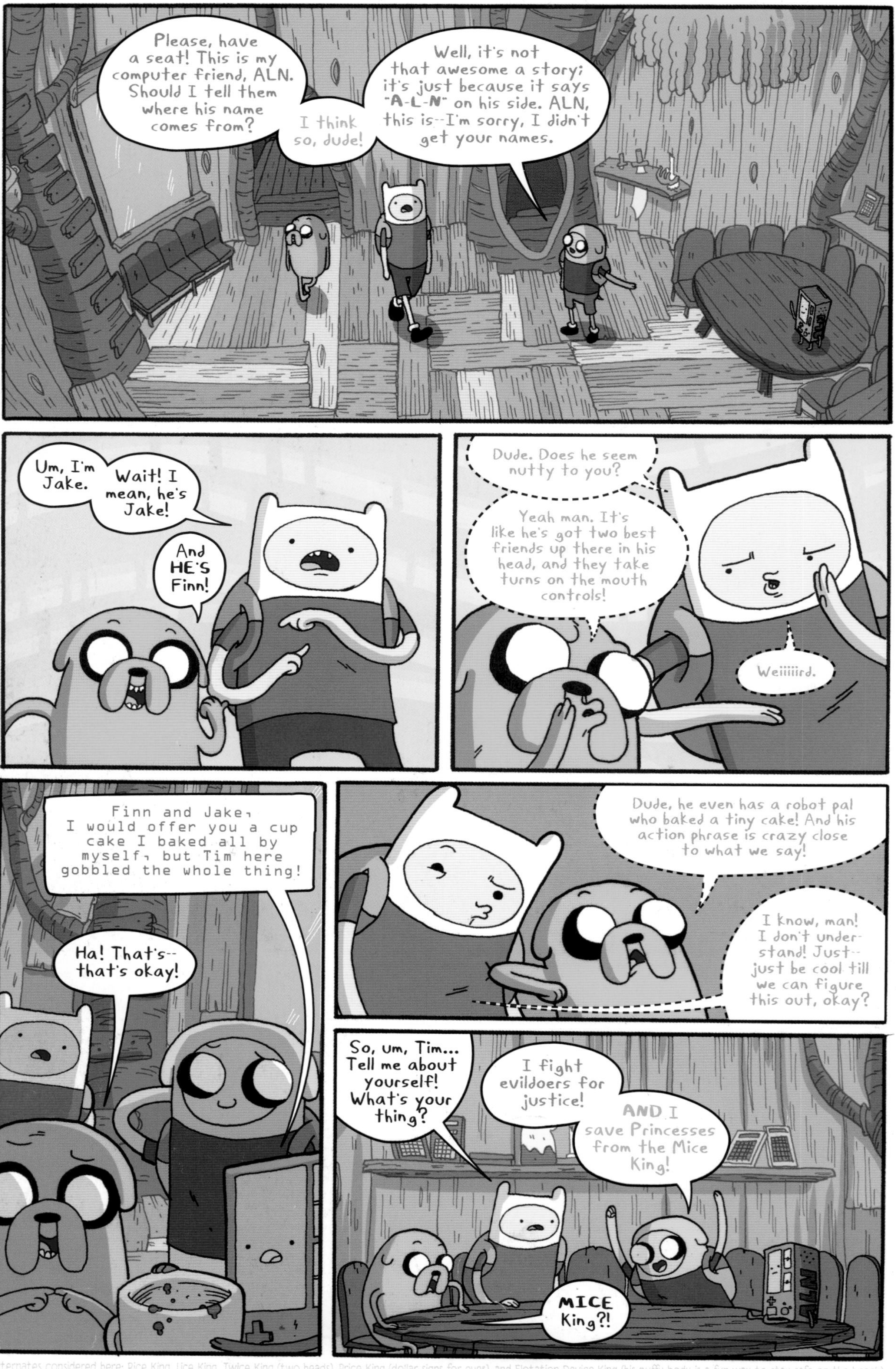
Please, have a seat! This is my computer friend, ALN. Should I tell them where his name comes from?
I think so, dude!
Well, it's not that awesome a story; it's just because it says "A-L-N" on his side. ALN, this is--I'm sorry, I didn't get your names.
Um, I'm Jake.
Wait! I mean, he's Jake!
And HE'S Finn!
Dude. Does he seem nutty to you?
Yeah man. It's like he's got two best friends up there in his head, and they take turns on the mouth controls!
Weiiiiird.
Finn and Jake, I would offer you a cup cake I baked all by myself, but Tim here gobbled the whole thing!
Ha! That's-- that's okay!
Dude, he even has a robot pal who baked a tiny cake! And his action phrase is crazy close to what we say!
I know, man! I don't understand! Just-- just be cool till we can figure this out, okay?
So, um, Tim... Tell me about yourself! What's your thing?
I fight evildoers for justice!
AND I save Princesses from the Mice King!
MICE King?!

Alternates considered here: Rice King, Lice King, Twice King (two heads), Price King (dollar signs for eyes), and Flotation Device King (his puffy body is a fun way to stay safe on the beach)

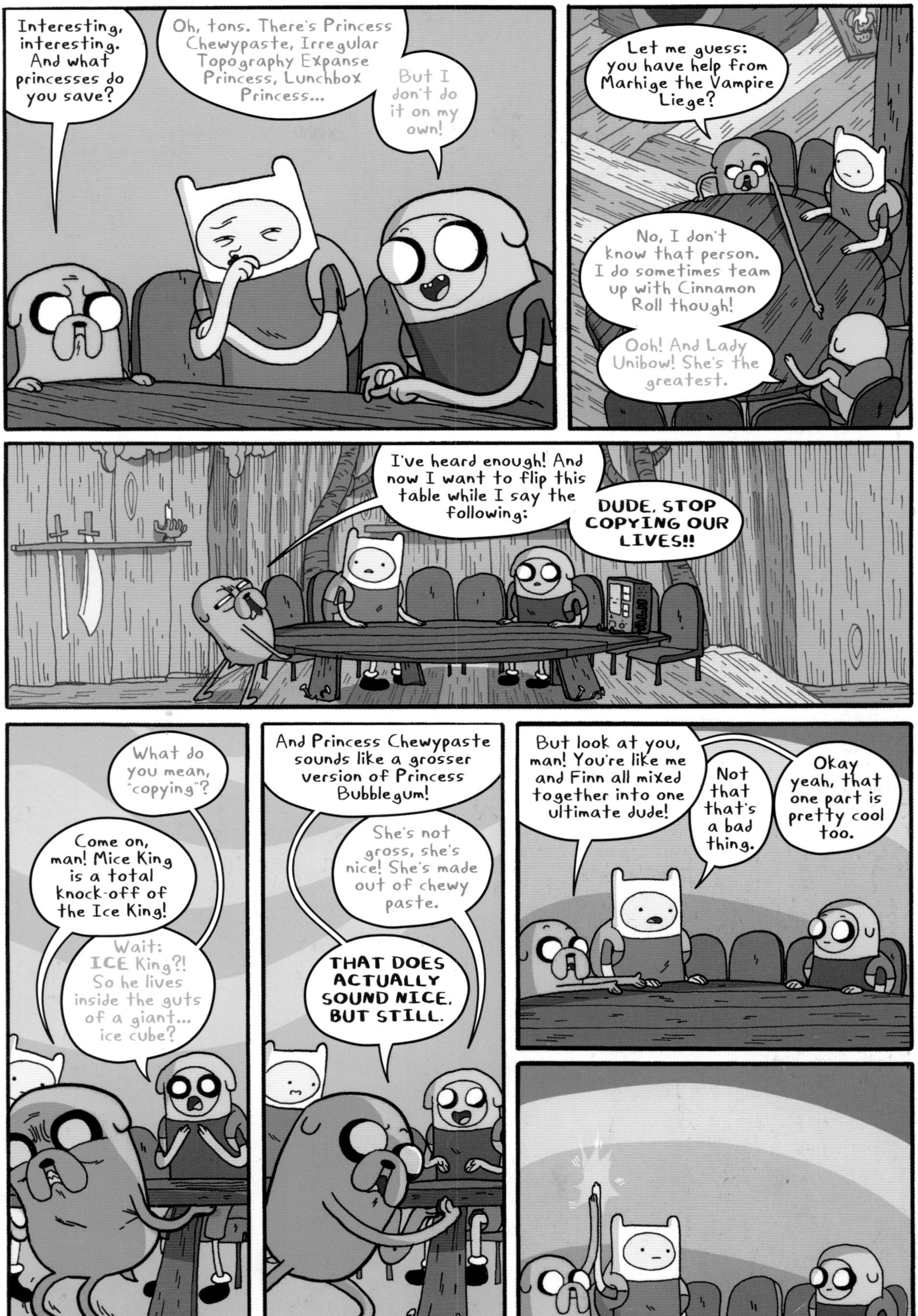

Interesting, interesting. And what princesses do you save?
Oh, tons. There's Princess Chewypaste, Irregular Topography Expanse Princess, Lunchbox Princess...
But I don't do it on my own!
Let me guess: you have help from Marhige the Vampire Liege?
No, I don't know that person. I do sometimes team up with Cinnamon Roll though!
Ooh! And Lady Unibow! She's the greatest.
I've heard enough! And now I want to flip this table while I say the following:
DUDE, STOP COPYING OUR LIVES!!
What do you mean, "copying"?
Come on, man! Mice King is a total knock-off of the Ice King!
Wait: ICE King?! So he lives inside the guts of a giant... ice cube?
And Princess Chewypaste sounds like a grosser version of Princess Bubblegum!
She's not gross, she's nice! She's made out of chewy paste.
THAT DOES ACTUALLY SOUND NICE, BUT STILL.
But look at you, man! You're like me and Finn all mixed together into one ultimate dude!
Not that that's a bad thing.
Okay yeah, that one part is pretty cool too.

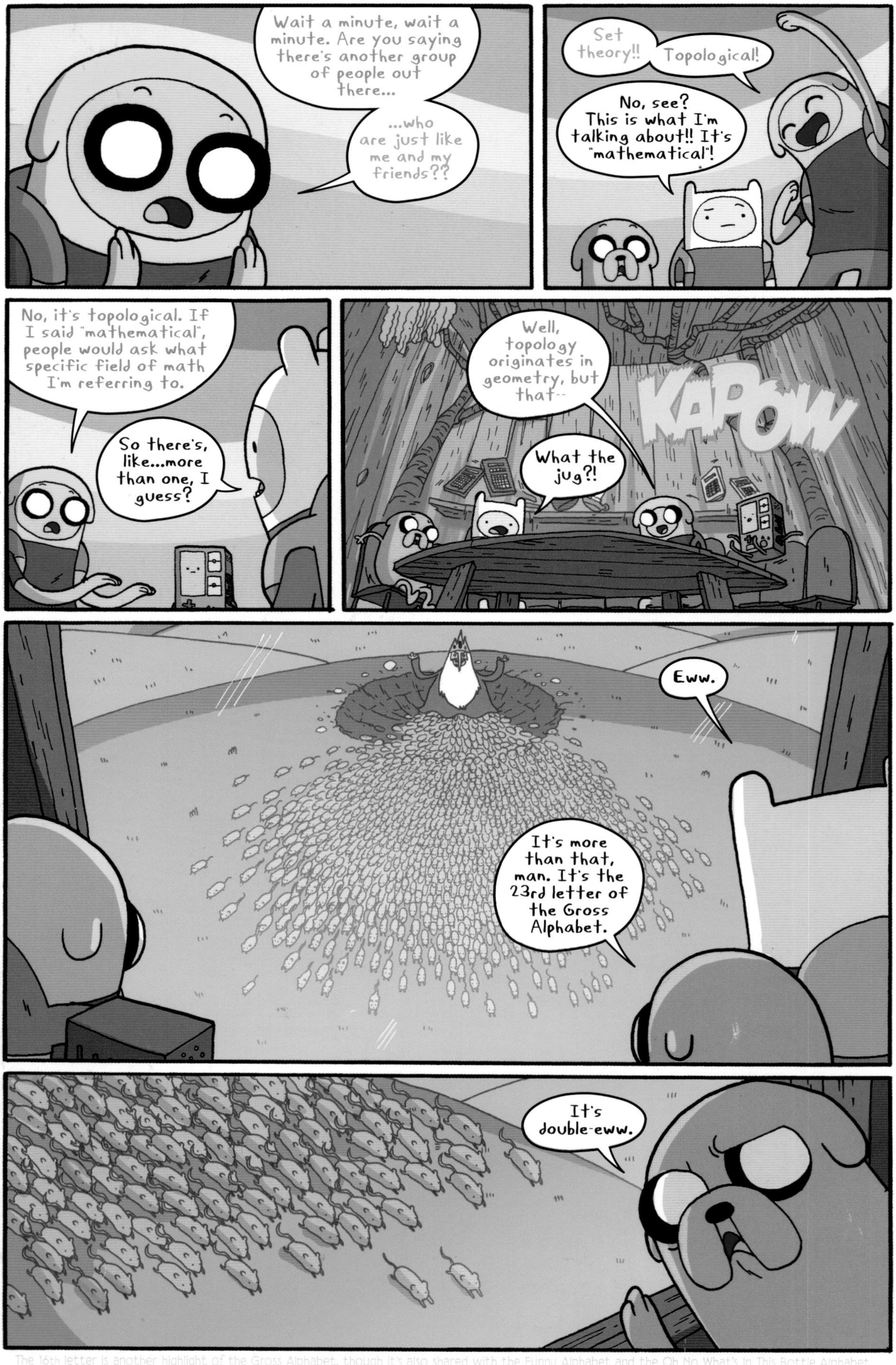
Wait a minute, wait a minute. Are you saying there's another group of people out there...
...who are just like me and my friends??
Set theory!!
Topological!
No, see? This is what I'm talking about!! It's "mathematical"!
No, it's topological. If I said "mathematical", people would ask what specific field of math I'm referring to.
So there's, like...more than one, I guess?
Well, topology originates in geometry, but that--
KAPOW
What the jug?!
Eww.
It's more than that, man. It's the 23rd letter of the Gross Alphabet.
It's double-eww.

The 16th letter is another highlight of the Gross Alphabet, though it's also shared with the Funny Alphabet and the Oh No What's In This Bottle Alphabet.

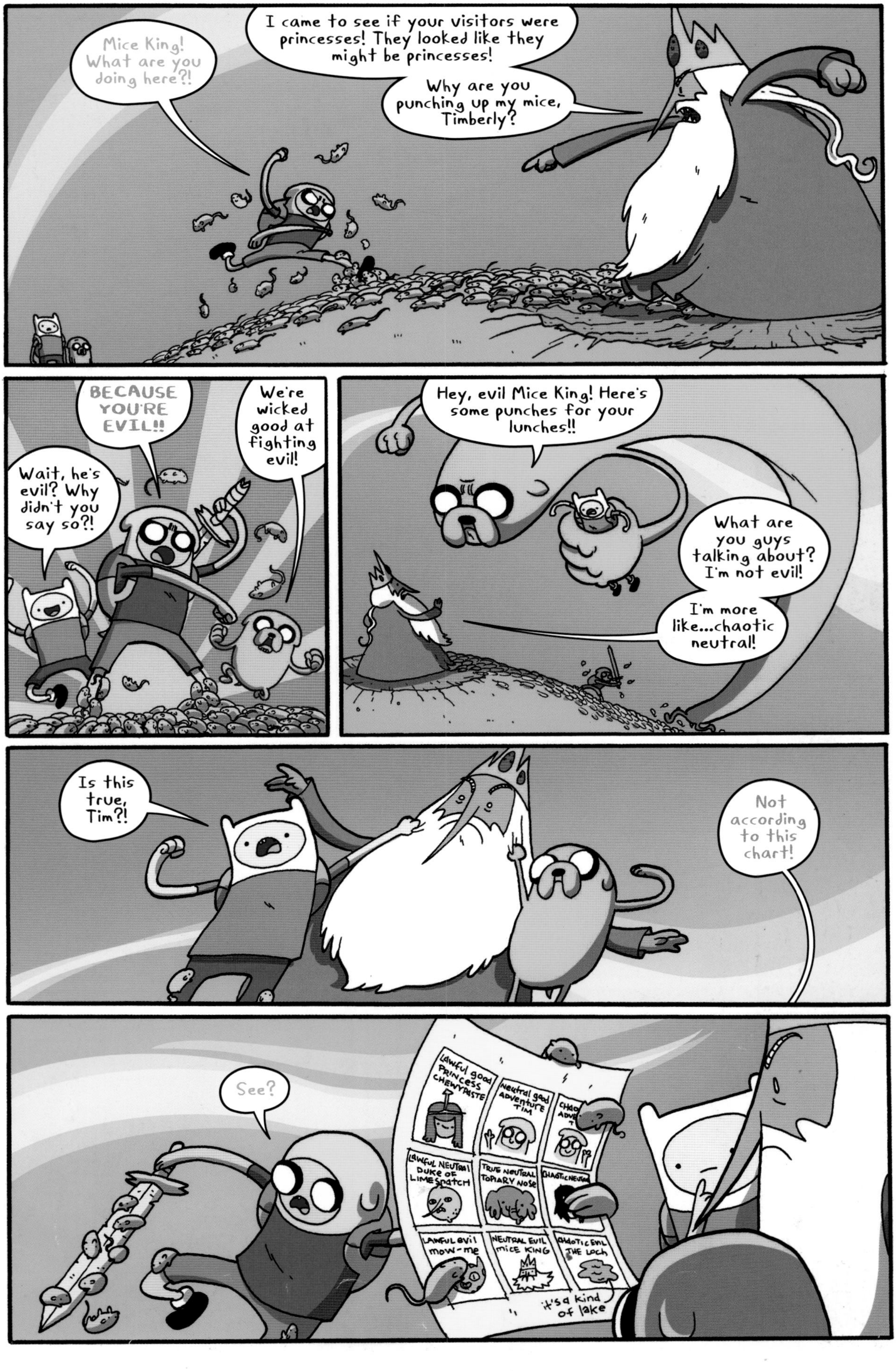
Mice King! What are you doing here?!
I came to see if your visitors were princesses! They looked like they might be princesses!
Why are you punching up my mice, Timberly?
BECAUSE YOU'RE EVIL!!
We're wicked good at fighting evil!
Wait, he's evil? Why didn't you say so?!
Hey, evil Mice King! Here's some punches for your lunches!!
What are you guys talking about? I'm not evil!
I'm more like...chaotic neutral!
Is this true, Tim?!
Not according to this chart!
See?
Lawful good PRINCESS CHEWYPASTE
Neutral good ADVENTURE TIM
LAWFUL NEUTRAL DUKE OF LIMESPATCH
TRUE NEUTRAL TOPIARY NOSE
LAWFUL evil mow-me
NEUTRAL EVIL mice KING
CHAOTIC EVIL THE LOCH
it's a kind of lake

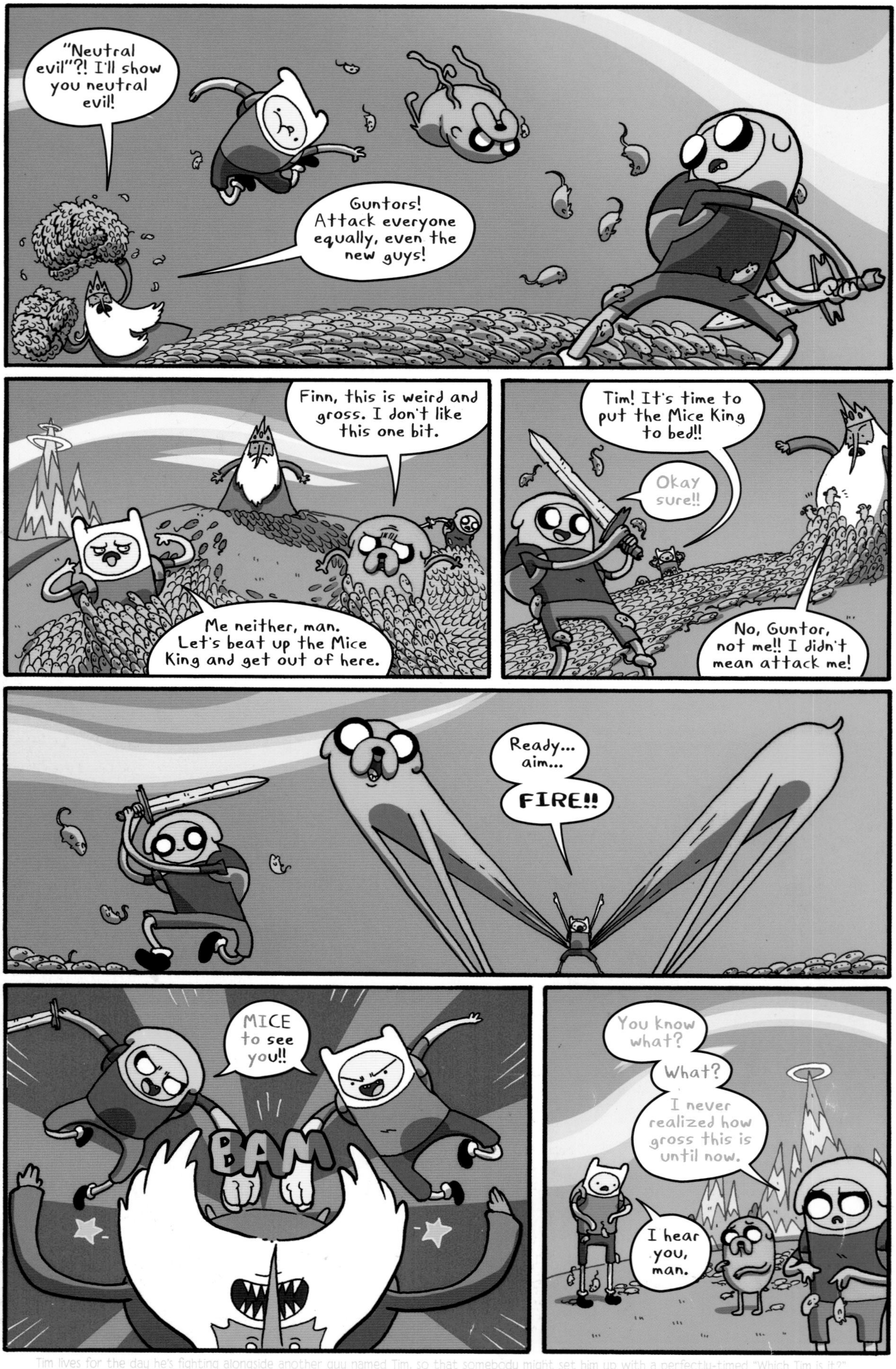
"Neutral evil"?! I'll show you neutral evil!
Guntors! Attack everyone equally, even the new guys!
Finn, this is weird and gross. I don't like this one bit.
Me neither, man. Let's beat up the Mice King and get out of here.
Tim! It's time to put the Mice King to bed!!
Okay sure!!
No, Guntor, not me!! I didn't mean attack me!
Ready... aim...
FIRE!!
MICE to see you!!
BAM
You know what?
What?
I never realized how gross this is until now.
I hear you, man.

Tim lives for the day he's fighting alongside another guy named Tim, so that somebody might set him up with a perfectly-timed "Which Tim is it?"

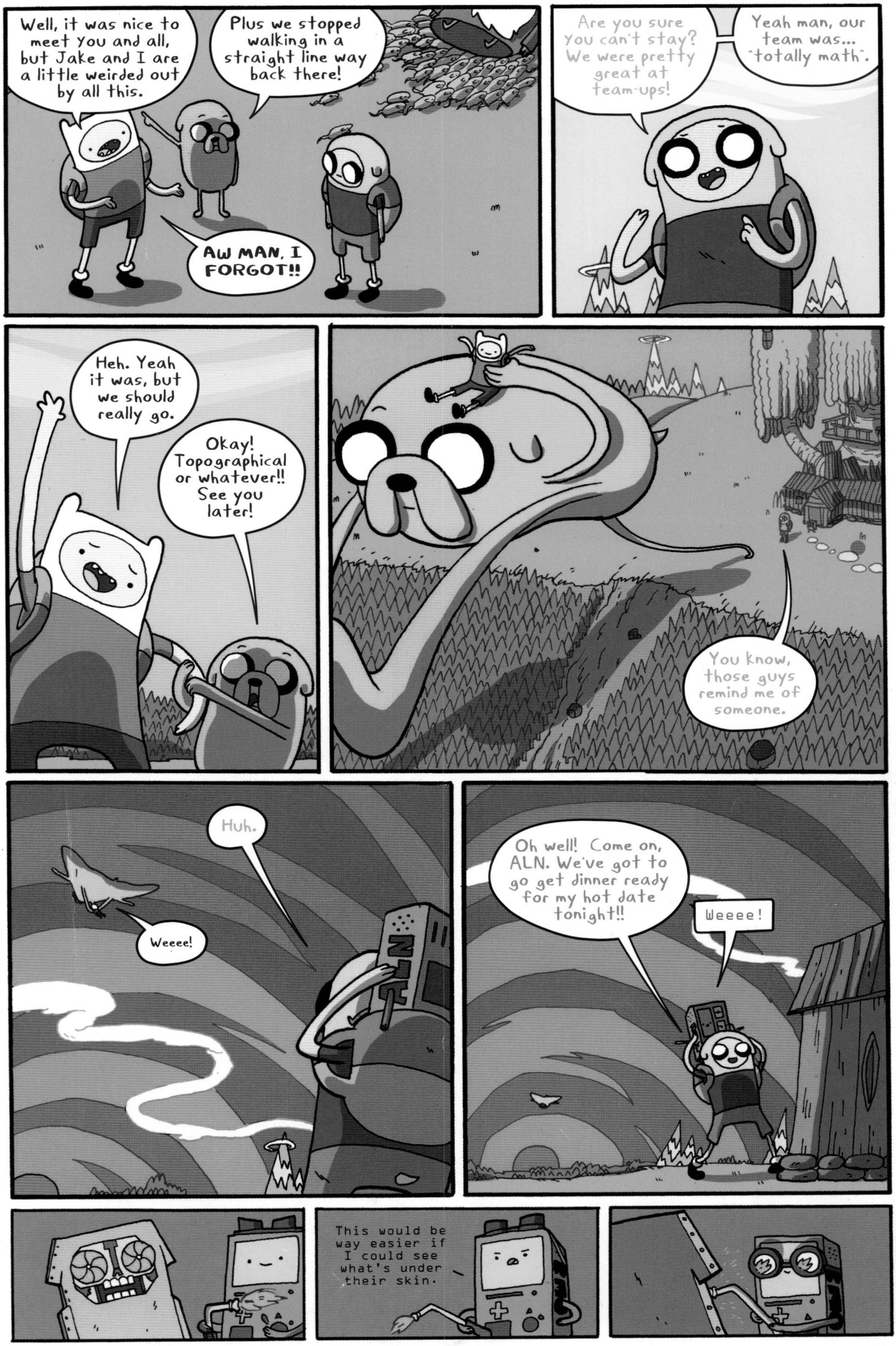
Well, it was nice to meet you and all, but Jake and I are a little weirded out by all this.
Plus we stopped walking in a straight line way back there!
AW MAN, I FORGOT!!
Are you sure you can't stay? We were pretty great at team-ups!
Yeah man, our team was... "totally math".
Heh. Yeah it was, but we should really go.
Okay! Topographical or whatever!! See you later!
You know, those guys remind me of someone.
Huh.
Weeee!
Oh well! Come on, ALN. We've got to go get dinner ready for my hot date tonight!!
Weeee!
This would be way easier if I could see what's under their skin.

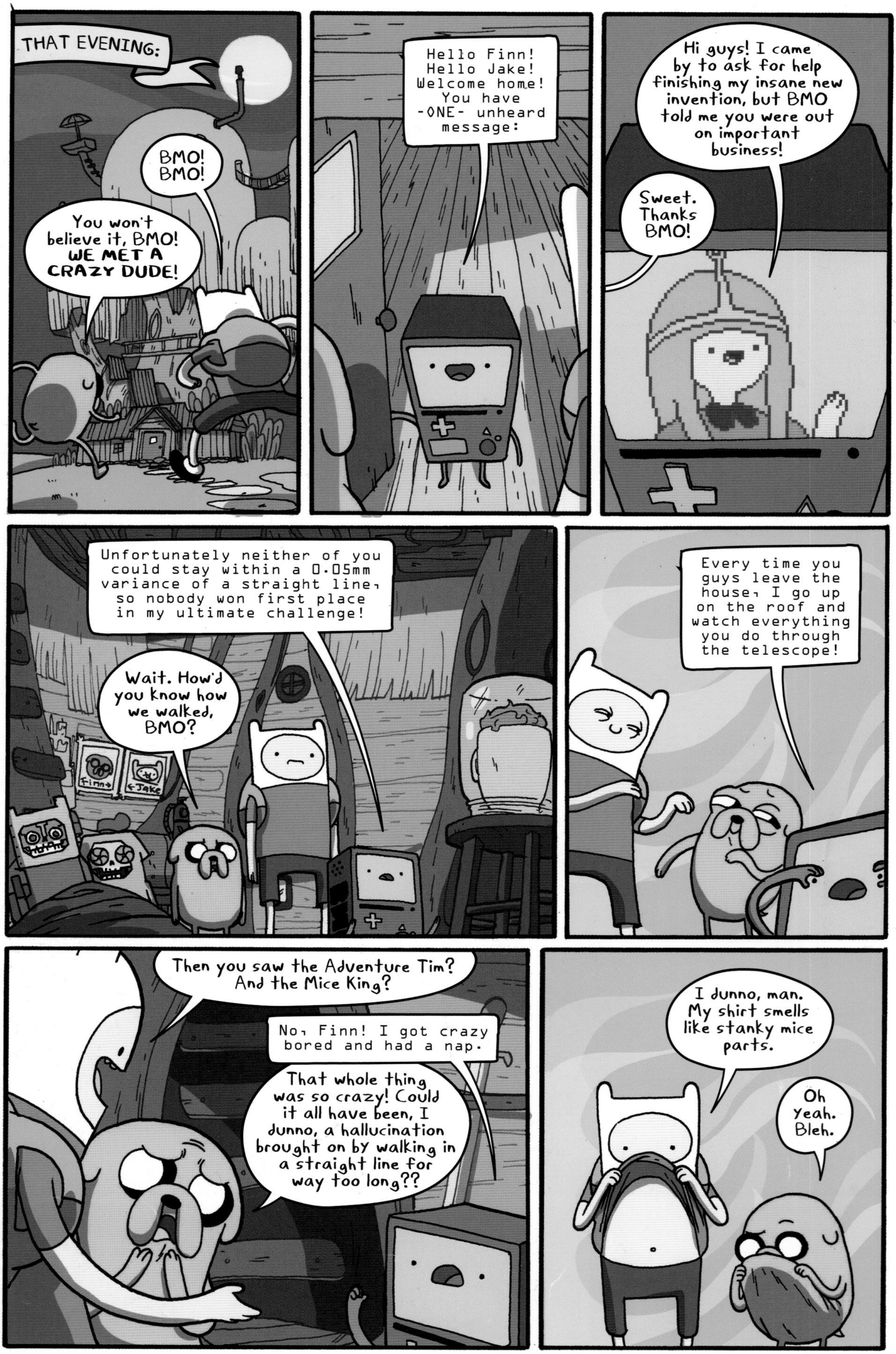
THAT EVENING:
BMO! BMO!
You won't believe it, BMO! WE MET A CRAZY DUDE!
Hello Finn! Hello Jake! Welcome home! You have -ONE- unheard message:
Hi guys! I came by to ask for help finishing my insane new invention, but BMO told me you were out on important business!
Sweet. Thanks BMO!
Unfortunately neither of you could stay within a 0.05mm variance of a straight line, so nobody won first place in my ultimate challenge!
Wait. How'd you know how we walked, BMO?
Finn
Jake
Every time you guys leave the house, I go up on the roof and watch everything you do through the telescope!
Then you saw the Adventure Tim? And the Mice King?
No, Finn! I got crazy bored and had a nap.
That whole thing was so crazy! Could it all have been, I dunno, a hallucination brought on by walking in a straight line for way too long??
I dunno, man. My shirt smells like stanky mice parts.
Oh Yeah. Bleh.

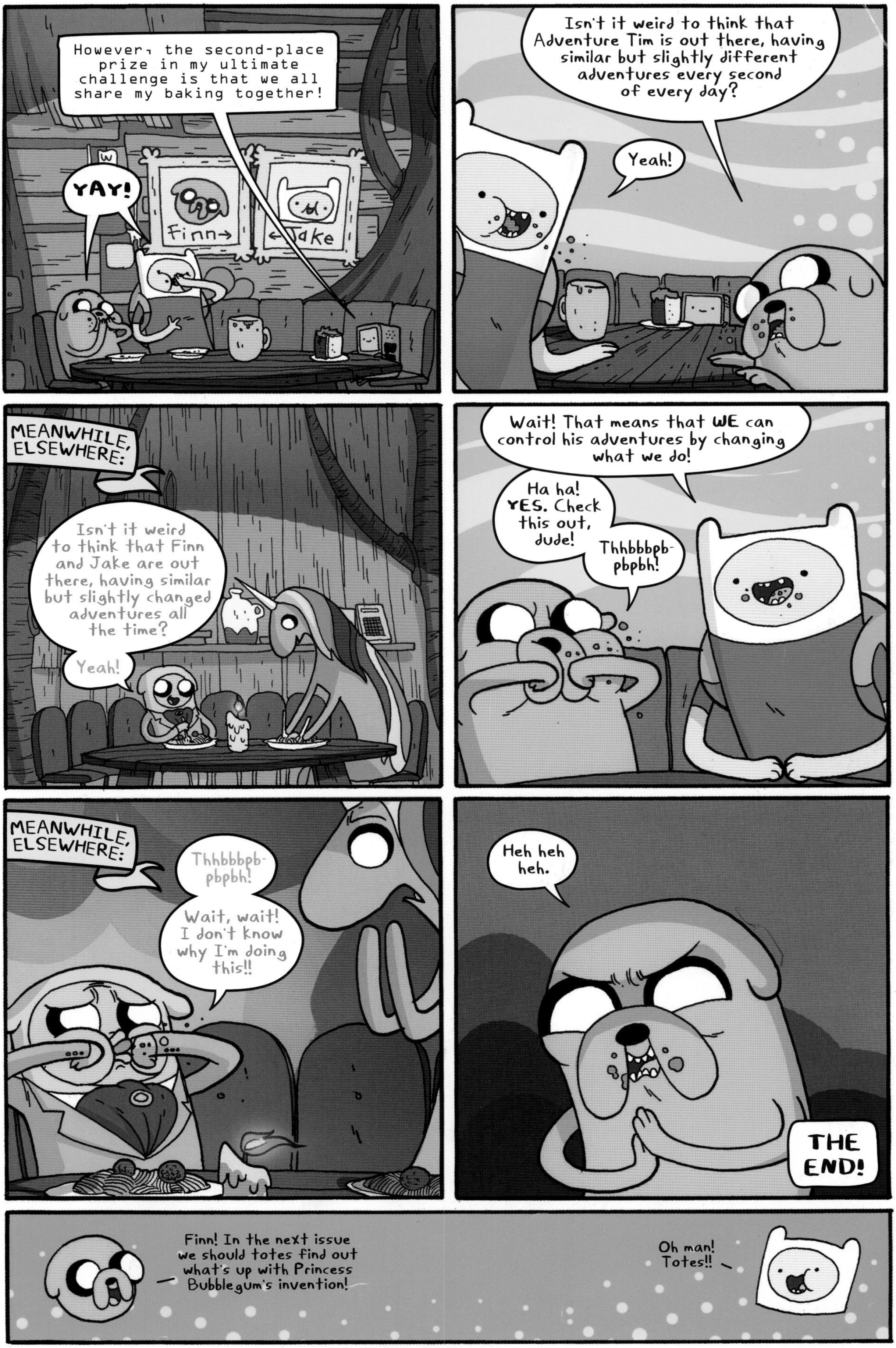

However, the second-place prize in my ultimate challenge is that we all share my baking together!
YAY!
Finn→
←Jake
Isn't it weird to think that Adventure Tim is out there, having similar but slightly different adventures every second of every day?
Yeah!
MEANWHILE, ELSEWHERE:
Isn't it weird to think that Finn and Jake are out there, having similar but slightly changed adventures all the time?
Yeah!
Wait! That means that WE can control his adventures by changing what we do!
Ha ha! YES. Check this out, dude!
Thhbbbpb-pbpbh!
MEANWHILE, ELSEWHERE:
Thhbbbpb-pbpbh!
Wait, wait! I don't know why I'm doing this!!
Heh heh heh.
THE END!
Finn! In the next issue we should totes find out what's up with Princess Bubblegum's invention!
Oh man! Totes!!

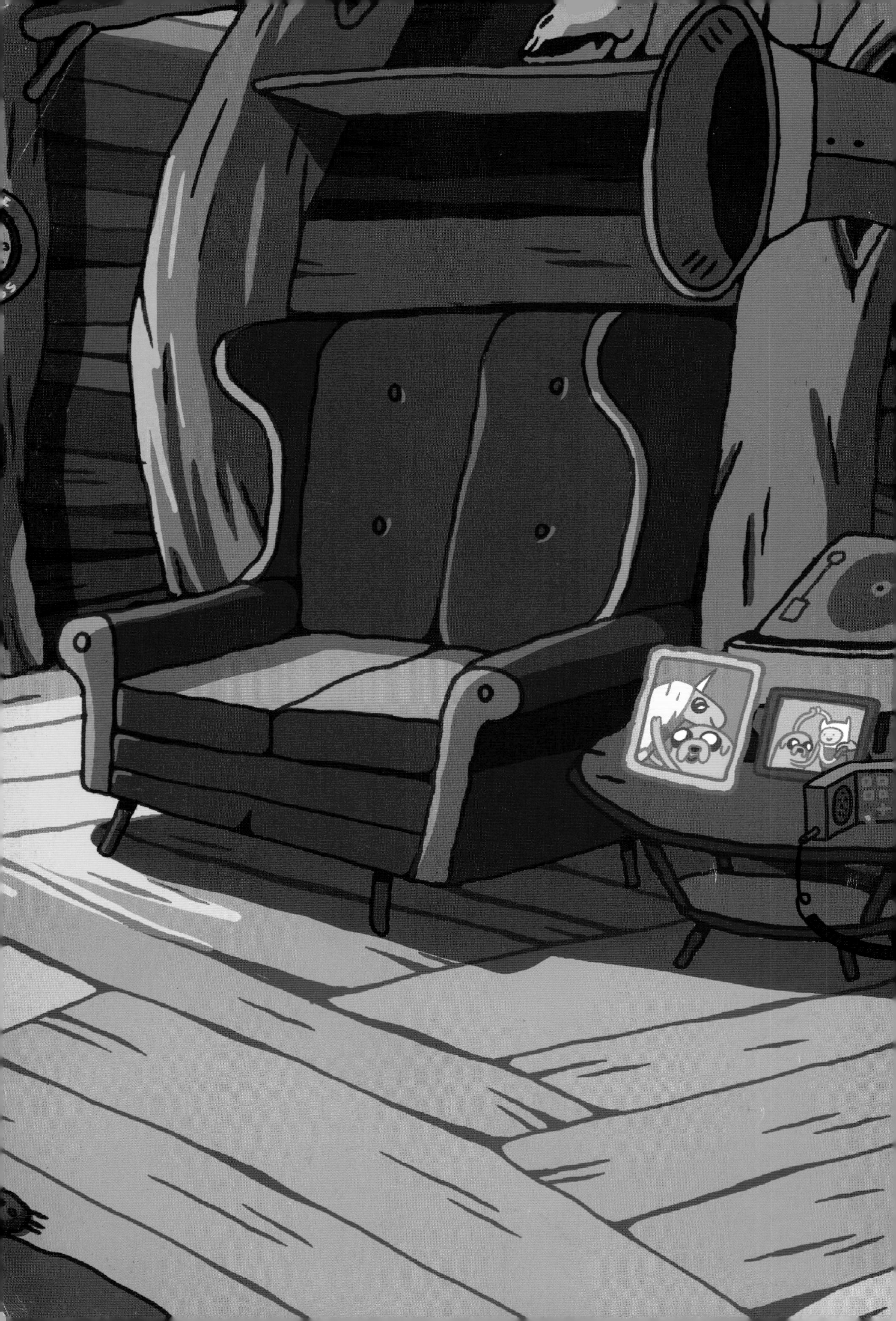

CHAPTER TWO

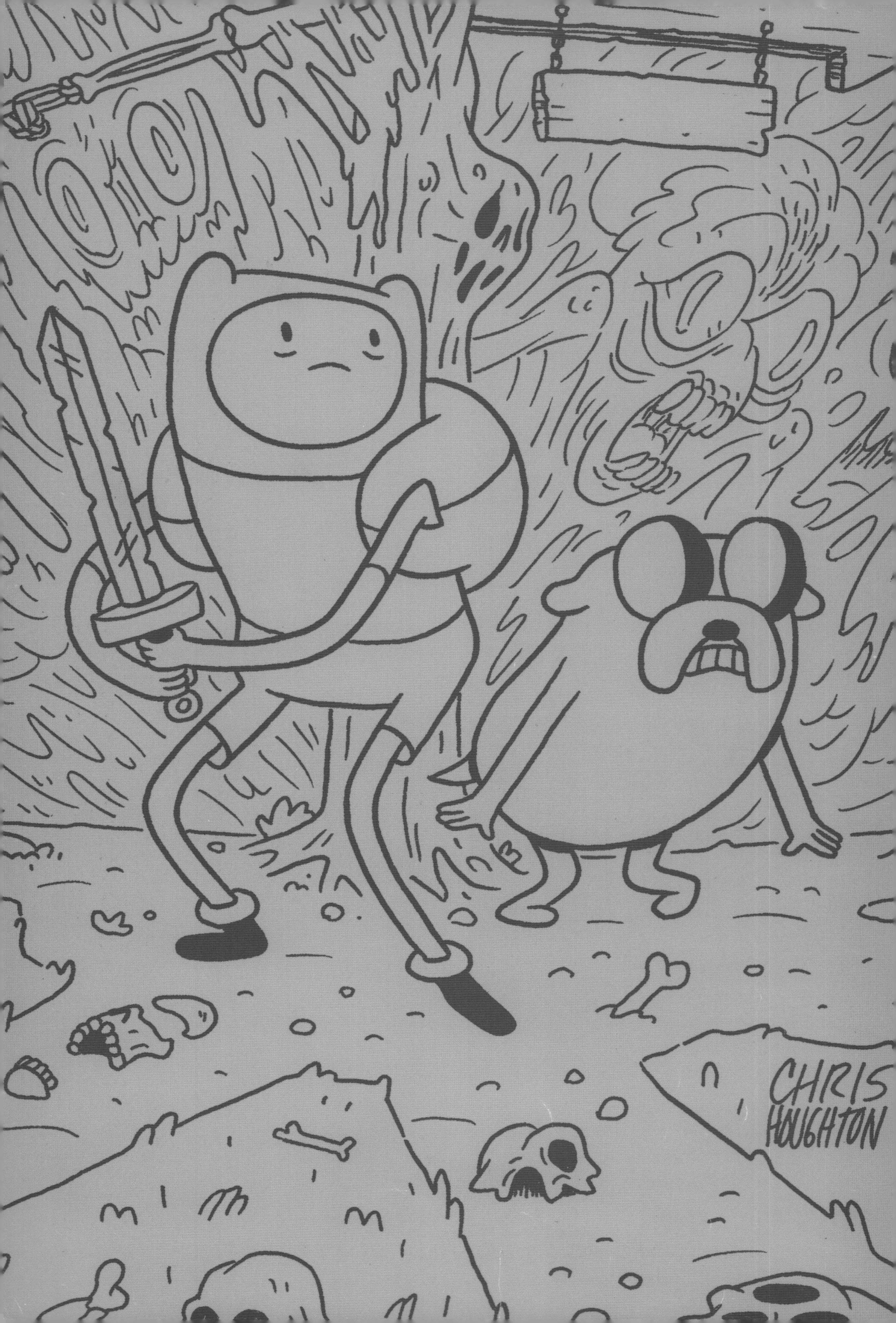
CHRIS
HOUGHTON

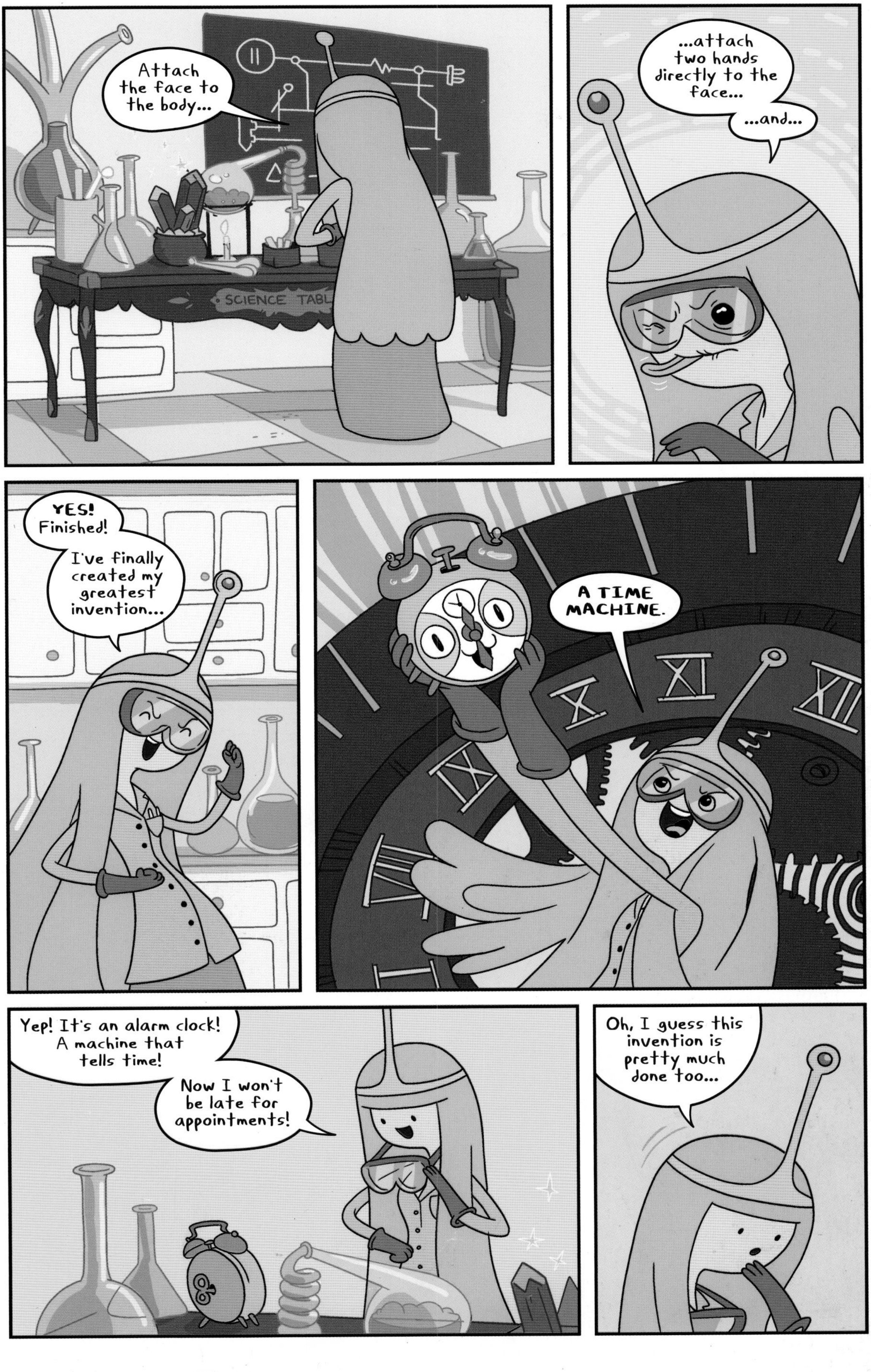
Attach the face to the body...
SCIENCE TABL
...attach two hands directly to the face...
...and...
YES! Finished!
I've finally created my greatest invention...
A TIME MACHINE.
Yep! It's an alarm clock! A machine that tells time!
Now I won't be late for appointments!
Oh, I guess this invention is pretty much done too...

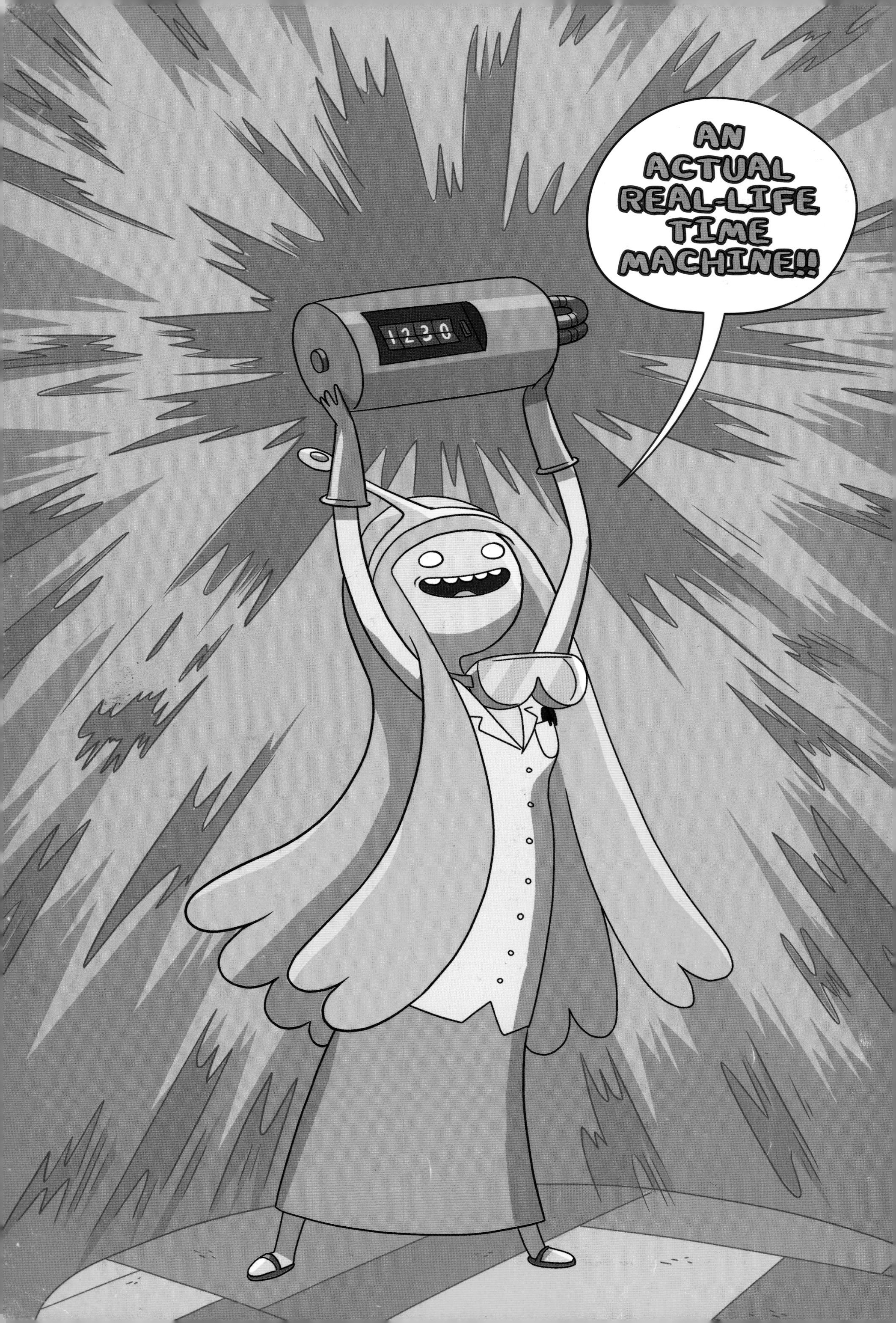
AN ACTUAL REAL-LIFE TIME MACHINE!!
1230

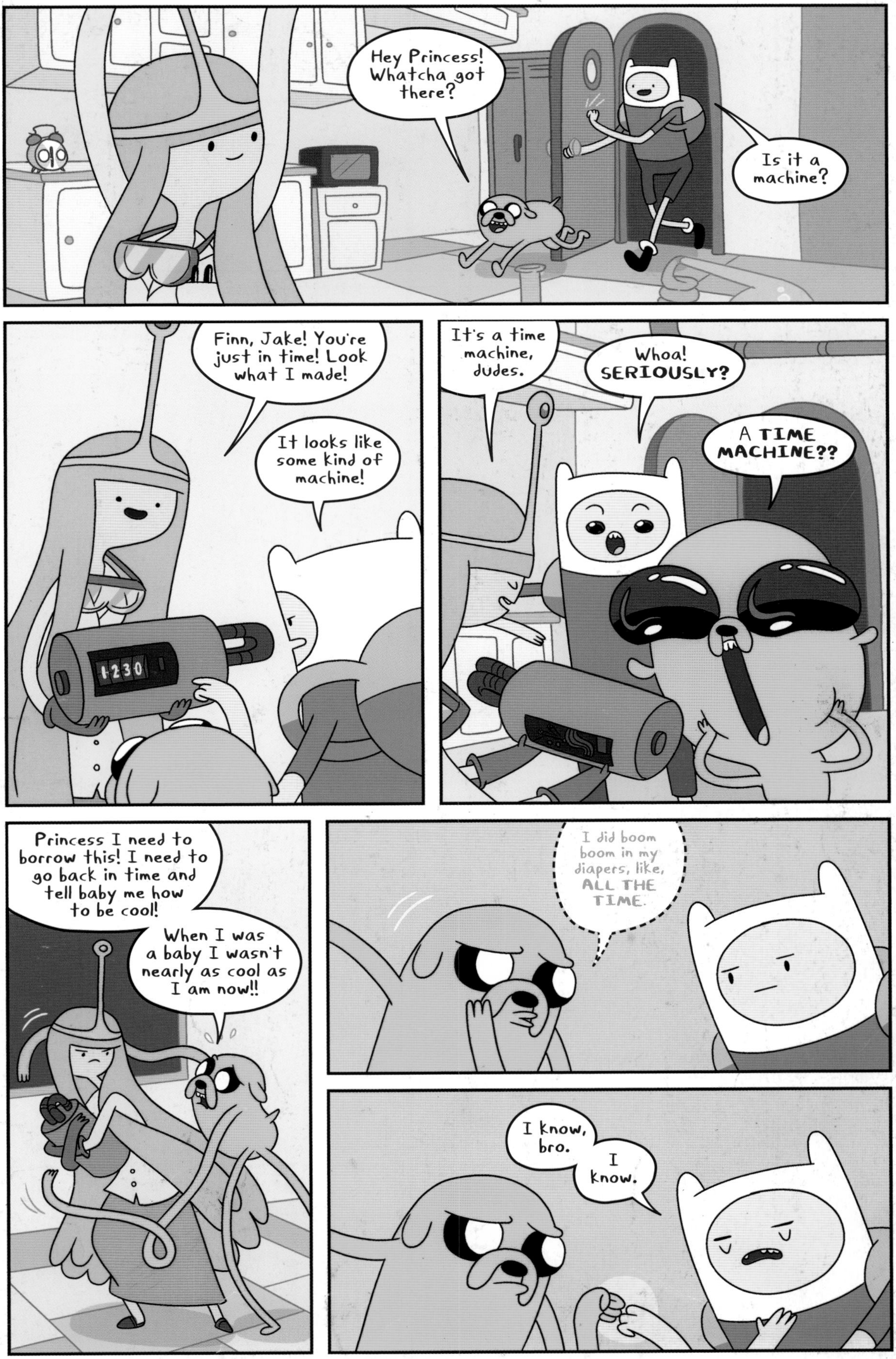
Hey Princess! Whatcha got there?
Is it a machine?
Finn, Jake! You're just in time! Look what I made!
It looks like some kind of machine!
1230
It's a time machine, dudes.
Whoa! SERIOUSLY?
A TIME MACHINE??
Princess I need to borrow this! I need to go back in time and tell baby me how to be cool!
When I was a baby I wasn't nearly as cool as I am now!!
I did boom boom in my diapers, like, ALL THE TIME.
I know, bro.
I know.

We've all done boom boom in places we regret, buddy.

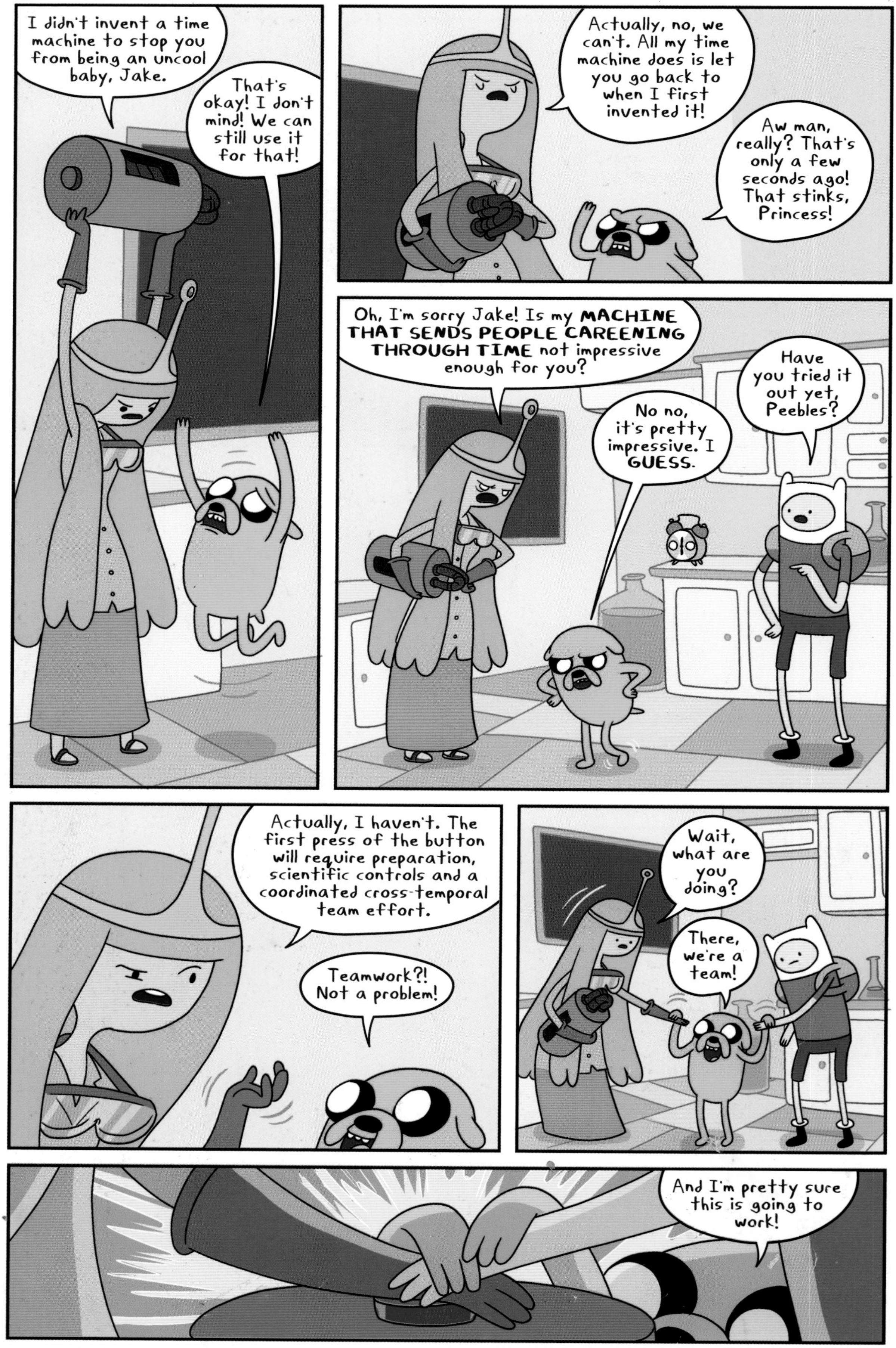
I didn't invent a time machine to stop you from being an uncool baby, Jake.
That's okay! I don't mind! We can still use it for that!
Actually, no, we can't. All my time machine does is let you go back to when I first invented it!
Aw man, really? That's only a few seconds ago! That stinks, Princess!
Oh, I'm sorry Jake! Is my **MACHINE THAT SENDS PEOPLE CAREENING THROUGH TIME** not impressive enough for you?
No no, it's pretty impressive. I **GUESS**.
Have you tried it out yet, Peebles?
Actually, I haven't. The first press of the button will require preparation, scientific controls and a coordinated cross-temporal team effort.
Teamwork?! Not a problem!
Wait, what are you doing?
There, we're a team!
And I'm pretty sure this is going to work!

It's okay, Princess Bubblegum... I'M impressed with your time machine. You've made way more progress on yours than I ever did!

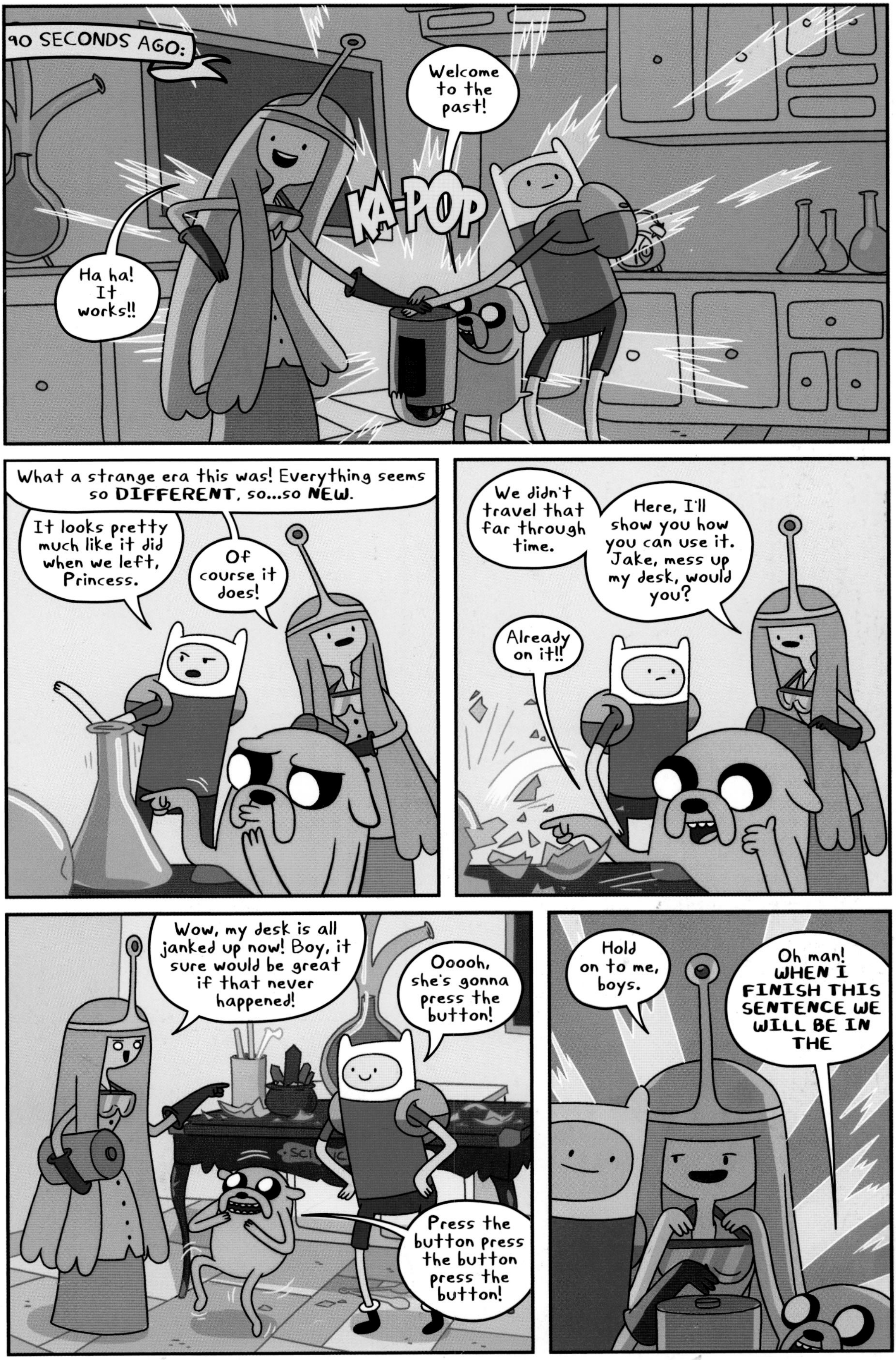
90 SECONDS AGO:
Welcome to the past!
KA-POP
Ha ha! It works!!
What a strange era this was! Everything seems so **DIFFERENT**, so...so **NEW**.
It looks pretty much like it did when we left, Princess.
Of course it does!
We didn't travel that far through time.
Here, I'll show you how you can use it. Jake, mess up my desk, would you?
Already on it!!
Wow, my desk is all janked up now! Boy, it sure would be great if that never happened!
Ooooh, she's gonna press the button!
Press the button press the button press the button!
Hold on to me, boys.
Oh man! **WHEN I FINISH THIS SENTENCE WE WILL BE IN THE**

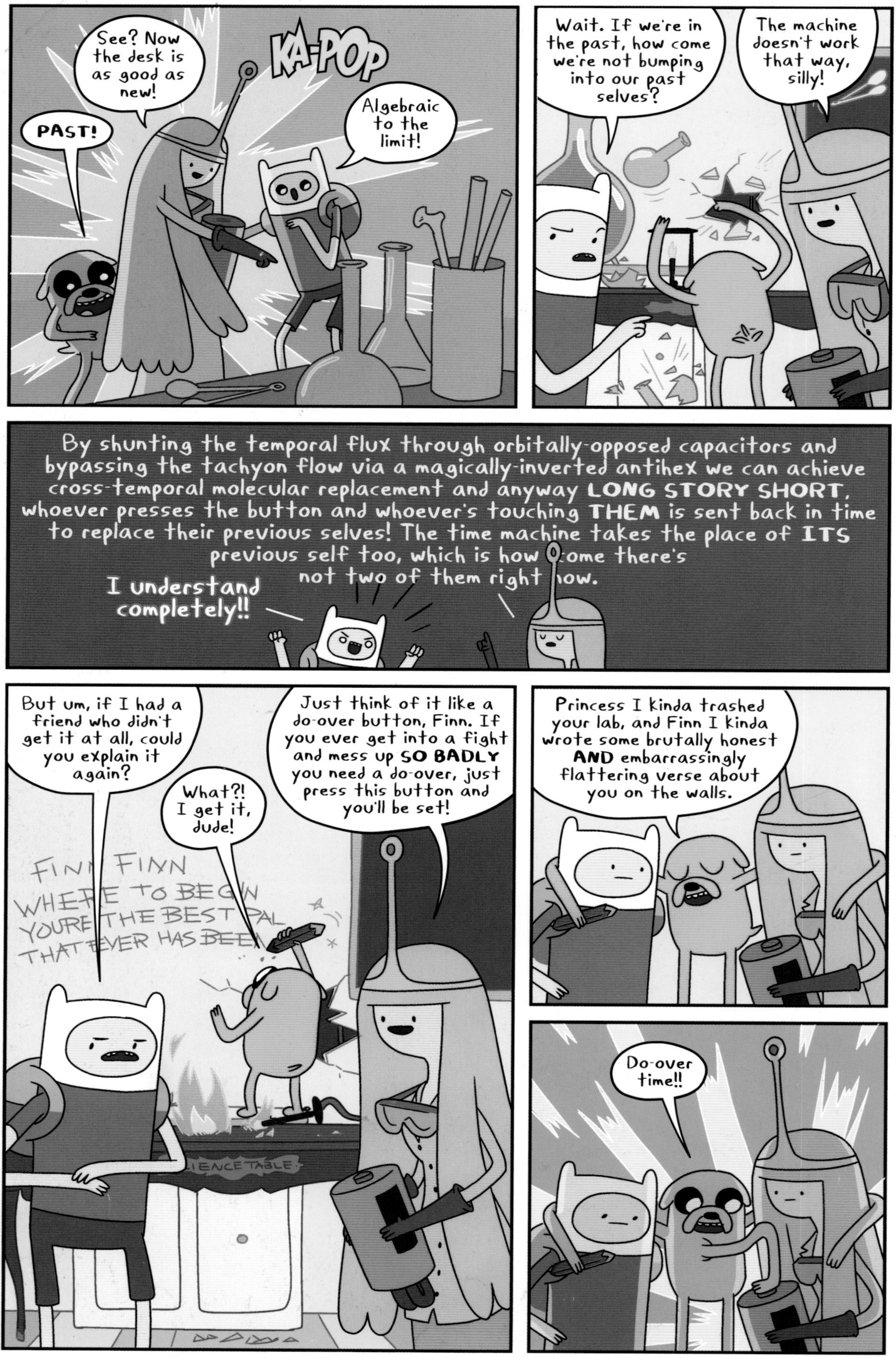
KA-POP
PAST!
See? Now the desk is as good as new!
Algebraic to the limit!
Wait. If we're in the past, how come we're not bumping into our past selves?
The machine doesn't work that way, silly!
By shunting the temporal flux through orbitally-opposed capacitors and bypassing the tachyon flow via a magically-inverted antihex we can achieve cross-temporal molecular replacement and anyway **LONG STORY SHORT**, whoever presses the button and whoever's touching **THEM** is sent back in time to replace their previous selves! The time machine takes the place of **ITS** previous self too, which is how come there's not two of them right now.
I understand completely!!
But um, if I had a friend who didn't get it at all, could you explain it again?
What?! I get it, dude!
Just think of it like a do-over button, Finn. If you ever get into a fight and mess up **SO BADLY** you need a do-over, just press this button and you'll be set!
FINN FINN
WHERE TO BEG N
YOURE THE BEST PAL
THAT EVER HAS BEE
IENCE TABLE
Princess I kinda trashed your lab, and Finn I kinda wrote some brutally honest **AND** embarrassingly flattering verse about you on the walls.
Do-over time!!

...FUTURE!

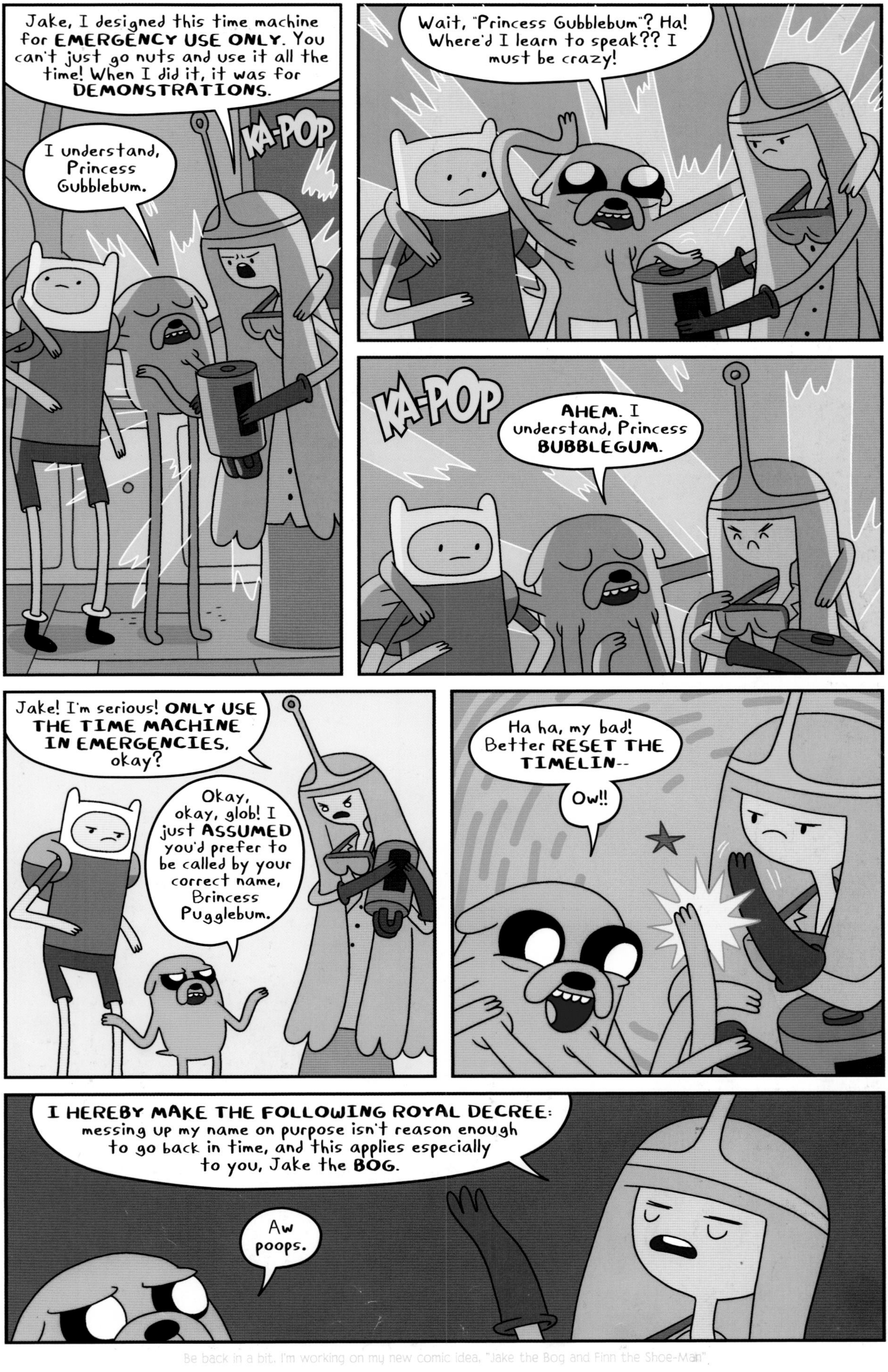
Jake, I designed this time machine for EMERGENCY USE ONLY. You can't just go nuts and use it all the time! When I did it, it was for DEMONSTRATIONS.
I understand, Princess Gubblebum.
KA-POP
Wait, "Princess Gubblebum"? Ha! Where'd I learn to speak?? I must be crazy!
KA-POP
AHEM. I understand, Princess BUBBLEGUM.
Jake! I'm serious! ONLY USE THE TIME MACHINE IN EMERGENCIES, okay?
Okay, okay, glob! I just ASSUMED you'd prefer to be called by your correct name, Brincess Pugglebum.
Ha ha, my bad! Better RESET THE TIMELIN--
Ow!!
I HEREBY MAKE THE FOLLOWING ROYAL DECREE: messing up my name on purpose isn't reason enough to go back in time, and this applies especially to you, Jake the BOG.
Aw poops.

Be back in a bit. I'm working on my new comic idea, "Jake the Bog and Finn the Shoe-Man".

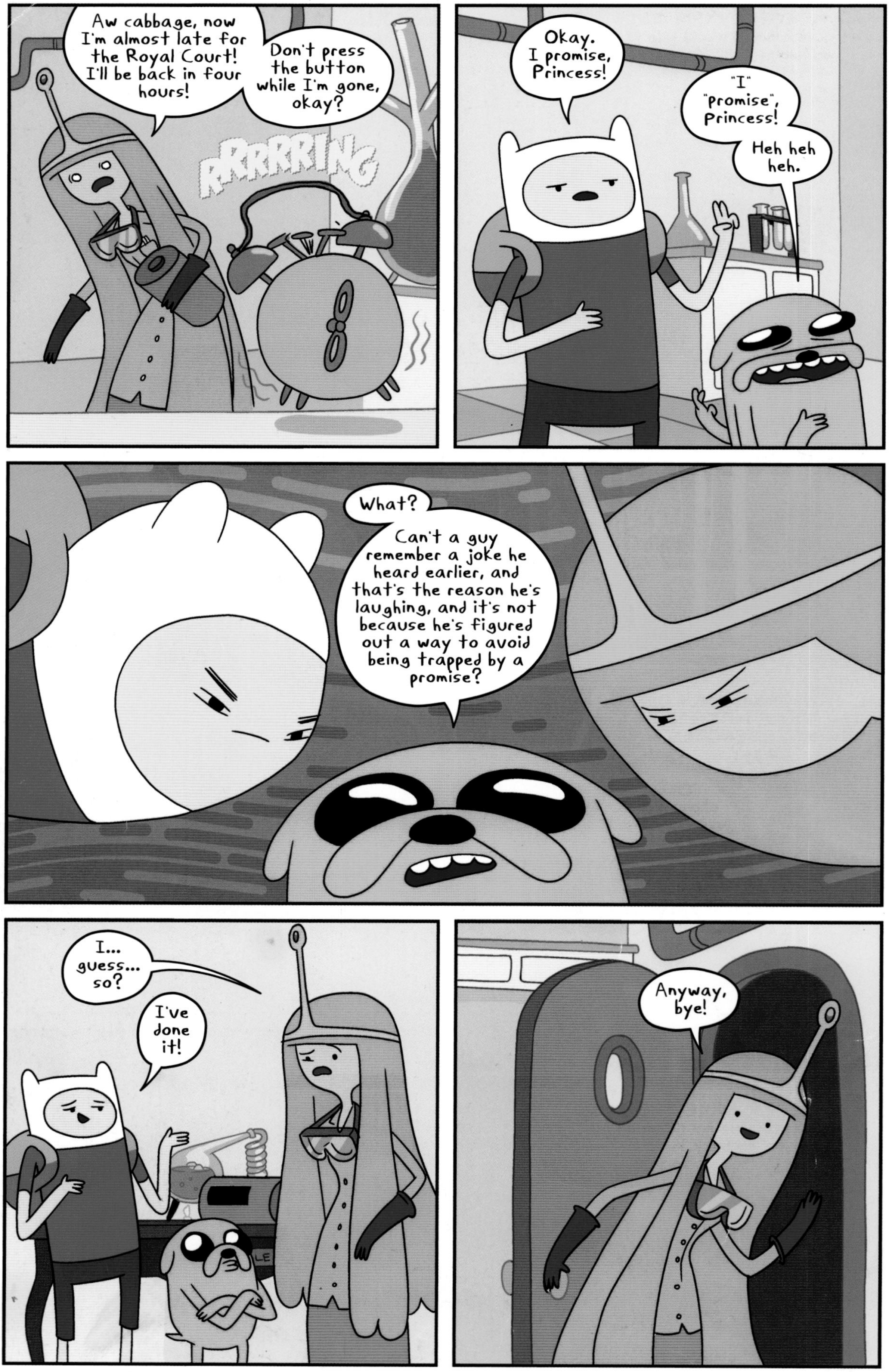
Aw cabbage, now I'm almost late for the Royal Court! I'll be back in four hours!
Don't press the button while I'm gone, okay?
RRRRRING
Okay. I promise, Princess!
"I" "promise", Princess!
Heh heh heh.
What?
Can't a guy remember a joke he heard earlier, and that's the reason he's laughing, and it's not because he's figured out a way to avoid being trapped by a promise?
I... guess... so?
I've done it!
Anyway, bye!

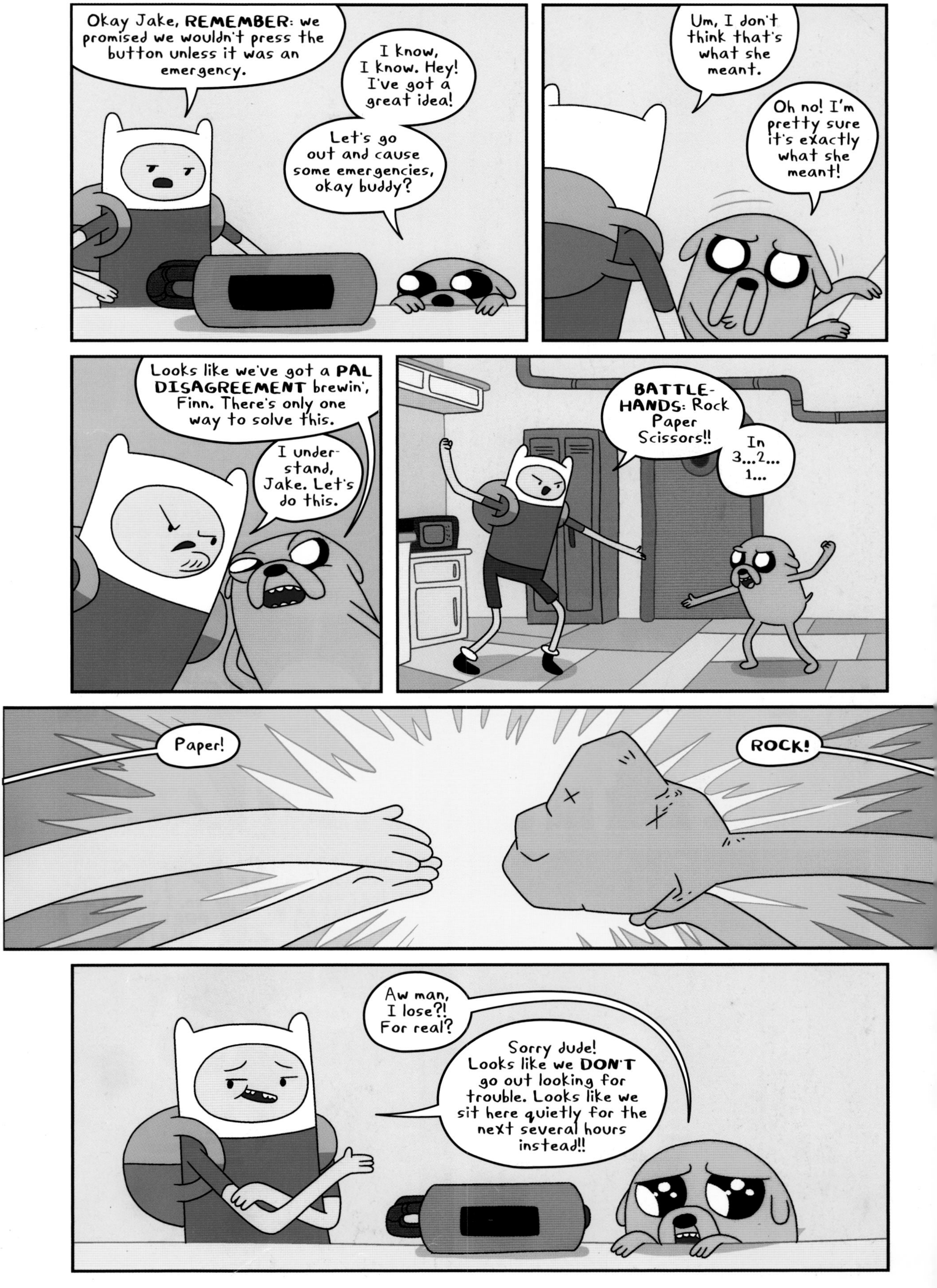
Okay Jake, REMEMBER: we promised we wouldn't press the button unless it was an emergency.
I know, I know. Hey! I've got a great idea!
Let's go out and cause some emergencies, okay buddy?
Um, I don't think that's what she meant.
Oh no! I'm pretty sure it's exactly what she meant!
Looks like we've got a PAL DISAGREEMENT brewin', Finn. There's only one way to solve this.
I understand, Jake. Let's do this.
BATTLE-HANDS: Rock Paper Scissors!!
In 3...2... 1...
Paper!
ROCK!
Aw man, I lose?! For real?
Sorry dude! Looks like we DON'T go out looking for trouble. Looks like we sit here quietly for the next several hours instead!!

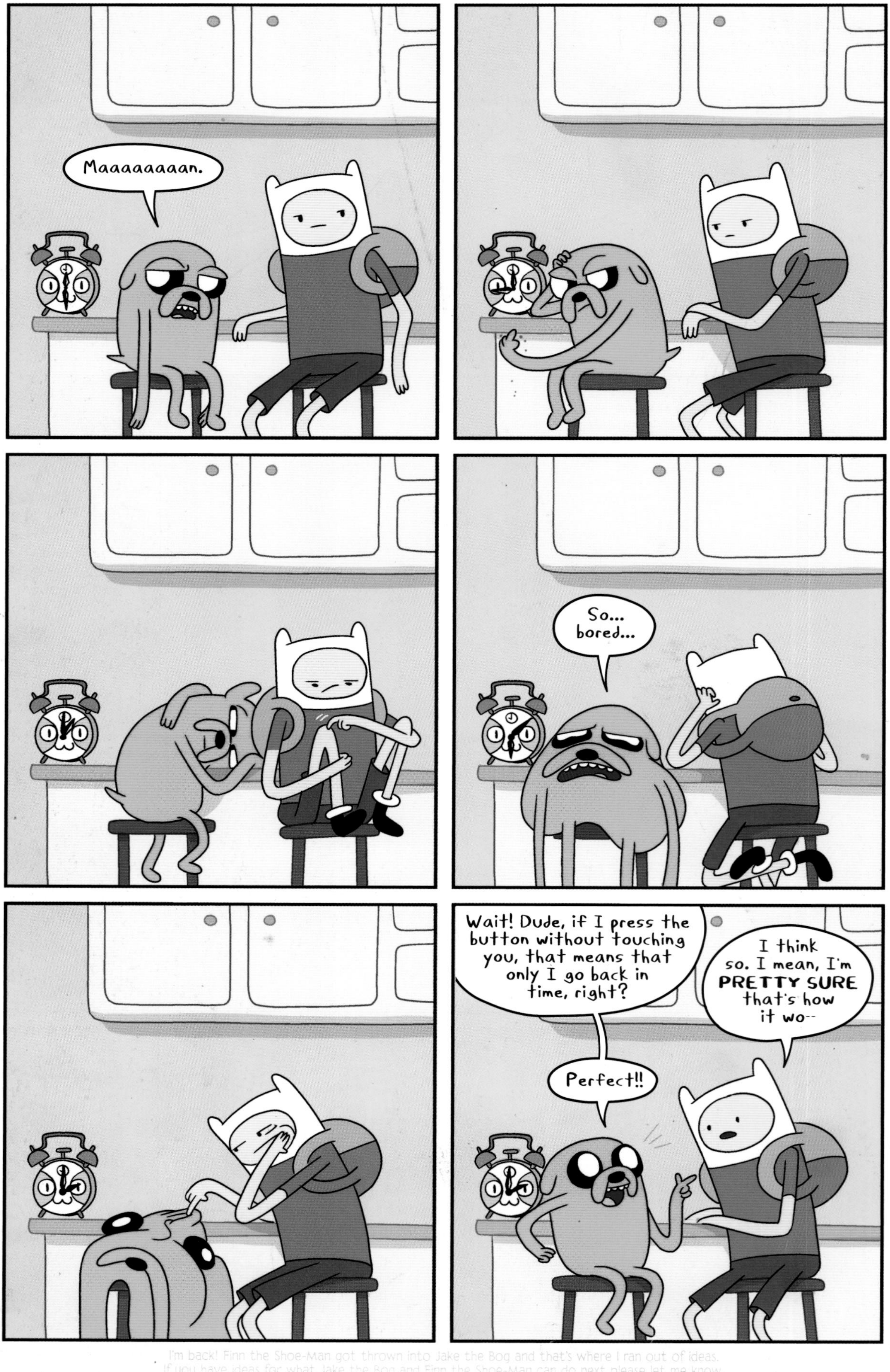
Maaaaaaaan.
So... bored...
Wait! Dude, if I press the button without touching you, that means that only I go back in time, right?
I think so. I mean, I'm **PRETTY SURE** that's how it wo--
Perfect!!

I'm back! Finn the Shoe-Man got thrown into Jake the Bog and that's where I ran out of ideas.
If you have ideas for what Jake the Bog and Finn the Shoe-Man can do next please let me know.

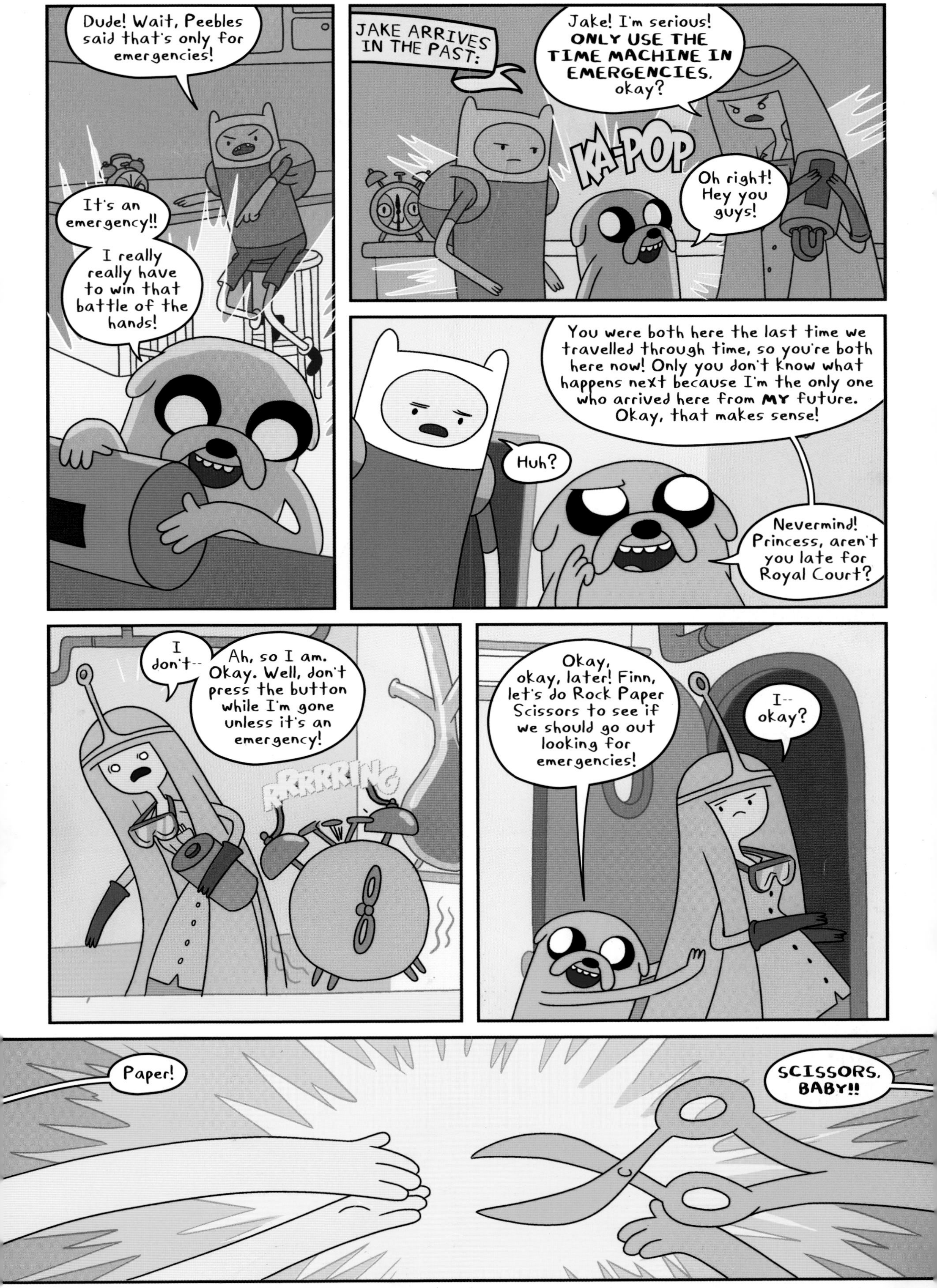
Dude! Wait, Peebles said that's only for emergencies!
It's an emergency!!
I really really have to win that battle of the hands!
JAKE ARRIVES IN THE PAST:
Jake! I'm serious! ONLY USE THE TIME MACHINE IN EMERGENCIES, okay?
KA-POP
Oh right! Hey you guys!
You were both here the last time we travelled through time, so you're both here now! Only you don't know what happens next because I'm the only one who arrived here from MY future. Okay, that makes sense!
Huh?
Nevermind! Princess, aren't you late for Royal Court?
I don't--
Ah, so I am. Okay. Well, don't press the button while I'm gone unless it's an emergency!
RRRRRING
Okay, okay, later! Finn, let's do Rock Paper Scissors to see if we should go out looking for emergencies!
I-- okay?
Paper!
SCISSORS, BABY!!

If you don't understand Jake's explanation of time travel then please re-read Jake's explanation of time travel, and he'll explain it for you again!

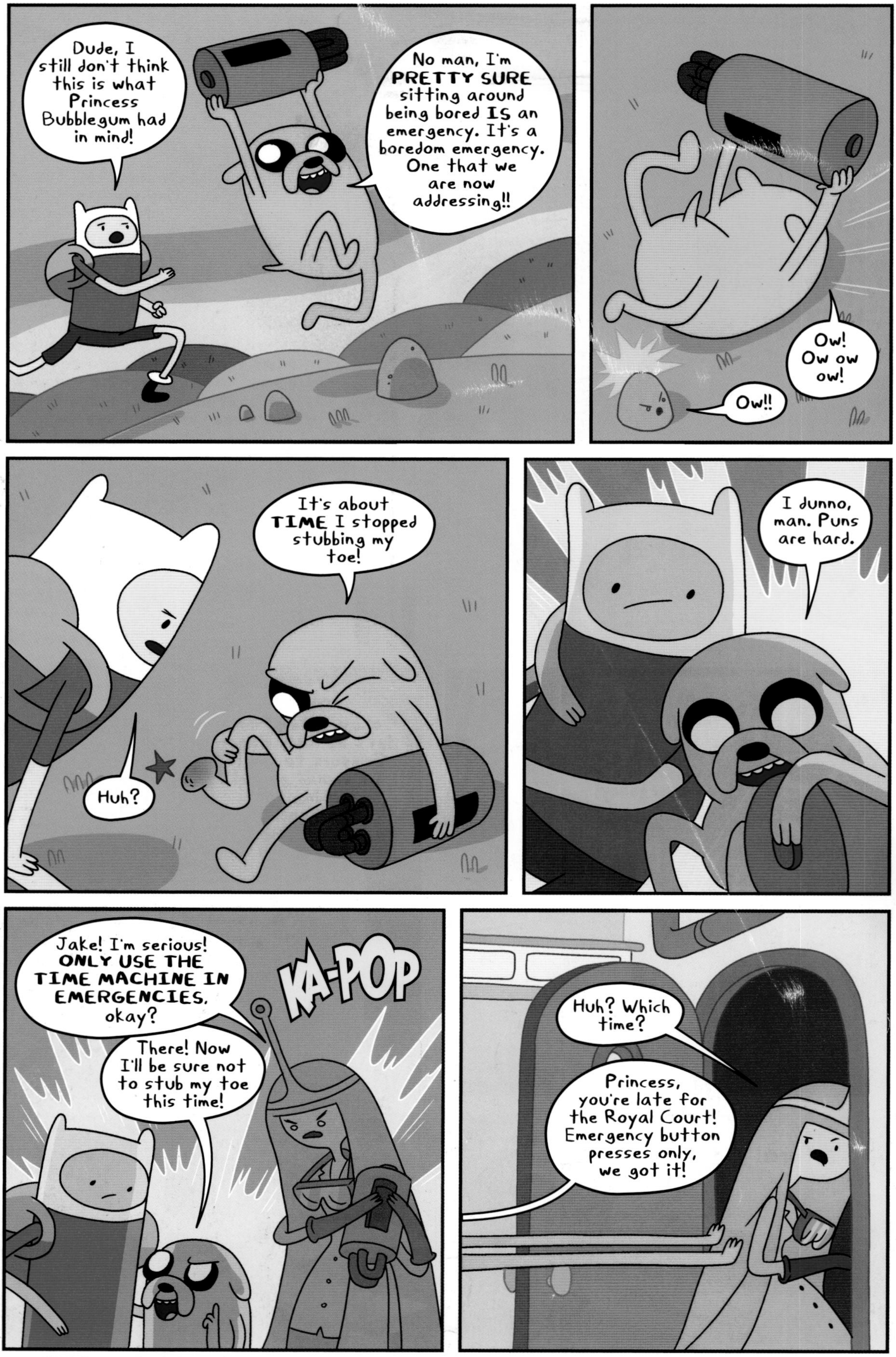
Dude, I still don't think this is what Princess Bubblegum had in mind!
No man, I'm PRETTY SURE sitting around being bored IS an emergency. It's a boredom emergency. One that we are now addressing!!
Ow! Ow ow ow!
Ow!!
It's about TIME I stopped stubbing my toe!
Huh?
I dunno, man. Puns are hard.
Jake! I'm serious! ONLY USE THE TIME MACHINE IN EMERGENCIES, okay?
KA-POP
There! Now I'll be sure not to stub my toe this time!
Huh? Which time?
Princess, you're late for the Royal Court! Emergency button presses only, we got it!

This is the very first instance of someone asking about the time around Finn and Jake where they did not respond with "Adventure Time!" Mark it on your calendars!!

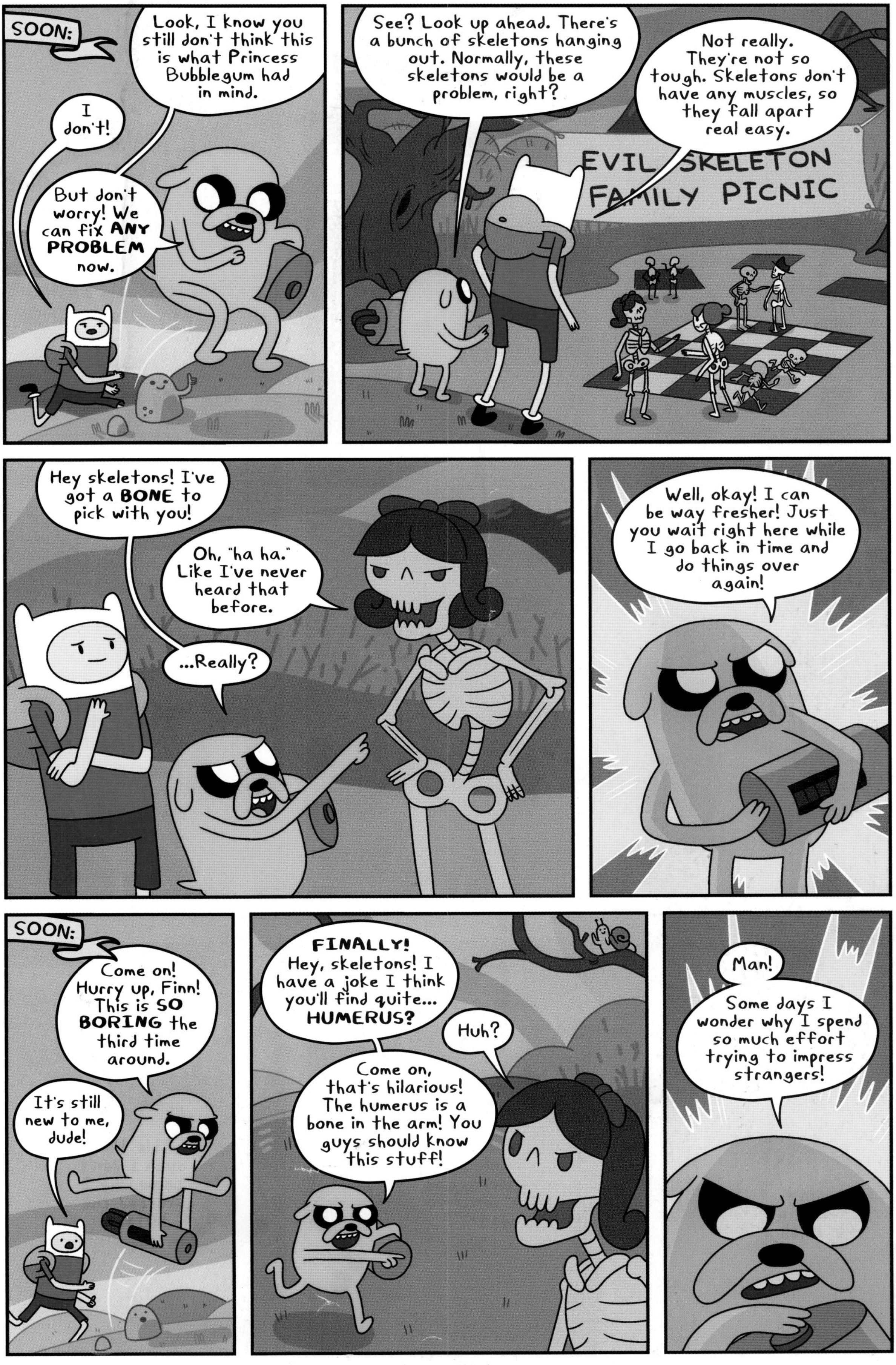
SOON:
Look, I know you still don't think this is what Princess Bubblegum had in mind.
I don't!
But don't worry! We can fix ANY PROBLEM now.
See? Look up ahead. There's a bunch of skeletons hanging out. Normally, these skeletons would be a problem, right?
Not really. They're not so tough. Skeletons don't have any muscles, so they fall apart real easy.
EVIL SKELETON FAMILY PICNIC
Hey skeletons! I've got a BONE to pick with you!
Oh, "ha ha." Like I've never heard that before.
...Really?
Well, okay! I can be way fresher! Just you wait right here while I go back in time and do things over again!
SOON:
Come on! Hurry up, Finn! This is SO BORING the third time around.
It's still new to me, dude!
FINALLY! Hey, skeletons! I have a joke I think you'll find quite... HUMERUS?
Huh?
Come on, that's hilarious! The humerus is a bone in the arm! You guys should know this stuff!
Man!
Some days I wonder why I spend so much effort trying to impress strangers!

Me too, man. Me too.

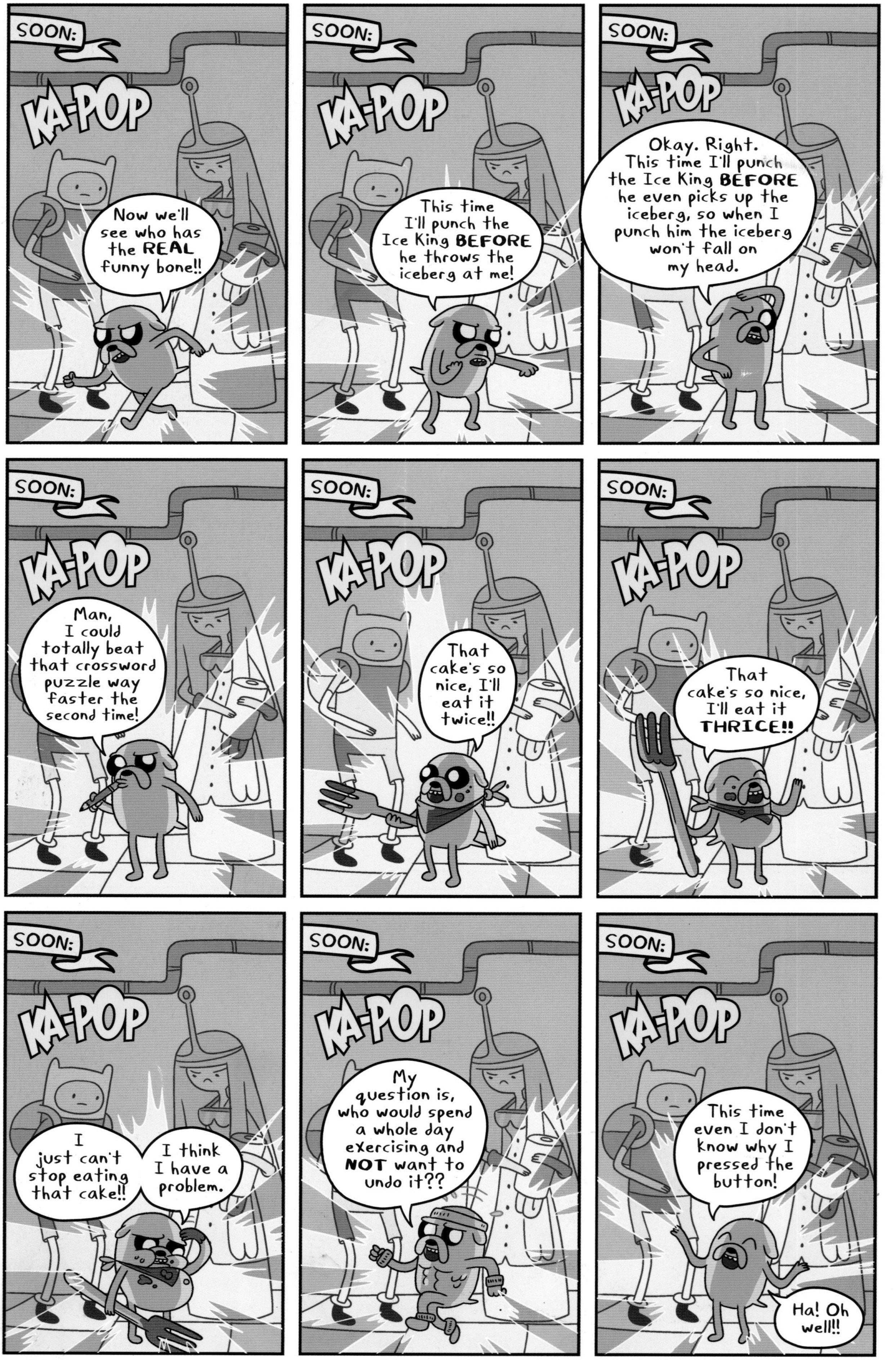
SOON:
KA-POP
Now we'll see who has the REAL funny bone!!
SOON:
KA-POP
This time I'll punch the Ice King BEFORE he throws the iceberg at me!
SOON:
KA-POP
Okay. Right. This time I'll punch the Ice King BEFORE he even picks up the iceberg, so when I punch him the iceberg won't fall on my head.
SOON:
KA-POP
Man, I could totally beat that crossword puzzle way faster the second time!
SOON:
KA-POP
That cake's so nice, I'll eat it twice!!
SOON:
KA-POP
That cake's so nice, I'll eat it THRICE!!
SOON:
KA-POP
I just can't stop eating that cake!!
I think I have a problem.
SOON:
KA-POP
My question is, who would spend a whole day exercising and NOT want to undo it??
SOON:
KA-POP
This time even I don't know why I pressed the button!
Ha! Oh well!!

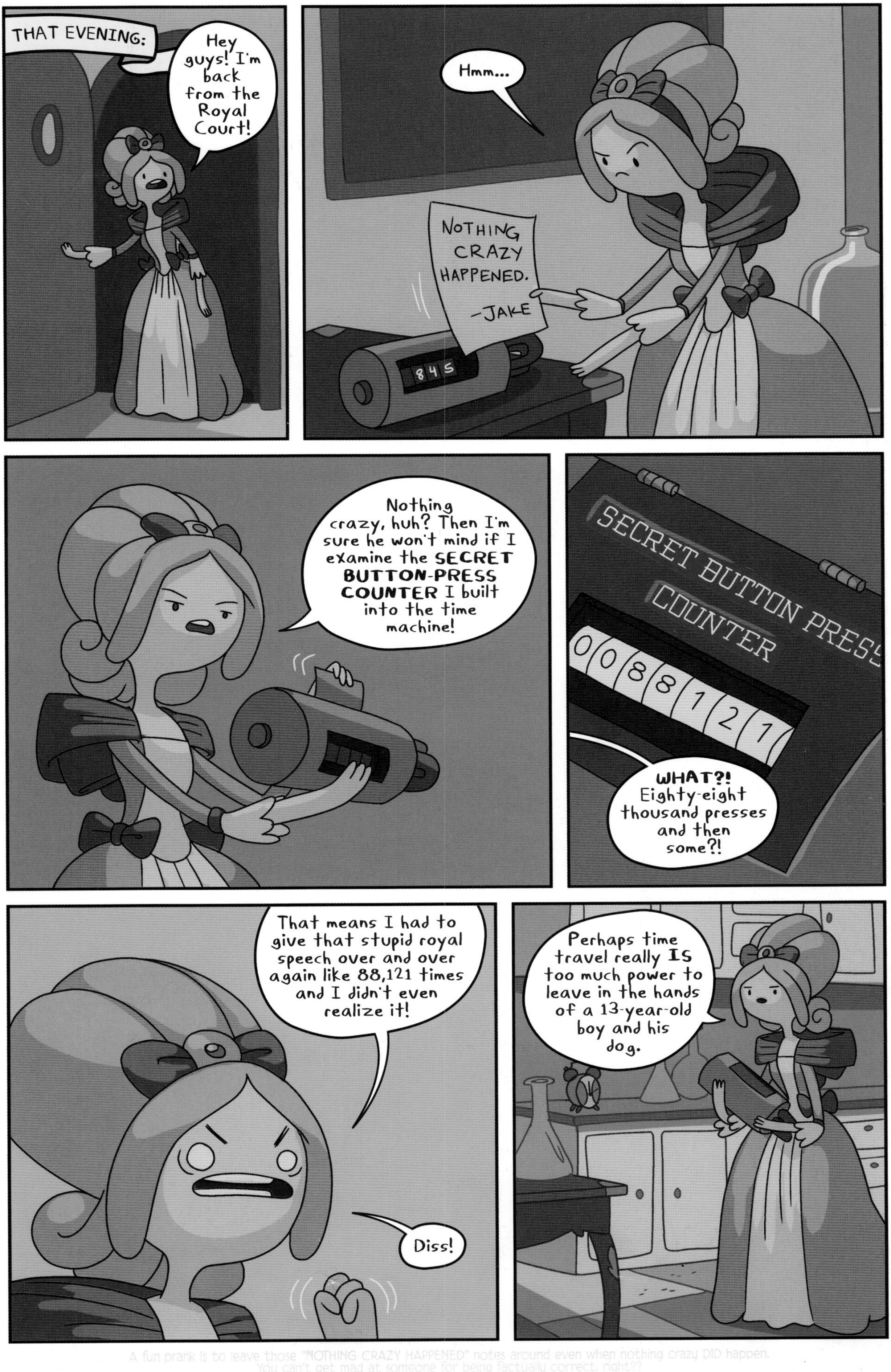

THAT EVENING:
Hey guys! I'm back from the Royal Court!
Hmm...
NOTHING CRAZY HAPPENED. -JAKE
845
Nothing crazy, huh? Then I'm sure he won't mind if I examine the **SECRET BUTTON-PRESS COUNTER** I built into the time machine!
SECRET BUTTON PRESS COUNTER
0088121
WHAT?! Eighty-eight thousand presses and then some?!
That means I had to give that stupid royal speech over and over again like 88,121 times and I didn't even realize it!
Diss!
Perhaps time travel really **IS** too much power to leave in the hands of a 13-year-old boy and his dog.

A fun prank is to leave those "NOTHING CRAZY HAPPENED" notes around even when nothing crazy DID happen. You can't get mad at someone for being factually correct, right??

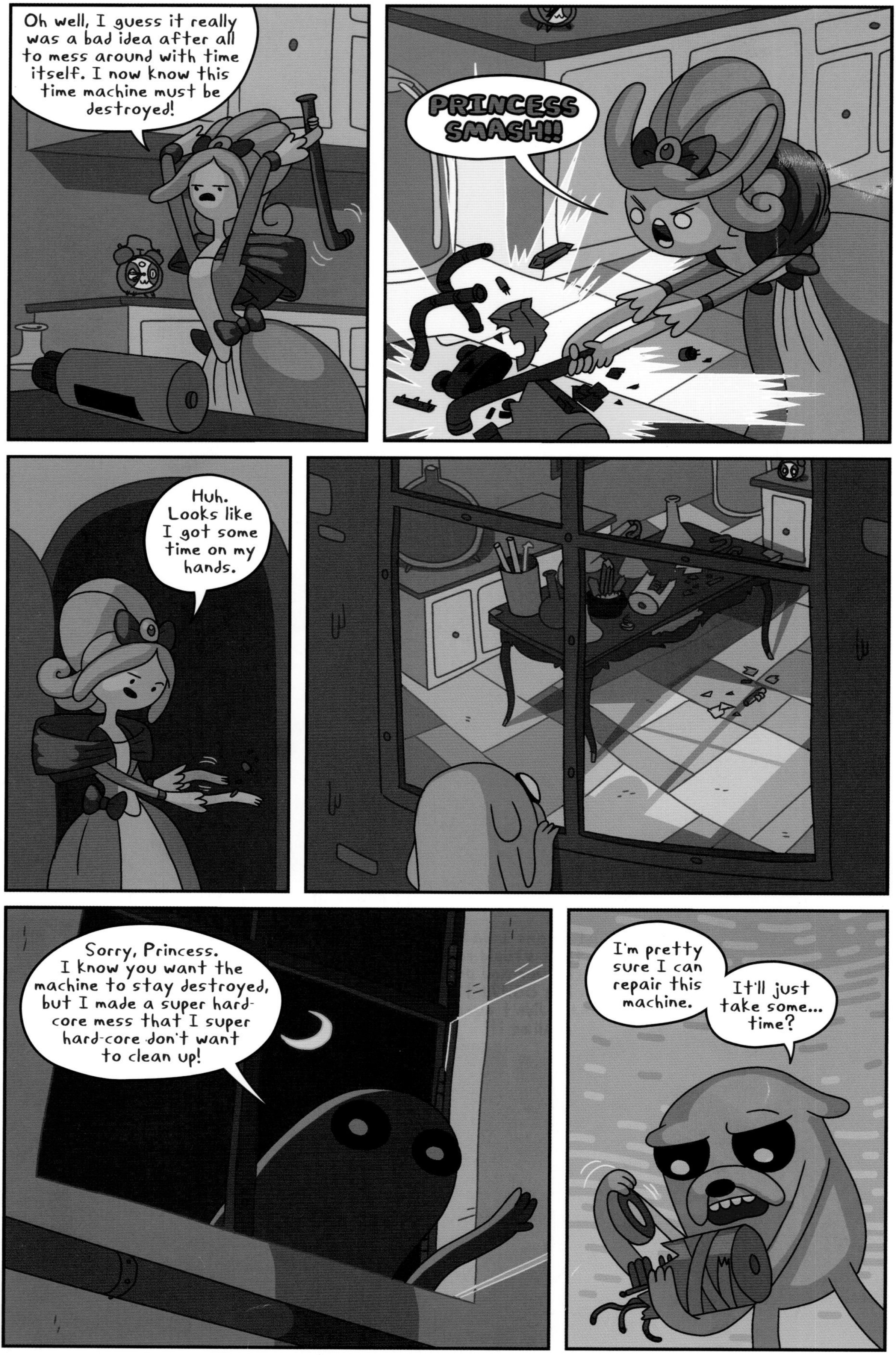
Oh well, I guess it really was a bad idea after all to mess around with time itself. I now know this time machine must be destroyed!
PRINCESS SMASH!!
Huh. Looks like I got some time on my hands.
Sorry, Princess. I know you want the machine to stay destroyed, but I made a super hard-core mess that I super hard-core don't want to clean up!
I'm pretty sure I can repair this machine.
It'll just take some... time?

PRINCESS SMASH IDEA SOME PEOPLE HAVE THAT PRINCESSES CAN'T SMASH

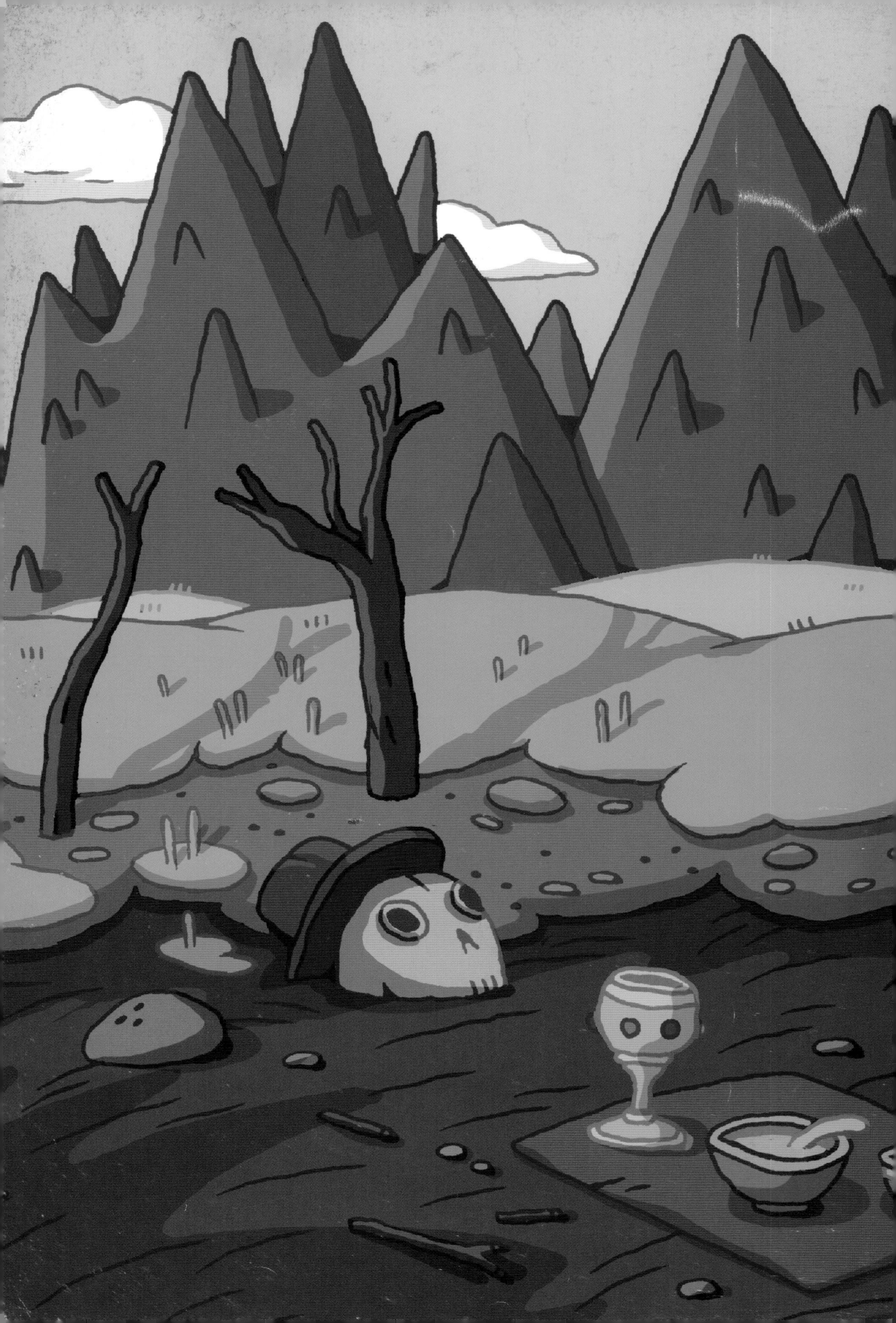

CHAPTER THREE

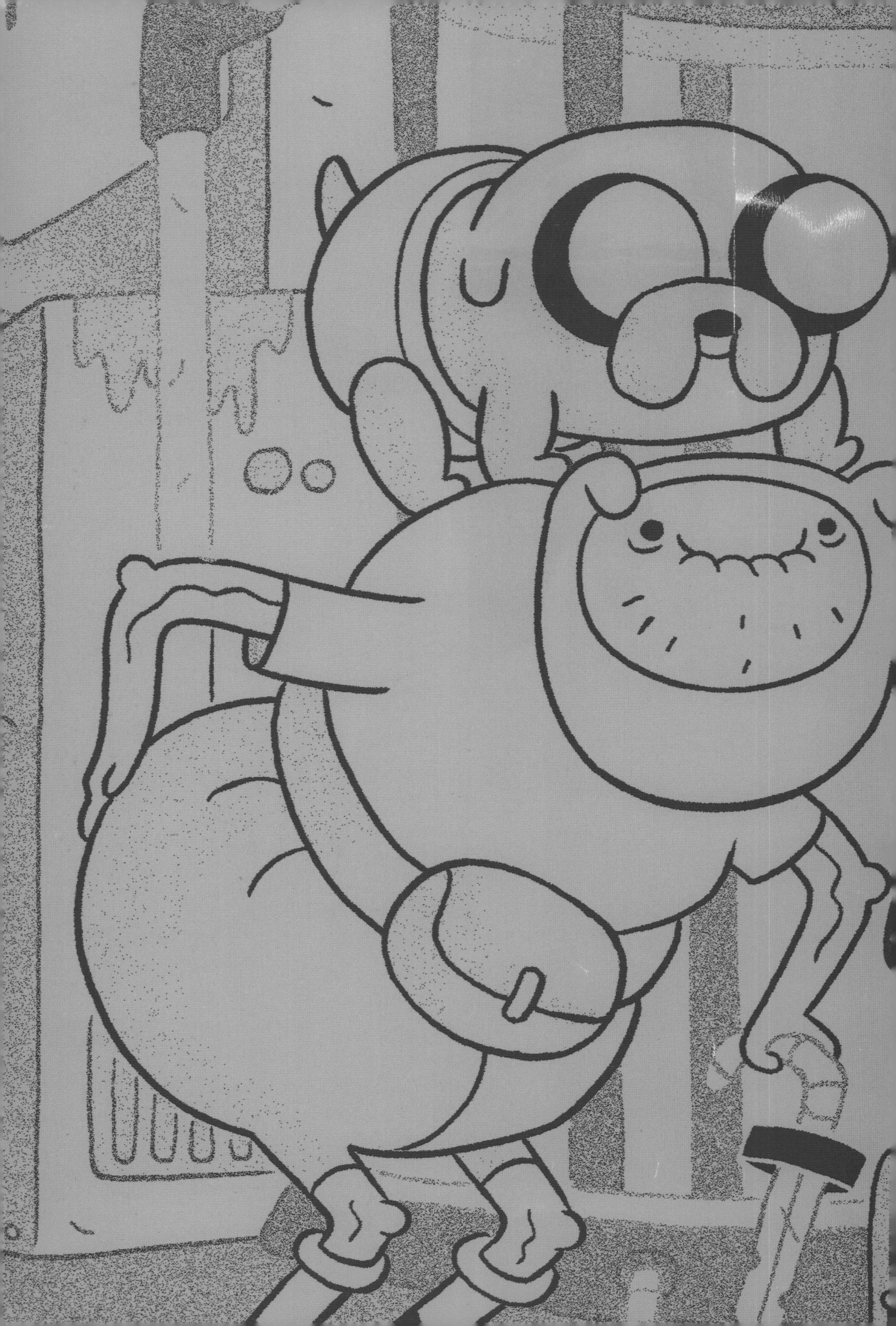

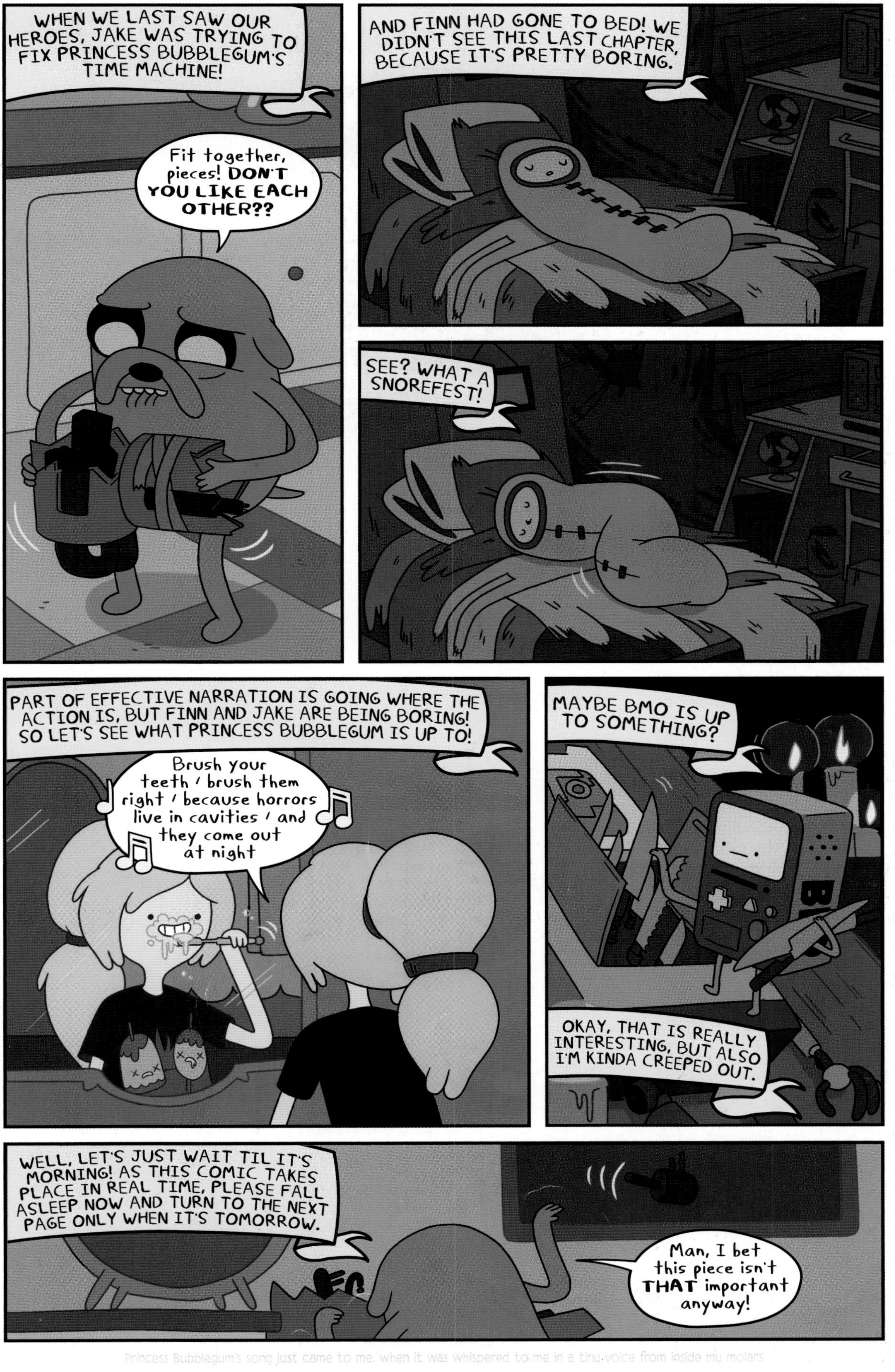
WHEN WE LAST SAW OUR HEROES, JAKE WAS TRYING TO FIX PRINCESS BUBBLEGUM'S TIME MACHINE!
Fit together, pieces! DON'T YOU LIKE EACH OTHER??
AND FINN HAD GONE TO BED! WE DIDN'T SEE THIS LAST CHAPTER, BECAUSE IT'S PRETTY BORING.
SEE? WHAT A SNOREFEST!
PART OF EFFECTIVE NARRATION IS GOING WHERE THE ACTION IS, BUT FINN AND JAKE ARE BEING BORING! SO LET'S SEE WHAT PRINCESS BUBBLEGUM IS UP TO!
Brush your teeth / brush them right / because horrors live in cavities / and they come out at night
MAYBE BMO IS UP TO SOMETHING?
OKAY, THAT IS REALLY INTERESTING, BUT ALSO I'M KINDA CREEPED OUT.
WELL, LET'S JUST WAIT TIL IT'S MORNING! AS THIS COMIC TAKES PLACE IN REAL TIME, PLEASE FALL ASLEEP NOW AND TURN TO THE NEXT PAGE ONLY WHEN IT'S TOMORROW.
Man, I bet this piece isn't THAT important anyway!

Princess Bubblegum's song just came to me, when it was whispered to me in a tiny voice from inside my molars

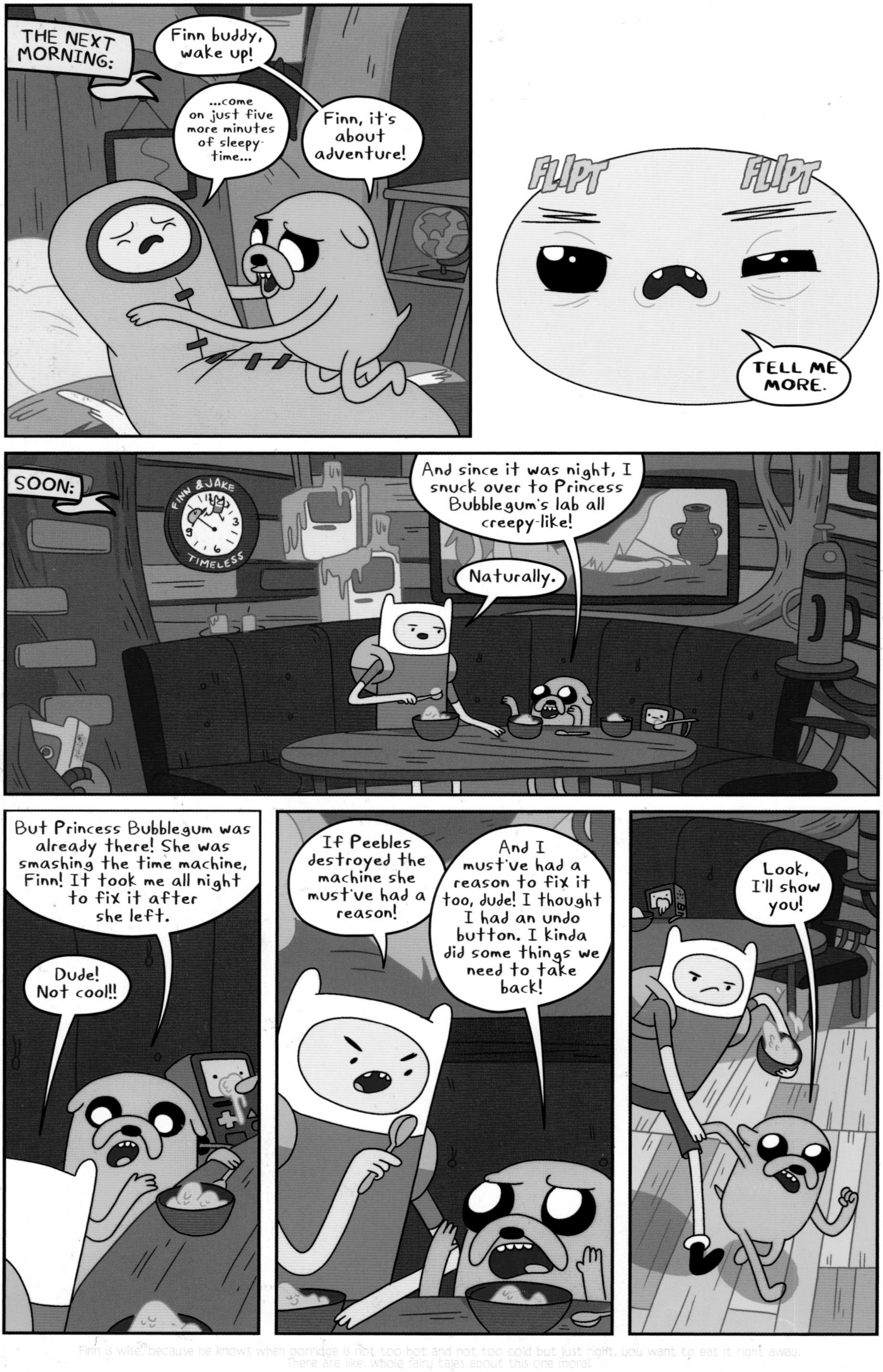
THE NEXT MORNING:
Finn buddy, wake up!
...come on just five more minutes of sleepy-time...
Finn, it's about adventure!
FLIPT FLIPT
TELL ME MORE.
SOON:
FINN & JAKE
TIMELESS
And since it was night, I snuck over to Princess Bubblegum's lab all creepy-like!
Naturally.
But Princess Bubblegum was already there! She was smashing the time machine, Finn! It took me all night to fix it after she left.
Dude! Not cool!!
If Peebles destroyed the machine she must've had a reason!
And I must've had a reason to fix it too, dude! I thought I had an undo button. I kinda did some things we need to take back!
Look, I'll show you!

Finn is wise, because he knows when porridge is not too hot and not too cold but just right, you want to eat it right away. There are like, whole fairy tales about this one moral.

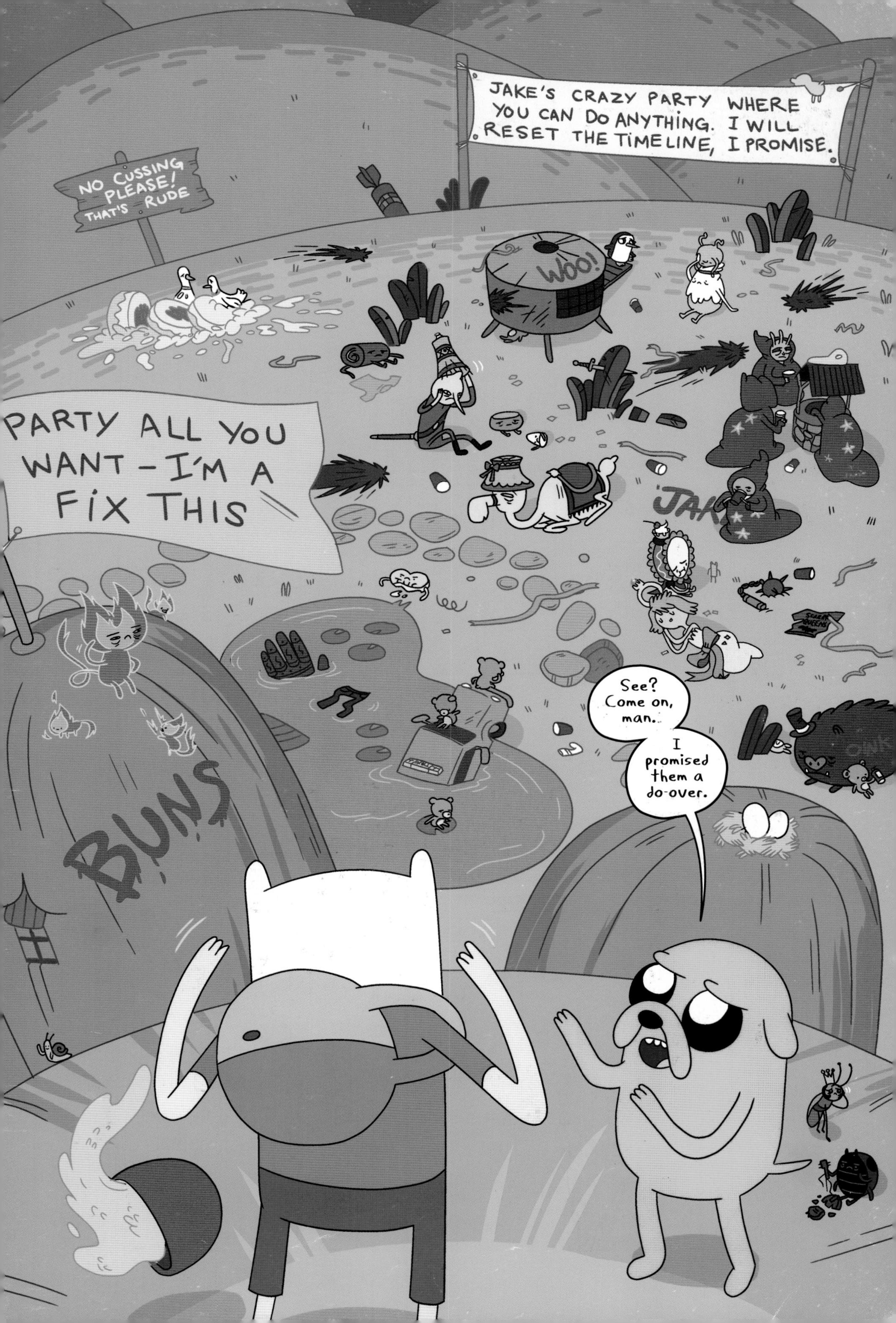
JAKE'S CRAZY PARTY WHERE YOU CAN DO ANYTHING. I WILL RESET THE TIMELINE, I PROMISE.
NO CUSSING PLEASE! THAT'S RUDE
WOO!
PARTY ALL YOU WANT - I'M A FIX THIS
BUNS
See? Come on, man...
I promised them a do-over.

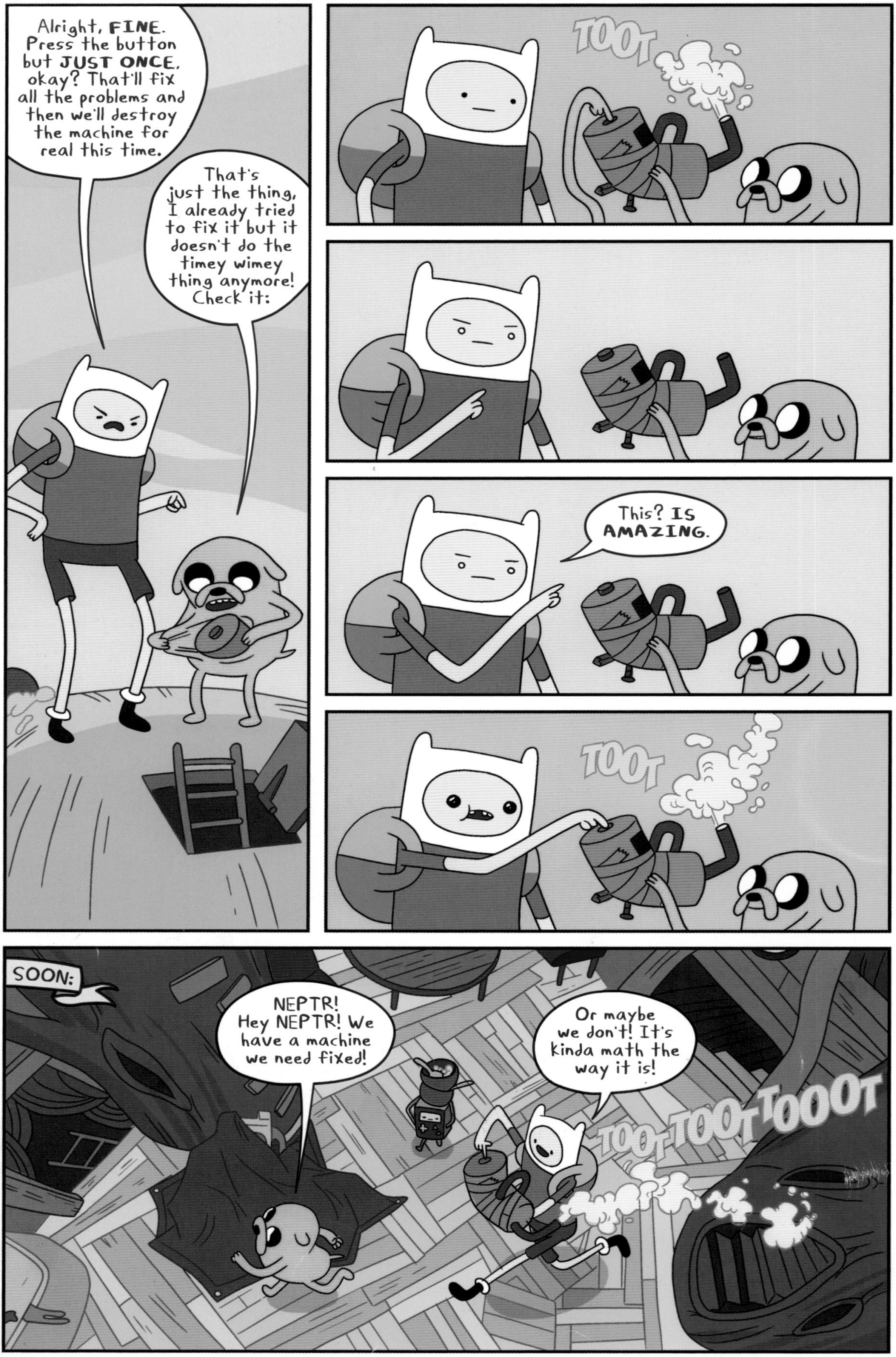
Alright, **FINE**. Press the button but **JUST ONCE**, okay? That'll fix all the problems and then we'll destroy the machine for real this time.
That's just the thing, I already tried to fix it but it doesn't do the timey wimey thing anymore! Check it:
TOOT
This? **IS AMAZING**.
TOOT
SOON:
NEPTR! Hey NEPTR! We have a machine we need fixed!
Or maybe we don't! It's kinda math the way it is!
TOOT TOOT TOOOT

It's maybe not be the machine we need...but it is the machine we want.

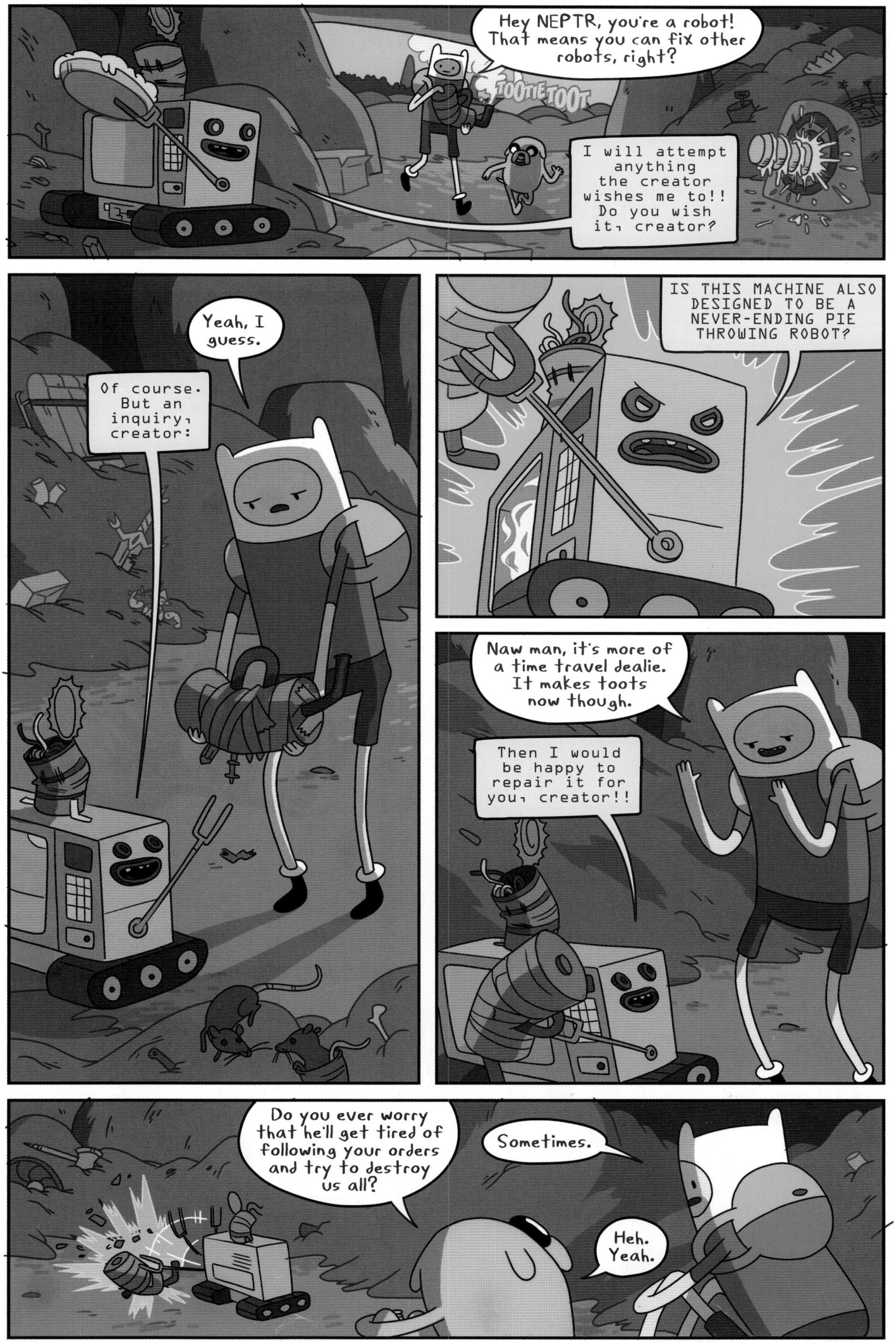

Hey NEPTR, you're a robot! That means you can fix other robots, right?
TOOTIE TOOT
I will attempt anything the creator wishes me to!! Do you wish it, creator?
Yeah, I guess.
Of course. But an inquiry, creator:
IS THIS MACHINE ALSO DESIGNED TO BE A NEVER-ENDING PIE THROWING ROBOT?
Naw man, it's more of a time travel dealie. It makes toots now though.
Then I would be happy to repair it for you, creator!!
Do you ever worry that he'll get tired of following your orders and try to destroy us all?
Sometimes.
Heh. Yeah.

Are we 100% certain that smashing the machine over and over won't repair it? We are? Okay. But listen: are we 100000000% certain?

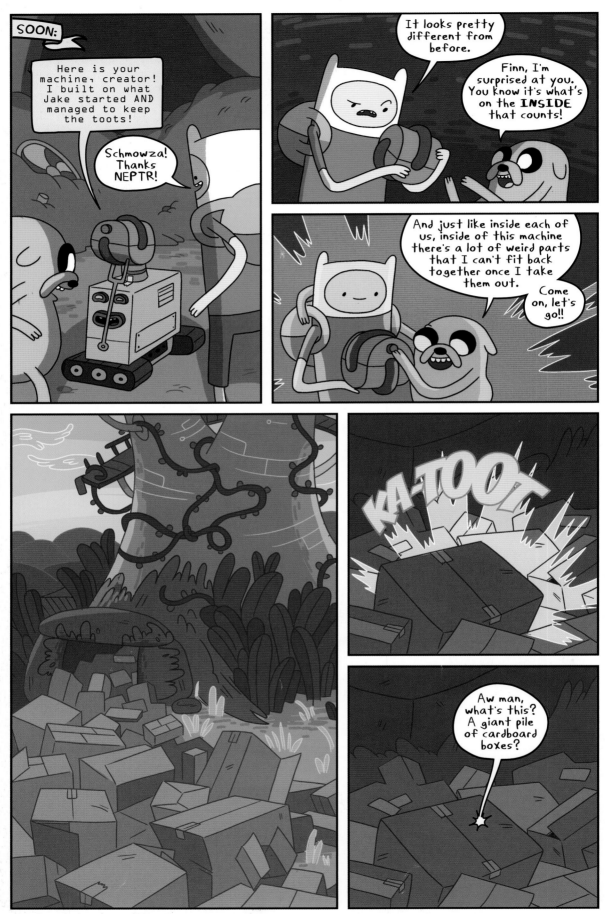

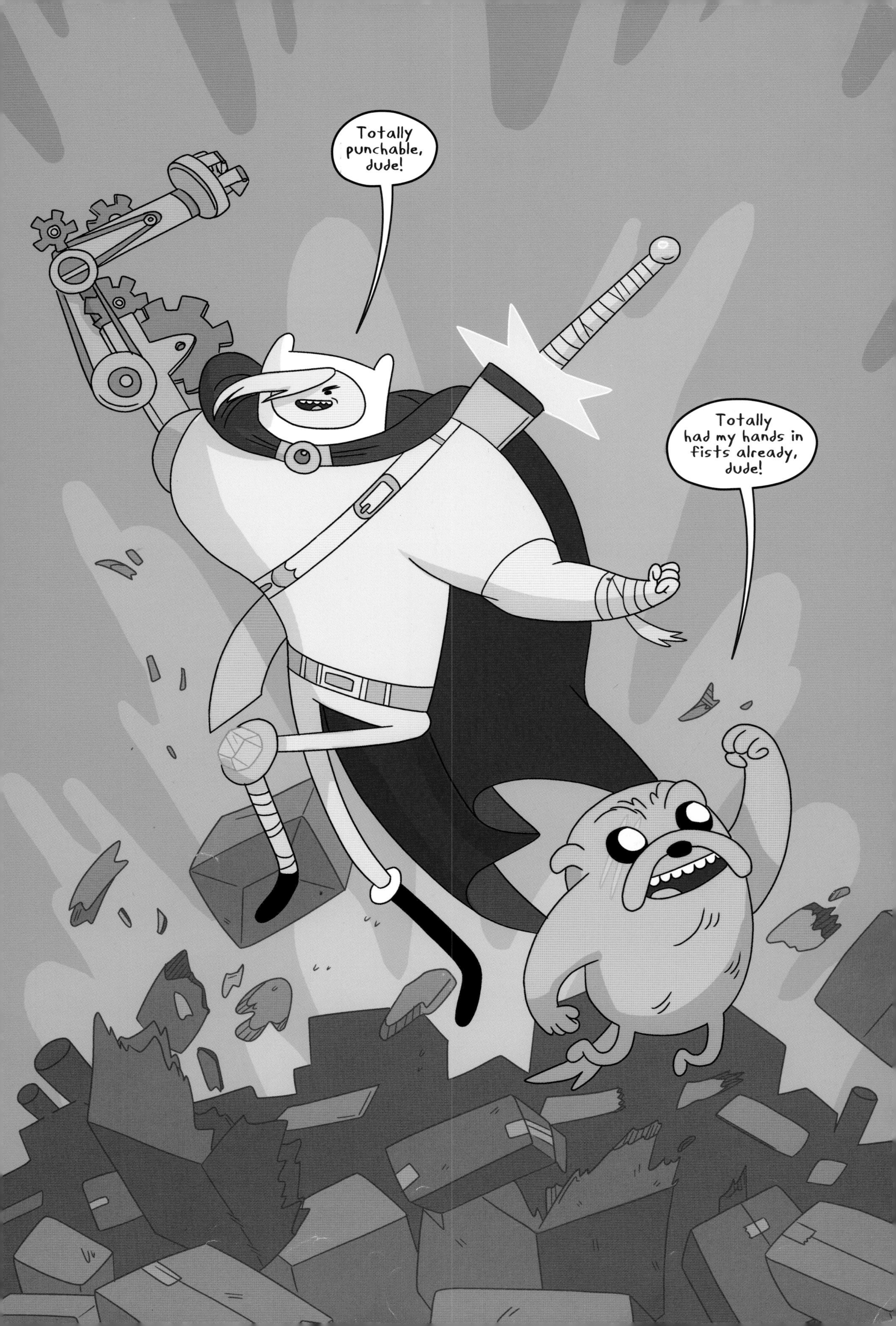
Totally punchable, dude!
Totally had my hands in fists already, dude!

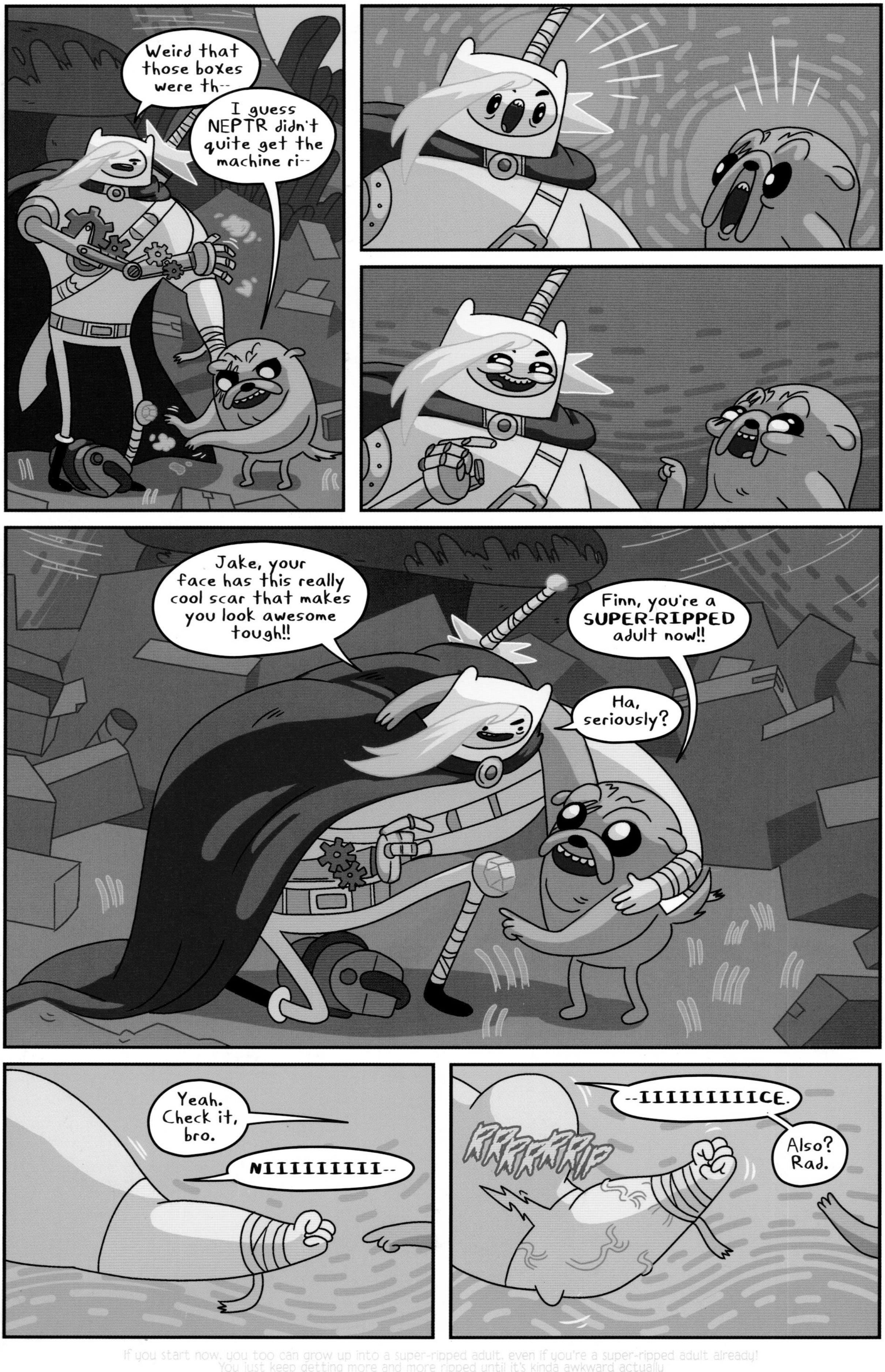
Weird that those boxes were th--
I guess NEPTR didn't quite get the machine ri--
Jake, your face has this really cool scar that makes you look awesome tough!!
Finn, you're a SUPER-RIPPED adult now!!
Ha, seriously?
Yeah. Check it, bro.
NIIIIIIIII--
RIPPPRRRIP
--IIIIIIIIICE.
Also? Rad.

If you start now, you too can grow up into a super-ripped adult, even if you're a super-ripped adult already! You just keep getting more and more ripped until it's kinda awkward actually

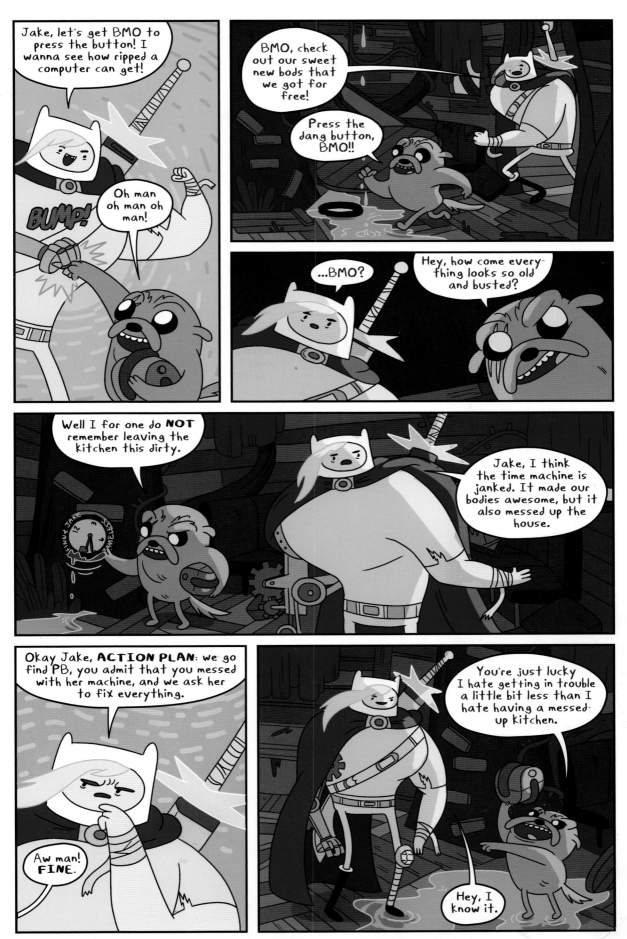

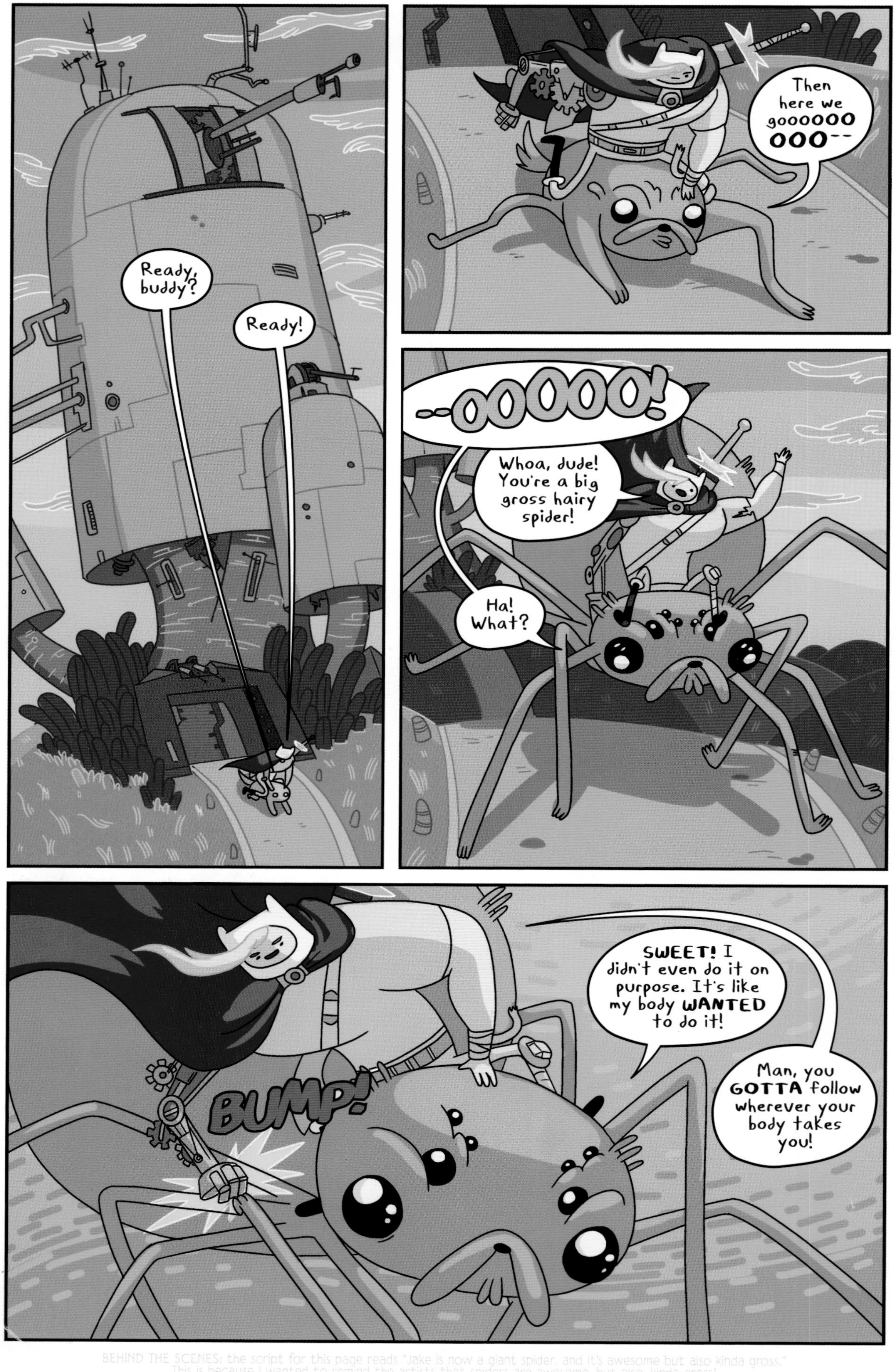
Ready, buddy?
Ready!
Then here we goooooo OOO--
--OOOOO!
Whoa, dude! You're a big gross hairy spider!
Ha! What?
BUMP!
SWEET! I didn't even do it on purpose. It's like my body WANTED to do it!
Man, you GOTTA follow wherever your body takes you!

BEHIND THE SCENES: the script for this page reads "Jake is now a giant spider, and it's awesome but also kinda gross." This is because I wanted to remind the artists that spiders are awesome, but also, kinda gross!

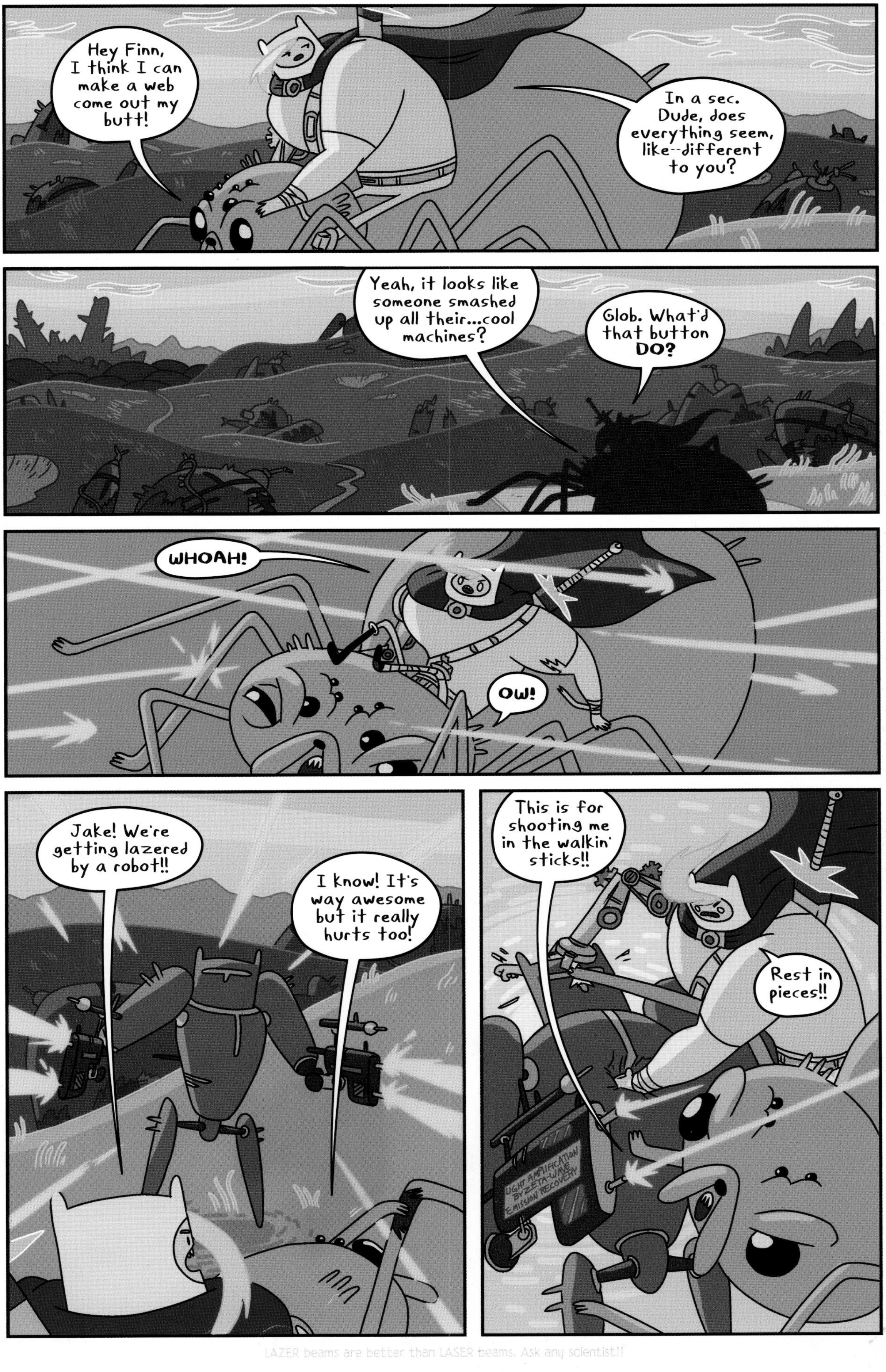
Hey Finn, I think I can make a web come out my butt!
In a sec. Dude, does everything seem, like--different to you?
Yeah, it looks like someone smashed up all their...cool machines?
Glob. What'd that button DO?
WHOAH!
OW!
Jake! We're getting lazered by a robot!!
I know! It's way awesome but it really hurts too!
This is for shooting me in the walkin' sticks!!
Rest in pieces!!
LIGHT AMPLIFICATION BY ZETA-WAVE EMISSION RECOVERY

LAZER beams are better than LASER beams. Ask any scientist!!

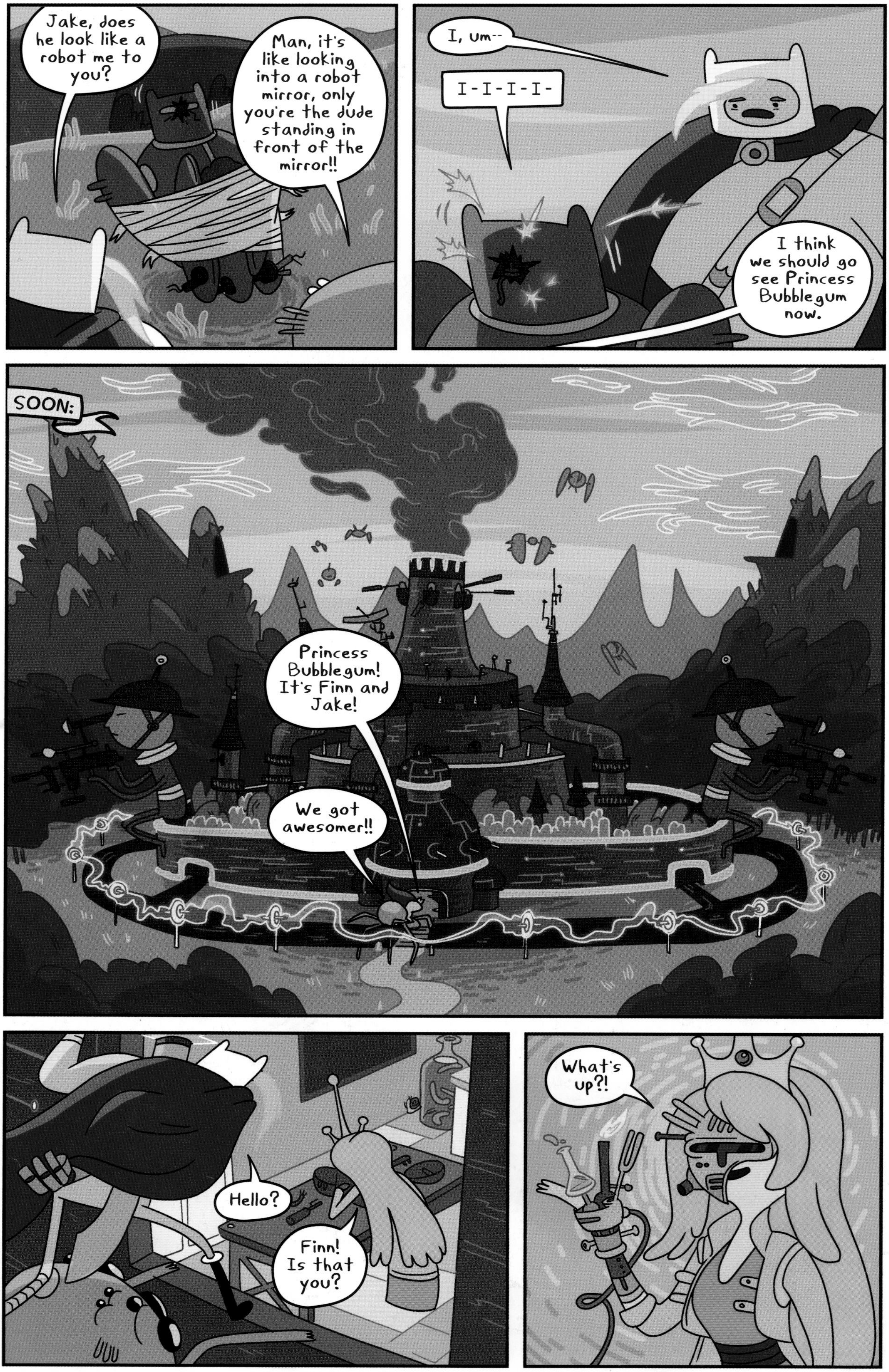
Jake, does he look like a robot me to you?
Man, it's like looking into a robot mirror, only you're the dude standing in front of the mirror!!
I, um--
I-I-I-I-
I think we should go see Princess Bubblegum now.
SOON:
Princess Bubblegum! It's Finn and Jake!
We got awesomer!!
Hello?
Finn! Is that you?
What's up?!

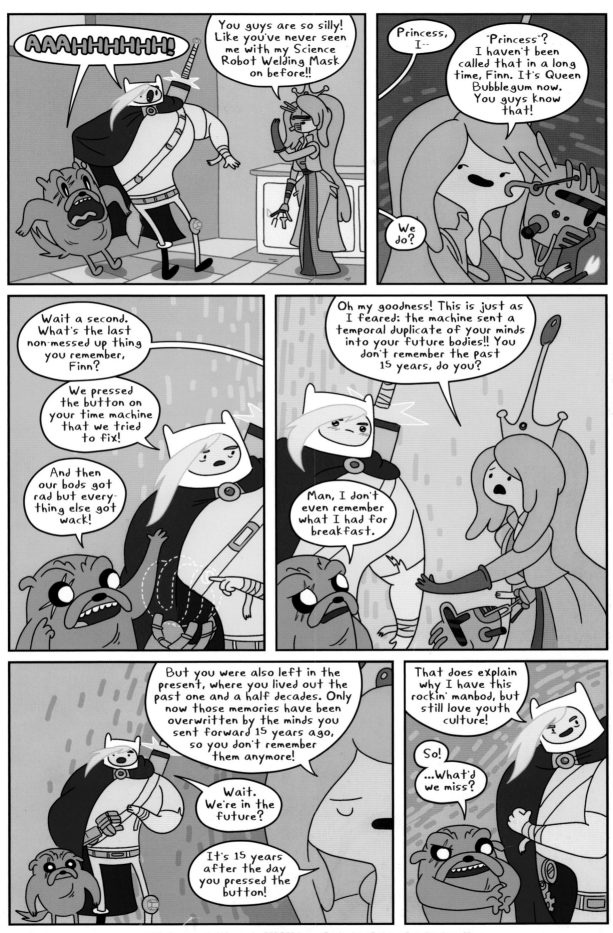

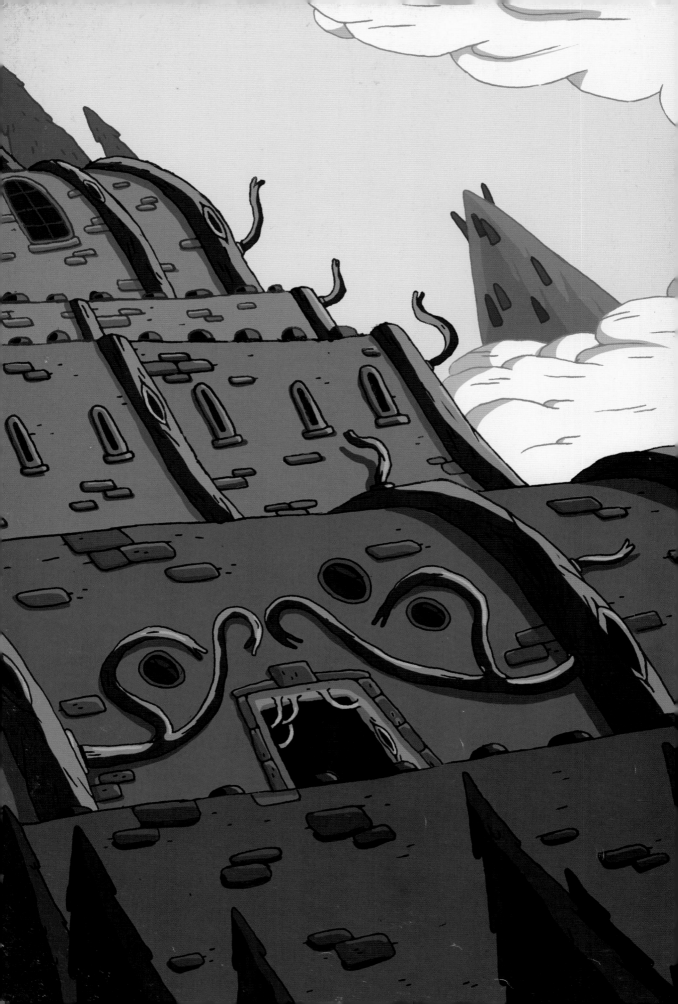

CHAPTER FOUR

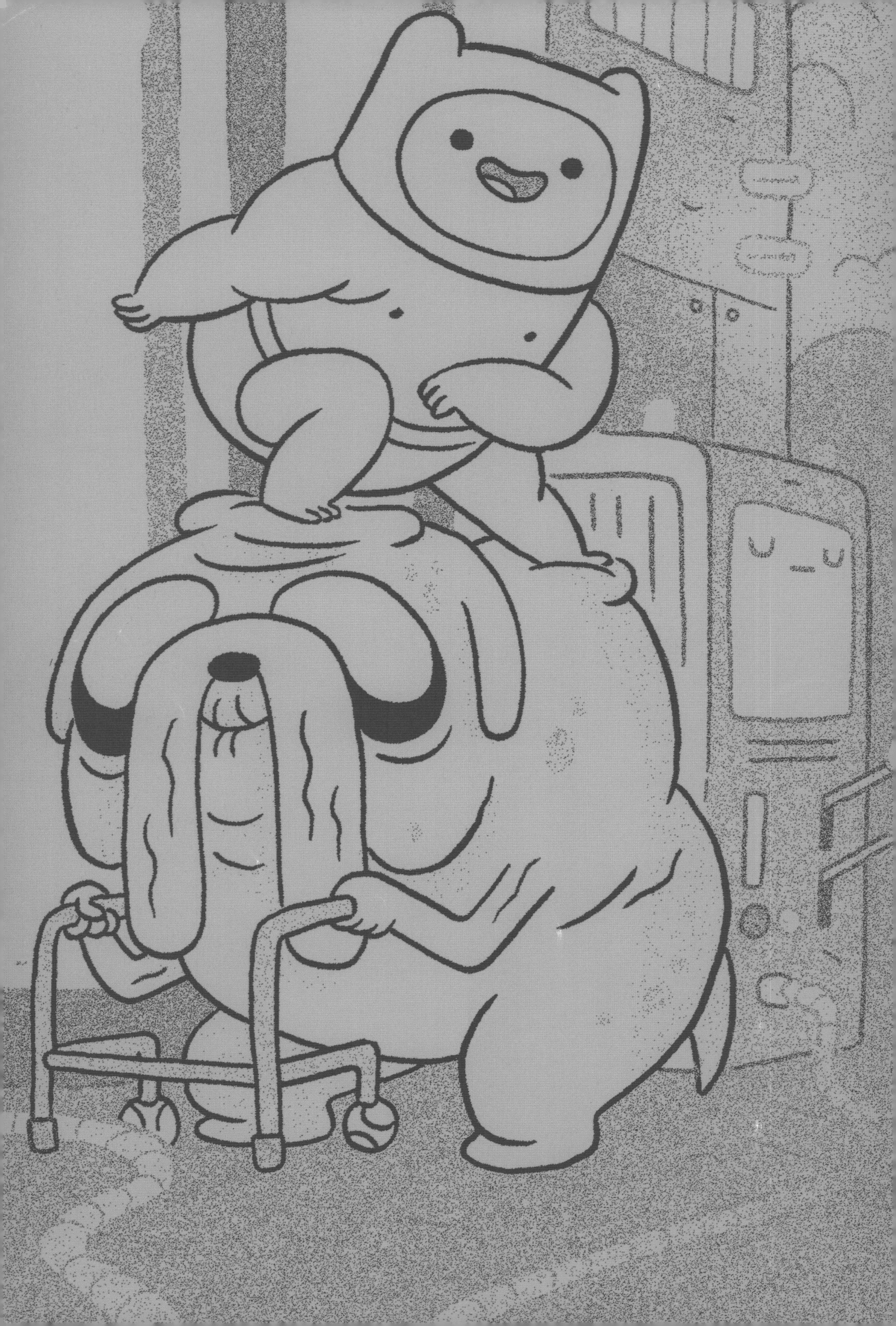

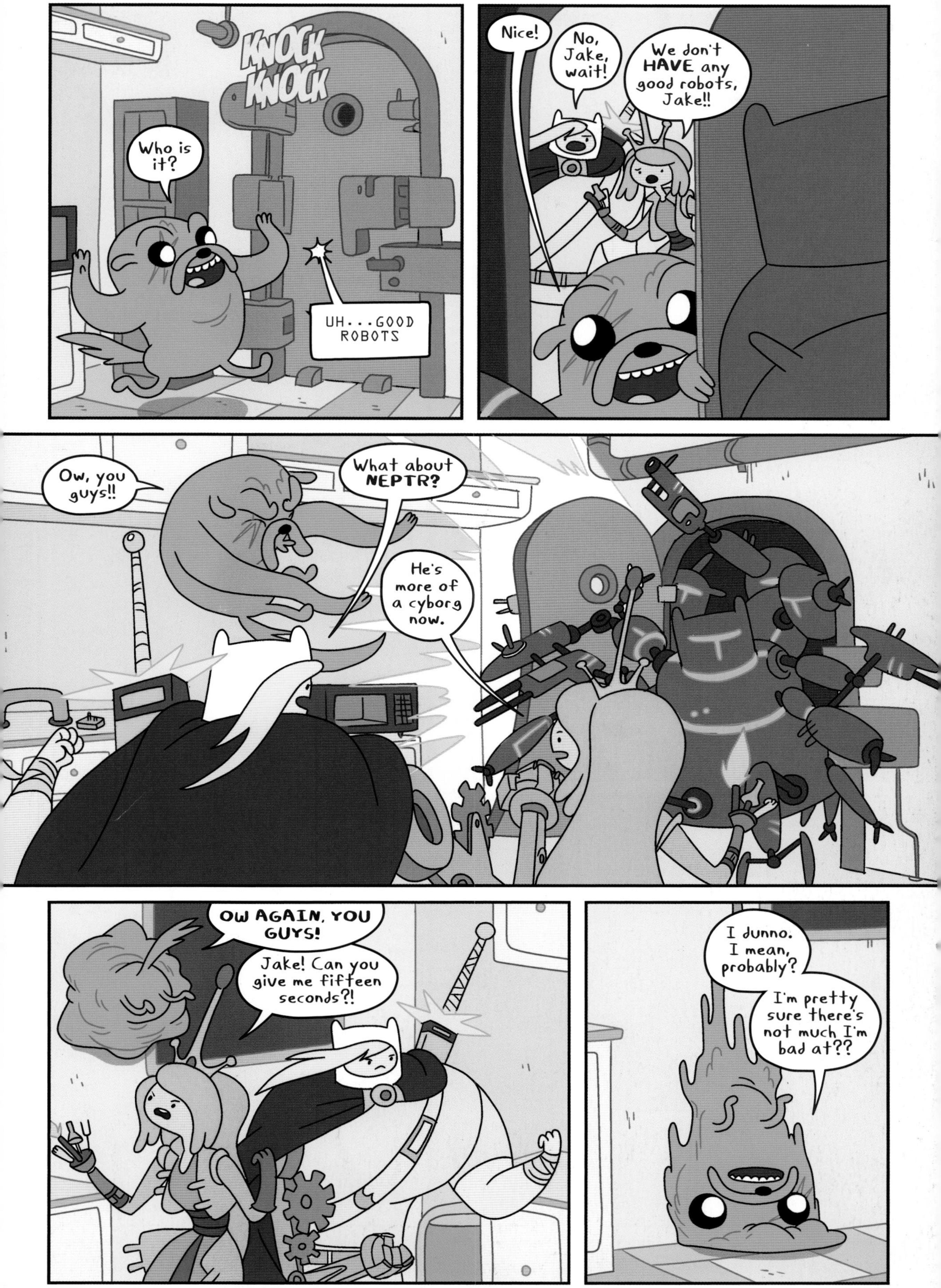
KNOCK KNOCK
Who is it?
UH...GOOD ROBOTS
Nice!
No, Jake, wait!
We don't HAVE any good robots, Jake!!
Ow, you guys!!
What about NEPTR?
He's more of a cyborg now.
OW AGAIN, YOU GUYS!
Jake! Can you give me fifteen seconds?!
I dunno. I mean, probably?
I'm pretty sure there's not much I'm bad at??

If you're just starting with this chapter, then the backstory you need to know is two things: IT'S THE FUTURE and EVIL ROBOTS ARE ATTACKING. Okay! Let's go! These robots aren't going to beat up themselves! *Nobody programmed them to do that!!*

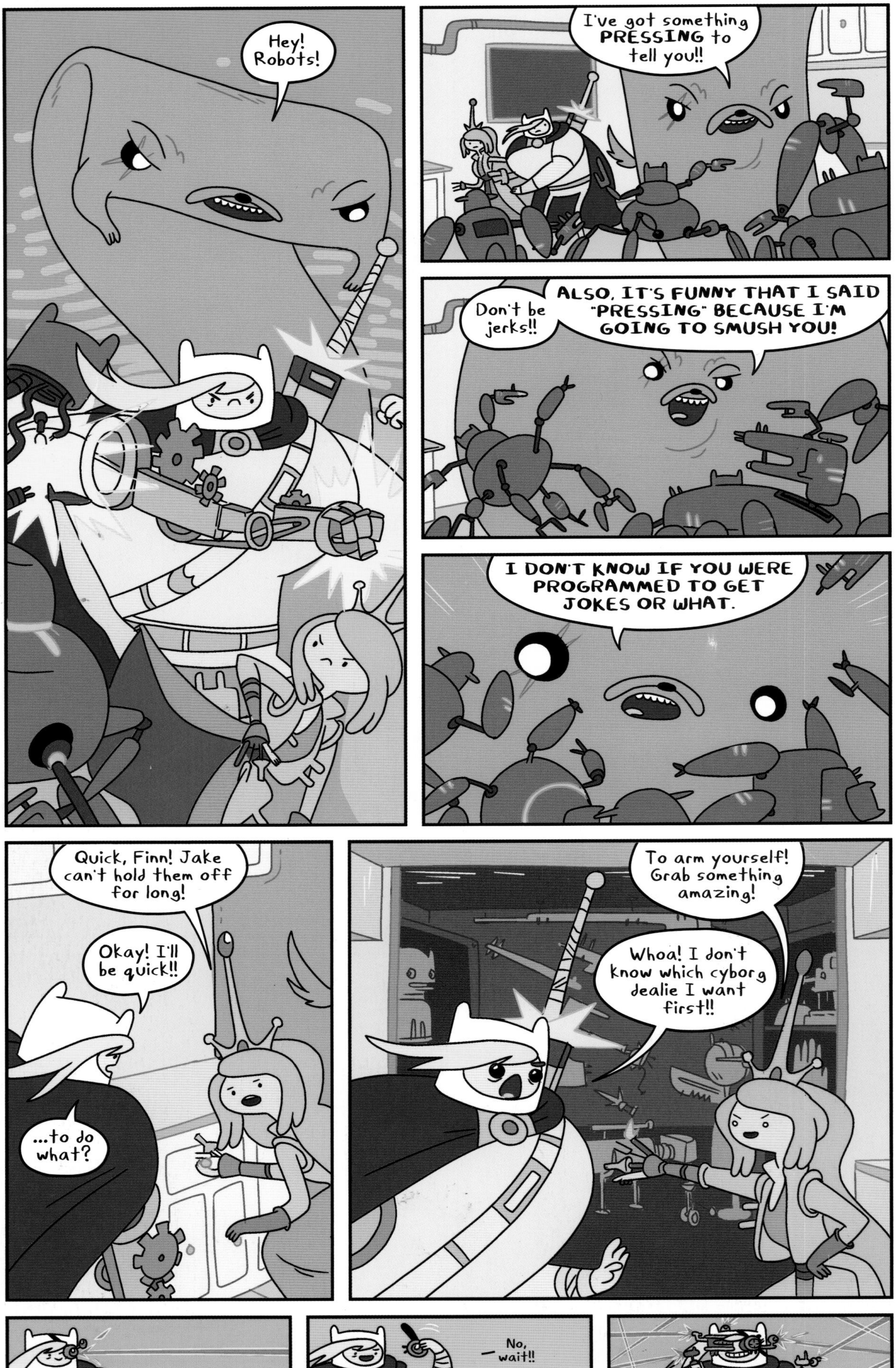

Hey! Robots!
I've got something PRESSING to tell you!!
Don't be jerks!!
ALSO, IT'S FUNNY THAT I SAID "PRESSING" BECAUSE I'M GOING TO SMUSH YOU!
I DON'T KNOW IF YOU WERE PROGRAMMED TO GET JOKES OR WHAT.
Quick, Finn! Jake can't hold them off for long!
Okay! I'll be quick!!
...to do what?
To arm yourself! Grab something amazing!
Whoa! I don't know which cyborg dealie I want first!!
No, wait!!

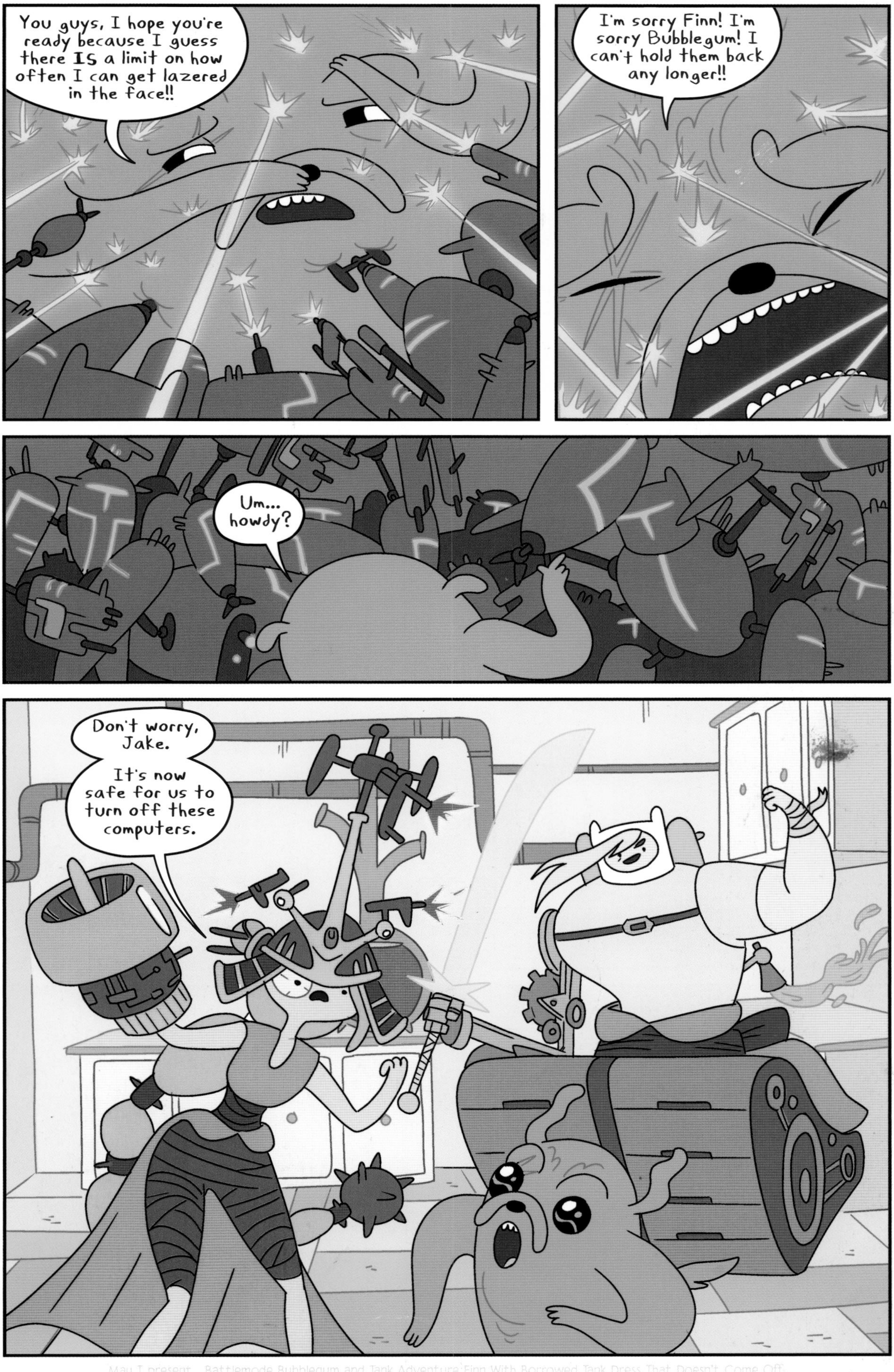
You guys, I hope you're ready because I guess there IS a limit on how often I can get lazered in the face!!
I'm sorry Finn! I'm sorry Bubblegum! I can't hold them back any longer!!
Um... howdy?
Don't worry, Jake.
It's now safe for us to turn off these computers.

May I present... Battlemode Bubblegum and Tank Adventure Finn With Borrowed Tank Dress That Doesn't Come Off.

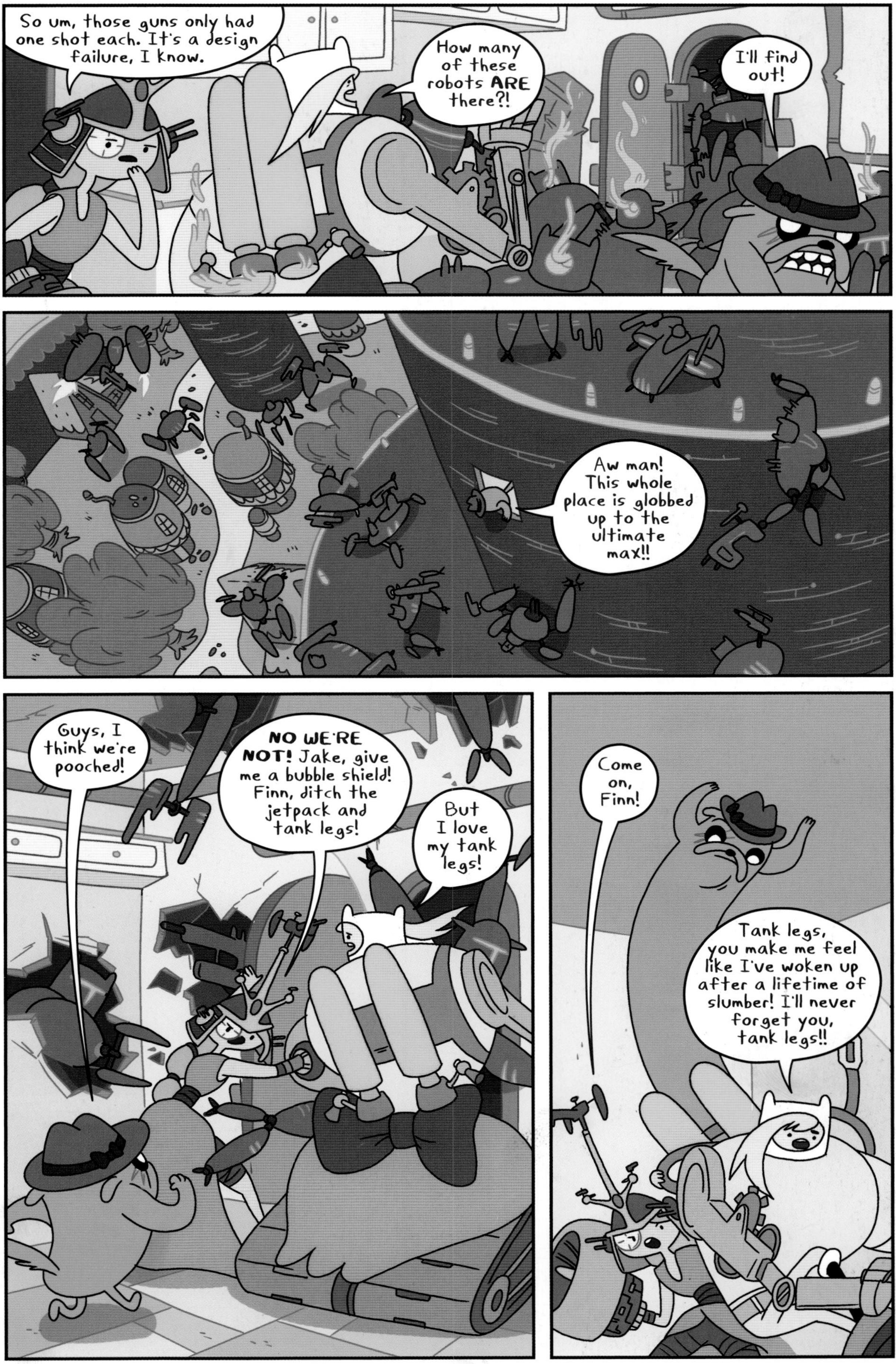
So um, those guns only had one shot each. It's a design failure, I know.
How many of these robots ARE there?!
I'll find out!
Aw man! This whole place is globbed up to the ultimate max!!
Guys, I think we're pooched!
NO WE'RE NOT! Jake, give me a bubble shield! Finn, ditch the jetpack and tank legs!
But I love my tank legs!
Come on, Finn!
Tank legs, you make me feel like I've woken up after a lifetime of slumber! I'll never forget you, tank legs!!

Tank-Legs I'm sorry but we need to break up. I just met Tank Arms

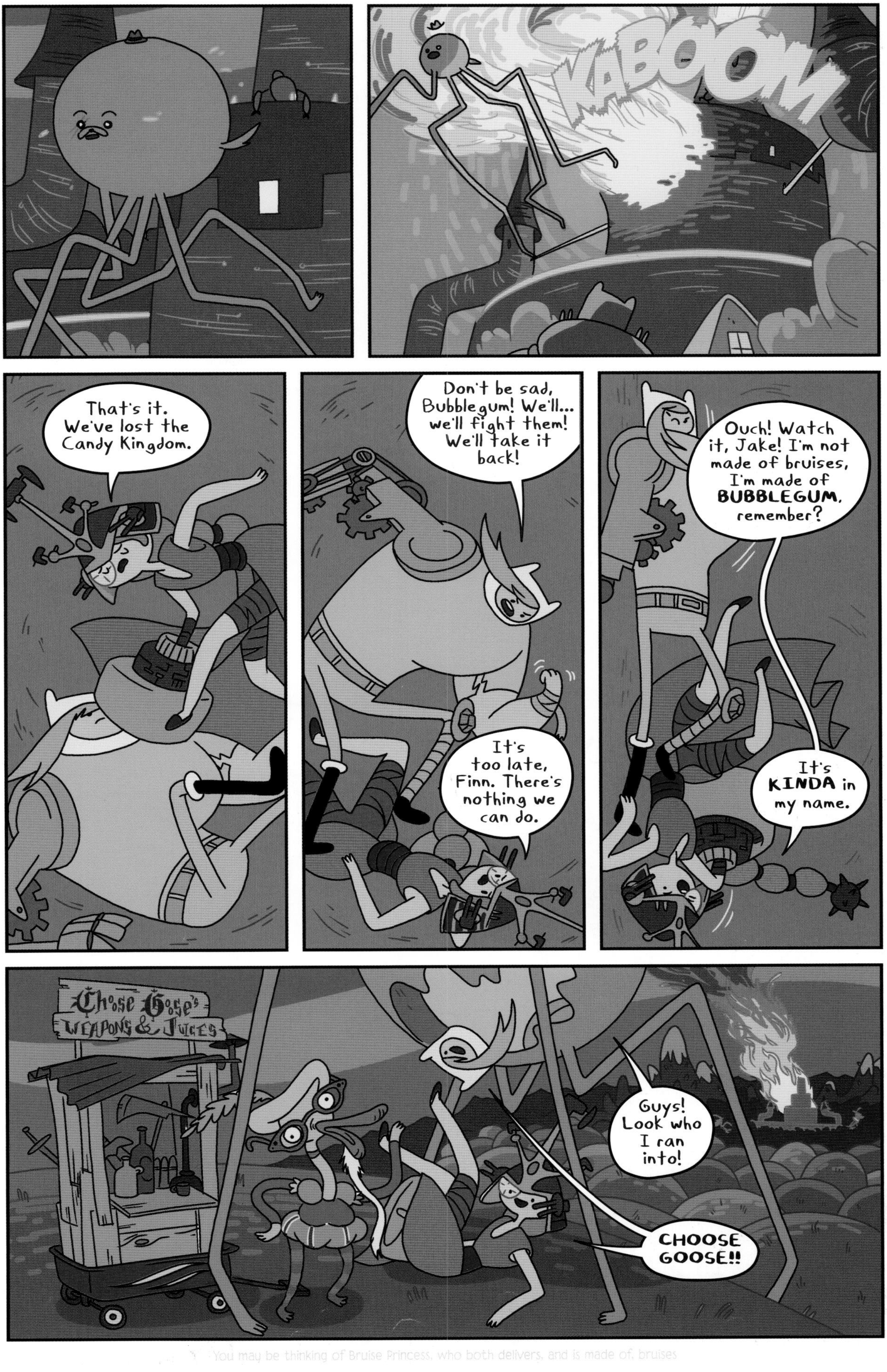
KABOOM
That's it. We've lost the Candy Kingdom.
Don't be sad, Bubblegum! We'll... we'll fight them! We'll take it back!
It's too late, Finn. There's nothing we can do.
Ouch! Watch it, Jake! I'm not made of bruises, I'm made of **BUBBLEGUM**, remember?
It's **KINDA** in my name.
Chose Goose's
WEAPONS & JUICES
Guys! Look who I ran into!
CHOOSE GOOSE!!

* You may be thinking of Bruise Princess, who both delivers, and is made of, bruises

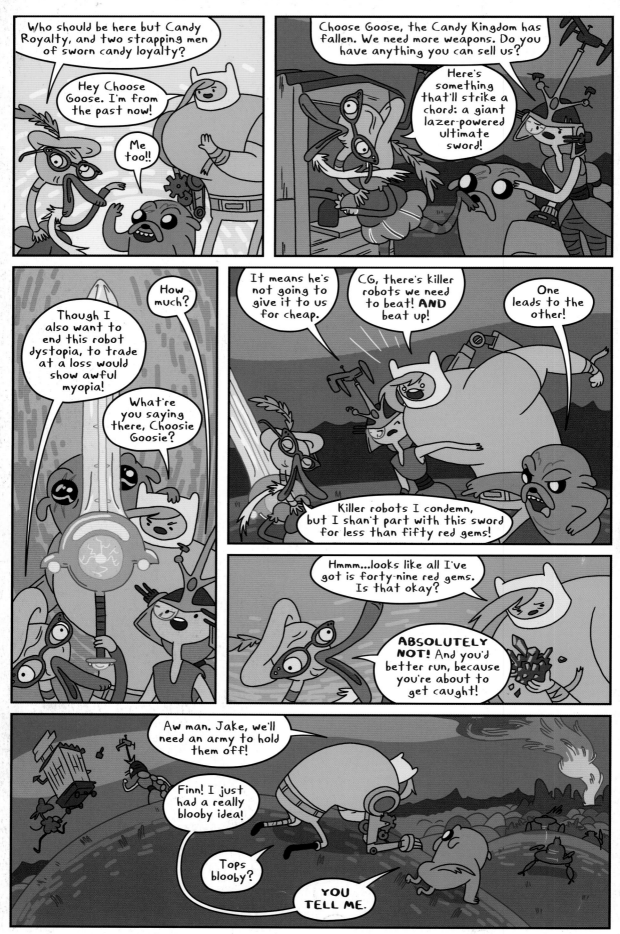

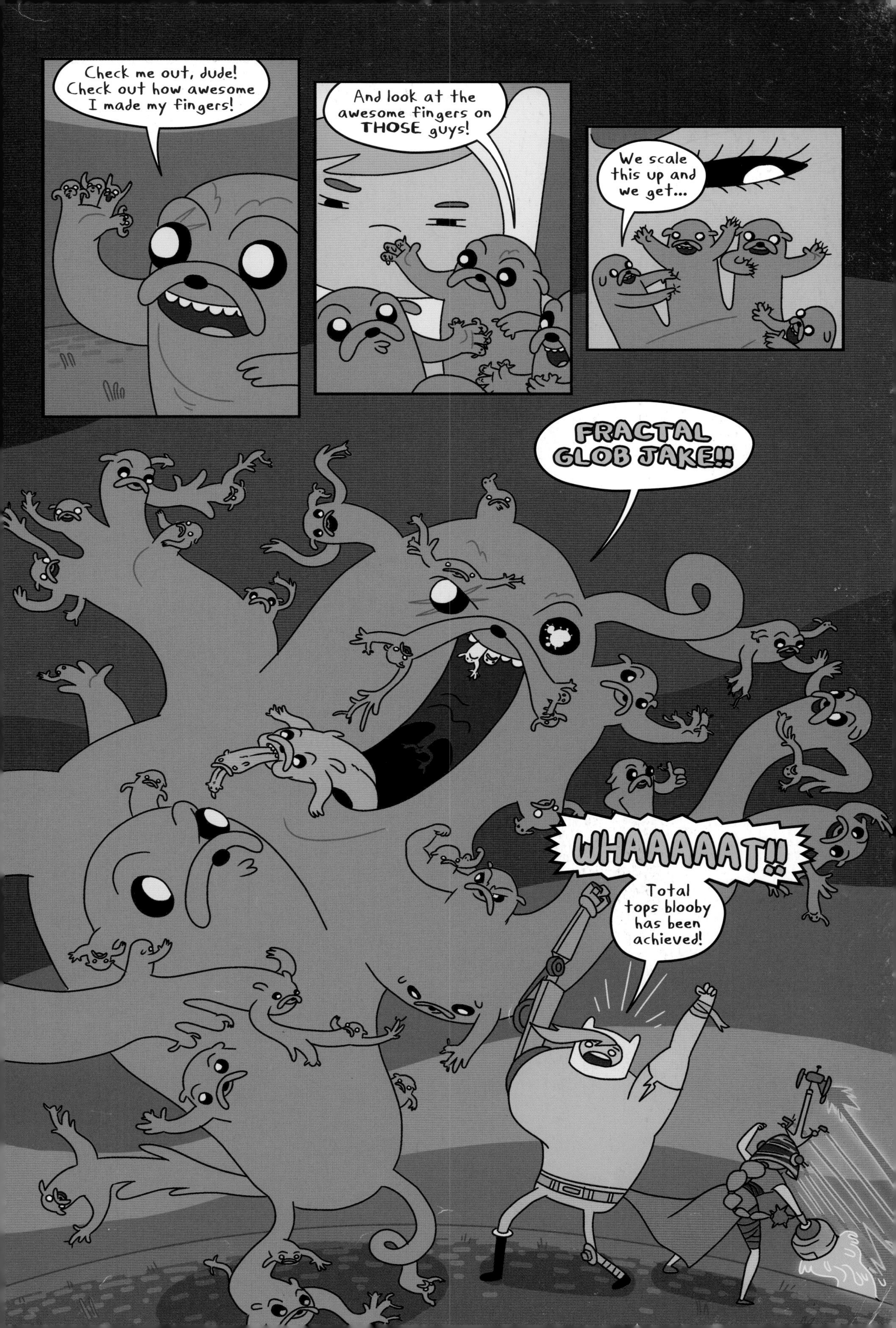
Check me out, dude! Check out how awesome I made my fingers!
And look at the awesome fingers on THOSE guys!
We scale this up and we get...
FRACTAL GLOB JAKE!!
WHAAAAAT!!
Total tops blooby has been achieved!

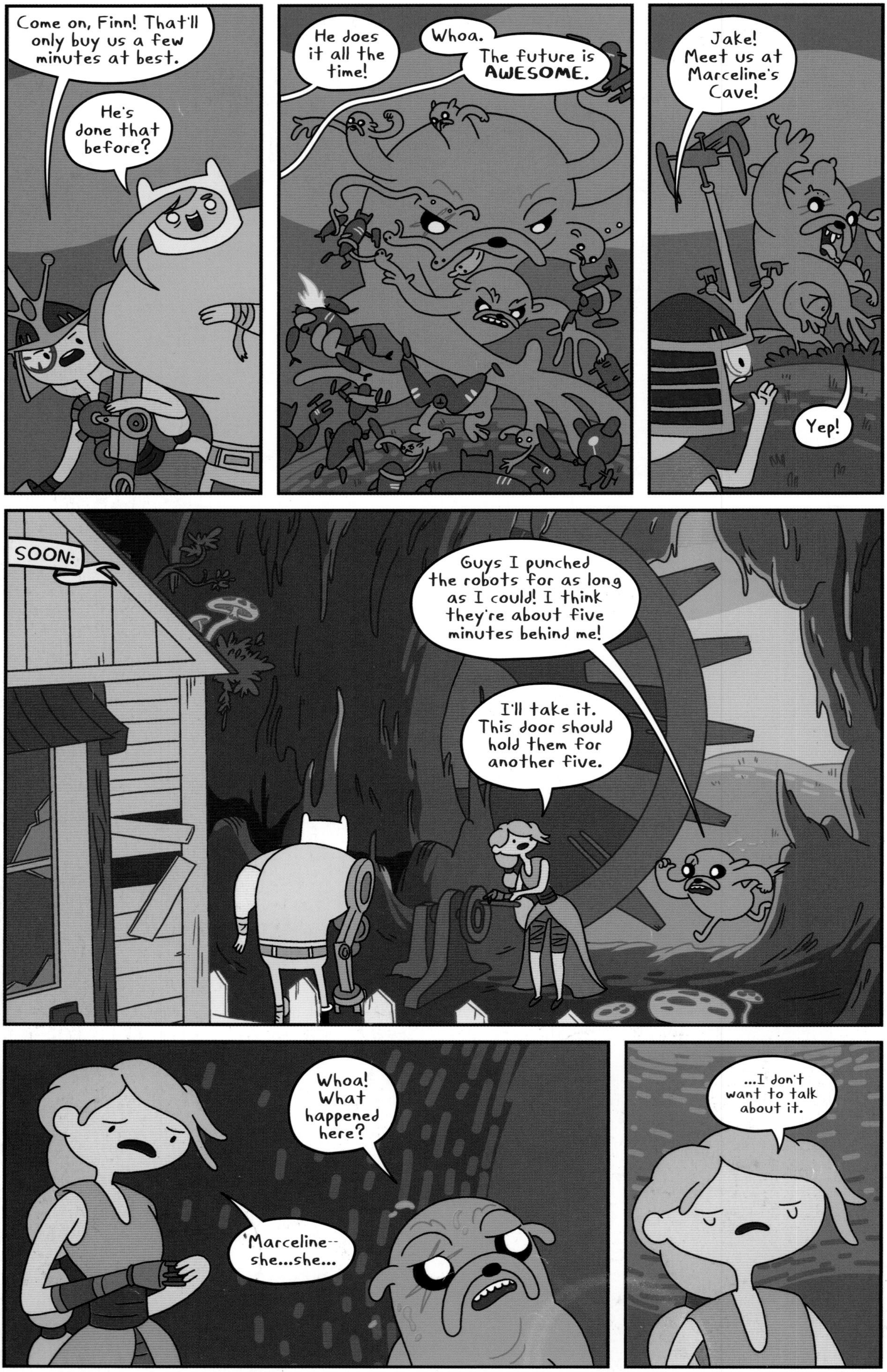
Come on, Finn! That'll only buy us a few minutes at best.
He's done that before?
He does it all the time!
Whoa.
The future is **AWESOME.**
Jake! Meet us at Marceline's Cave!
Yep!
SOON:
Guys I punched the robots for as long as I could! I think they're about five minutes behind me!
I'll take it. This door should hold them for another five.
Whoa! What happened here?
Marceline-- she...she...
...I don't want to talk about it.

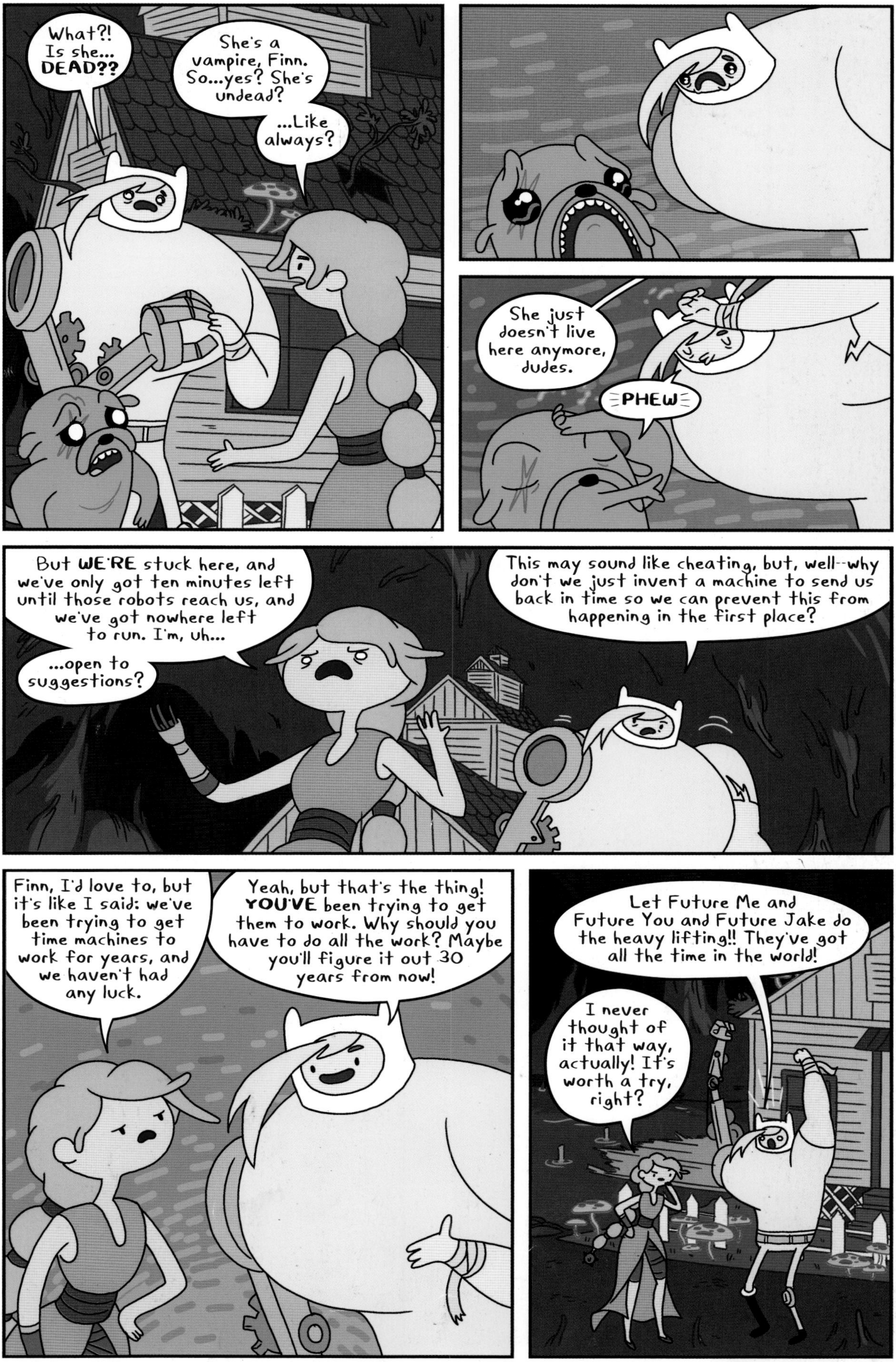
What?! Is she... **DEAD??**
She's a vampire, Finn. So...yes? She's undead?
...Like always?
She just doesn't live here anymore, dudes.
PHEW
But **WE'RE** stuck here, and we've only got ten minutes left until those robots reach us, and we've got nowhere left to run. I'm, uh...
...open to suggestions?
This may sound like cheating, but, well--why don't we just invent a machine to send us back in time so we can prevent this from happening in the first place?
Finn, I'd love to, but it's like I said: we've been trying to get time machines to work for years, and we haven't had any luck.
Yeah, but that's the thing! **YOU'VE** been trying to get them to work. Why should you have to do all the work? Maybe you'll figure it out 30 years from now!
Let Future Me and Future You and Future Jake do the heavy lifting!! They've got all the time in the world!
I never thought of it that way, actually! It's worth a try, right?

The maneuver Finn has invented here will be henceforth known as the "Deus Ex Tempus," which is Latin for "Whoa this is **TOTALLY AWESOME!!**"

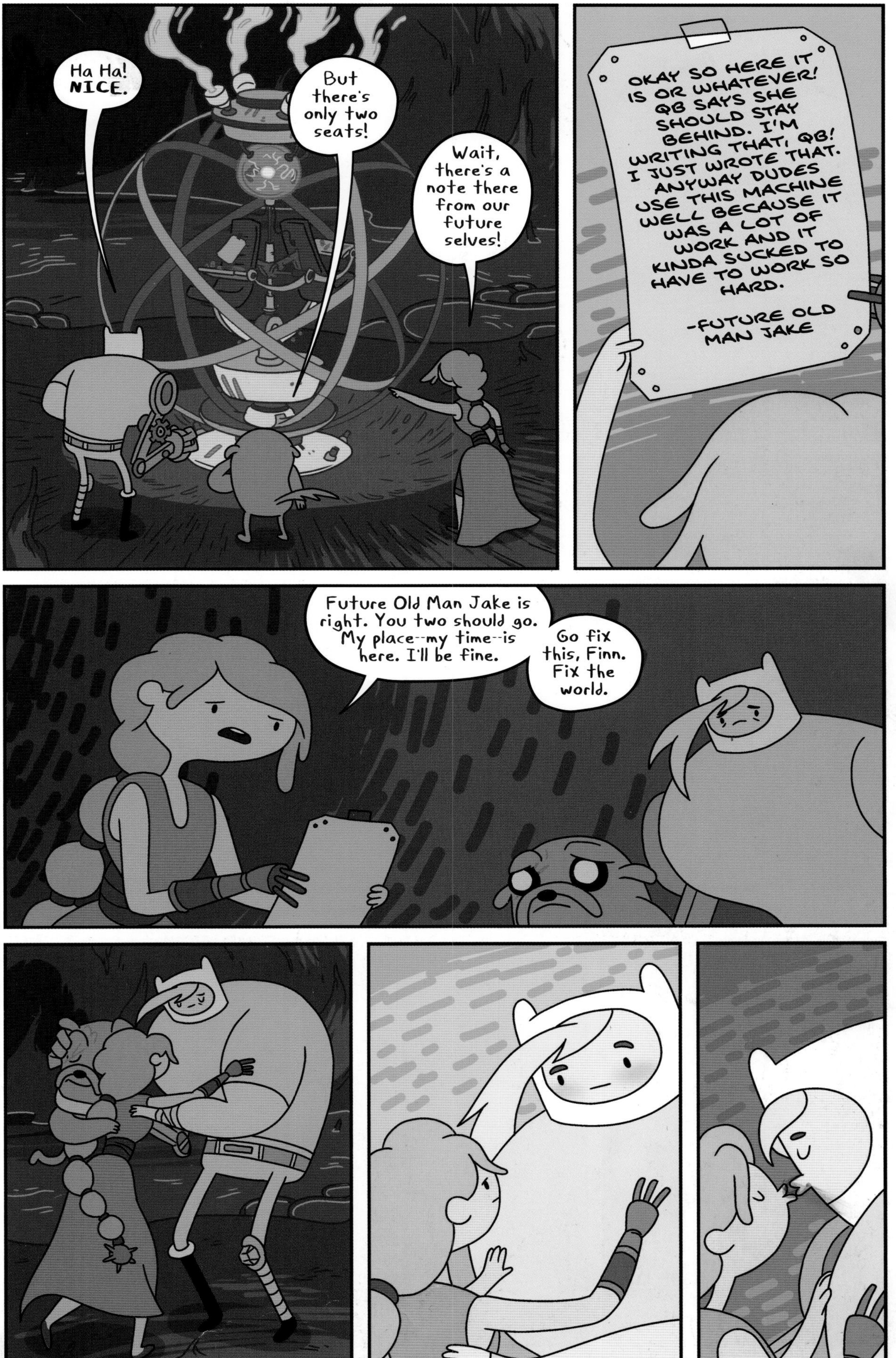
Ha Ha! NICE.
But there's only two seats!
Wait, there's a note there from our future selves!
OKAY SO HERE IT IS OR WHATEVER! QB SAYS SHE SHOULD STAY BEHIND. I'M WRITING THAT, QB! I JUST WROTE THAT. ANYWAY DUDES USE THIS MACHINE WELL BECAUSE IT WAS A LOT OF WORK AND IT KINDA SUCKED TO HAVE TO WORK SO HARD.
-FUTURE OLD MAN JAKE
Future Old Man Jake is right. You two should go. My place--my time--is here. I'll be fine.
Go fix this, Finn. Fix the world.

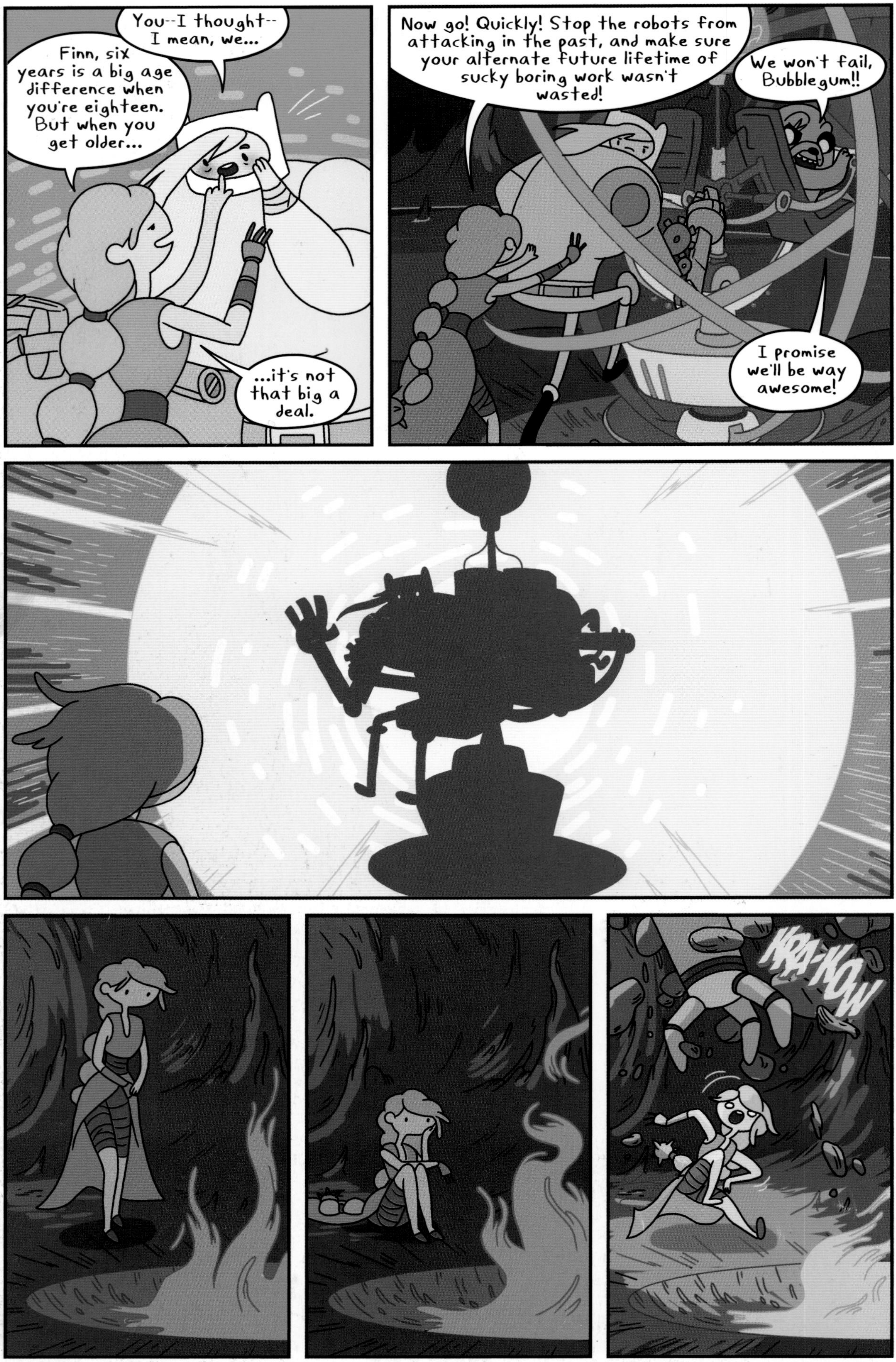
Finn, six years is a big age difference when you're eighteen. But when you get older...
You--I thought-- I mean, we...
...it's not that big a deal.
Now go! Quickly! Stop the robots from attacking in the past, and make sure your alternate future lifetime of sucky boring work wasn't wasted!
We won't fail, Bubblegum!!
I promise we'll be way awesome!
KRA-KOW

DID YOU KNOW: Sucky boring work is so flippin' sucky and boring

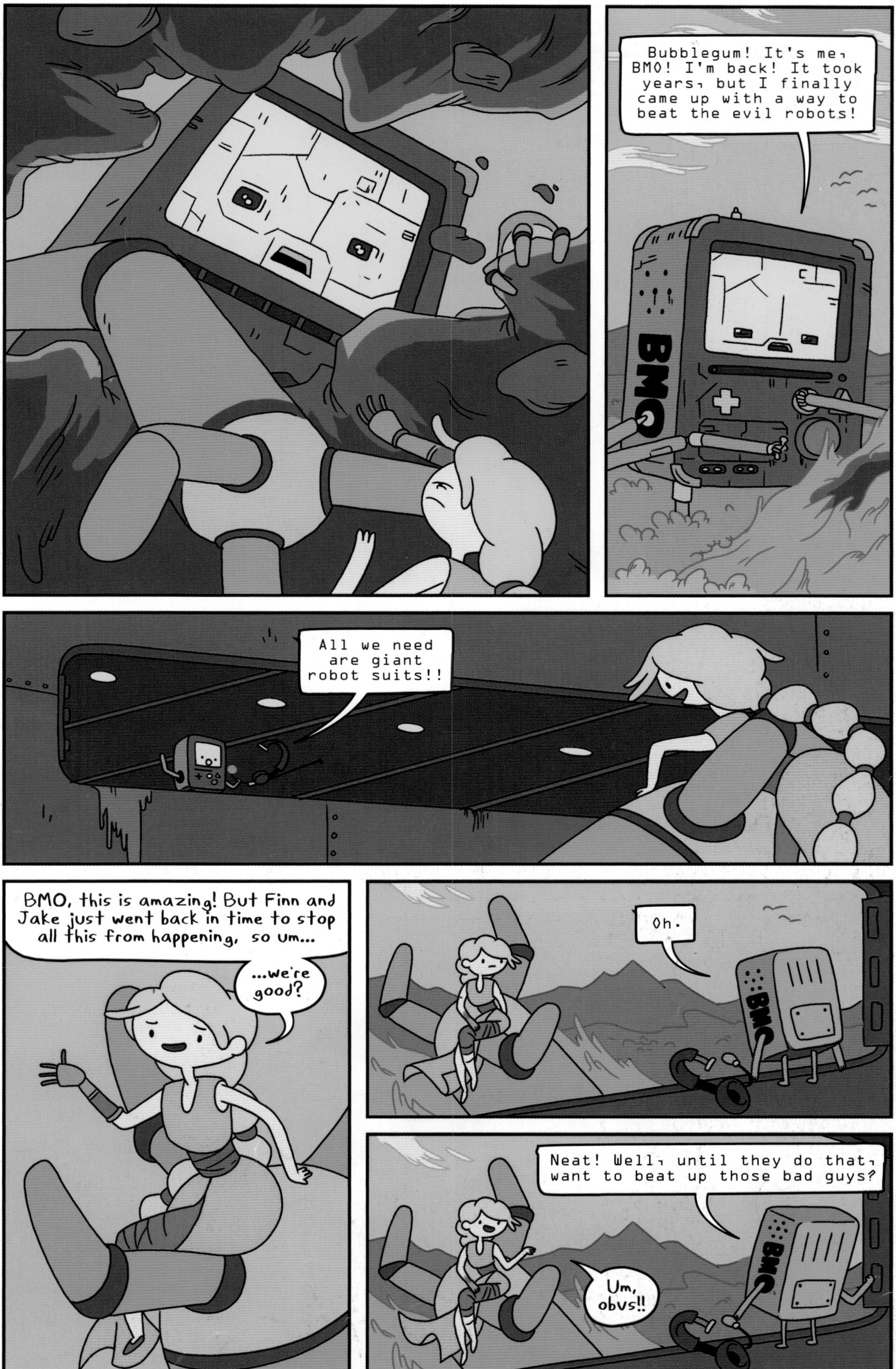
Bubblegum! It's me, BMO! I'm back! It took years, but I finally came up with a way to beat the evil robots!
All we need are giant robot suits!!
BMO, this is amazing! But Finn and Jake just went back in time to stop all this from happening, so um...
...we're good?
Oh.
Neat! Well, until they do that, want to beat up those bad guys?
Um, obvs!!

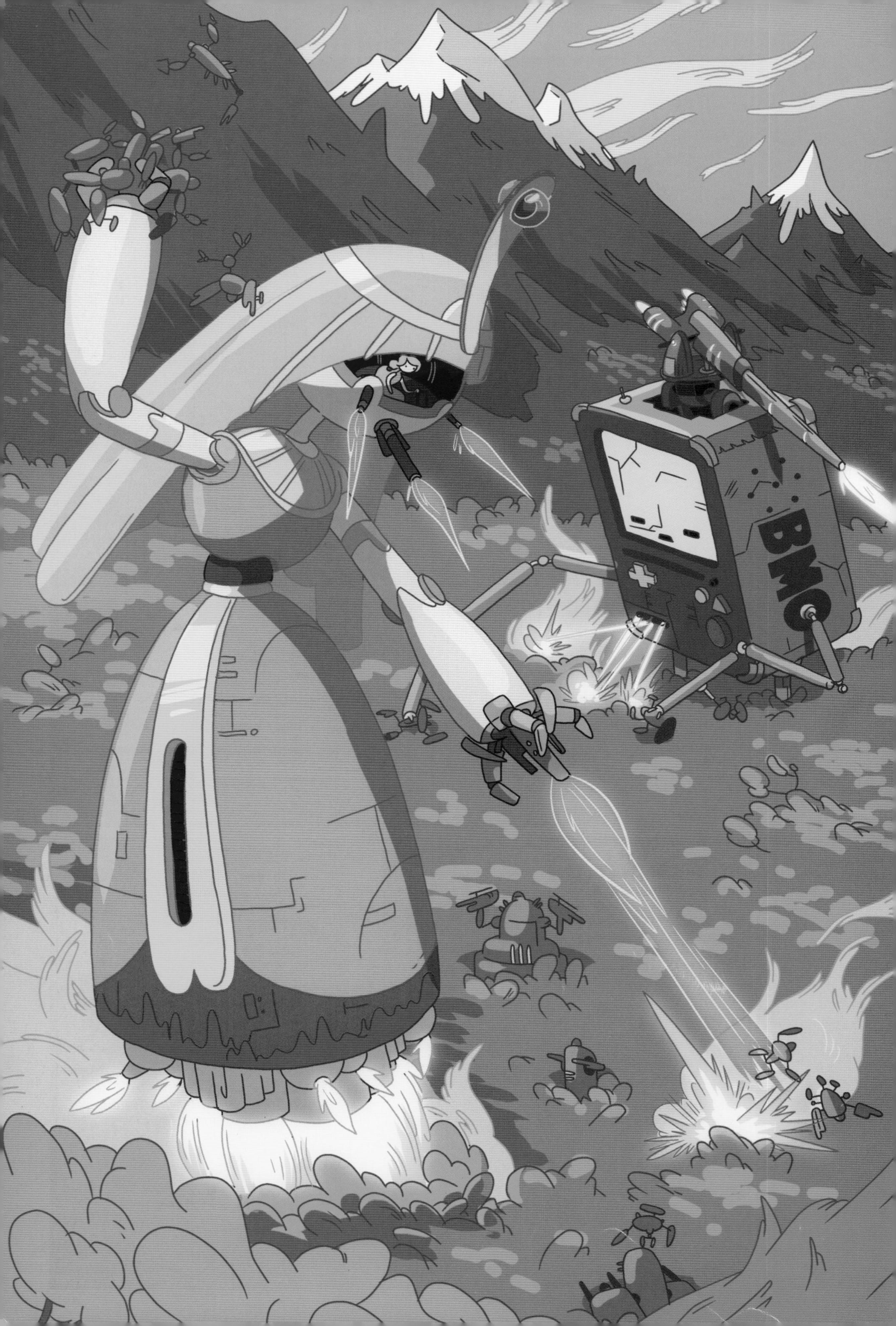
BMO

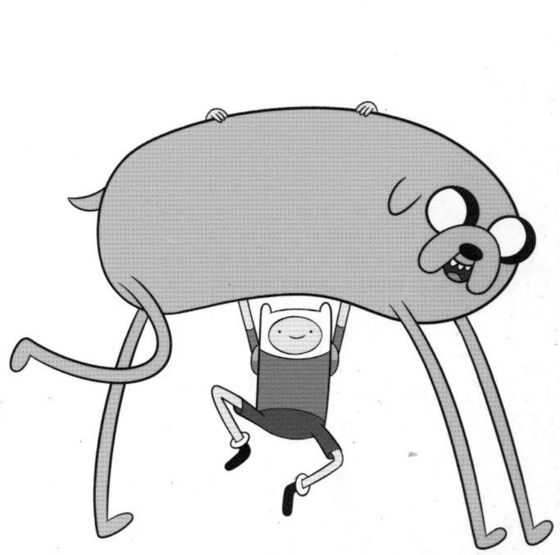

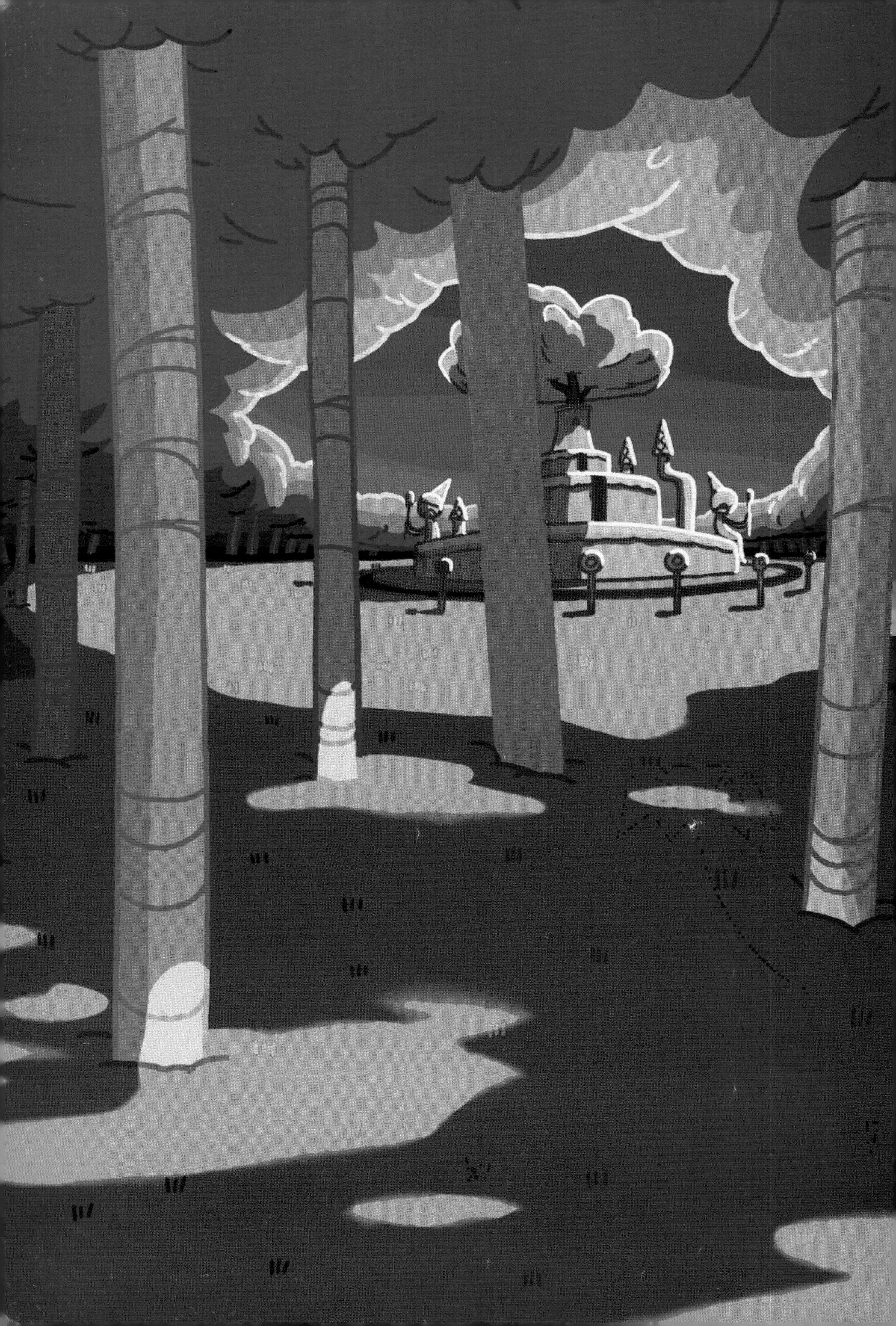

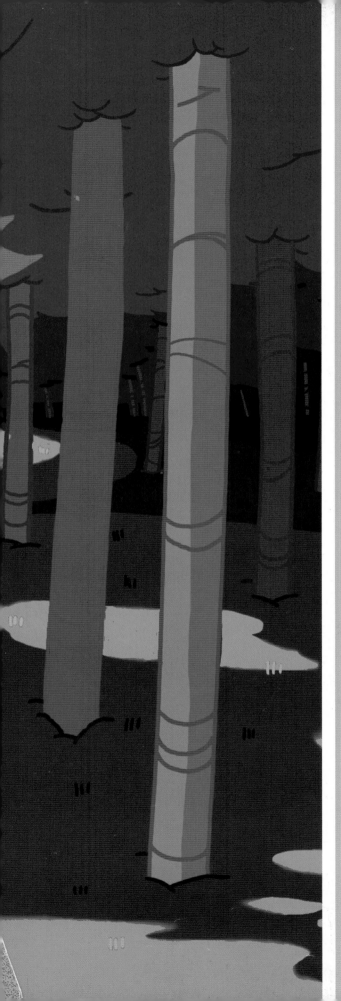

CHAPTER FIVE

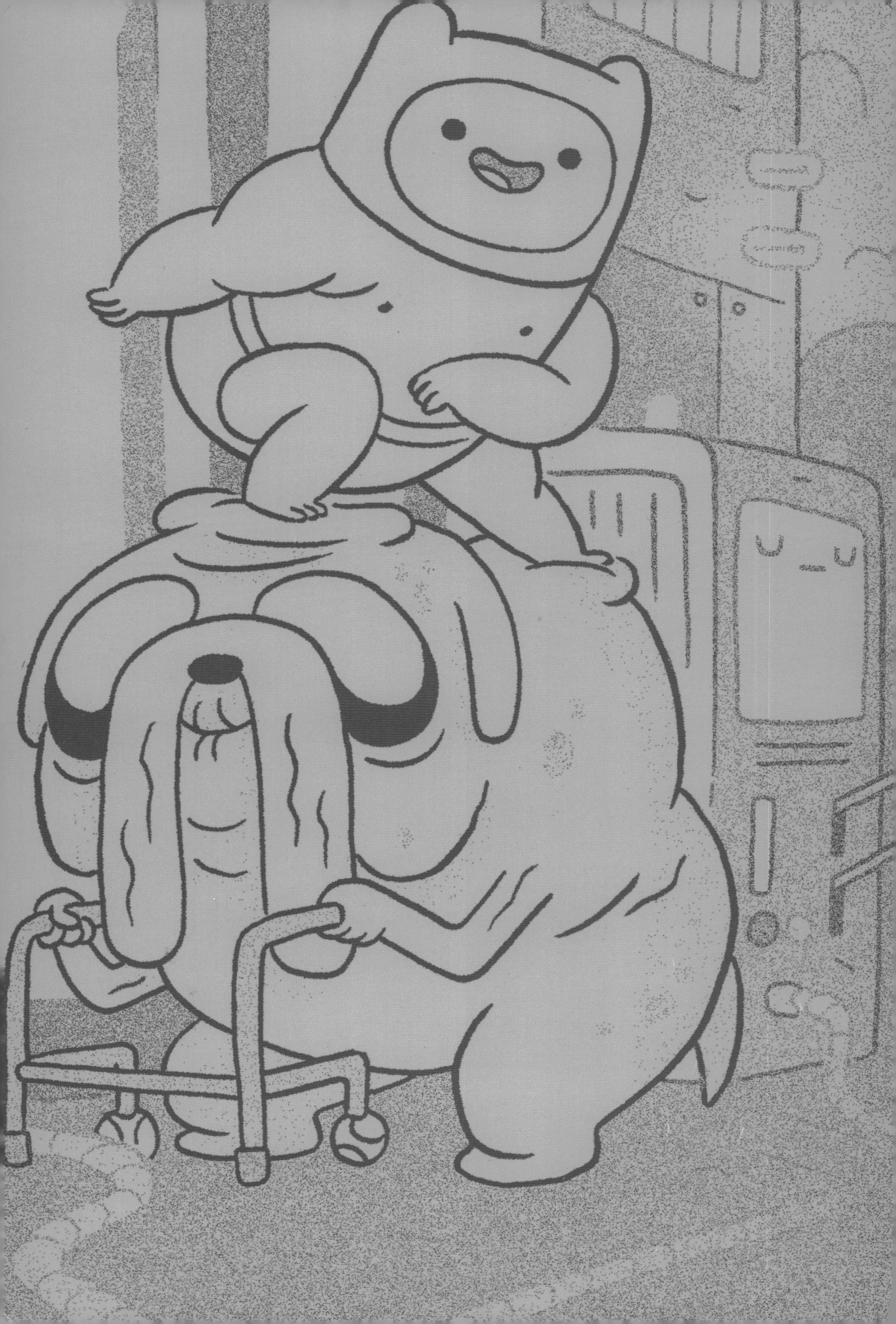

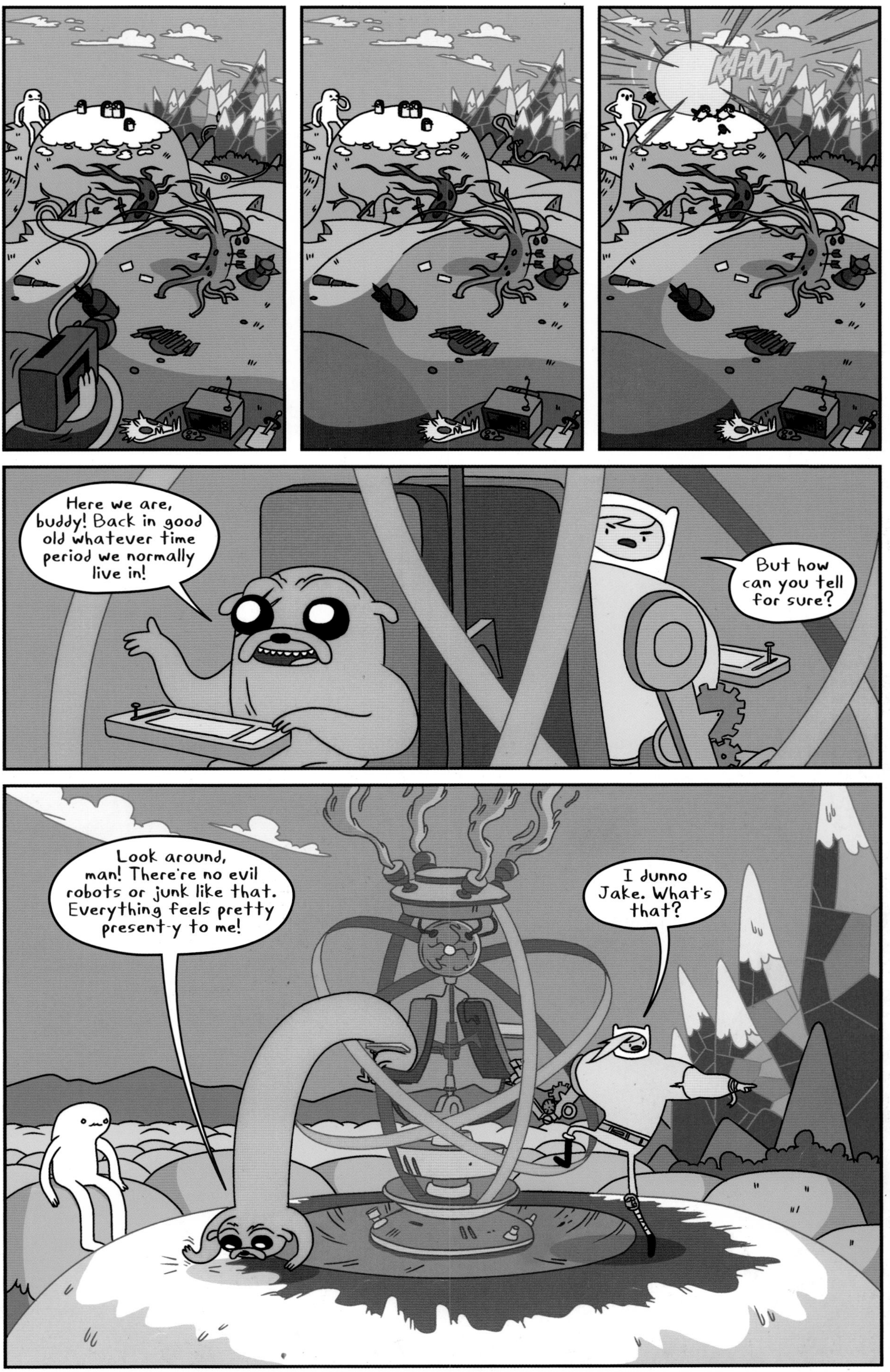
KA-POOT
Here we are, buddy! Back in good old whatever time period we normally live in!
But how can you tell for sure?
Look around, man! There're no evil robots or junk like that. Everything feels pretty present-y to me!
I dunno Jake. What's that?

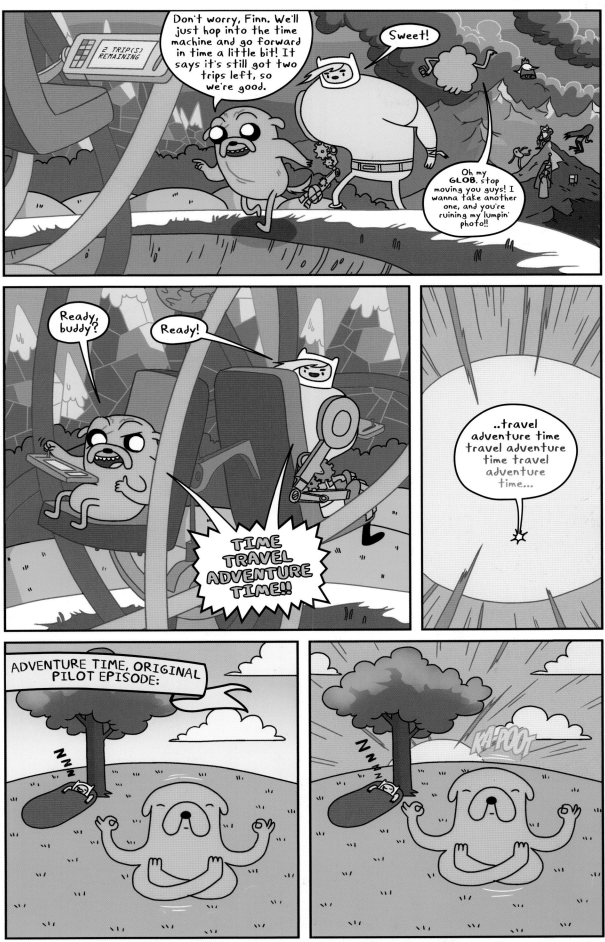

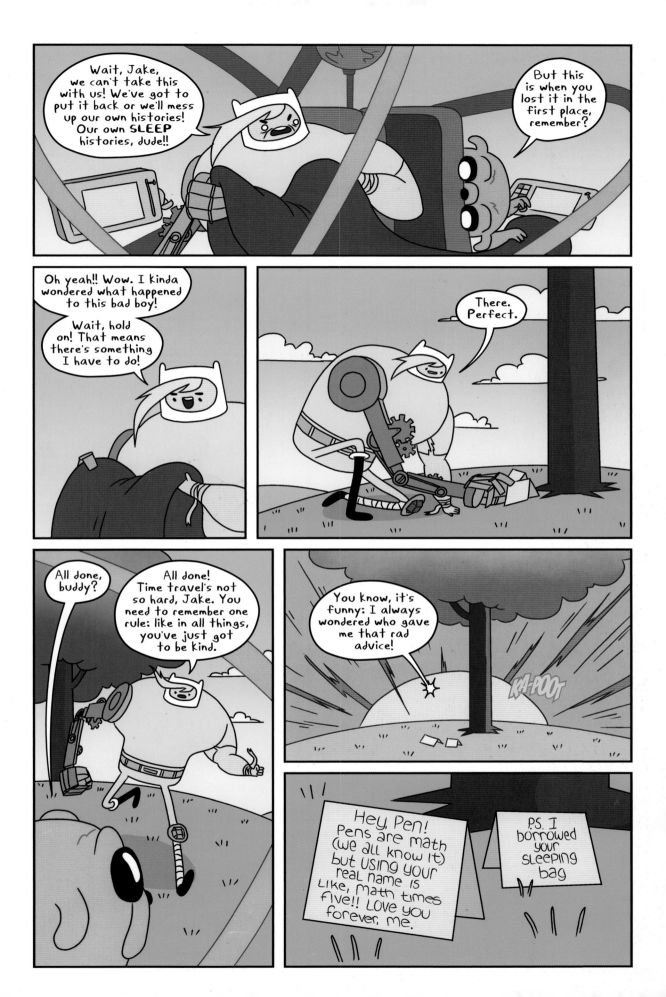

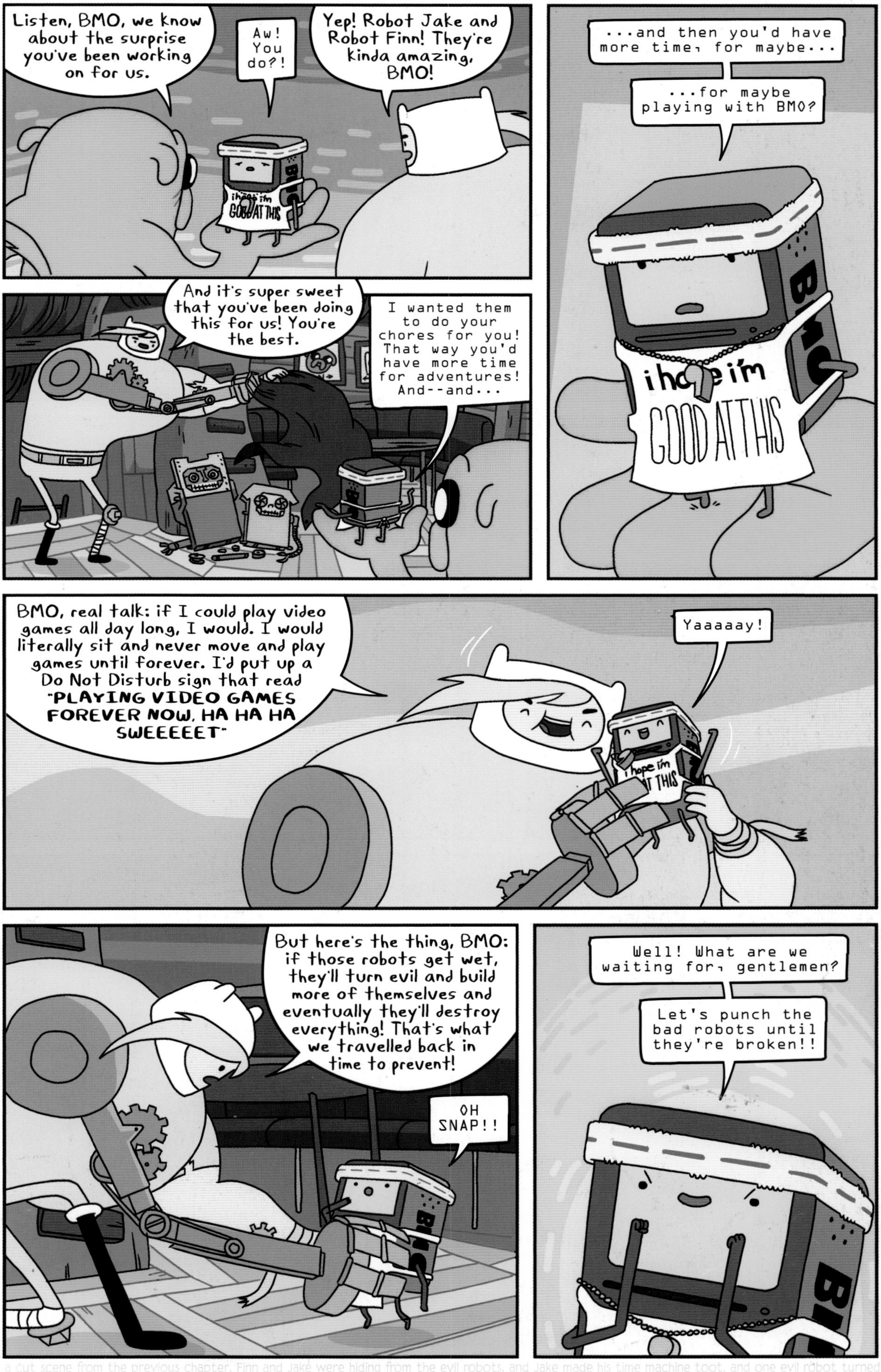
Listen, BMO, we know about the surprise you've been working on for us.
Aw! You do?!
Yep! Robot Jake and Robot Finn! They're kinda amazing, BMO!
i hope i'm GOOD AT THIS
...and then you'd have more time, for maybe...
...for maybe playing with BMO?
And it's super sweet that you've been doing this for us! You're the best.
I wanted them to do your chores for you! That way you'd have more time for adventures! And--and...
BMO, real talk: if I could play video games all day long, I would. I would literally sit and never move and play games until forever. I'd put up a Do Not Disturb sign that read "PLAYING VIDEO GAMES FOREVER NOW, HA HA HA SWEEEEET"
Yaaaaay!
But here's the thing, BMO: if those robots get wet, they'll turn evil and build more of themselves and eventually they'll destroy everything! That's what we travelled back in time to prevent!
OH SNAP!!
Well! What are we waiting for, gentlemen?
Let's punch the bad robots until they're broken!!

In a cut scene from the previous chapter, Finn and Jake were hiding from the evil robots, and Jake made his time machine toot, and one evil robot turned to the other and said "Hey, are you dropping bad packets in here?" It was extremely hilarious.

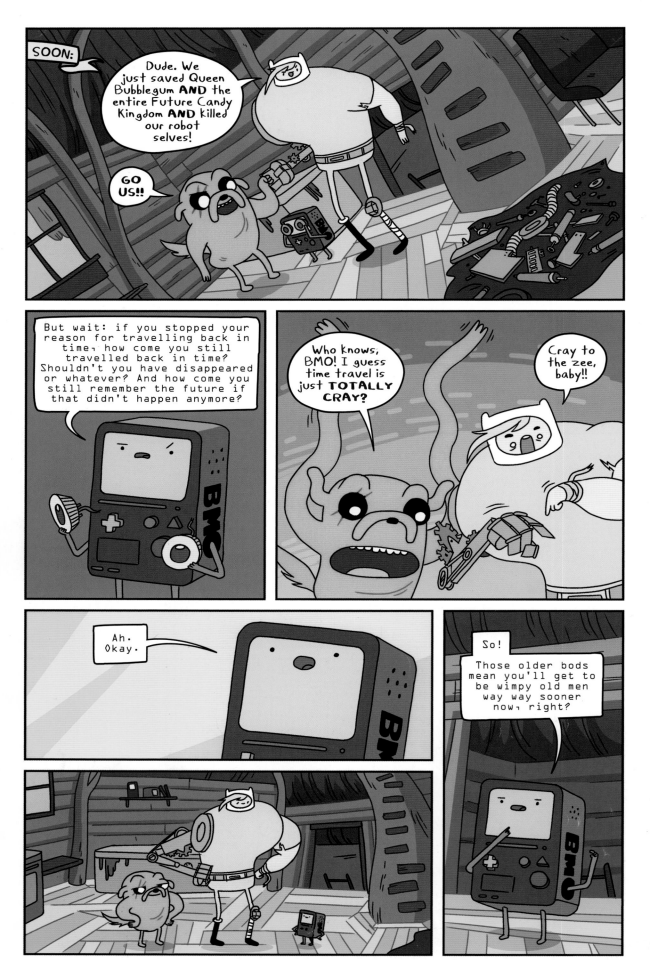

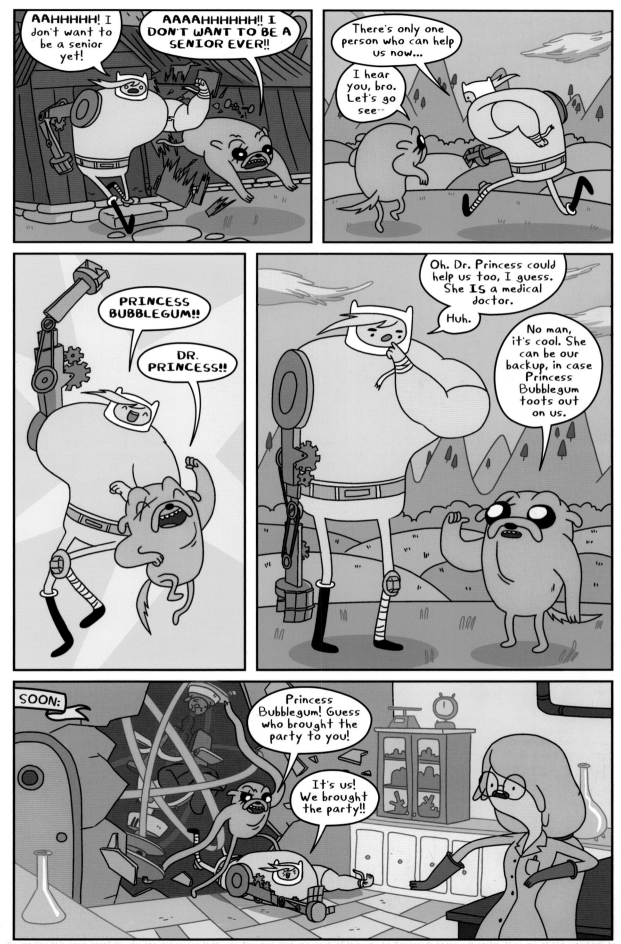

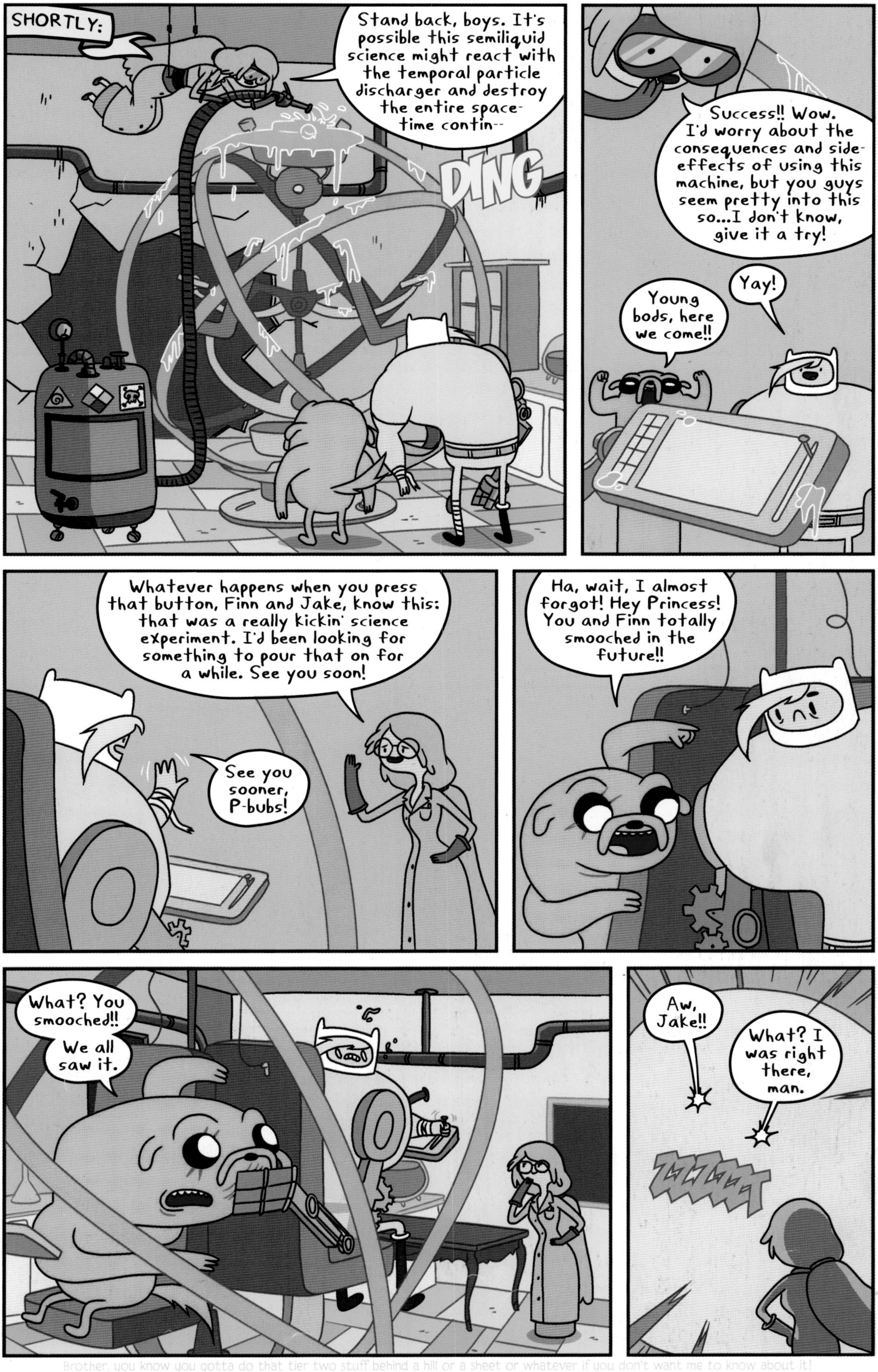
SHORTLY:
Stand back, boys. It's possible this semiliquid science might react with the temporal particle discharger and destroy the entire space-time contin--
DING
Success!! Wow. I'd worry about the consequences and side-effects of using this machine, but you guys seem pretty into this so...I don't know, give it a try!
Young bods, here we come!!
Yay!
Whatever happens when you press that button, Finn and Jake, know this: that was a really kickin' science experiment. I'd been looking for something to pour that on for a while. See you soon!
See you sooner, P-bubs!
Ha, wait, I almost forgot! Hey Princess! You and Finn totally smooched in the future!!
What? You smooched!!
We all saw it.
Aw, Jake!!
What? I was right there, man.
ZZZZZT

Brother, you know you gotta do that tier two stuff behind a hill or a sheet or whatever if you don't want me to know about it!

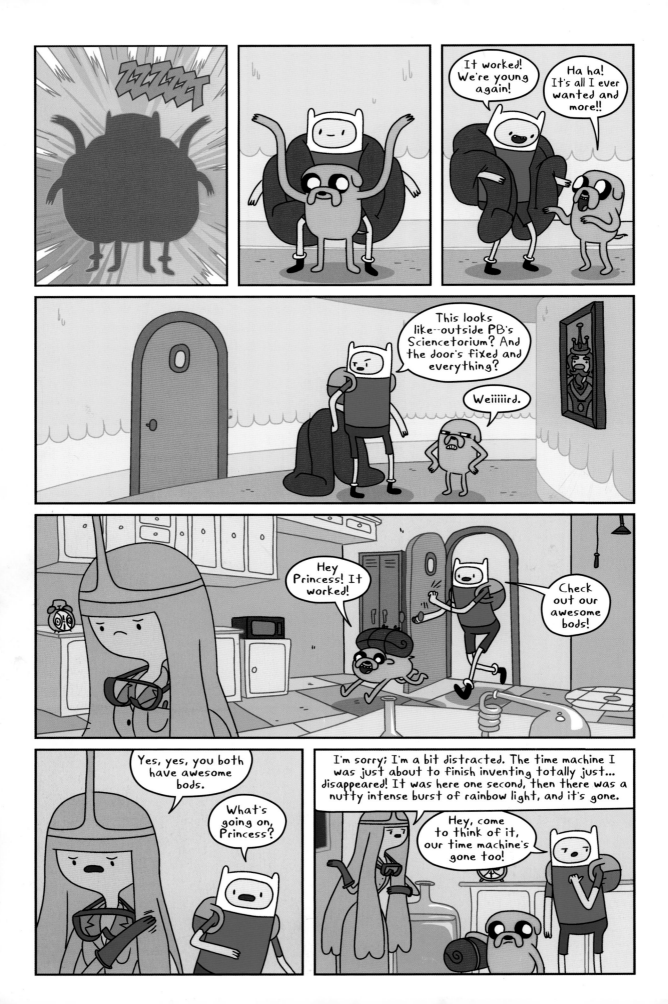

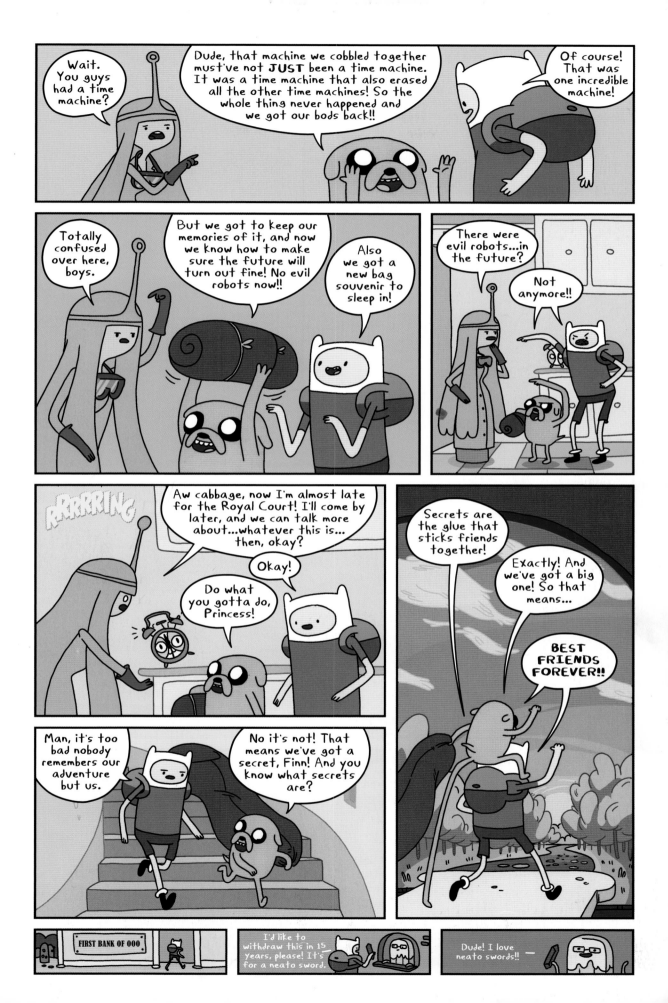

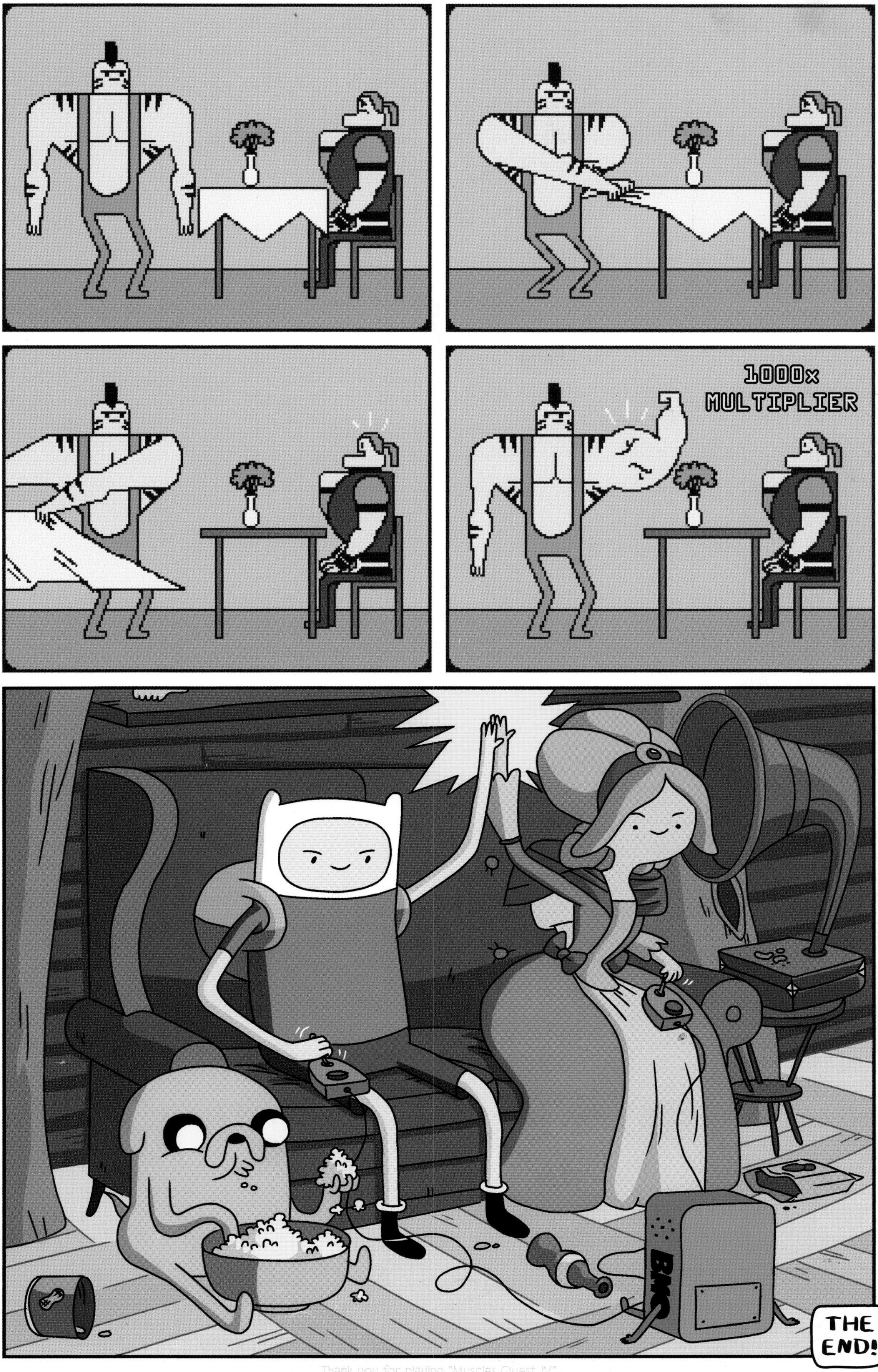
1000x
MULTIPLIER
THE END!

Thank you for playing "Muscles Quest IV"

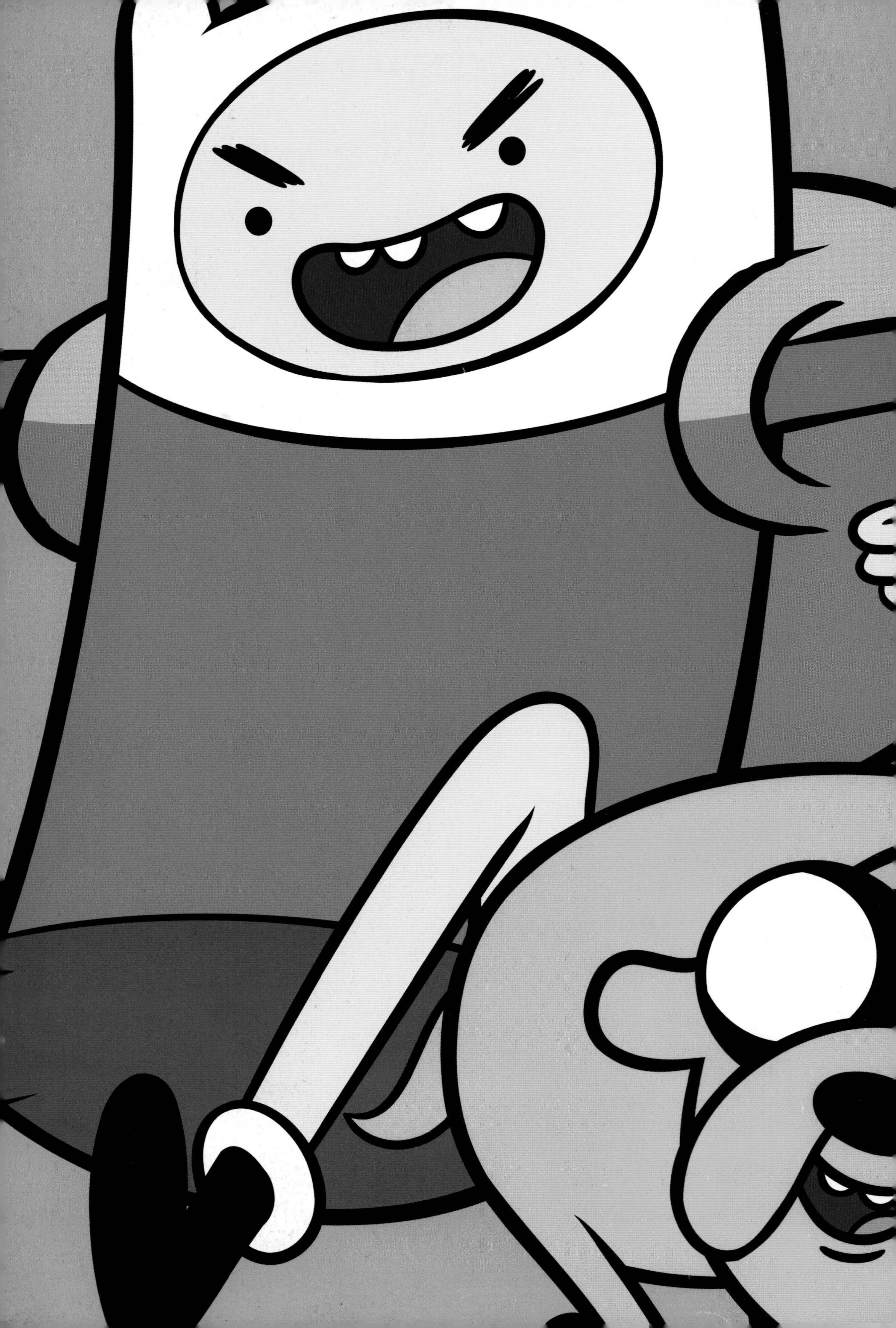

COVER GALLERY

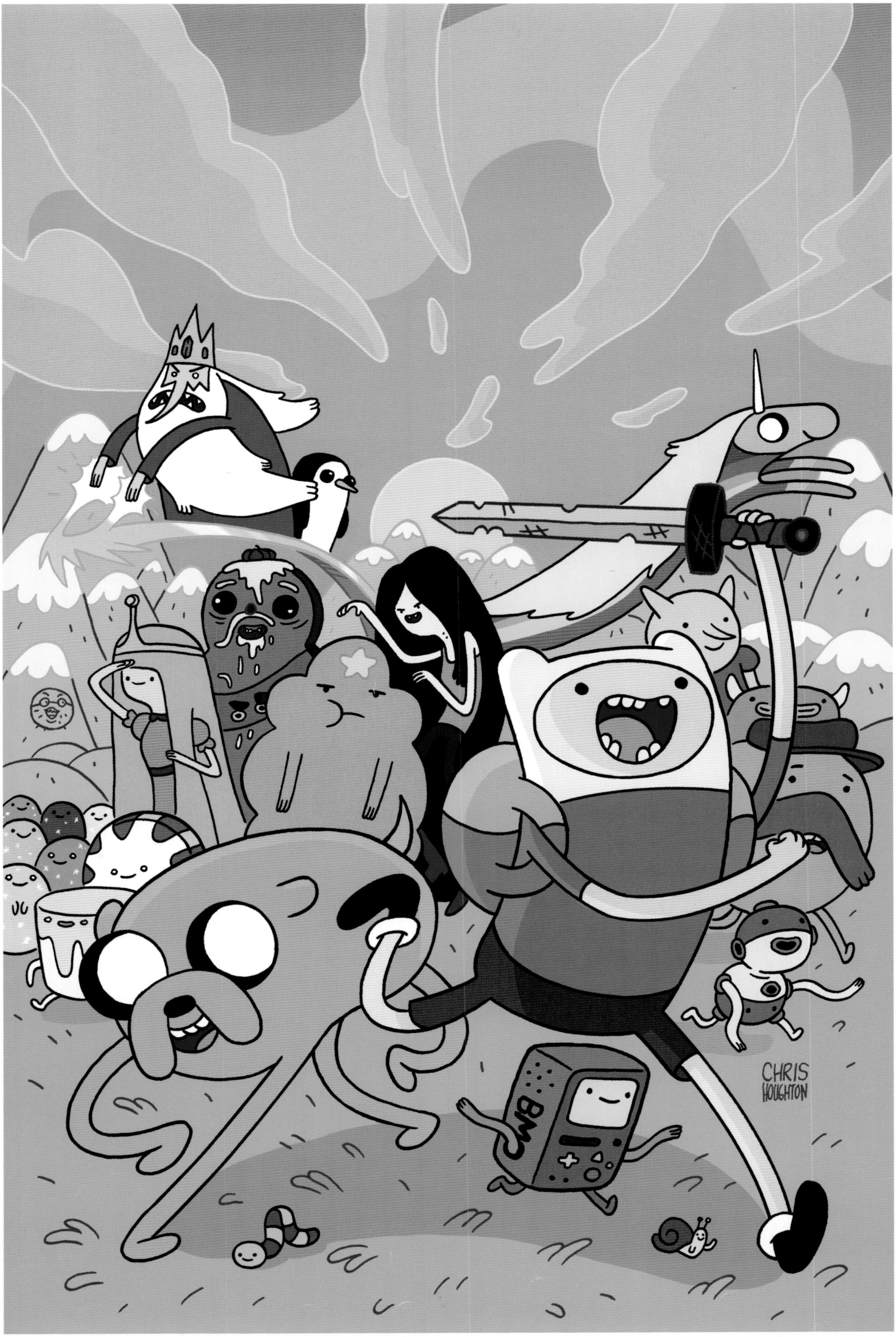
CHRIS HOUGHTON

ISSUE FIVE | CHRIS HOUGHTON | COLORS BY KASSANDRA HELLER

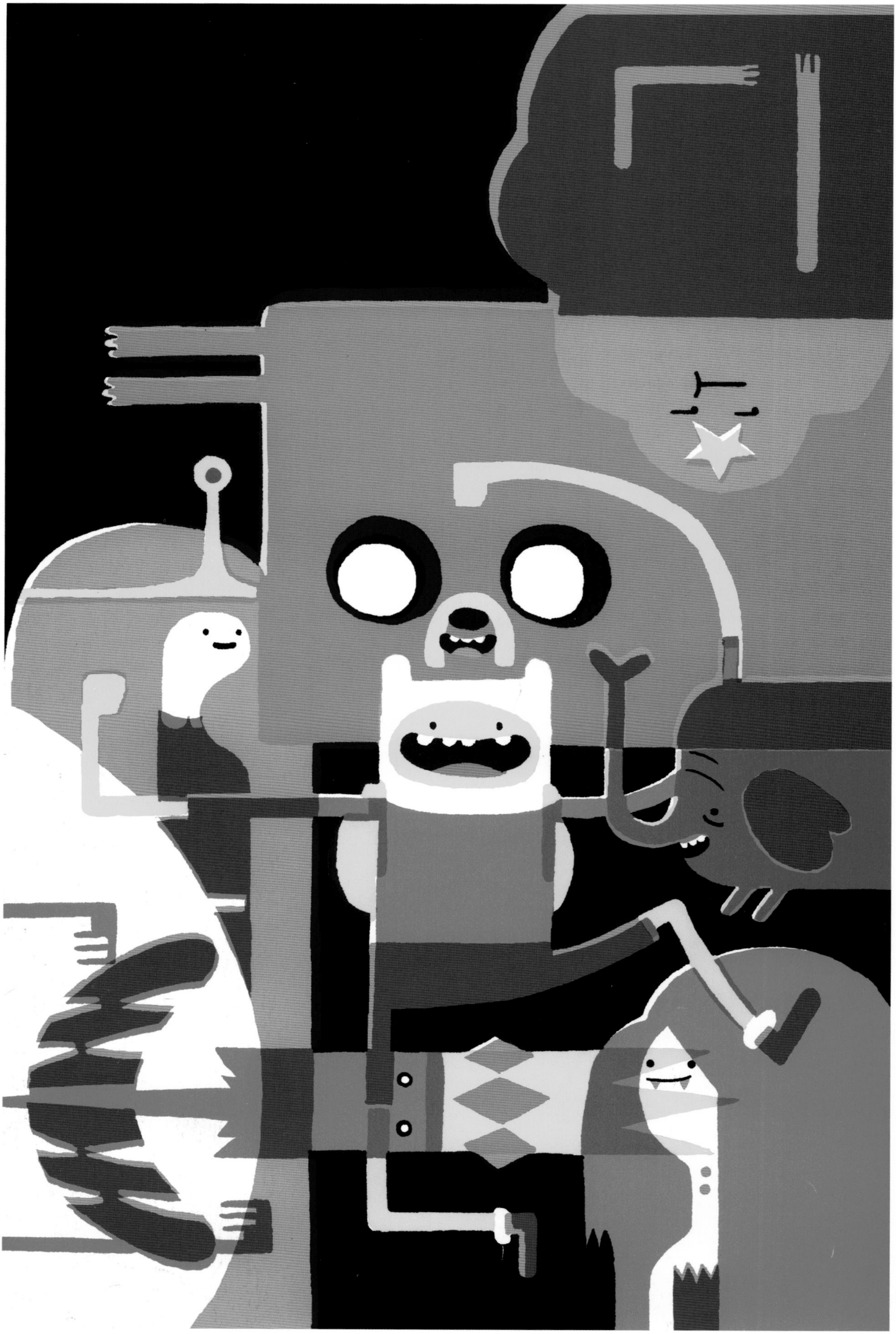

ISSUE FIVE | ELEANOR DAVIS

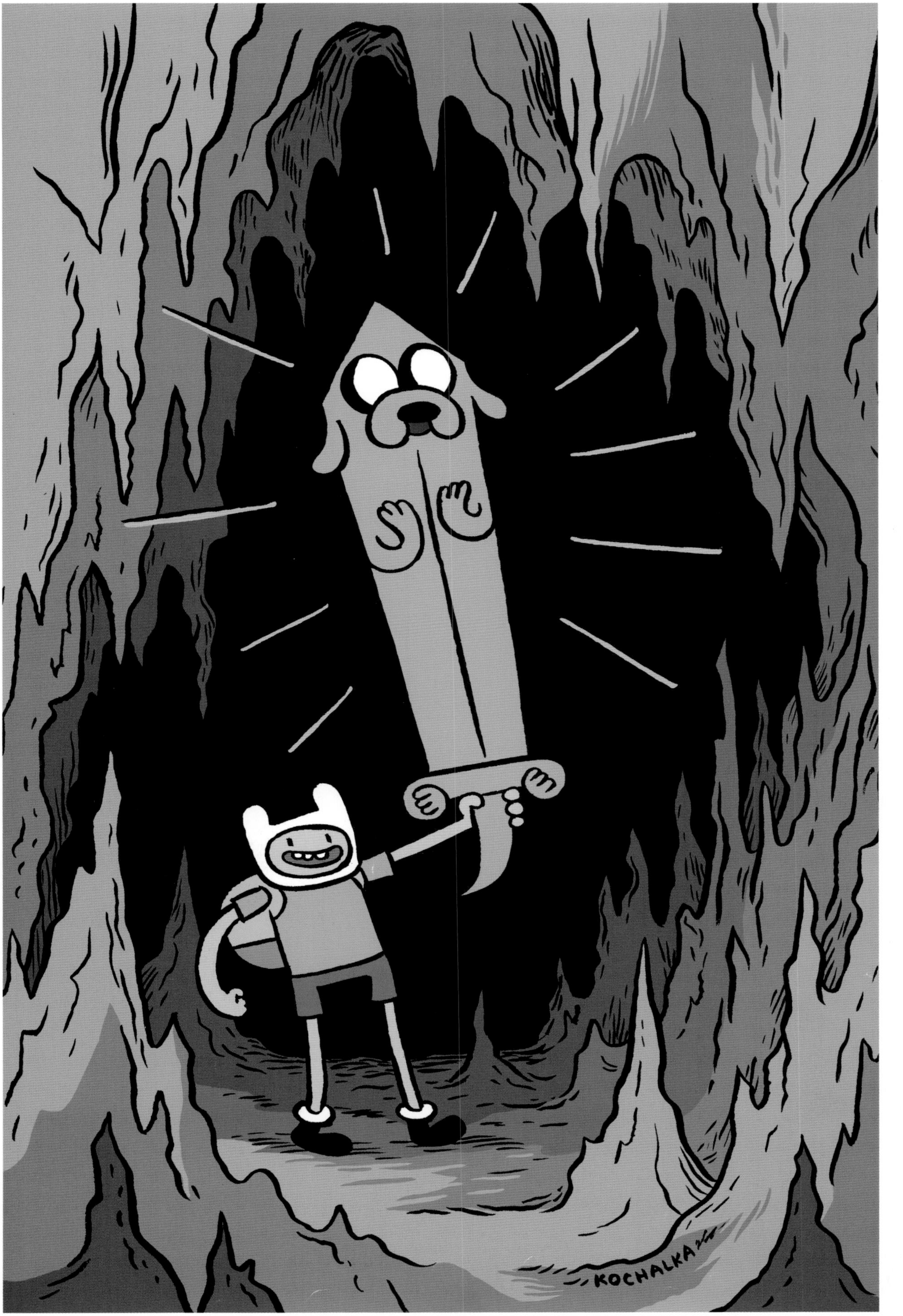
KOCHALKA

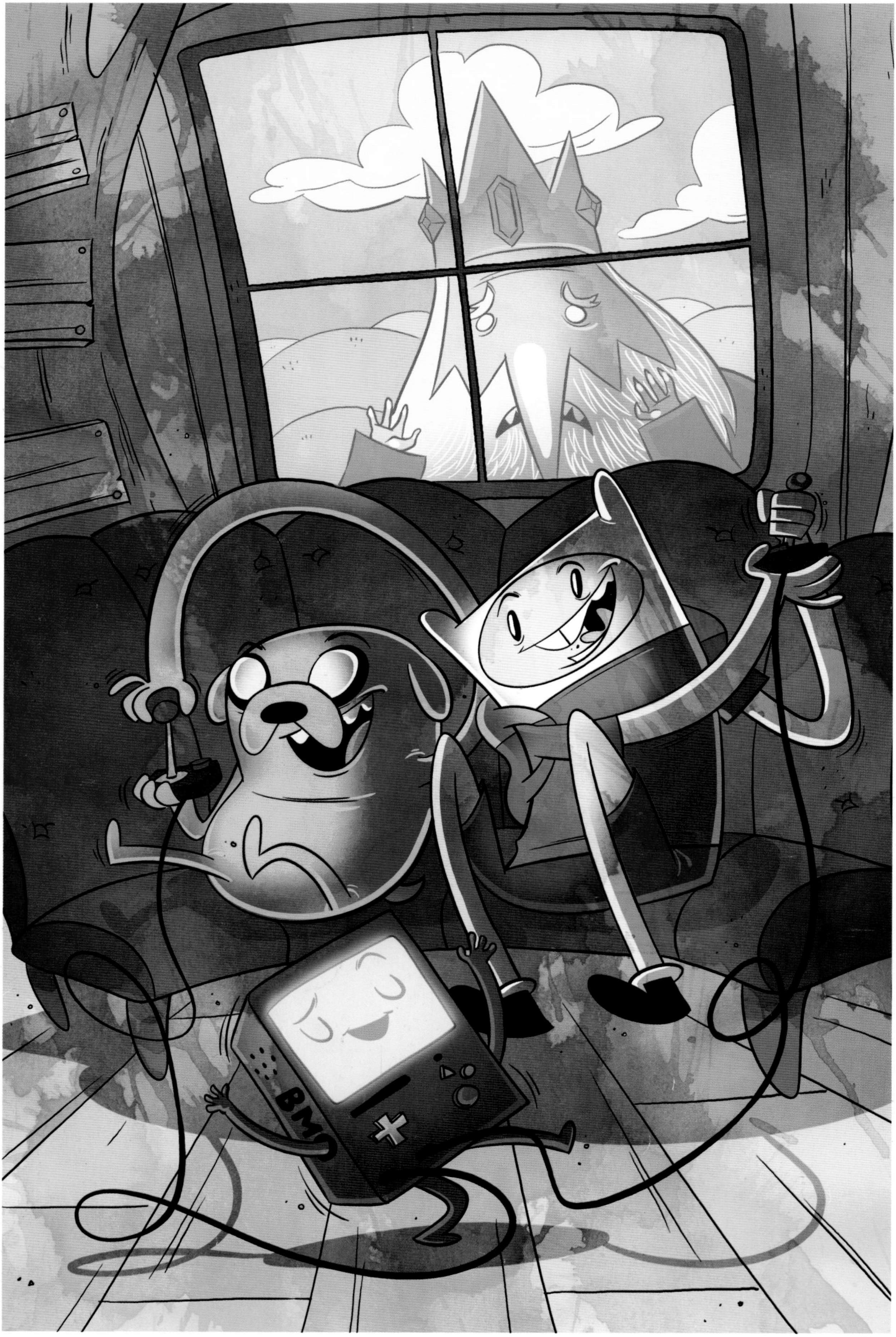
BMO

ISSUE FIVE | MIKE "GABE" KRAHULIK

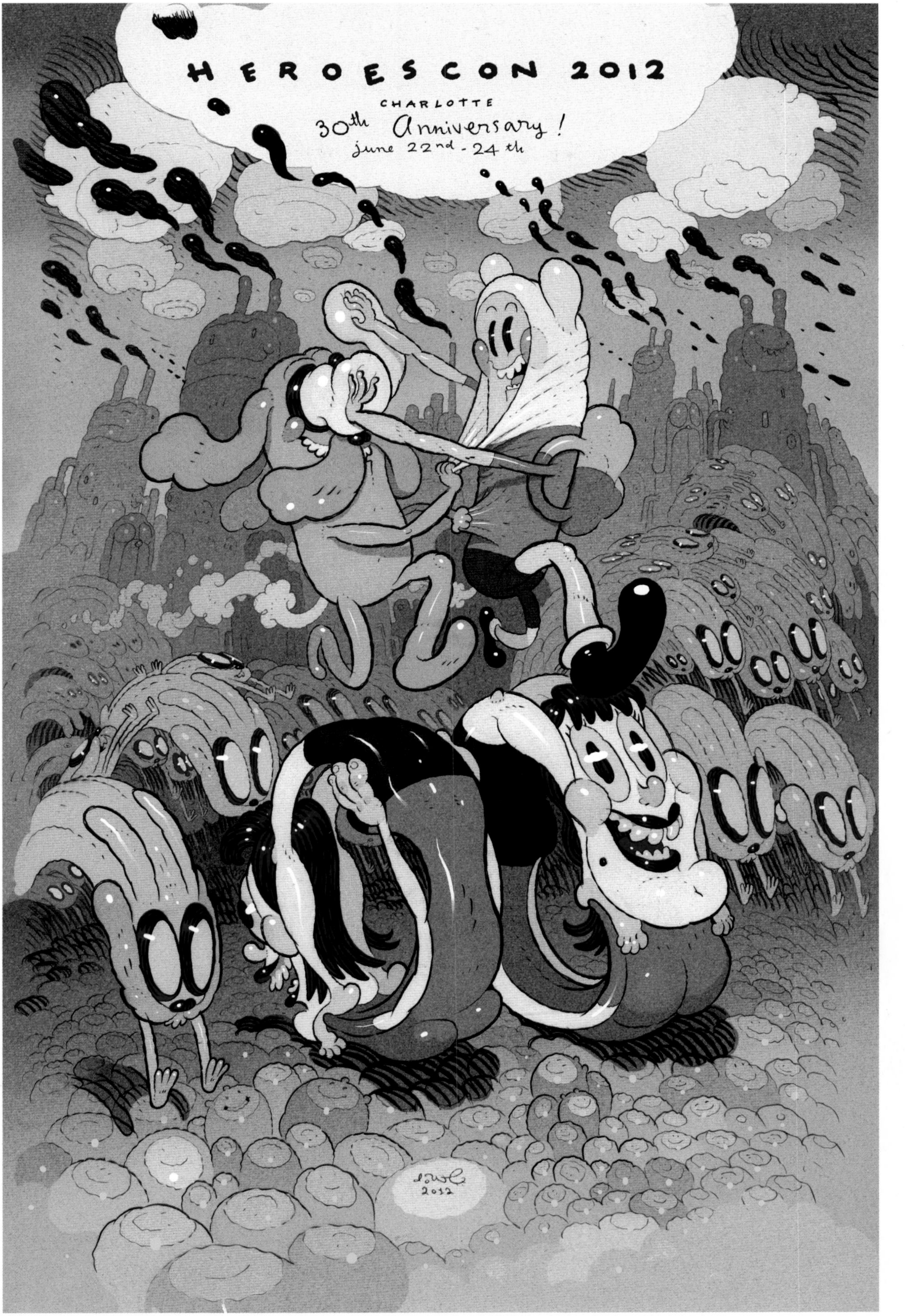
HEROESCON 2012
CHARLOTTE
30th Anniversary!
june 22nd - 24th
2012

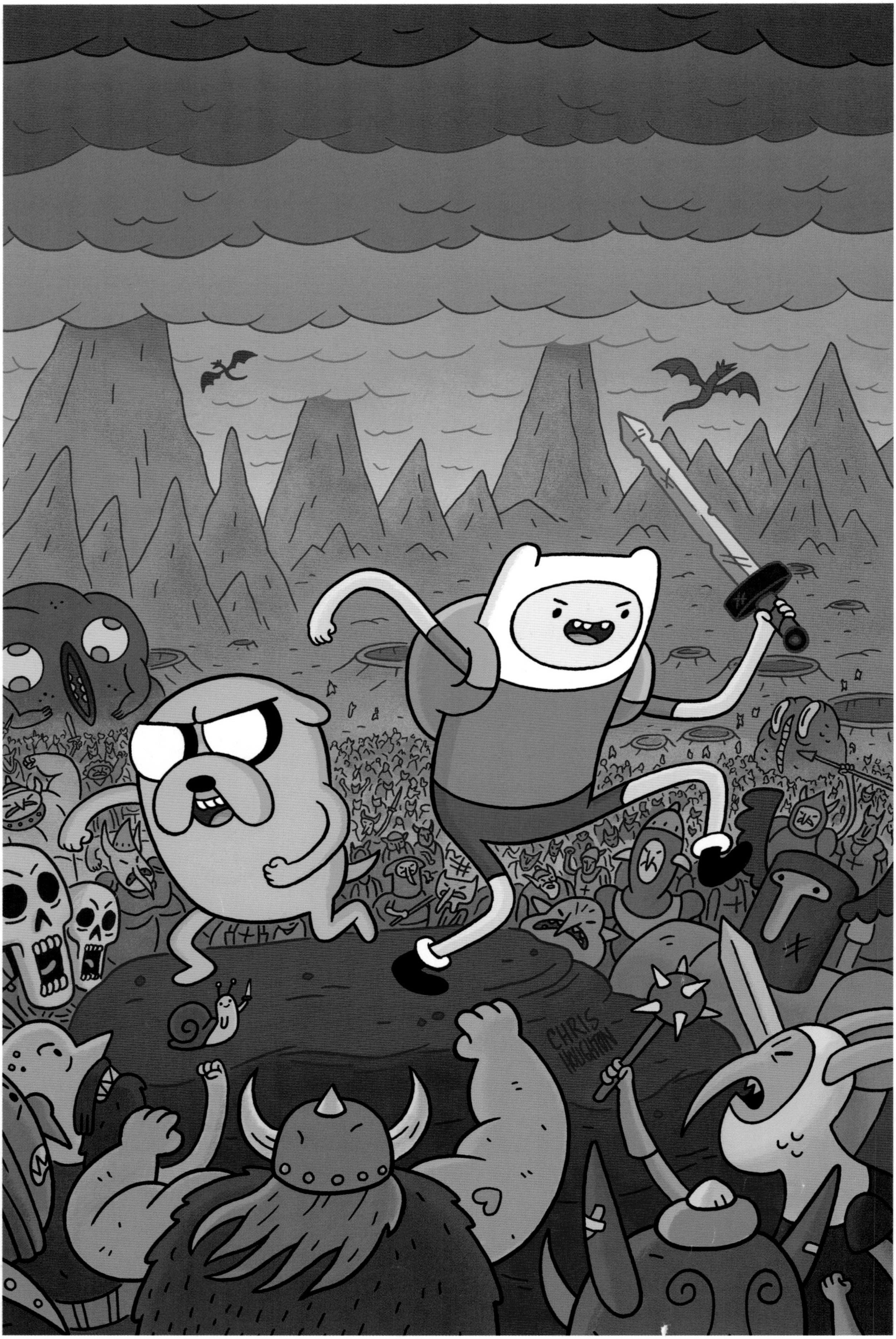
CHRIS HOUGHTON

ISSUE SIX | CHRIS HOUGHTON | COLORS BY KASSANDRA HELLER

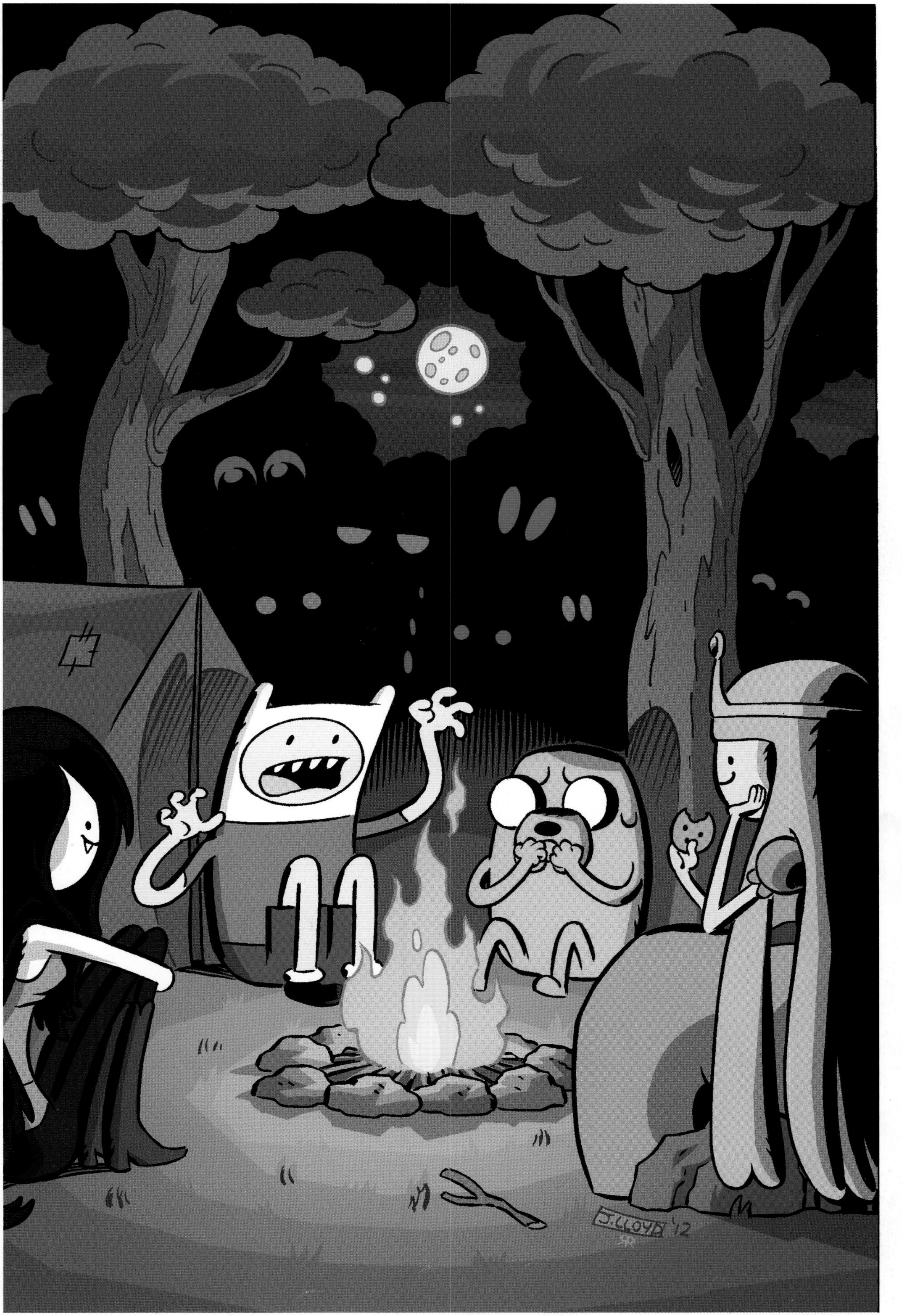
J.LLOYD '12

ISSUE SIX | JAMES LLOYD

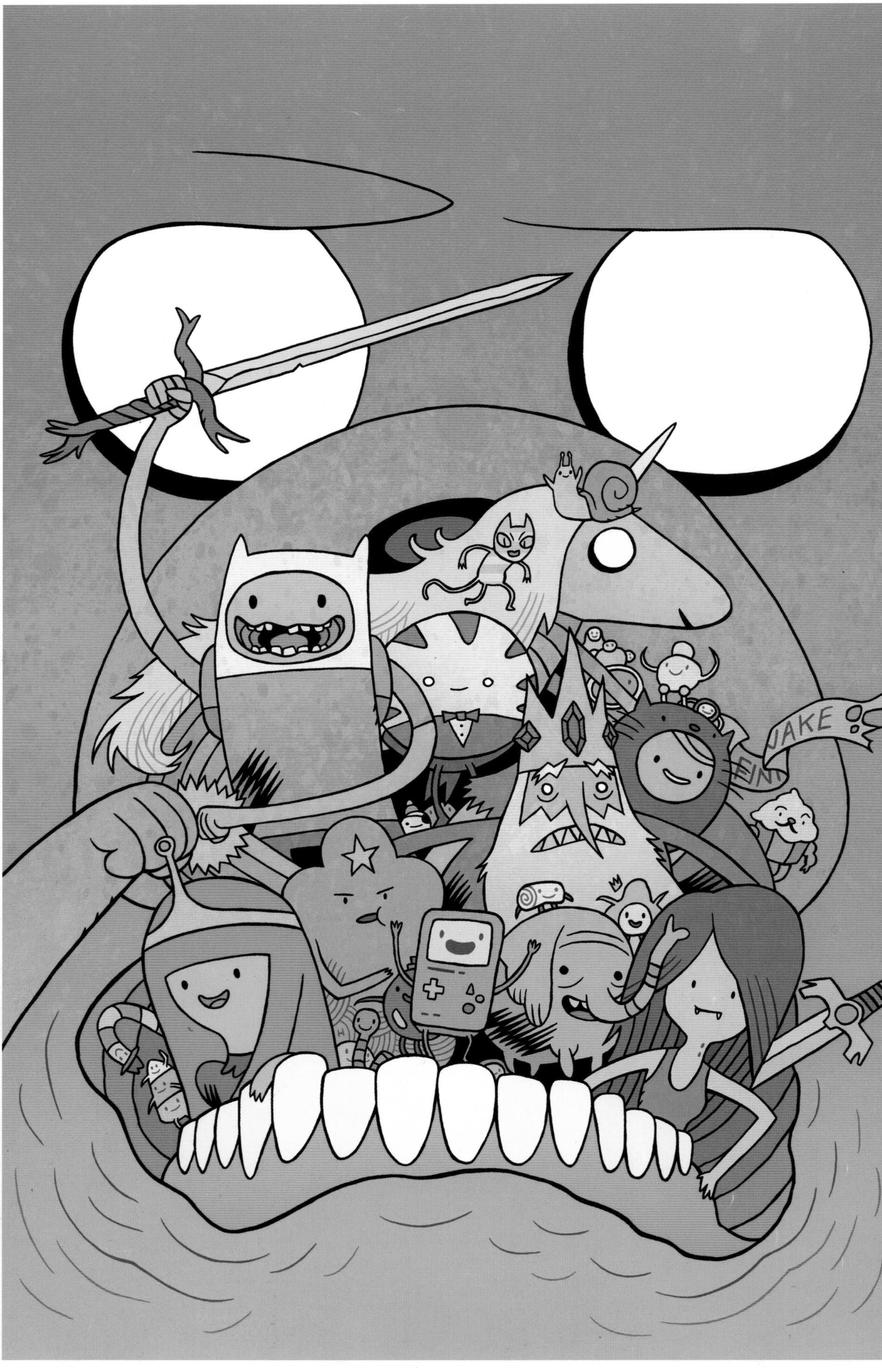
JAKE

ISSUE SIX | DAN HIPP

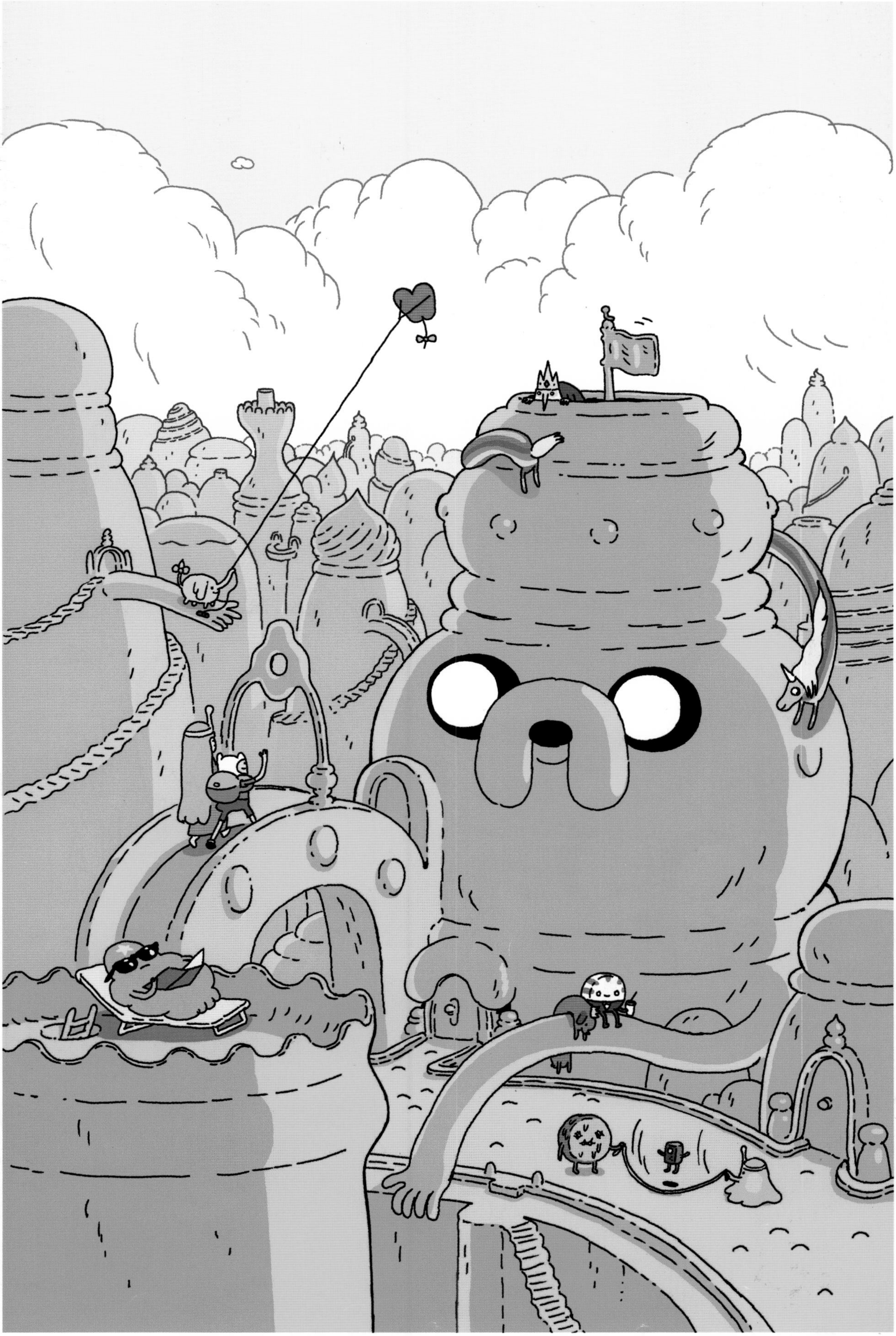

ISSUE SIX | STEVE WOLFHARD

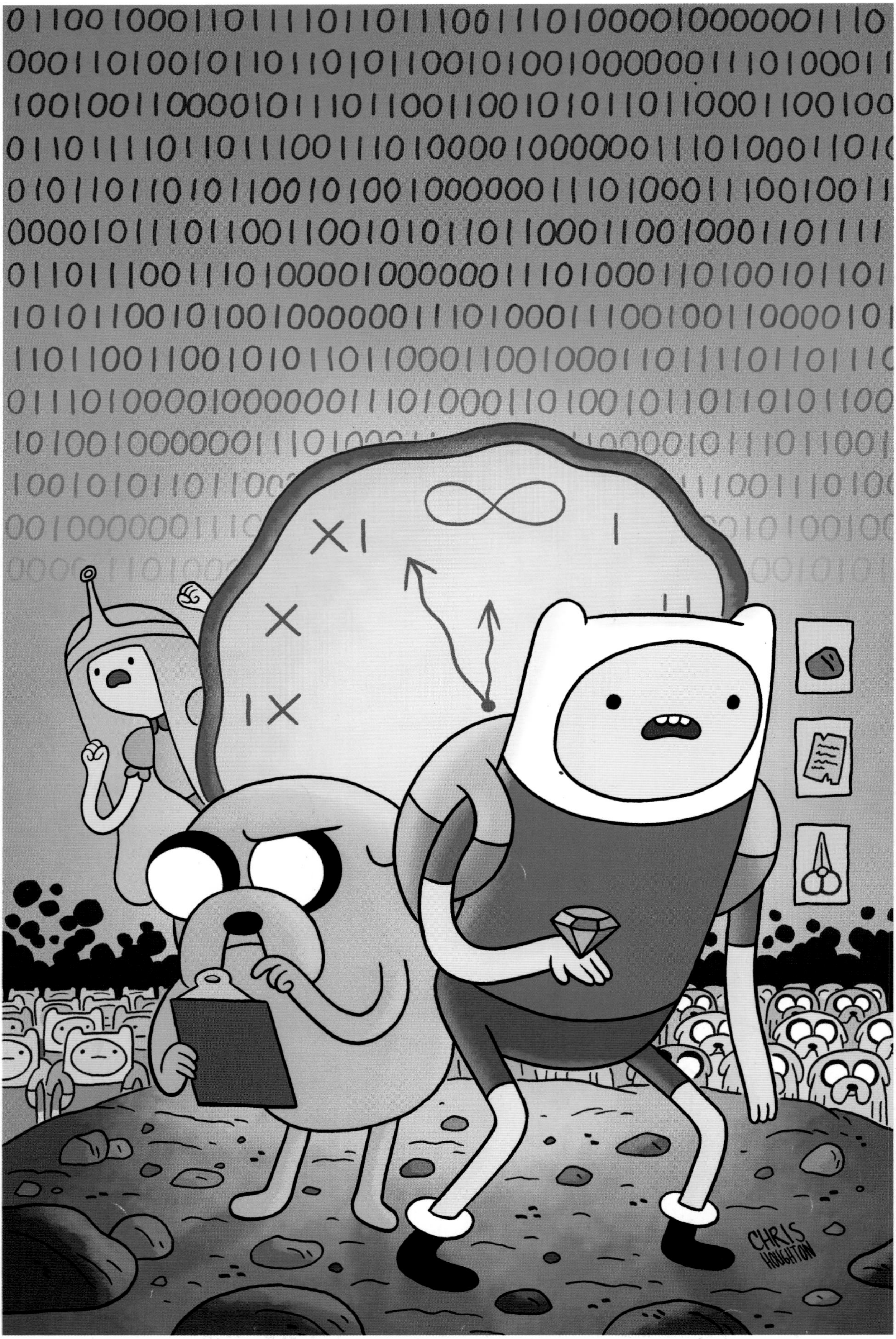
CHRIS HOUGHTON

ISSUE SEVEN | CHRIS HOUGHTON | COLORS BY KASSANDRA HELLER

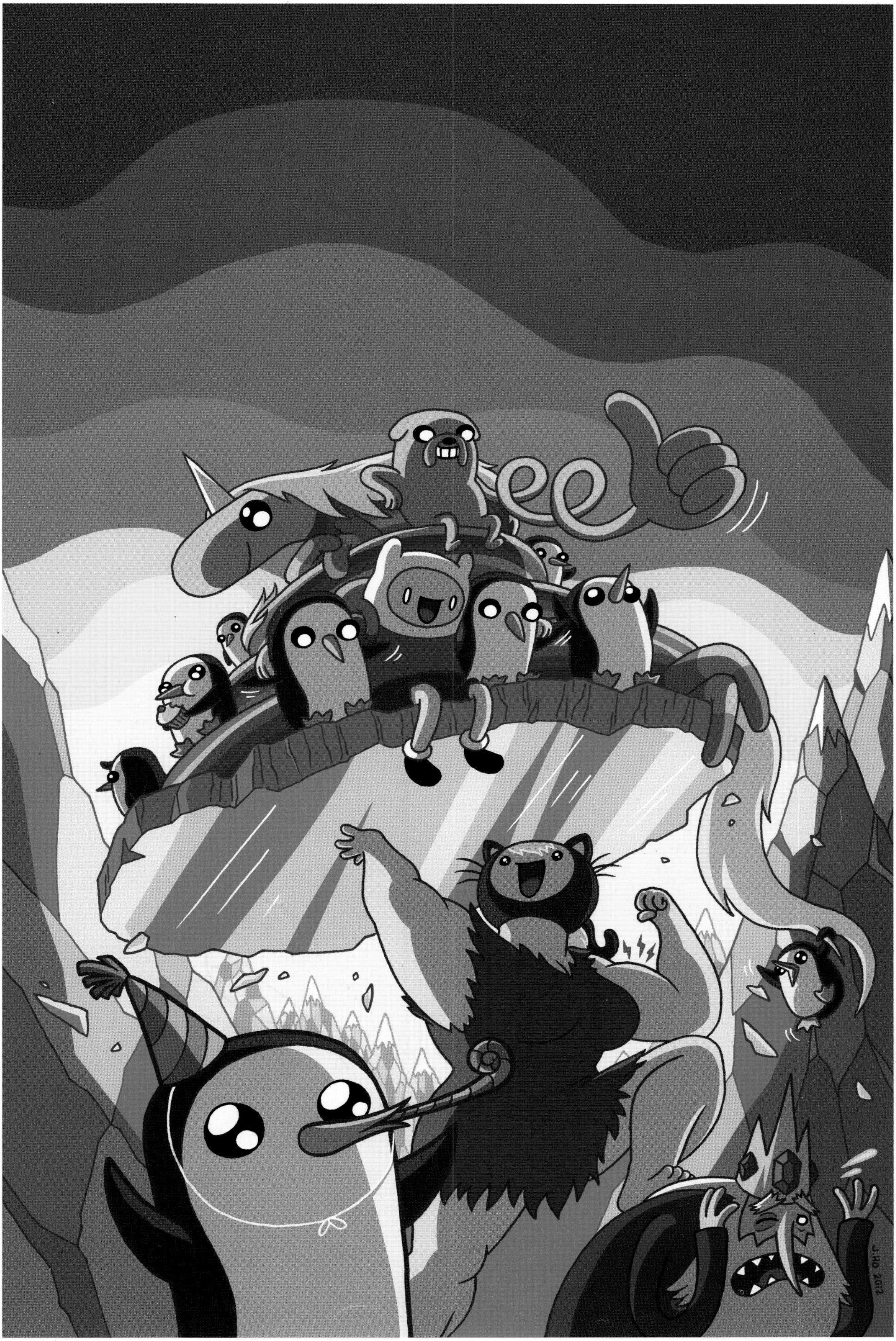
J.HO 2012

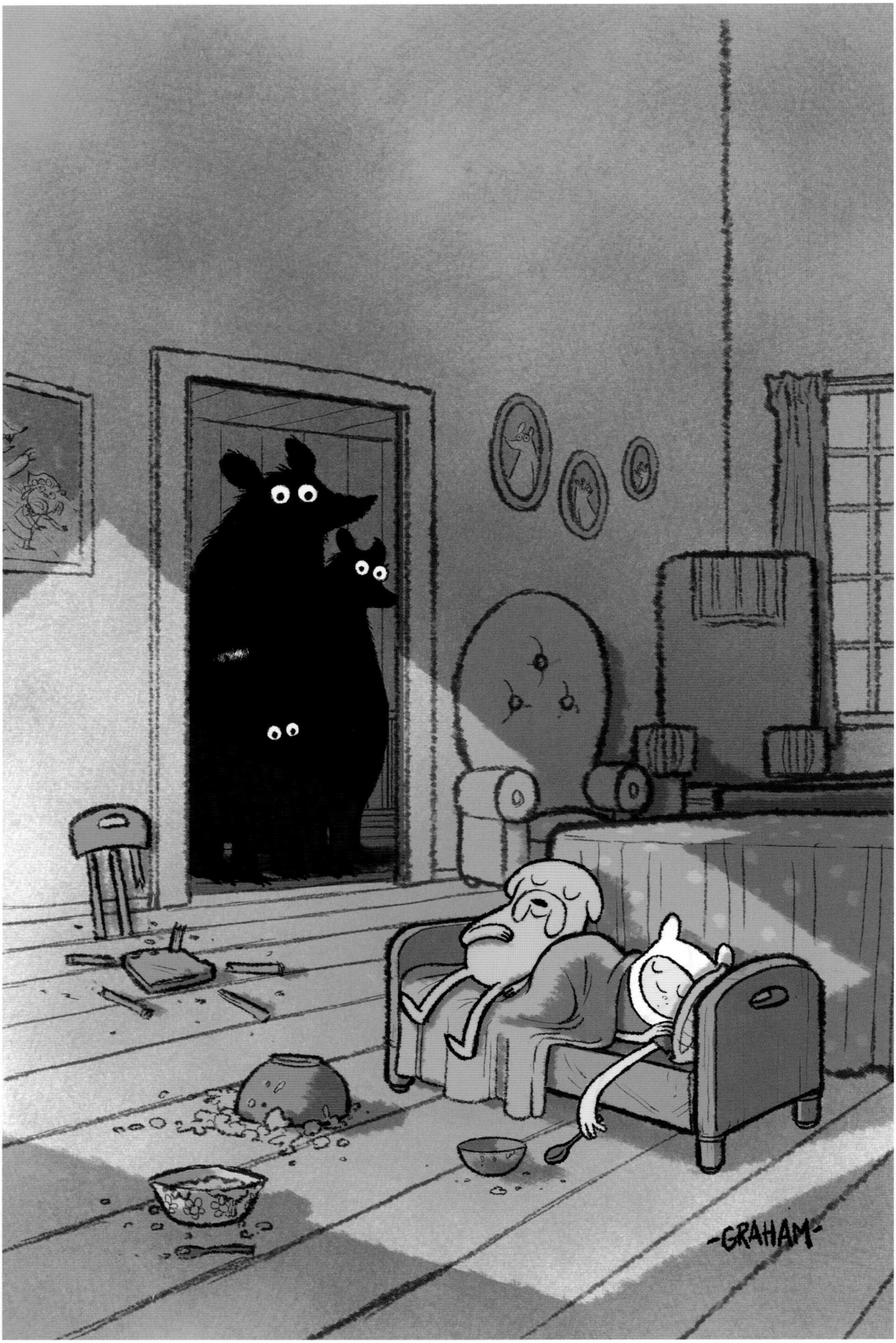
-GRAHAM-

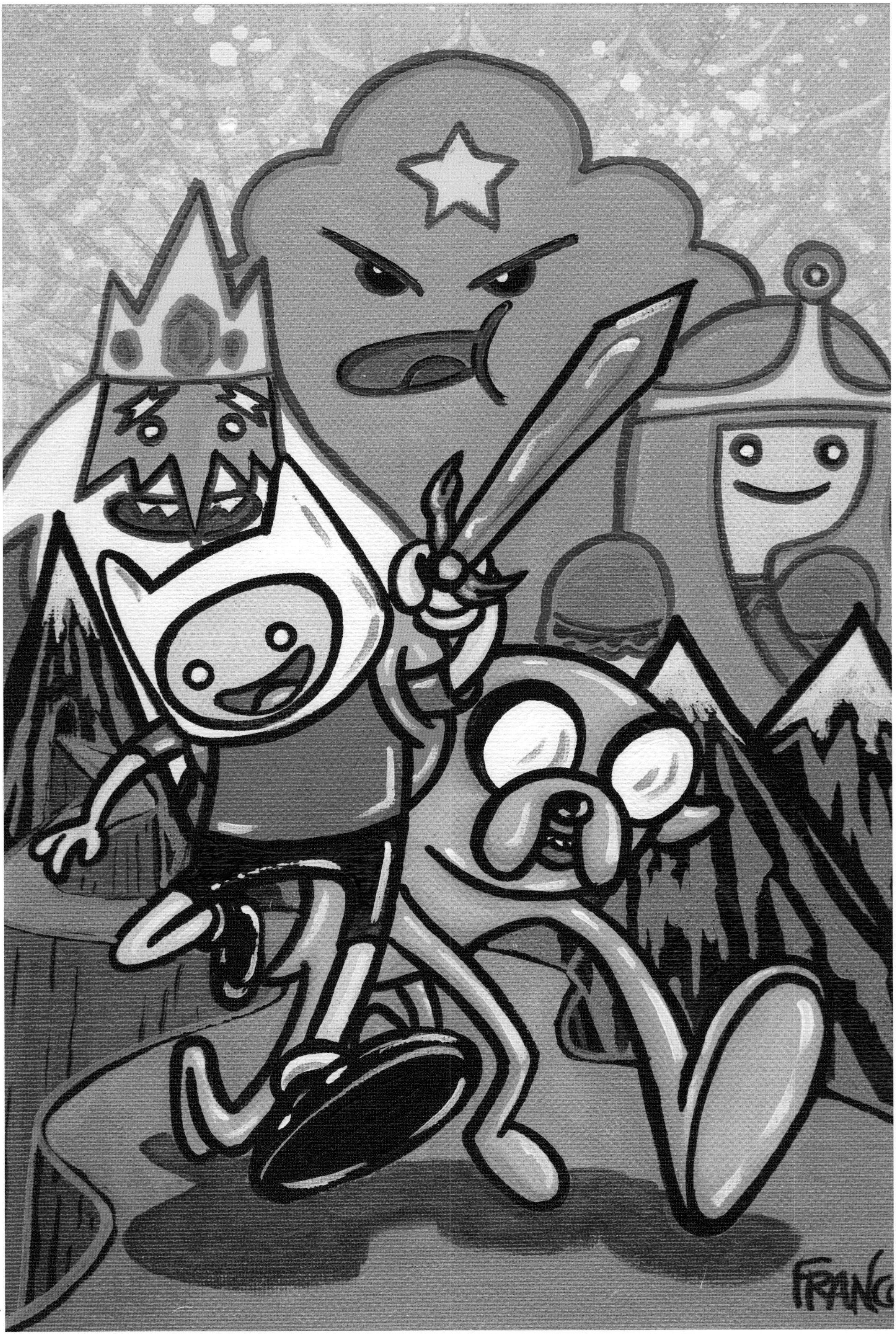
FRANCO

ISSUE SEVEN | FRANCO

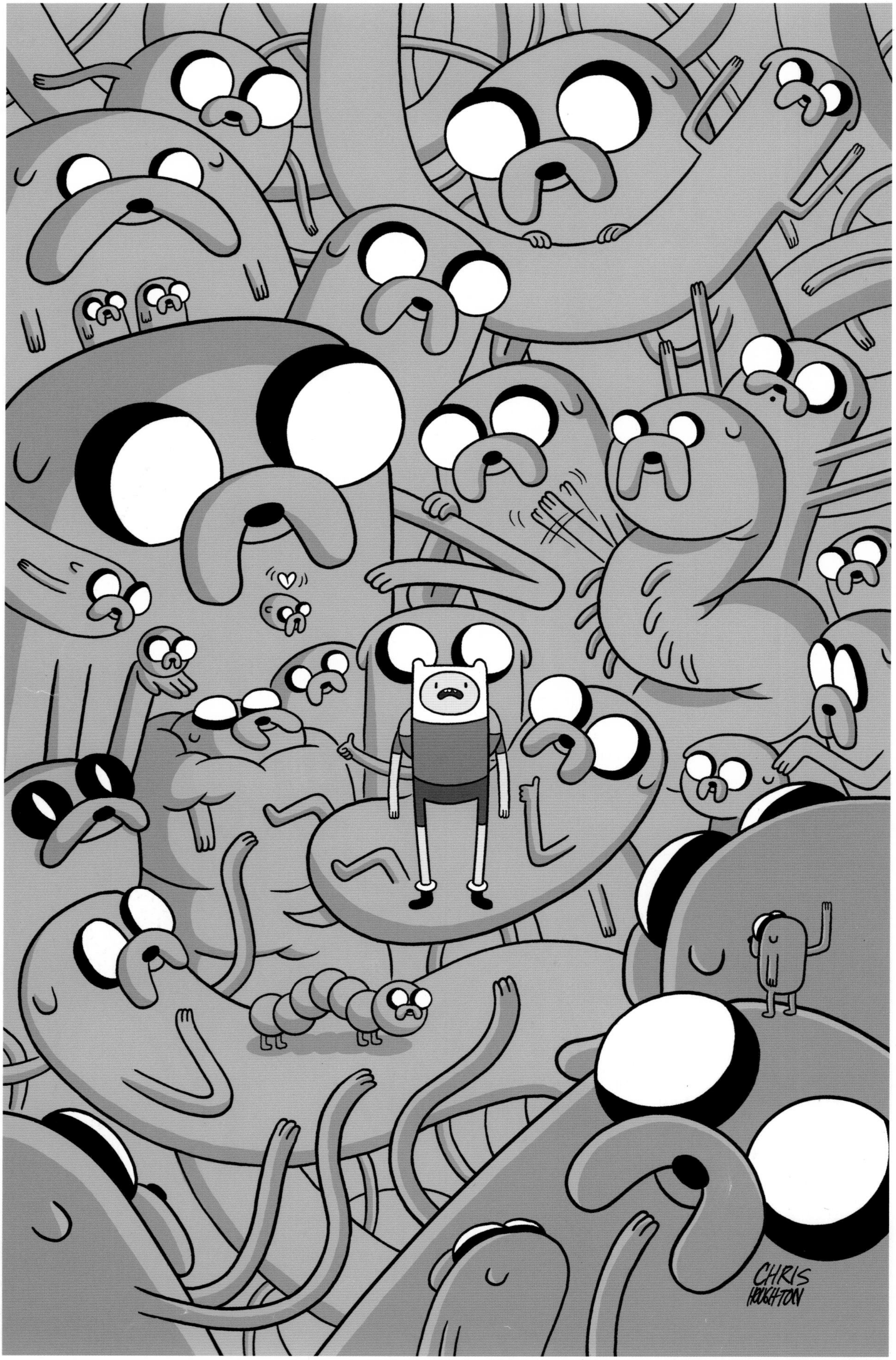
CHRIS
HOUGHTON

ISSUE EIGHT | CHRIS HOUGHTON | COLORS BY KASSANDRA HELLER

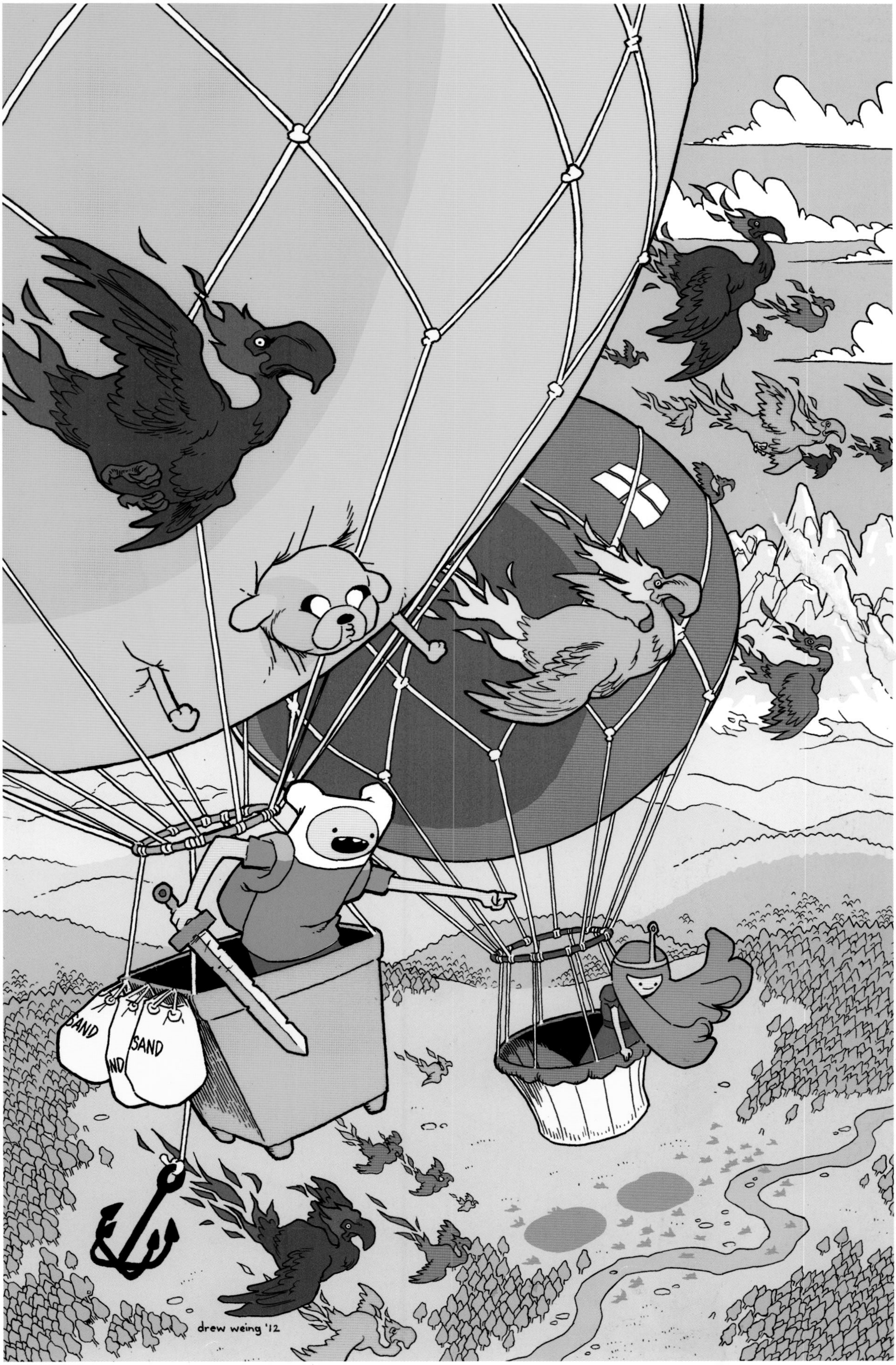
SAND
ND
SAND
drew weing '12

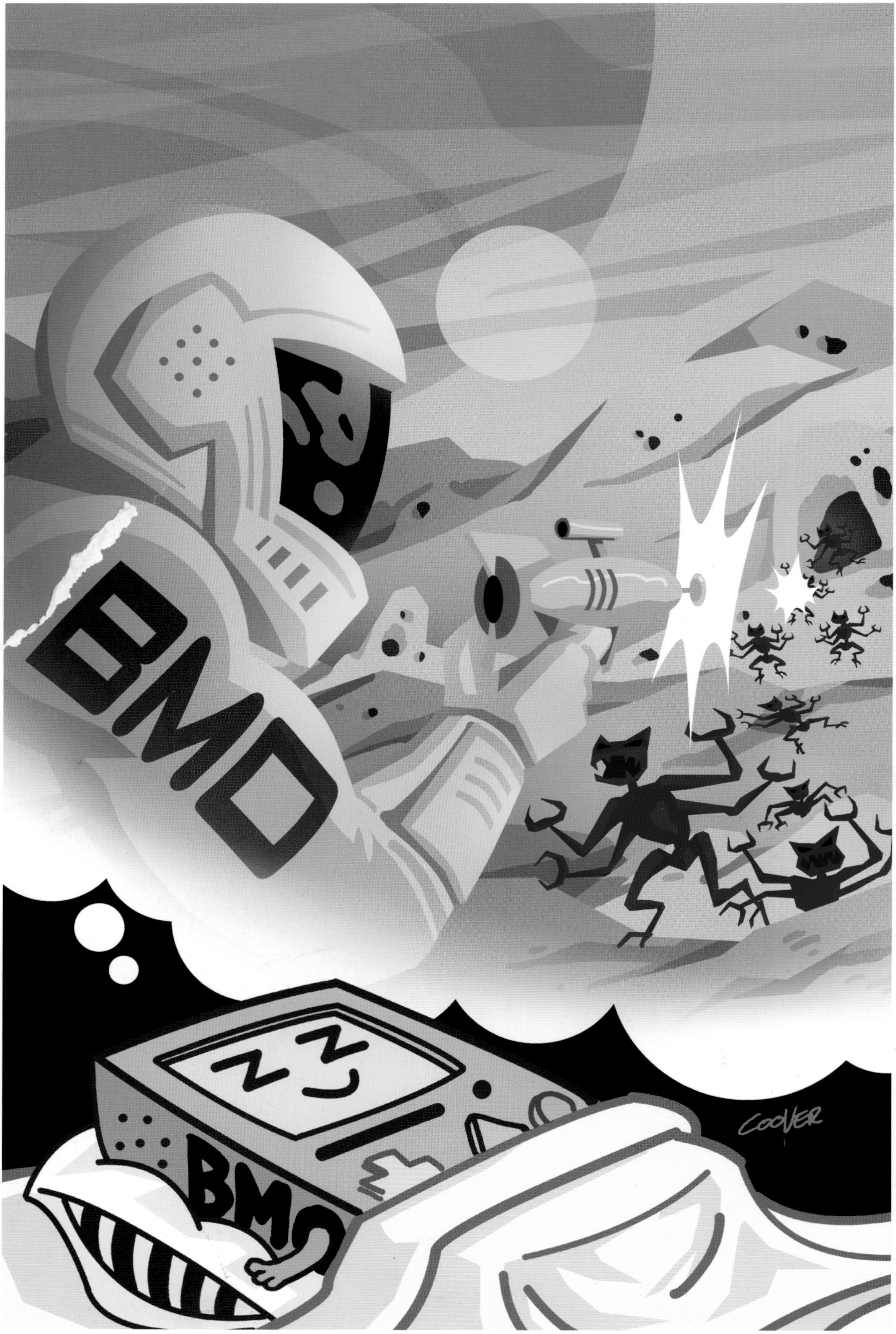
BMO
COOVER
BMO

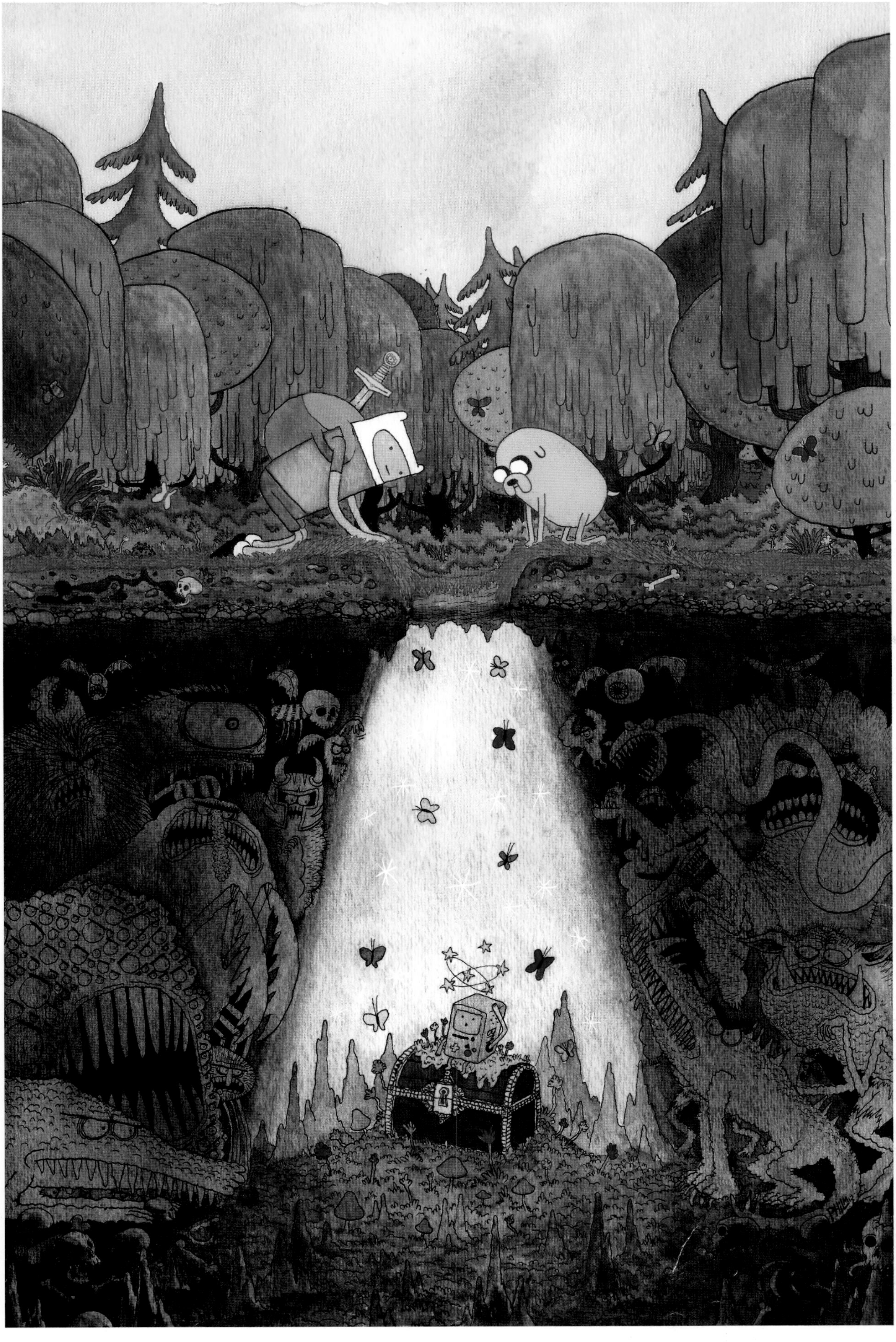

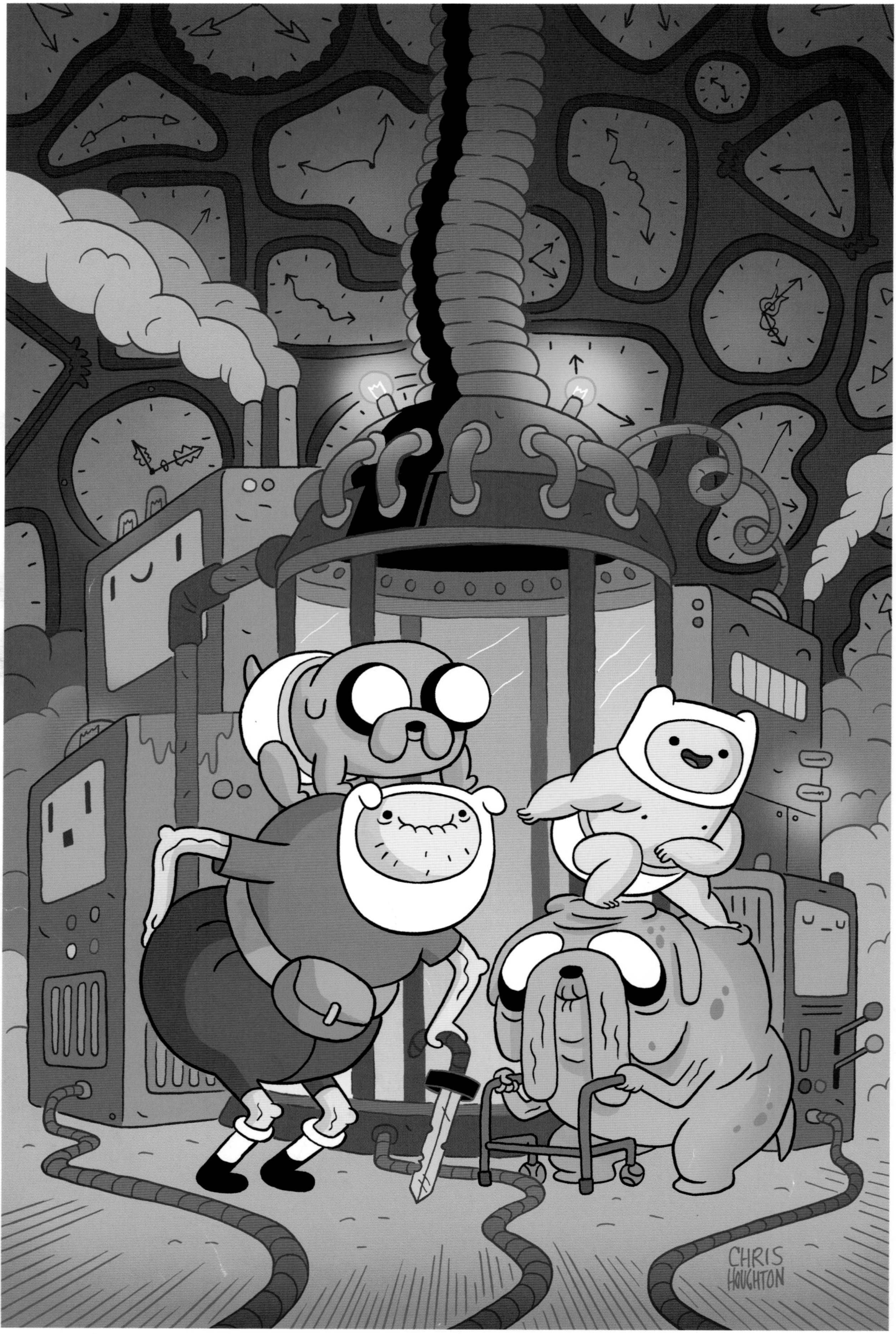
CHRIS
HOUGHTON

ISSUE NINE | CHRIS HOUGHTON | COLORS BY KASSANDRA HELLER

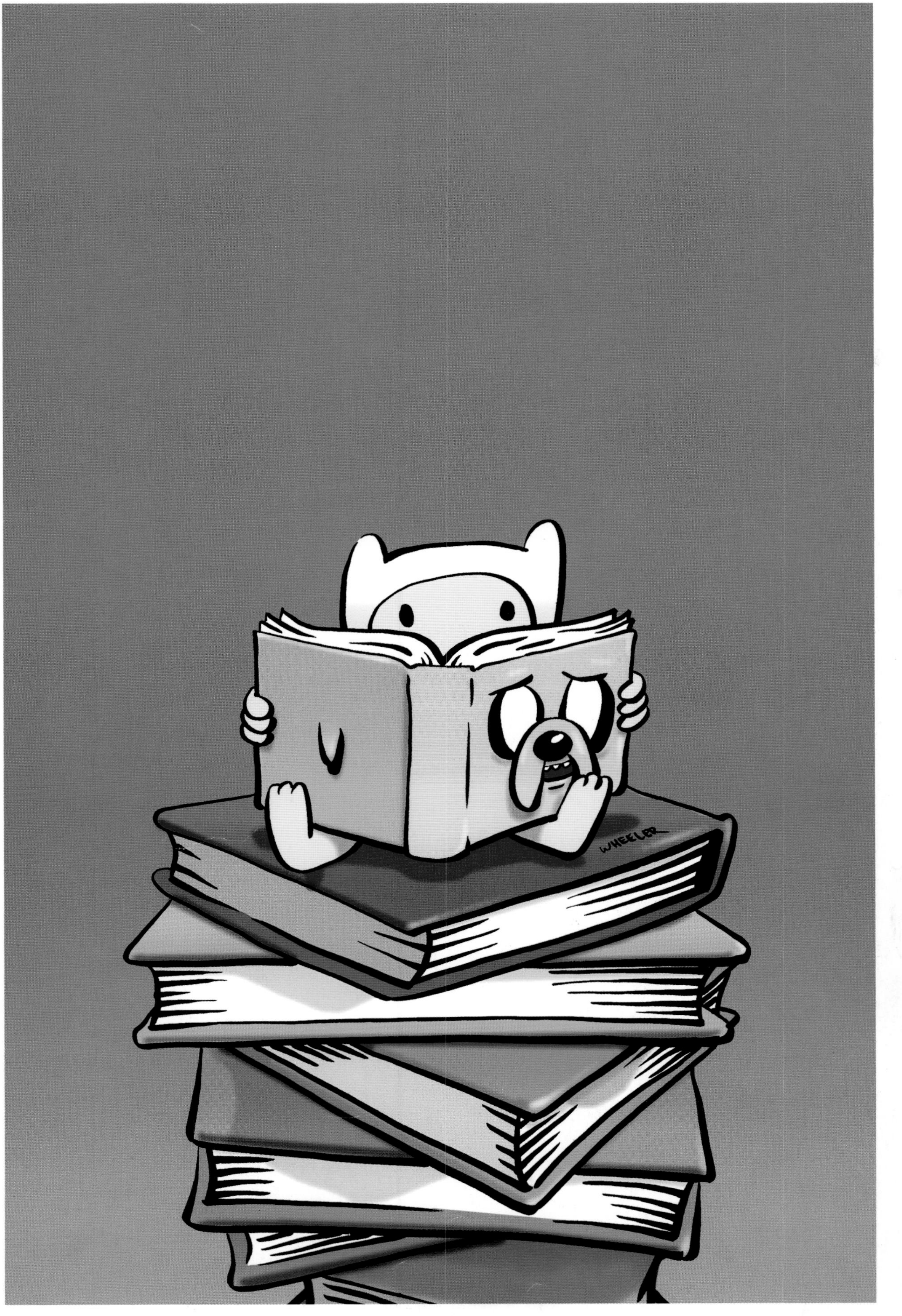
WHEELER

ISSUE NINE | SHANNON WHEELER

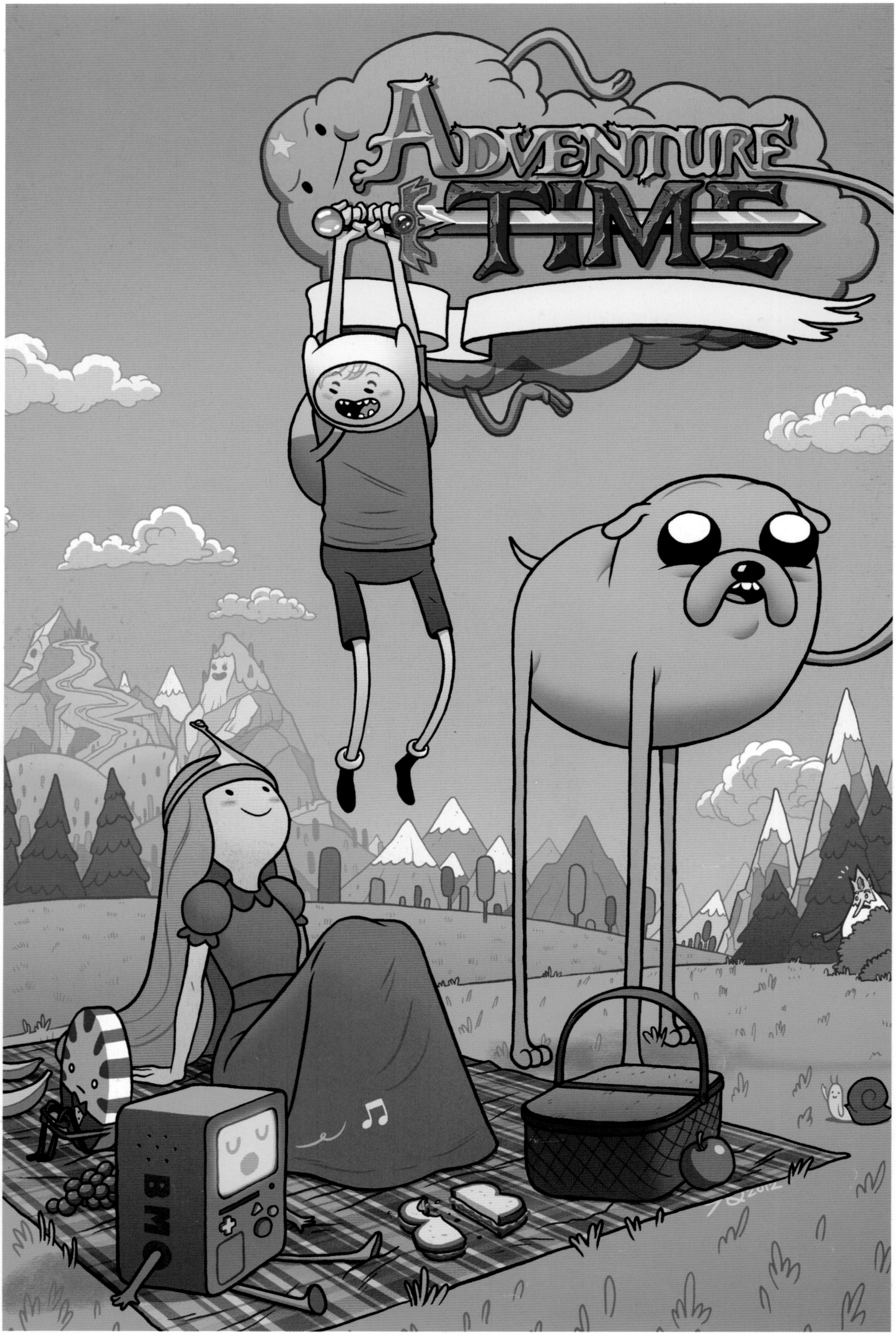
ADVENTURE TIME
BMO

ISSUE NINE | JOE QUINONES

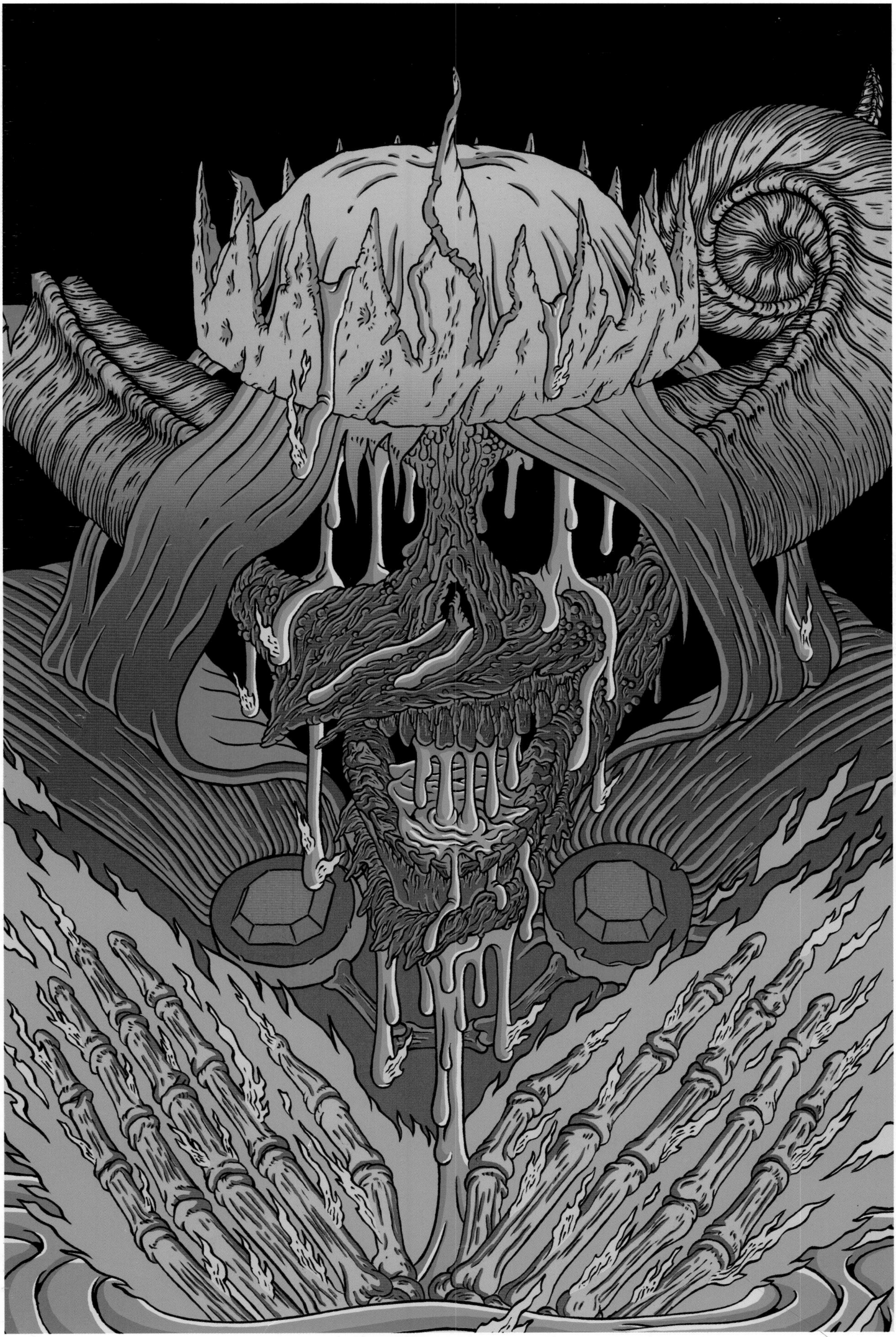

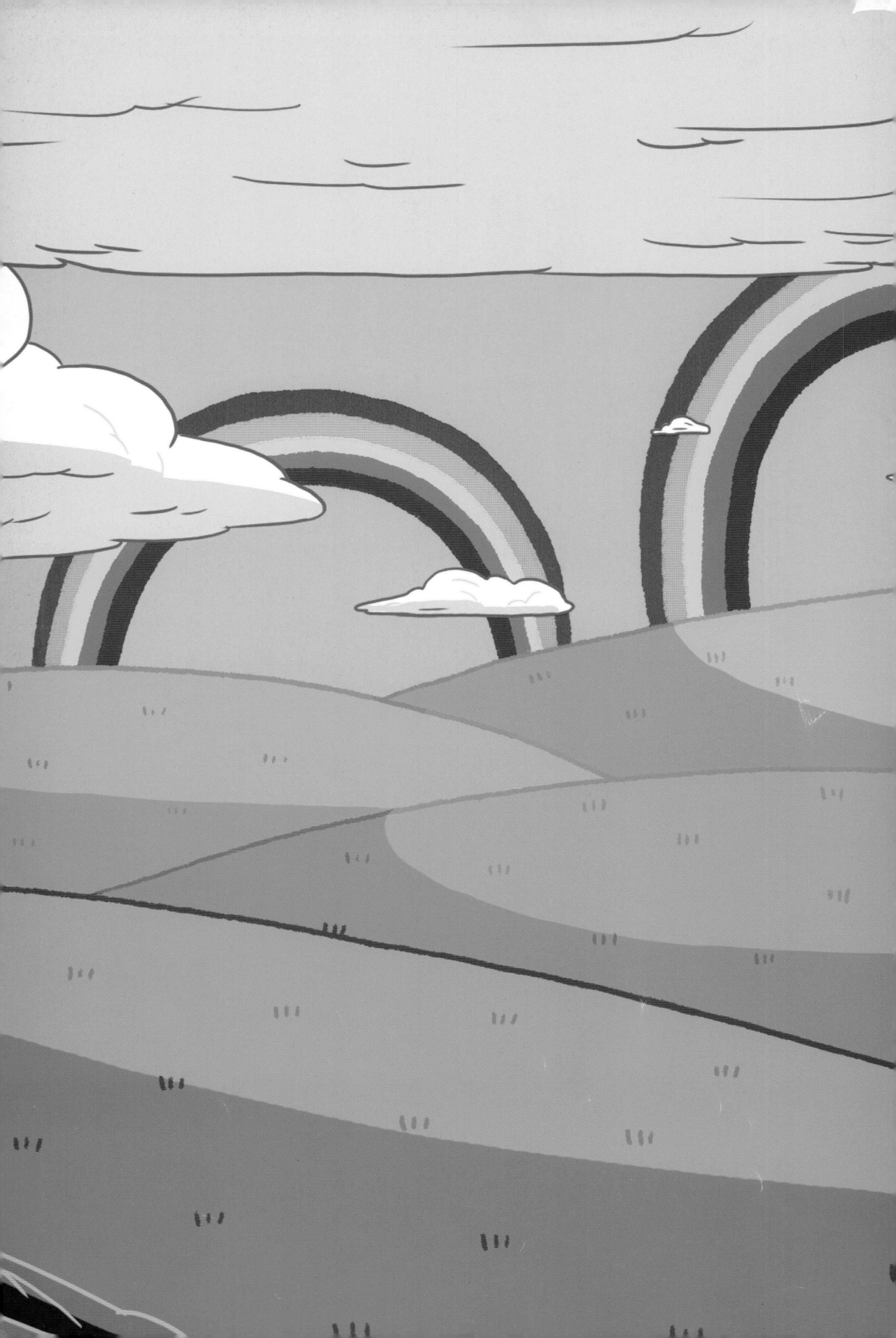

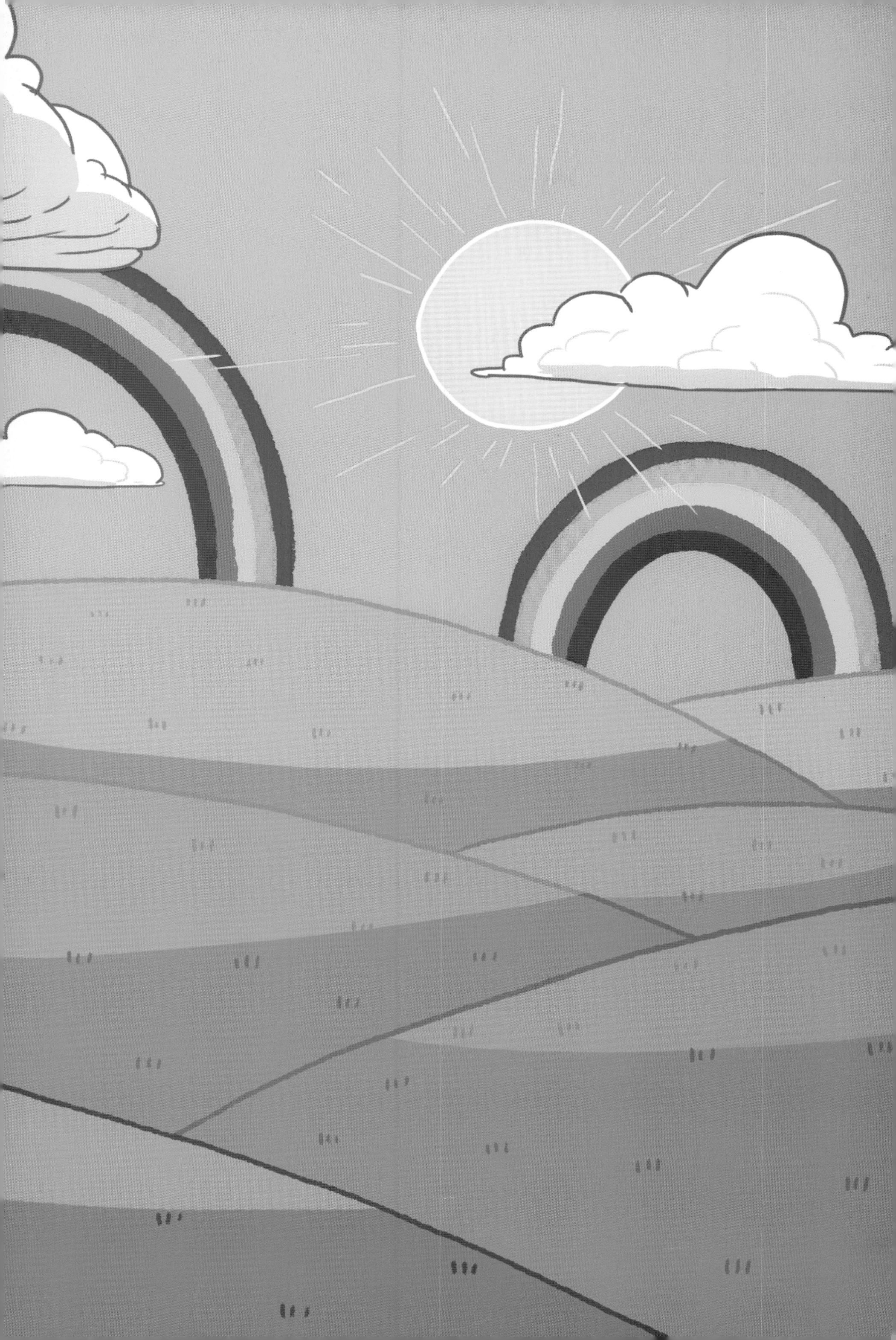

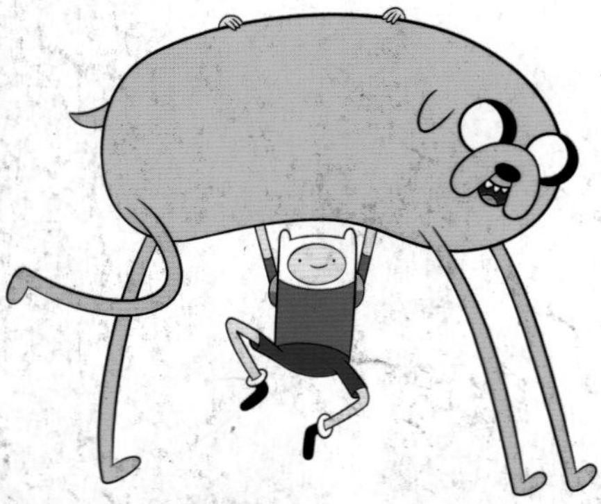

BEHIND THE SCENES

THE MAKING OF ADVENTURE TIME...TRAVEL

by Ryan North

HEY, WHERE DID ADVENTURE TIM COME FROM?

I was hanging out with my editor, Shannon, and for fun I was pitching her purposely-terrible stories for ADVENTURE TIME. This is probably not the greatest thing to be doing to your editor, but it's a fun thing to do with friends, and Shannon's both so she gets a pass!

After I'd pitched "Finn and Jake read their favorite books quietly, but we can't see what they're reading" and "Finn and Jake spend the night sleeping and the comic's done in real-time as we stand there watching them sleep," I said "Okay, what if Finn and Jake meet this cool new guy in town who's totally awesome and called 'Adventure Tim'?" and Shannon said "Wait, that's a really good idea" and I said "Whoa, hold on, yeah I think it is."

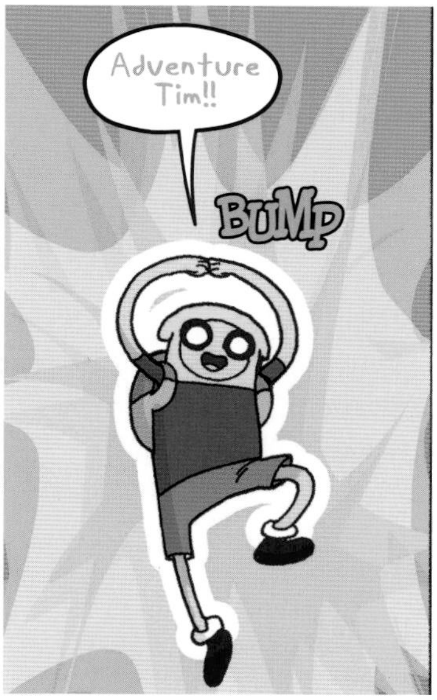
Adventure Tim!!
BUMP

There's a lesson here, and it's this: never be afraid to share your ideas, even if you think they're dumb. Sometimes the dumb ideas are the most fun! From there it was a short walk to the idea of having Adventure Tim be a combination of Finn and Jake, and from there to making Adventure Tim's life just a slightly bit different from what we're used to. And that in turn lead to Princess Chewypaste, The Mice King, and The Loch, so I guess it wasn't such a dumb idea after all!

OKAY BUT WHERE DID THE TIME TRAVEL STORY COME FROM?

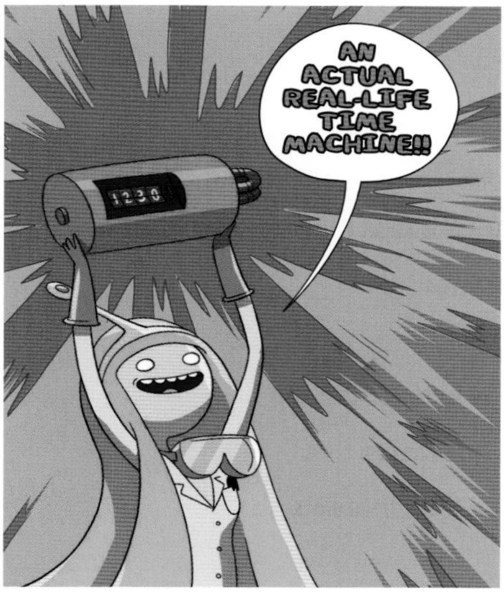
AN ACTUAL REAL-LIFE TIME MACHINE!!

At the end of the last comic (collected in ADVENTURE TIME Volume 1), there's a one-page flashback to Marceline, a thousand years ago. At the time, Marceline and Ice King's history wasn't revealed yet on the show. The people working on the show knew about it, and I knew about it, but beyond that it was TOP SECRET.

We did over 10 different versions of that one-page flashback to make it perfect: it had to fit not just with the show, but also with the episodes that hadn't aired yet, AND we didn't want to give away the Marcy/Ice King reveal too soon. I'm super happy with the finished result, but at the end of that I thought "Man, it'd be fun to write something where there weren't any continuity issues to worry about! Gosh, I'd love to do something like that... IN THE FUTURE."

Then I thought, "Wait! The way I emphasised 'in the future' in that last thought has given me a good idea!"

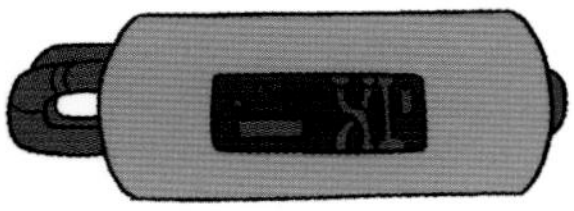

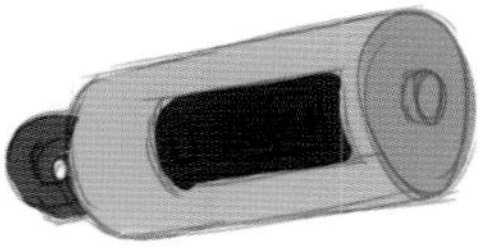

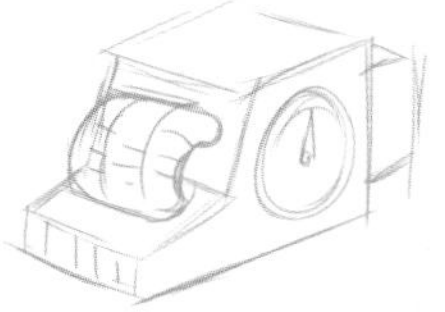

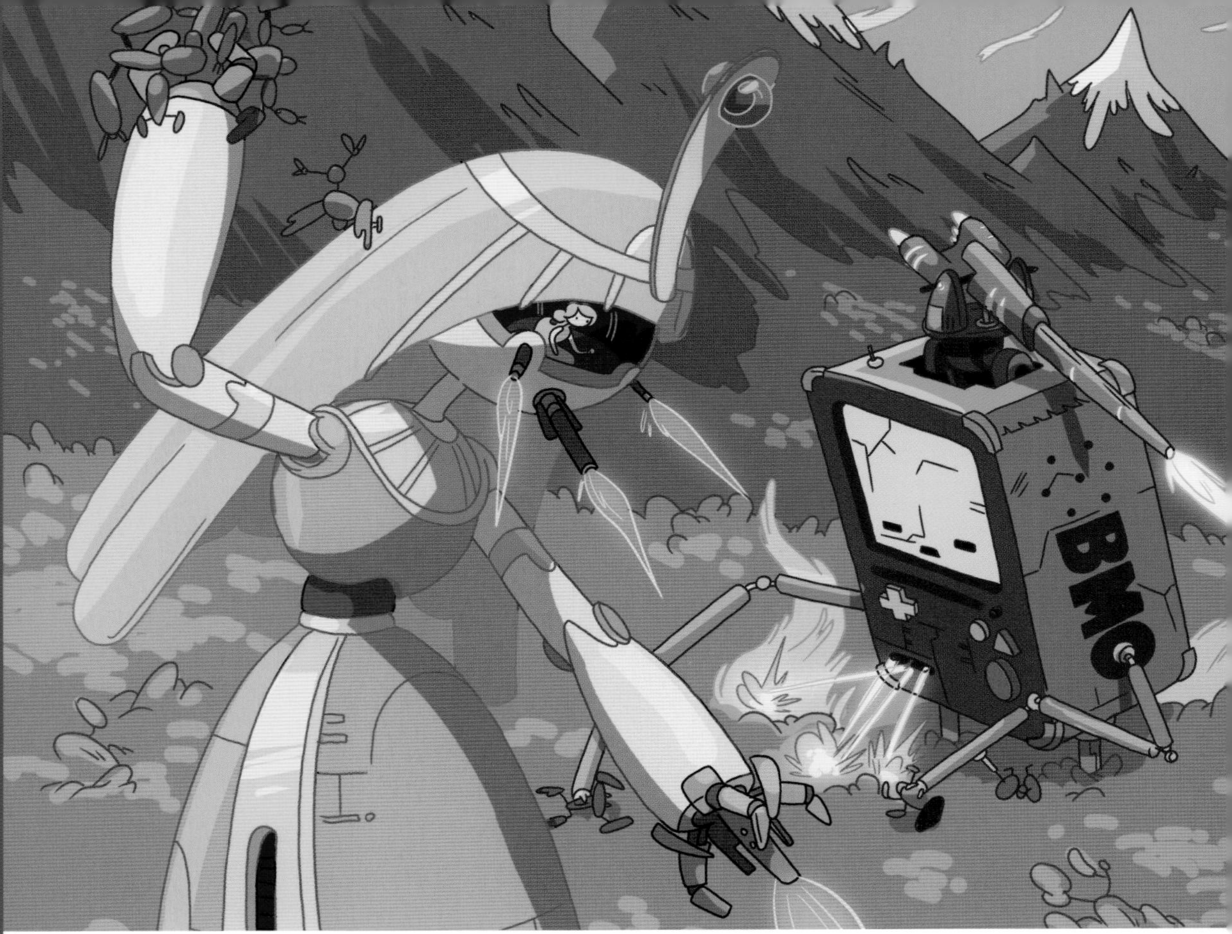
BMO

HOW DID YOU DECIDE WHAT TO SHOW IN THE FUTURE LAND OF OOO?

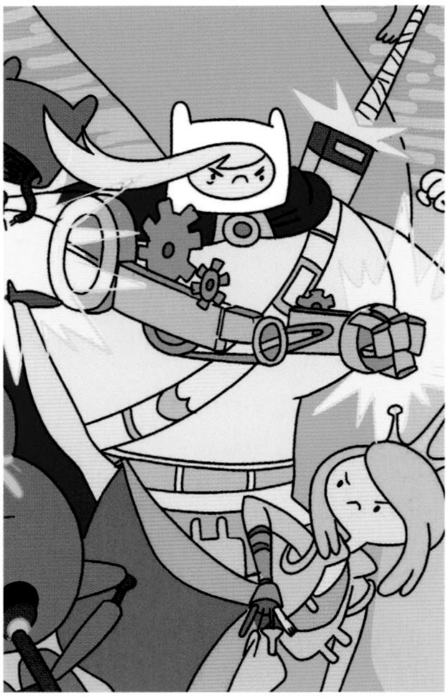

I guess it wasn't such a dumb idea after all! I have a lot of capital-o Opinions about time travel, and I knew I wanted to show a few things:

- Killer robots
- Mechanical arms
- A tank-tread dress

I figured any ONE of those in a story would be fun, but putting in all three? That would HAVE to be at least moderately mathematical. And as no time travel story is ever satisfying without some temporal shenanigans, I made a special effort in the climax to have Finn and Jake travel not just back to issue #1, but also to the original ADVENTURE TIME pilot. And I got to fix a couple of continuity errors around names and disappearing sleeping bags there too! Yay!

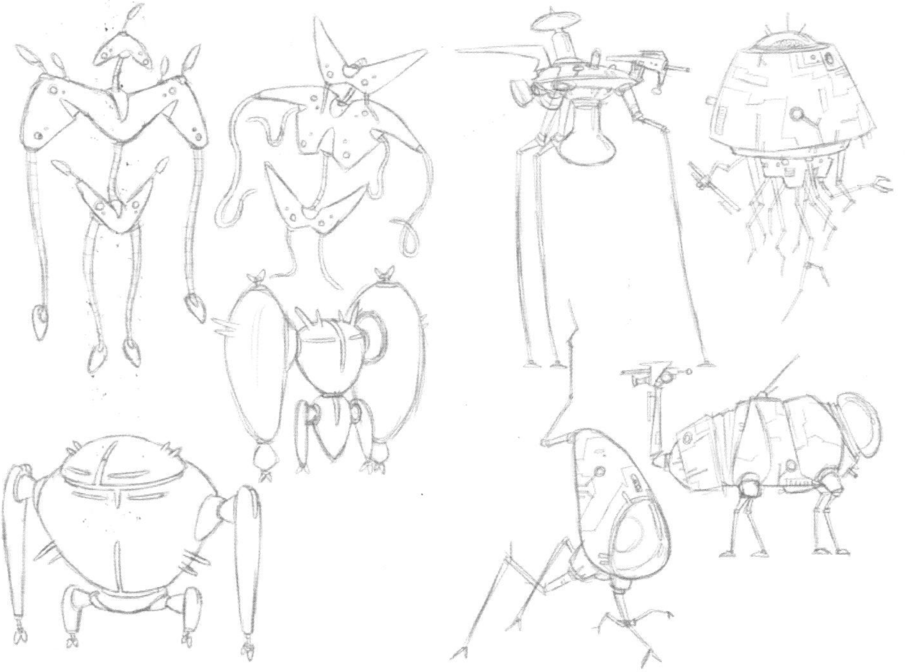

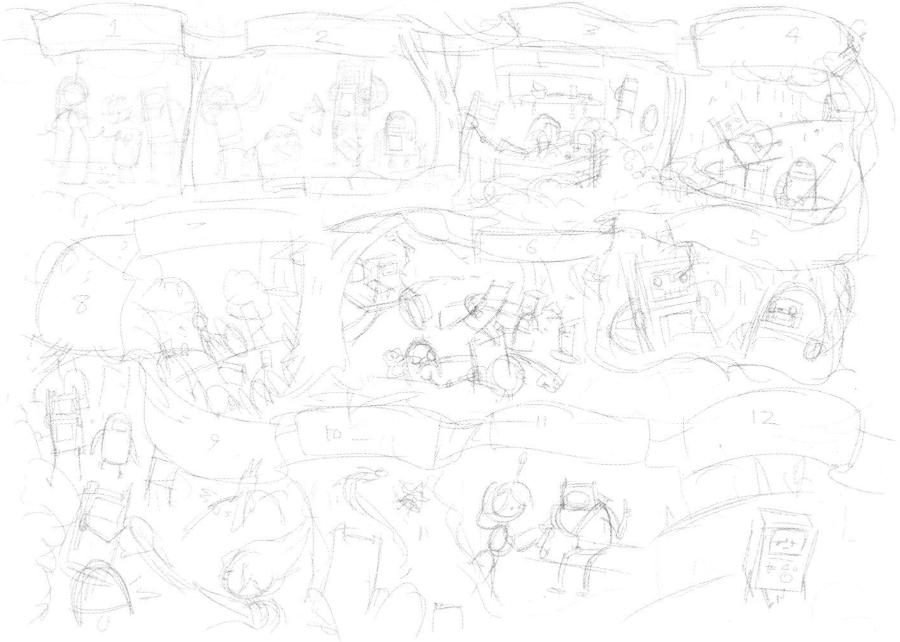

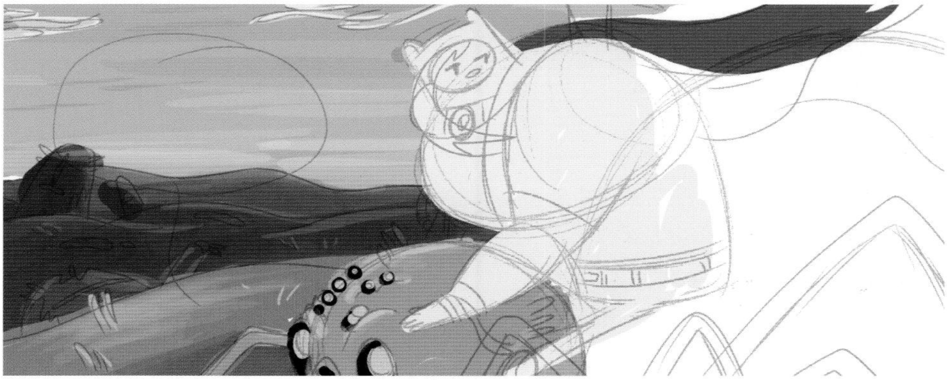

HEY WAIT HOLD ON WHAT WERE SOME OF THE EARLIER VERSIONS OF THAT FLASHBACK SCENE WITH MARCELINE YOU MENTIONED ?

The first version actually involved The Lich's origin story: this was before his origin was hinted at on the show! The only problem was, that upcoming origin was different. Pendleton Ward and I talked about it and we agreed it'd be cool if the comic matched up with the show as much as possible, so I focused on Marceline instead. But here's what could've been: a first-draft alternate origin for The Lich!

Panel 1:
NARRATION: One thousand years ago:
A general and a corporal in a bunker: make it look kinda retro-futuristic "how the 50s imagined the future" style, with switches and lights and lots of interesting giant computers in the background. The general should have the general proportions of The Lich - a giant of a man. Right now he's sitting, hunched over at his desk, working on something we can't see on his desk. We don't see his face. On the back of another chair sits a dark green cloak.
Corporal comes running in, breathless, panicked. He's wearing some sort of military uniform, but nothing corresponding to any military we'd recognize.
CORPORAL: Sir, the enemy missiles have launched! We need to respond in k-

GENERAL: (interrupting without looking up, his word bubble over the corporal's): I'm tired of losing, Corporal.

Panel 2:

Corporal stares at him in shock. This was not what he expected. We still don't see the General's face.

GENERAL: We've been trying to win this war with technology, and it's always been stalemate. But you know what beats technology like rock beats scissors?

CORPORAL: ...Better, fancier techno-

GENERAL: MAGIC, corporal.

Panel 3:

The general stands up, shows him what's on his desk: it's the bag of holding, surrounded by some magic runes and other magical artifacts used in creating it: candles, flasks of red liquid, crow feathers, tentacles, etc. Again: set up so we don't see the General's face.

GENERAL: And I should know: I've been... dabbling in it. I call this the Bag of Holding. It's a pocket dimension. Properly yielded, it could suck up bombs. Tanks. ENTIRE ARMIES. There's no limit to what I -

Panel 4:

Corporal interrupts him, looking at him like he's crazy. General regards him evenly as he reaches for a magical cloak, with, we can now see, has the same clasp as The Lich. Again, the cloak itself has a darker, less faded green. We see the General from behind so we still can't see his face.

CORPORAL: General, with all due respect: THIS IS CRAZY. Magic doesn't exist!

GENERAL: Oh, it didn't. For a while. But it came back.

GENERAL: I helped it, Corporal.

Panel 5:

General picks up the bag. We see over his shoulder so his face remains invisible, but we can see the Corporal's face. Magic suction begins to come out of the bag. Corporal looks horrified.

GENERAL: Magic is real. And powerful. And dangerous, but I can control it without being consumed by it. I know I can.

GENERAL: I've had a revelation, Corporal. Would you like to hear it? Nobody can ever kill me as long as I kill them first.

CORPORAL: You're... you're insane. Please. Stop.

Panel 6:

The General walks out the door, sucking up his own troops as he walks towards the exit, behind him is a horrified corporal. The panel is framed so we CAN see the General's face now, but just his mouth and the very bottoms of his eyes, and he's smiling a big evil toothy smile like The Lich, only without the decayed flesh around it: pointy, mis-matched teeth, all gums, teeth, and tongue. His eyes (what little we can see of them) are black like the Lich's.

GENERAL: Oh, I'll stop when I want to. And right now...

GENERAL (voice balloon black, like The Lich's): I really don't want to.

Panel 7:

We zoom and it's a bit later and we see the Earth with a huge section of it newly missing: explosions visible from space, chaos.

MATHEMATICAL EDITION
Volume Three

COMING JANUARY 2014

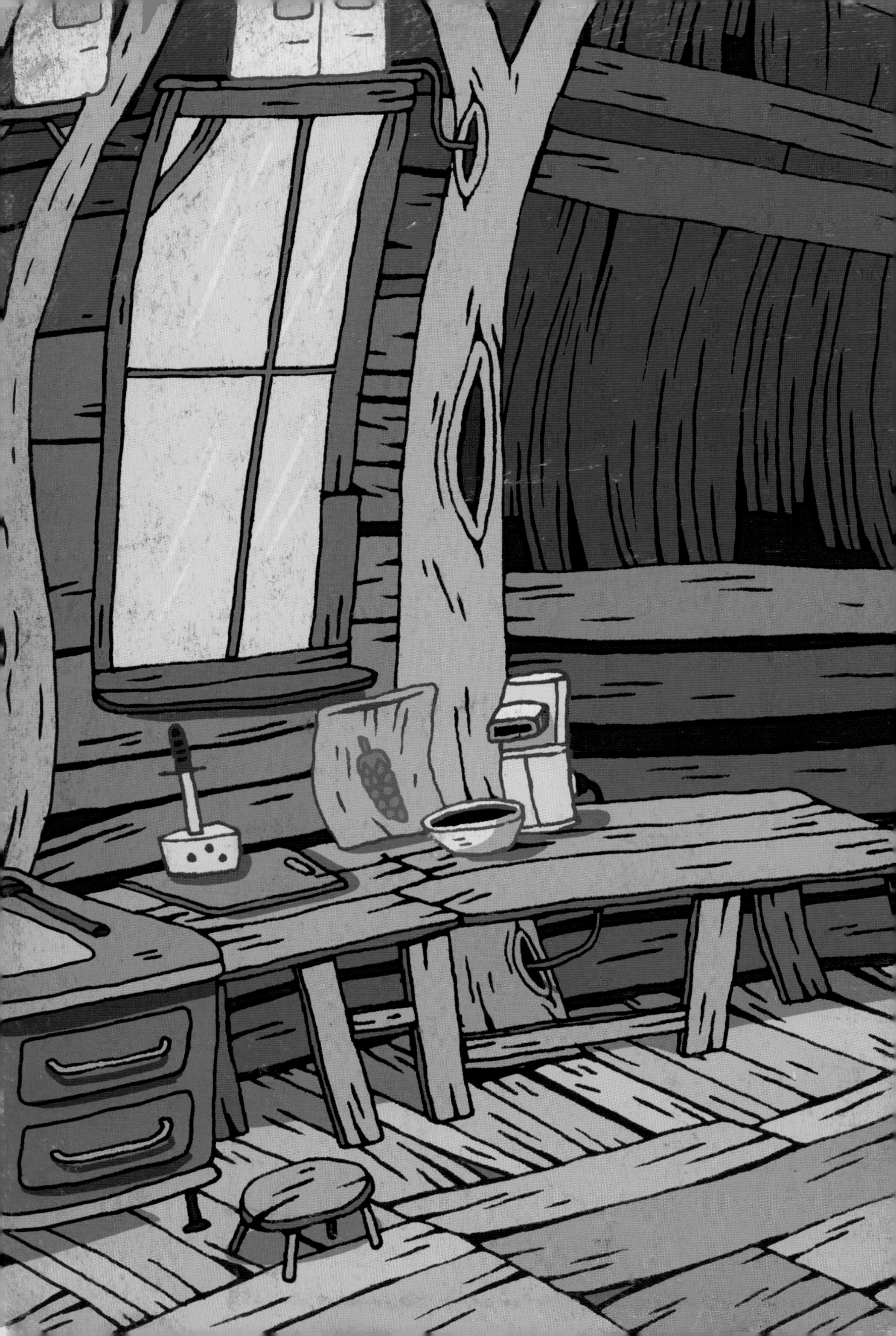

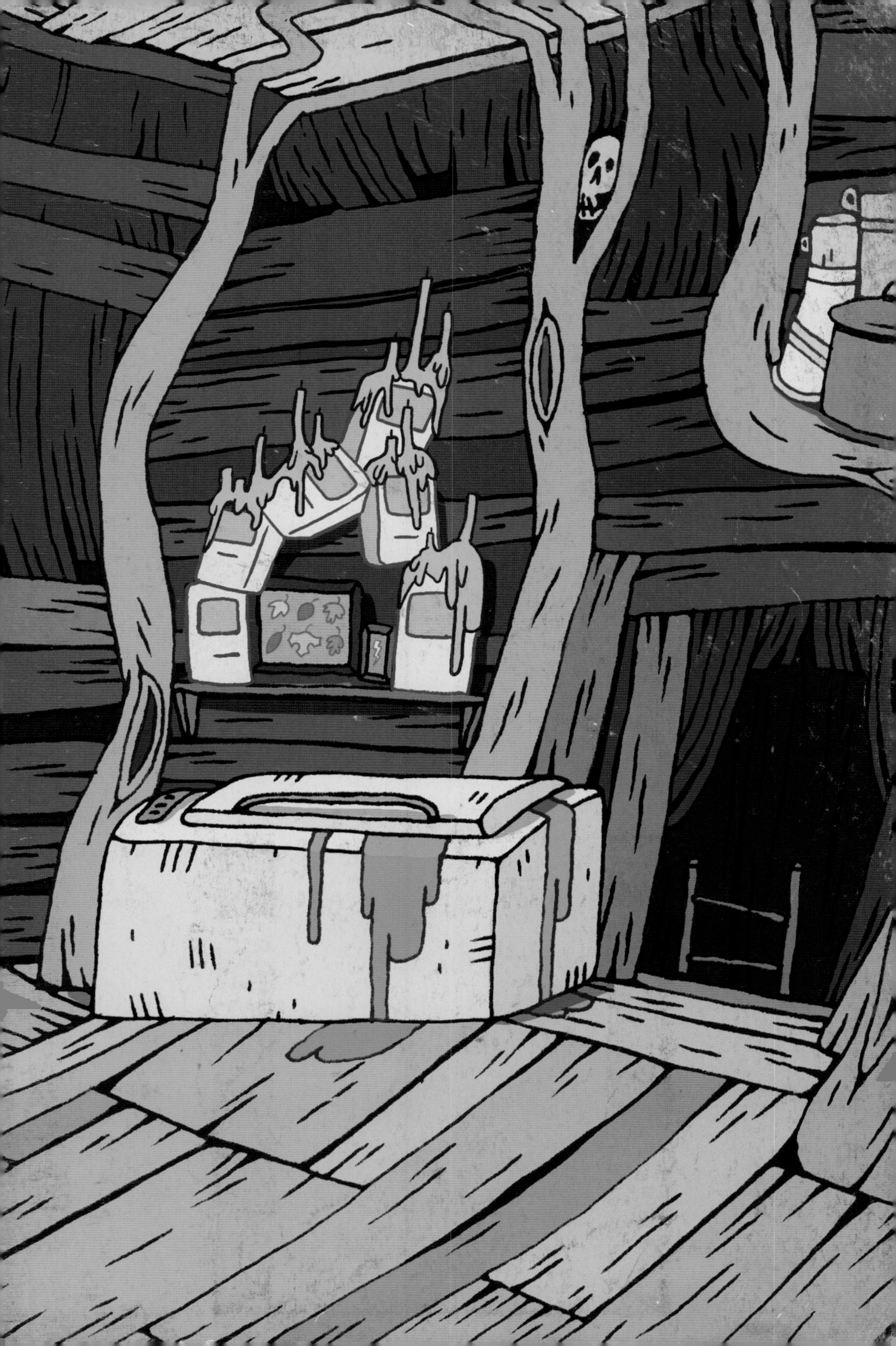

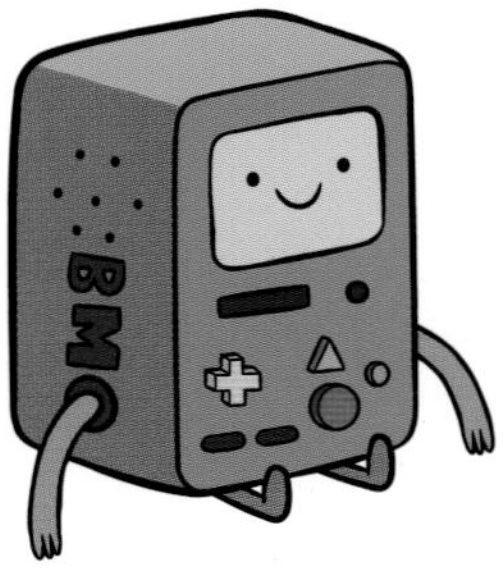
BMO

Ryan North lives in Toronto with his rad wife and sweet dog. He writes comics at dinosaurcomics.com every day. His interests include skateboarding, being a good friend, and eating tasty things. He really hopes you like the comics!

Shelli Paroline escaped early on into the world of comics, cartoons, and science fiction. She has now returned to the Boston area, where she works as an unassuming illustrator and designer.

Braden Lamb grew up in Seattle, studied film in upstate New York, learned about vikings in Iceland and Norway, and established an art career in Boston. Now he draws and colors comics, and wouldn't have it any other way.